THE HOPE NOT PLOT

THE HOPE NOT PLOT

A Novel of Churchill's Final Farewell

DAVID R. STOKES

The Hope Not Plot
A Novel of Churchill's Final Farewell

Copyright ©2025 by David R. Stokes

Broad Run Books
Haymarket, Virginia
www.broadrunbooks.com

1st Edition

ISBN: 979-8-9992040-0-4

Cover Design   Nilesh Prabhu
Interior Layout   Rachel Newhouse

For Karen, who has been my amazing wife and best friend for nearly 50 years. I agree completely with Winston Churchill when he said, "My ability to persuade my wife to marry me was quite my most brilliant achievement."

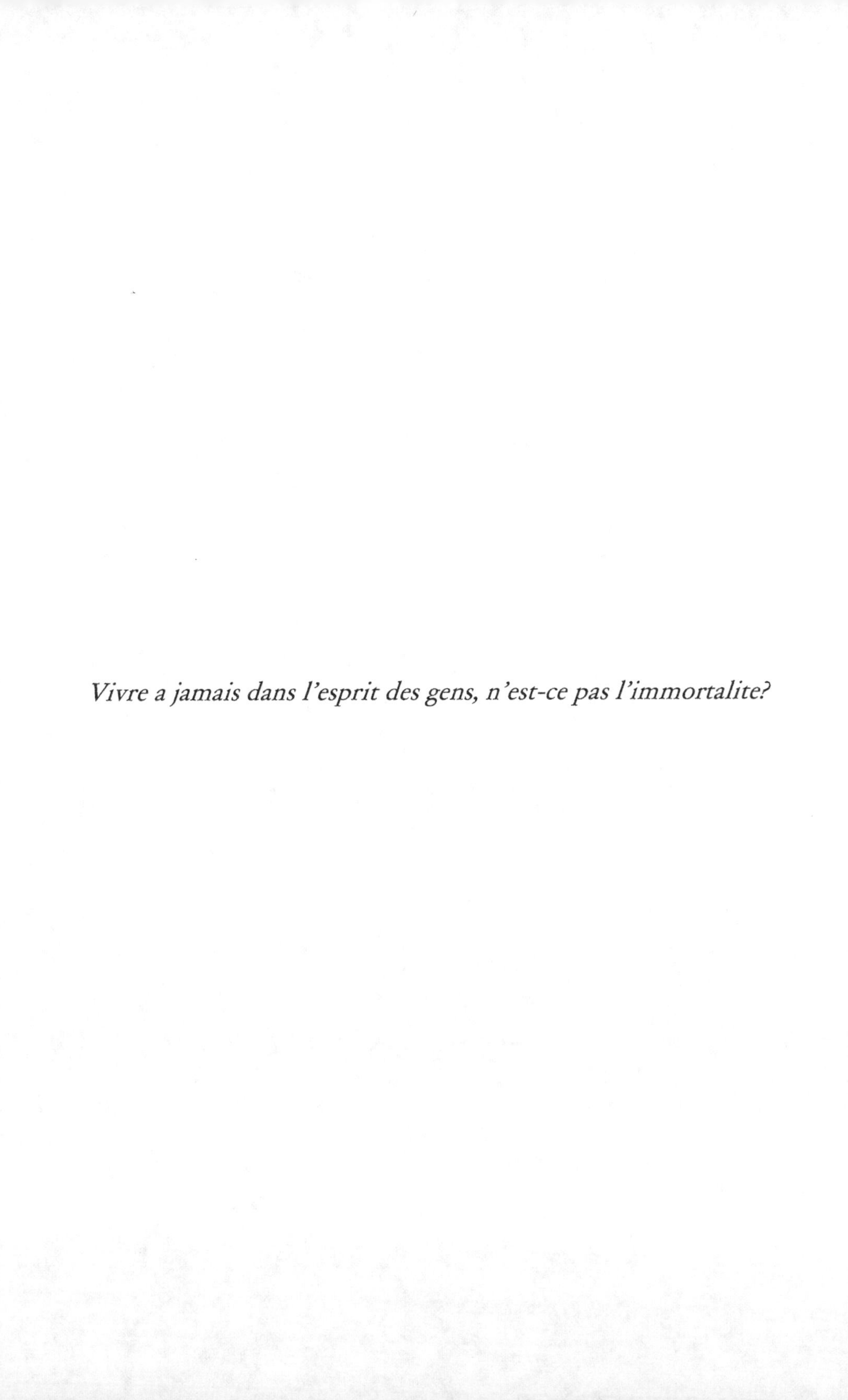

Vivre a jamais dans l'esprit des gens, n'est-ce pas l'immortalite?

CHAPTER ONE

London
10 Downing Street
Cabinet Room

January 15, 1965

EVERYONE ROSE TO their feet in acknowledgment and respect as the Prime Minister crossed the threshold into the room. Harold Wilson, a man who had ascended rapidly to the pinnacle of British political life, had taken his place as the master of Ten Downing Street only three months prior. The anointed leader of a new era, he sat in the storied Cabinet Room, its walls steeped in the gravitas of history and tradition.

Wilson was still becoming accustomed to the power he wielded and the new office he occupied, finding his way amid the labyrinthine responsibilities of governance. He seated himself at the large mahogany conference table, which commanded most of the room's space, full of purpose and intent.

This was no ordinary meeting; he had summoned his ministers to discuss a momentous event that would soon envelop the nation.

Wilson took the center chair nearest the door, the sole seat with armrests, a place that bespoke authority. Behind him, shelves filled with leather-bound volumes framed a fireplace where embers glowed like the fading pulse of a bygone era.

A pipe lay before him on the table. He picked it up, calmly stuffed it with tobacco, and lit it with the deliberation of a man who knew the value of creating the right atmosphere before speaking. Only then did he begin to address the gathered officials. It was a ritual, one with which the assembled ministers were all too familiar, but which carried new urgency today.

"Thank you all for coming," he began, his tone suffused with the British precision for which he was known. "We are on the threshold of an extraordinary moment in the history of the realm. I have called this special meeting because each one of you will play vital roles in what is shortly to come."

The ministers exchanged glances around the table, each aware of the gravity of the situation.

He continued, "It is clear that Sir Winston's days are numbered. There is no doubt that his death will mark the end of an era," he said, the words hanging heavily in the air. "It will also be an important moment for the nation and our new government. Let us be determined to give the great man the farewell he deserves, regardless of political affiliation or personal feelings. The eyes of the entire world will be upon us. I am determined we will be at our very best!"

Wilson's declaration was met with a forceful and orchestrated response. The ministers slapped the massive table with open palms, an audible seal of their commitment as they shouted in unison, "Hear, hear!"

Wilson continued, encouraged by the unified display of support. "Thank you, gentlemen. Much appreciated." His voice carried the authority of his office and the urgency of the moment. "Now, I've asked two men who aren't usually in this room for meetings to join us today. First, the Director General of the Security Service, Roger Hollis, will discuss measures being taken to protect the honored guests and world leaders who are certain to travel here."

The presence of Hollis betokened the unprecedented scale of the operation they were undertaking.

"Also, please welcome Stuart Palmer. He's the chief assistant to Mr. Fitzalan-Howard, the Earl Marshall who will oversee funeral events. The plans that have been in place for many years are being dusted off and updated." As he spoke, Wilson's measured gaze paused on the face of each minister, ensuring that each man understood the monumental task awaiting them. "Palmer will address the complexities of coordinating such a historic occasion," he concluded.

ALTHOUGH HAROLD WILSON was a youthful and energetic force in British politics, he was a pragmatic one above all. He understood the symbolic power of Winston Churchill, even as he sought to distance his government from Churchill's legacy. The room was replete with his closest advisors: men who had stood by him and shared in his vision for a modern Britain. Yet each of them had their own private thoughts and concerns about what was to come.

Some, like the Chancellor of the Exchequer, worried about the economic implications of a major state event and the cost of hosting a gathering of foreign dignitaries. Others, like the Home Secretary, were more concerned about potential demonstrations from groups opposed to Churchill's policies. However, none were unaware of the immense historical significance of the task at hand. Their collective experience in statecraft would be tested in the coming days as the world turned its eyes toward London once again.

"Mr. Palmer?"

"Thank you, Prime Minister," Stuart Palmer replied, his voice tinged with nervousness as he rose from his seat. At sixty-two years of age, Palmer was a man of noticeable presence. His conservative suit and bowtie marked him as distinctly traditional amidst the more modern dress of the ministers. He paused, affixed a pair of half-frame reading glasses precariously near the end of a rather imposing nose, and looked around the room. "With your permission, Sir, I'd like to first give some background as to how all of this has developed." He hesitated for a moment, aware of all eyes upon him as he slid a thin file folder from his briefcase and placed it on the table.

"That's a grand idea, Palmer. Proceed," Wilson replied between deliberate puffs on his pipe.

"Again, thank you, Prime Minister," Palmer continued. His tone grew slightly more confident as he aimed to seize the ministers' attention. "The plans for Mr. Churchill's funeral date back to just after Her Majesty's glorious coronation in 1953. You all know that she dubbed Mr. Churchill a Knight of the Garter, but what you may not know is that Sir Winston suffered a stroke a few days later. This news was never released to the public. Certain circles were made aware, but secrecy was paramount."

"That's an outrage," whispered a voice. It belonged to James Callaghan, the Chancellor of the Exchequer—regarded by most as the *second* most powerful office in the government. "I was in the Shadow Cabinet then, and we never heard a word about such a thing." His indignation was palpable.

There were murmurs of consensus as several men exchanged looks. And a murmur of conversation broke out across the table. Many wore expressions of disbelief, others of anger.

Prime Minister Wilson raised his hand, bringing them back to order with the gesture. "Gentlemen, I understand your anger. But I do not think any good purpose will be served at this time by second-guessing Mr. Churchill's service and career. He has always been a crafty survivor, I think we can all agree. Please, Mr. Palmer, continue."

"Thank you, Prime Minister." Palmer was visibly relieved. "As I indicated, the illness was not made public at the time, but those closest to him thought Mr. Churchill might very well have to resign. He confounded them, however, with a speedy and full recovery. The Queen was well aware of the Prime Minister's health challenges and was very concerned." He paused to wipe his glasses, now slightly fogged, and then earnestly spoke again. "By all accounts, she has always had great respect, even affection, for Mr. Churchill. Regards him almost as a beloved uncle."

"This is a vital point to bear in mind, Gentlemen," Wilson interjected with urgency, feeling the tide turn and seeking to remind them of the larger picture. "If any of you find any part of this distasteful because of political and personal disagreements with Sir Winston, I suggest you remember Her Majesty's feelings and wishes," Wilson said.

"Hear, hear," they all replied, the echo of voices now more subdued, if still slightly conflicted. The political implications loomed large, and Wilson wanted to ensure that their personal and partisan inclinations did not obscure the royal esteem in which Churchill was held.

Wilson looked around the table and said, "Again, Mr. Palmer, please go on. There will be no more interruptions."

Palmer continued his thoughts about the close relationship between Sir Winston Churchill and Her Majesty the Queen, their personal bond a matter of great public interest and frequent speculation. "As we all know, when he was once asked what he and the Queen talked about for so long on so many occasions, he replied, 'Mostly horse racing,'" Palmer said.

A series of barely suppressed chuckles from around the table followed this well-known story. Those assembled could imagine the scene quite clearly: the great man of state and the young queen, sharing confidences with humor and respect.

"At the time of his initial illness," Palmer continued, "Her Majesty was on the verge of planning her first official excursion abroad as the reigning monarch." As he spoke, the men around the table became absorbed in the intrigue of this early episode, leaning slightly forward as if Palmer was sharing a titillating secret. "So it is hardly surprising that she had a discreet discussion beforehand about what should happen if Sir Winston did indeed pass during her absence from England. She instructed her staff to give him a public funeral on a scale befitting his position in history and to spare no effort in doing so."

A voice interrupted Palmer's flow. "May I ask a question, Mr. Palmer?" said George Brown, the Secretary of State for Economic Affairs. The words seemed to hang in the air as all eyes shifted to the Prime Minister. No one was sure what to expect, especially from Brown, a man known for brazenness, drunkenness, and impulsiveness.

The Prime Minister frowned slightly.

He didn't quite know what to do with his unpredictable colleague. No one did. Brown had a history of putting both feet in his mouth, usually because of his excessive drinking. His worst moment remained vivid in everyone's memory. In the aftermath of John F. Kennedy's assassination, Brown—who often exaggerated his closeness to the Kennedy family—had appeared on national television as part of a tribute to the fallen leader. He was drunk, and an incoherent stream of slurred words resulted in a humiliating day-after apology.

It was quite a fall from grace. Before that incident, his political star had been on the rise. He was considered Prime Minister material, and many felt that if not for his public disgrace, it might be Brown addressing them today.

Wilson nodded to Brown, indicating that he could go ahead with his question. "Thank you, Harold, er, I'm sorry—I mean, Prime

Minister." The familiar gaffe drew some eye rolls and speaking looks that Brown had already initiated his daily alcohol consumption.

However, despite his demeanor, the Secretary of State forged ahead. "Wouldn't a full state funeral require a request from the Queen to the House of Commons and an affirmative vote after Old Winnie's death? Has Her Majesty indicated that she plans to do this?"

The others cast surprised glances at one another. By some miracle, Brown was coherent, and the question was legitimate. Most had expected a foggy, alcohol-laden preamble from him and a longer, more awkward foray into something controversial. Instead, he seemed lucid.

"Yes, she has," Palmer replied, relieved the question was easy to answer. "I expect that such a motion will be made in the House within a few hours of Mr. Churchill's passing, and it will be, of course, promptly approved." Brown sat back in his chair, quite pleased with himself.

Stuart Palmer then summed up his briefing. "So the wheels were set in motion for Winston Churchill's grand farewell approximately a dozen years before his death. With Her Majesty's initial directive, our preparations started in earnest. Those early instructions were soon enhanced to include a variety of contingencies. Over time, what began as a simple notion was formalized into a comprehensive working plan.

Because Sir Winston did not step aside with his first serious illness, it was decided that most elements of the plan should be kept out of his view. After his retirement, even though he had lingering health issues, he remained active for several years. We thought it would be best if he did not know what we were doing, and Her Majesty agreed. By the late 1950s the process was highly organized, and a detailed blueprint was in place. The plan is called, appropriately, Operation Hope Not."

"Thank you, Mr. Palmer," Wilson said. Then he addressed the rest of the men around the table and glanced at Roger Hollis, head of MI5. "Each of you will receive a numbered and bound copy of this plan as you leave today. You are to keep this in your sole possession and guard it carefully. Are we agreed?"

In unison, they said, "Yes, Prime Minister."

Wilson then spoke directly to the intelligence chief: "Roger, I assume you will oversee security preparations at St. Paul's, as well as the other elements of the plan?"

Hollis, who had been making a few notes, simply looked up and replied, "Indeed, Sir. I will keep you fully informed."

A moment later, the Prime Minister pushed his chair back and stood up, signaling the end of the meeting. There was a scraping and shuffling of chairs as the ministers, one by one, followed their leader's example. They had their assignments, and now all of them would return to their various offices and ministries to make sure they were prepared. But their tasks were of secondary importance at this point to the new Prime Minister.

HAROLD WILSON HAD deliberately cleared his schedule, setting aside time to work alone in his private study at Ten Downing Street. Making his way there after dismissing the ministers, he pondered the speech he had begun and knew he must soon complete. Wilson did not have the certainty of precisely *when* he would need to deliver it, yet he was acutely aware that the speech must be finished before Churchill was laid to rest.

Close on the heels of Sir Winston's passing, Wilson would undoubtedly face a significant moment in the House of Commons. As the bearer of a message from Her Majesty the Queen, he would be responsible for speaking in favor of her motion to host a grand farewell for the old bulldog. Knowing the House Chamber would be packed with peers and members, he was determined not to waste this crucial political opportunity. It would be a definitive occasion for his new government.

The Prime Minister had spent his entire adult life in politics. He understood what would be expected of him when Churchill's moment finally came. However, he sensed that it was something quite out of the ordinary. He would be eulogizing one of the most eloquent figures ever to have crafted a phrase in the English language, and the difficulty of the task was not lost on him.

The floor of the Commons will no doubt be rowdy and combative, he thought, but it was the vast reach of the BBC that worried him even more. His speech would be broadcast live to households throughout the United Kingdom; indeed, it would be seen by millions around the globe. Wilson felt the pressure mounting, and he was deeply conscious that his words would be part of the story of the realm.

He knew he had to create memorable words about an unforgettable man, and he was determined to make certain that every syllable was his own. No speechwriters. Churchill had written everything himself, and Wilson was resolute that he would do the same, no matter how challenging the task.

Many of Sir Winston's speeches seemed to be so casual, so spontaneous. But Wilson knew that was not the case. Churchill had been known to labor over each word, each turn of phrase, every single time. Wilson reasoned that the man who had led the nation through perilous times with his brilliant oratory had set the standard high, perhaps impossibly so. He could almost hear the echo of the old warrior's voice in his mind, "We shall fight them on the beaches...." Harold Wilson refocused his thoughts and told himself that he must write about Churchill the way Churchill wrote about Britain. But he wasn't sure he could do it.

He sat at his desk and stared at the half-written speech, feeling its inadequacy and fearing that the world would see him as an amateur beside a giant. He put his pipe to his lips and puffed on it, considering a few more lines that seemed derivative and weak. Then he put the pipe in an ashtray, picked up his pen, and resumed writing.

He began with a simple statement. *"We meet today in this moment of tribute; of spontaneous sympathy this House feels for Lady Churchill and all the members of his family...."*

CHAPTER TWO

EDMUND MURRAY LOOKED on with the steady gaze that came from decades of vigilance. Standing post as a protection officer was in some ways second nature to him now, having been committed to it for fifteen years. He preferred the term "protection officer" to the more common "bodyguard," finding it more aligned with the dignity of his elevated charges. He had spent the most thrilling season of his career as the shadow of the most formidable man in the country—the Prime Minister of Great Britain.

For a lawman, it had been an exciting chapter, but that whirlwind existence had been fading for several years. Those frenetic earlier days felt like they belonged to another life—and the demands of such work had required sacrifices not only from him but from his patient spouse, as well. He owed his wife more than he could measure, beginning with a honeymoon that had been put off for the better part of twenty years. He indulged in a fleeting, affectionate smile at the thought of their unorthodox marital journey—the kind of smile that rarely made an appearance these days, especially on this particular morning that promised to grow heavy.

The Detective Sergeant pondered his posting. He had been on this distinctive assignment for a long time. It was 1950 when his responsibilities began. Now, reluctantly, he could see the end of this remarkable era drawing near. Which was not to say he approached it with any bitterness.

Quite the contrary.

Murray counted himself fortunate—blessed, even—to have witnessed history unfold from such a privileged vantage point. He'd had the luxury of a front-row view of some of the most significant events of the modern age. Such as today, when he took his station outside an unassuming house at the iconic address of 28 Hyde Park Gate in the affluent area of Kensington, West London.

IT WAS JANUARY, and the sun was being its usual shy self. The sky was overcast, full of metallic grey that threatened to unleash a storm. Although not yet frigid, the moisture in the air distorted the temperature, turning the clouds into a thick, cold mist that transformed the day into a wintery scene. Drizzle hung in the air with the promise that it might turn into snow at any moment.

Three men dressed in the crisp uniforms of the local police made their way through the growing commotion on the street. One of them spoke up, his voice a mix of deference and curiosity. "Sir, we've been sent by headquarters and told to report to Detective Sergeant Murray. You him?"

Murray scrutinized the trio briefly. Unlike he, who wore his customary dark business suit, they were clad in the everyday uniforms of police constables, complete with shining silver buttons that glinted even in the weak light. His reply was brisk and authoritative. "Indeed, I am."

"What do you want us to do?" one of the men asked, eager to be useful.

"Well, officers, not much is happening at the moment. Just stand here with me and look official," Murray instructed, his voice resonating with the assurance of a man accustomed to command. "And whatever you do, don't smile. This is likely going to develop into quite the sad day."

The officers snapped to attention.

Their presence was necessary, the crowd gathering around the storied address was swelling by the minute. And it was likely to grow much larger before day's end. Among the assembled were some on professional assignment—journalists wielding their notepads, photographers with cameras slung around their necks, and representatives from the BBC adjusting their cumbersome recording equipment.

But most were ordinary citizens, intrigued passersby eager to catch a glimpse of something monumental. They were hungry to connect with a moment of great historic weight, knowing that it could be their only chance. They braved the cold, drawn by a mix of curiosity and reverence.

The officers did their best to shield their eyes from the occasional harsh glare of television lights now trained on the house and to stay warm as they felt the mercury steadily inch down the thermometer. They shuffled to keep their circulation going, huddling a little closer together with each passing minute.

EARLIER THAT MORNING, the front door of 28 Hyde Park Gate had opened just enough to reveal a dim interior, and Detective Sergeant Murray had taken the opportunity to lean in for news. The pale light from inside cast a feeble glow on his face. He heard a woman's voice echo softly, "Mr. Murray, one of the doctors will be out after lunch with a statement."

He responded with a customary tip of his hat, "Thank you, ma'am."

But the promised hour had come and gone without any further communication, leaving him and the gathering throng outside to their own assumptions and speculations. Murray understood well the unpredictability of any affairs connected to Winston Churchill. The legendary figure had always possessed a unique relationship with the marching of time, seeming to exist in his own universe where the rigid structure of clocks and calendars scarcely held dominion over his activities. Time was elastic in the Churchillian world—a flexible, negotiable entity that could bend to inspiration or will. It was as if he commanded his own chronology, his life unfolding on a grand tapestry where moments were embroidered by importance rather than sequence.

Most in the crowd felt the bite of the moody weather, but none had chosen to leave. They were waiting for word about the man who had presided over a turbulent century like no one else, and the chill in their bones seemed a small price to pay. The mist now clung like a wet shroud, and they pulled their collars higher and wrapped scarves tighter.

The curtains were pulled over most of the home's windows, yet the determined in the crowd strained to catch any glimpse of what might be happening inside. A floral wallpaper could be seen through two of the windows that were not completely covered, faintly visible against the shifting winter light. People craned their necks, moving in small clusters, hoping for a better vantage. A swirl of anticipation mixed with a sense of dread filled the air, a muted buzz of whispers and shuffling.

Occasionally, speculation rippled among them, like the quiet words from one lady, "I think I saw something. Is that him coming to the window?" Her voice carried with a tremor of hopefulness, and others looked too. But it was only their imaginations playing tricks. Even the little flashes of supposed movement through the windows proved illusory. There seemed to be a ghostliness to the waiting, as if history itself hovered on the brink of being made and revealed.

"I was here a while back. That was a much happier day," another woman said, almost as if speaking to her own memory. Her nostalgia cast a subtle warmth amid the chill. "It was for his birthday. He came to the window and smiled. Then he flashed that victory sign. We all cheered. It was a lovely thing," she continued, her voice blooming with the recollection. A tear welled at the corner of her eye, and she brushed it away with a gloved hand, not wanting to let it linger. The momentary lightness of her reminiscence seemed to be swallowed quickly by the gravity of the present mood.

"Don't go looking for any victory sign today," a man near her said, his voice a muted response. It was meant as an acknowledgment of the somber reality, yet it held its own kind of tenderness. Several others nodded in wordless agreement, the weight of the moment shared among them. Pensively, some bowed their heads, and their lips moved in silent prayer, offering what comfort they could in the uncertainty.

CHAPTER THREE

CHURCHILL HAD MADE what would become his final public appearance the night before he turned 90. The theory behind heralding the event a day early was that a Sunday would make it easier for people to come. They would be less likely to have work or other obligations than on Monday, Winston's actual birthday—November 30. Notices appeared in the press. Once the word was out, the people showed up.

Clementine was as attentive and as doting as ever. She had done what she could to make the house look lovely, festively adorning it with her husband's favorite flowers and placing them in strategic locations throughout. She let others attend to the important matters of television and photography, and focused most of her own energies toward getting Churchill ready for what she sensed would be his last performance.

When she asked which outfit he would like to wear for his big moment, his answer was ready. "Surprise me," he said, perhaps sarcastically. But after more than fifty-six years of marriage, she knew him well enough to know that on this occasion, he was content to be in her hands. She returned a few minutes later, having selected one of his eight siren suits—the full-body zipper outfits he immortalized during the war. Each was tailored from the finest material. Several months earlier, when rumors floated through London about his ill health, Churchill's response had been to order three more of them—maroon, navy blue, and green velvet.

"Tell the tailor," he said, "I intend to wear them out and order new ones."

Clementine selected the green velvet suit. Her favorite. It also matched the dress she had on that day. She zipped him up, and though the effort clearly tired him, she said he looked rather heroic. "Just like when you were in charge," she told him. She was deeply fond of those happy and hectic times, and there was a part of her that yearned for them even more now than when they were unfolding at a dizzying pace. She fiddled with the bowtie and made a playful statement to lighten the moment.

"Your public awaits, Sir Winston!"

She worried how he would handle the brief walk through the house from his bedroom to the drawing room where he would greet the crowd, and was grateful the effort would involve only the main floor. Two years earlier, after Churchill had broken his hip in a nasty fall at the Hotel de Paris in Monte Carlo, the home had undergone a massive retrofit.

Never again would he be required to climb a set of stairs.

His cane in hand, the old man ambled through the halls, past books and paintings that hinted about his remarkable life. Though his steps were small, each one of them attempted to be as sprightly as possible. He let out a loud harrumph with each shuffling click of his walking stick and before he was ready, he stopped in front of the decanter Mary had placed in the room and poured a generous measure of whisky into a nearby glass.

He took several moments to catch his breath and poured himself a second. As Clementine looked on, she was relieved to see that Sir Winston had full intentions of meeting the day with the impishness and resolve that had carried him through the wars and served him well with the family.

THE STAFF AT 28 Hyde Park Gate orchestrated everything with meticulous precision for his birthday appearance. They hovered near the front window, curtains drawn, resolute not to let a single glimpse of Churchill reach the eager eyes gathered outside until the precise moment. They were determined that neither the passage of years nor any mundane struggle to reach his place would cast a shadow over the day's image of the venerated statesman.

The suspense grew in the crowd outside as the hour passed and the curtains remained shut. But the delay heightened anticipation, lending theatrical tension to the event. Then, dramatically, the curtains were thrown open. The murmur of expectation outside transformed into a resonant cheer. There, in the brilliant glow of the midday light, stood Winston and Clementine Churchill. At first, the elderly man's expression was one of almost childlike wonder, a momentary hint of bewilderment crossing his face at the size of the throng that had gathered to salute him. Yet within seconds, this gave way to the famous smile which seemed to unite with his audience.

A singular voice rose from the density of people tightly packed in the cul-de-sac, shouting above the others in a jubilant greeting, "Happy birthday, Sir Winston!" And then the crowd was one enormous choir. They sang in triumphant unison, "For He's a Jolly Good Fellow—" and the tune rolled onward until, inevitably, it morphed to the familiar notes of "Happy Birthday, Dear Winston."

A little girl tugged at her mother's sleeve. Her eyes were wide with curiosity and surprise. "Who is that, Mummy?" she asked, her gaze fixed on the stooped figure at the window. "Who are those old people?"

With a smile, her mother answered, "Sweetheart, that is Sir Winston Churchill and his wife, Lady Churchill."

The girl frowned, her young mind working to make sense of it all. "Is he a Knight or something?" she persisted, wanting to understand the significance of this spectacle. Her mother laughed softly.

"In a way, yes. Her Majesty made him a knight many years ago. He's a great and brave man who has done many great things for our country." The girl accepted her mother's words without further question. But they would linger in her memory and gain new meaning many years later, after history's lessons filled in the gaps of her childhood understanding. She listened and watched as the scene unfolded, too young to grasp the magnitude but still absorbing the vibrant atmosphere.

Inside the house, hidden from the eyes of the crowd, Roy Howells, Churchill's loyal valet, discreetly supported the old man's right arm. His grip was steady but gentle, offering balance without intruding on the elder statesman's dignity. On the opposite side, Clementine was a pillar of strength and grace, bracing her husband's left as the moment of joyful homage unfolded outside. They exchanged a private look, an entire lifetime of shared triumphs and trials passing silently between them.

From the street, the chorus of voices reached an exuberant crescendo, and Winston, visibly moved, turned from the window. Tears—perhaps a mixture of joy, nostalgia, and awareness of time's relentless march—glistened in his eyes. The curtains drew closed again. A hush of expectancy and hope went through the onlookers, a collective breath held in anticipation. Would they have another glimpse of the great man, or was that the final sight of the day?

They didn't have to wait long.

Like any master performer acknowledging his audience's ardor, the curtains reopened. The mood shifted from somber to spirited as Sir Winston reappeared and gave the crowd what they had dared not even fully hope for—his iconic V for victory sign. The hand gesture, once a symbol of defiance and determination during Britain's darkest hour, now conveyed gratitude and farewell with poignant resonance. He held the sign aloft, fingers steady yet tender with age, while the voices below rose anew in jubilant response.

Some half-expected Winston to speak, but no words were necessary. The moment, elegantly orchestrated and imbued with reverence, spoke volumes. It was a visual and emotional symphony, bearing witness to a man who had become the embodiment of indomitable will. The crowd's noise swelled and then ebbed as Churchill, with an actor's flawless sense of timing, turned from the window again.

One final time, the curtains fell to veil the scene. An echo of cheers lingered in the air even as people began to disperse, their hearts full because of what they had witnessed. It was to be Sir Winston Churchill's last public appearance, a moment inadvertently eternalized, destined to be recalled by a generation in the days to come.

NOW, TWO MONTHS later—January 1965—two doctors quietly attended to Winston Churchill in a modestly furnished room at the back of the house. They took turns listening to the old man's labored breathing, watching Clementine as she sat by her husband's bed holding his listless hand. When she looked up at them hoping for the reassurance they could not give, one of the doctors finally broke the silence. "We're very sorry," he said to Clementine, speaking on behalf of them both, "but this latest episode looks to be too much for him to overcome. It's just a matter of time, now."

Clementine, her voice small but resolute, asked, "How much time?"

The other doctor merely shrugged and sighed. "Could be hours. Could be days. Very hard to predict in such cases. We know he's been long thought of as an English bulldog and such, but even the strongest of their breed reach an end at some point."

Her eyes grew red, and again she asked, desperately clinging to the hope that these men might be mistaken, "How is this different from the other episodes?"

"It's a matter of degree, simple as that." The first doctor replied gently. "It would appear that your husband is getting ready to meet his Maker."

Clemmie began to weep and in a wavering voice said, "He's always wondered if his Maker would ever be prepared to meet him."

MEANWHILE, THE MULTITUDE outside stood frozen, collectively caught up in the historic significance of the moment. It was a diverse gathering, one that sometimes elbowed and jostled for a better view of the window. It included those who had lived through the bombing of London as well as teenagers who had only learned about Churchill's wartime leadership in school.

They knew about how he had rallied their parents and grandparents during the Blitz. They knew about the stirring speeches and how he came to symbolize the resolve of an entire nation. "Never give in," the old man had said. They never had. But now, some thought sadly, it was Winston Churchill's turn to surrender to the inevitable.

The growing crowd also included a number of foreigners on assignment, reporters from America, France, and other parts of Europe. There was a certain irony in their presence. It was not even a year earlier, after President Kennedy's death, that it was said there would never again be such an outpouring of world interest in the passing of one man.

The crowd in front of 28 Hyde Park Gate knew otherwise.

CHAPTER FOUR

FOR DAYS, THE news of Churchill's decline reverberated around the globe, splashed prominently on the front pages of newspapers from Paris to New York, and Tokyo to Buenos Aires. In a country known for keeping calm and carrying on, a whole nation seemed to hold its breath, waiting for the last chapter of his storied life to conclude.

Harold Wilson wanted to show that he was not only astute but also gracious in the face of the impending tragedy. He cleared his schedule so that he could personally visit his failing predecessor, lingering at the house for over an hour and telling reporters assembled outside that the circumstances were dire and that his prayers were with Churchill and his family.

Others also filed in and out of the Churchill home under clouds of sadness. Violet Bonham Carter, who had known Churchill longer than most, paid her respects but stayed only briefly, as the sight of her old friend on his deathbed proved too much to bear. The scene overwhelmed her and she hastily bid him farewell before her emotion escaped her control. Although she was aware of the decades-long speculation surrounding her opinion of Clementine's suitability as a match for Winston, her feelings on the subject were irrelevant now.

At this crucial hour, she told Clementine she was lucky to have shared so much of her life with him. But even that bit of sentiment couldn't keep Violet at the house for very long. An old friend of sixty years, she knew there was nothing she could do to help, other than say her tearful "Goodbye, Winston" and escape before she broke down.

The public kept its own vigil, lining the street and outlasting even the most dedicated reporters. Many exhaled misty clouds with each chilled breath, but they stayed put, knowing that they were witnessing a pivotal moment in history. Larger with each passing hour, the gathering showed little interest in dispersing.

AN ELDERLY COUPLE, he with rather pronounced war medals on his coat, gingerly approached one of the constables Murray had assigned to duty. They walked the short distance with deliberate thin-ice care and, once at the house, handed over a bouquet of flowers.

A voice that was barely above a whisper said, "He would have liked tulips, don't you think?"

Her husband, who wore thick glasses and hearing aids, replied "Yes, my dear."

"B-but is this OK, Constable? We just want to leave these for him."

The officer smiled gently and said, "Certainly, ma'am. I'll see to it that they are delivered directly."

The lady, expressing gratitude, looked up at the policeman and said, "I was here during the bloody Blitz, we both were. And my husband was also in the First War and then through that awful mess at Dunkirk. We just felt we had to come. We're so very grateful for what he done for us."

The crowd was a study in generations.

Some, like that elderly couple, had lived through both global conflicts, others had memories only of the most recent one. Still others were so young they had to depend on parental or grandparental stories to help them sort out Churchill's significance in the grand scheme of things. Their very presence helped them connect with those stories.

One young man, who had been just a boy when Churchill gave his stirring speeches, turned to his friend and said, "Ya know, if it wasn't for Winnie, God bless 'im, we'd have bloody Germans jack-booting up and down these very streets with swastikas on their lapels. My pop always says he saved everybody's life."

OMINOUSLY, YET SIGNIFICANTLY, also part of the throng across from the house at Hyde Park Gate, standing silently among the masses were two poker-faced men dispatched by the Soviet Embassy to monitor things. The Russians had just as much interest, if not more, in the developments surrounding Churchill as his own countrymen. Their involvement, however, had a very *different* character to it.

They had orders to keep a close watch, like vultures or undertakers—some would say like the KGB spies they indeed were. They were entirely focused on the declining health of the old man who had been a thorn in their side since the day he made that Iron Curtain speech in America. And even before that. In fact, they had anticipated and waited for this moment for years.

Every hour, sometimes more frequently, one or the other made his way to a red telephone box a block away. They rang their embassy to report the latest, always with a bleak picture of what they observed: "No improvement," they said, in both English and in Russian. "Not long." The two of them could not be on the scene constantly. Their long leather coats stood out in a crowd, even in a crowd as large as the one assembled outside the Churchill home, and too many trips to the telephone might impress those in the crowd as suspicious.

Eventually, their bosses at the embassy assigned other comrades to replace them. Then more. The cadre of Soviets grew by the day, watching the Churchill vigil with great interest. But these men had motivations that went far beyond simply learning the latest news, or even accurately transmitting it back to their superiors.

The Soviets were playing a long and sinister game.

DURING THE GREAT Patriotic War against Hitler, they had proved themselves as enduring and resilient fighters. Their endurance at Hyde Park Gate was not a matter of physical stamina, however. It was just a matter of making sure they were ready to take their cue when the time came. By the time others had tired and gone home, they would still be on the scene.

But their part in the vigil had nothing to do with paying tribute, nor did it involve reverence or respect of any kind. The men had a mission and an agenda. Each of them was convinced that the entire world, and especially the Eastern part of it, would change soon—in a big way.

Even in his most lucid and aware moments, Winston Churchill, despite his penchant for intrigue, could never have envisioned the plot that was about to unfold. It was a scheme that had been around and waiting for more than a dozen years, ever since the British Lion had lost his roar and the Conservatives had lost their power. Despite all his brilliance, all his expansive understanding of history, the man who described the Soviets as "a riddle, wrapped in a mystery, inside an enigma," had no idea of the full set of plans his death would set off.

A plot that would use his death as a *trigger.*

CHAPTER FIVE

Washington, D.C.
January 16, 1965

THE BRITISH AMBASSADOR to the United States sat alone at his desk in the sparsely furnished study of the imposing embassy residence, an expansive mansion located on one the most prestigious avenues in Washington, D.C. A fire crackled in the nearby hearth, shedding the only light in the room.

Though it was morning and the sun was shining brightly in a cloudless sky, the drapes had been drawn to match the mood of the room's solitary occupant. He was making careful preparations to step down from his role and return to England. But fate seemed to be dealing him one more hand to play before he could do so.

He had, of course, been closely following the news from home about the final decline of Winston Churchill. But it was more than a professional or patriotic sense of things that now filled his thoughts, though they were indeed a part of what he was feeling. What preoccupied him most at this moment, as the world awaited the passing of a giant, was a personal crisis of conscience that had been steadily plaguing him for more than a year.

David Ormsby-Gore had been the Ambassador since 1961. In an unprecedented move, President John F. Kennedy had personally recommended David to Prime Minister Macmillan during a meeting at Key West, Florida. Macmillan had appeared taken aback by the boldness of the request, but in truth, he had been expecting it all along.

The man sometimes referred to as "Supermac" had been keenly aware of the remarkably close friendship between Kennedy and Ormsby-Gore. In fact, Macmillan had been present back in 1938 in Scotland the weekend the two young men met for the very first time. And, in a strange twist of both history and genetics, Macmillan was actually distantly related by blood to Kennedy *and* Ormsby-Gore.

That 1938 occasion was a typically British late summer gathering hosted by Lord Harlech—David's father—at his sprawling estate near Oban. That particular weekend turned out to be unforgettable in large part because of how it ended, with Harlech and most of the others in attendance scrambling to get back to London. Prime Minister Neville Chamberlain had just announced that he was flying to meet personally with Hitler about Czechoslovakia.

At Munich.

IN ATTENDANCE THAT long-past weekend, though hardly noticed, was twenty-one-year-old John Fitzgerald Kennedy, who much preferred to be called "Jack." He and his older brother, Joe, were sons of the controversial United States Ambassador to Great Britain, Joseph P. Kennedy.

Jack usually found himself in the shadow of his popular and extroverted brother. Possibly this is what drew him to the son of Lord Harlech, who, like Jack, was the second son of a powerful man.

In David's case, though, the older brother had died tragically in an automobile accident three years earlier. It was now left to the bookish and boyish younger brother who had none of the kind of charisma possessed by the elder, to carry the mantle for the fallen sibling.

The two of them—Kennedy and Ormsby-Gore—were sometimes referred to as "slacker second sons," but both were developing skills to enable them to surprise all who made the mistake of underestimating them. They formed an instant bond that weekend around conversations about world affairs, not to mention the ever-present ladies. It was friendship at first sight. Of course, there was a war looming in their future, one that Jack's older brother would not survive. That would serve to further cement the friendship between Jack and David for years to come.

IN 1961, WHEN David arrived in Washington to commence his official duties following Macmillan's appointment, it quickly became apparent that his was a post like no other. This was much more than a diplomatic relationship. More than an assignment of political convenience, his presence in the nation's capital was emblematic of the personal bond he shared with America's youngest and most charismatic President.

In addition to the myriad formal interactions between the British Embassy and the White House, there were too many intimate and "off-the-record" moments with Jack to count—late night meetings in the Oval Office, travel aboard Air Force One, and winter weekends at the Kennedy compound in Palm Beach. David was warmly embraced by the Kennedy family. They shared secrets. They talked about Cuba, the Soviets, and the world. Even Jackie adored the man they affectionately called "the British Ambassador to Camelot."

However, David didn't share *all* his secrets with Jack.

Especially the big one about how he had been working in London with a small group of young and well-born British students who had been recruited by Soviet Intelligence since a short while before he and Jack had met. That work was dangerous and it continued into his days as Ambassador.

And what was eating at David, and would continue to do so for the rest of his days, was that he had known his friend's life had been in jeopardy. While he didn't know all the details, he had known enough that he could have warned Jack not to go to Dallas.

NOW, DAVID HAD more intelligence from the same Soviet source. It was about yet another plot involving yet another President of the United States. But even more than that, it was also a threat to dozens of world leaders, not to mention peace on the planet.

He had been asked to discover Lyndon Johnson's plans with regard to Churchill's impending funeral. And he had experienced a chill at the thought of what such a request possibly meant. Would David allow history to repeat itself, or worse, to expand itself to include the lives of many?

So in the darkness of his study, and born of the bitterness that overwhelmed his soul, Ambassador David Ormsby-Gore made a decision, brave on the one hand, and cowardly on the other. He would find a way to betray the people for whom he had secretly been working for nearly thirty years. He would find the courage to pay the price for redemption. It was the only way he felt he could continue to live with himself.

THE OLD BAKELITE rotary telephone sat on an ornately carved desk made of dark mahogany. David stared at it with a mix of determination and dread, knowing that the call he was about to make could alter the course of many lives, including his own. He picked up the receiver.

"Yes, Mr. Ambassador. How may I help you?" The voice of one of his trusted staff members responded promptly and politely.

"Please contact a man named William Moyers at the White House. He's a Special Assistant to President Johnson. I need to meet privately with the President as soon as possible." David took a moment, careful to stress his next words. "But this needs to be private and 'unofficial.' Do you understand?"

"Yes, Mr. Ambassador. I'll make contact and let you know when you can pop over."

David imagined the informal phrase "pop over" would be enough to explain the nature of the visit. Still, he needed to be certain that his urgency and insistence on confidentiality had been conveyed.

"Thank you. And no one else around here, other than you and my driver—absolutely no one else—is to know anything about this visit." He added the last part with particular emphasis, ensuring that the gravity and secrecy of this mission were unmistakable.

"Of course, sir."

He replaced the receiver in its cradle and, for a moment, allowed himself to absorb the enormity of what he had just set in motion. There was no turning back now, he realized, no undoing the act of defiance into which he was now fully committed. It was a gamble, one that could either bring him the redemption he sought or lead to his ruin. He shivered slightly, feeling the room, and the entire embassy, grow colder around him.

A seed of doubt, small but persistent, gnawed at his conscience. But he suppressed it, knowing that lives, perhaps millions, depended on what he did in the coming hours. It was time for him to act, to take a risk larger than anything he had ever attempted. *Perhaps*, he thought, *it's a fitting end to my years of service.*

In that moment of silence, he wondered what kind of reception he would receive from Lyndon Johnson. His friendship with Jack Kennedy had given him carte blanche access to the President of the United States—even when it might have been better if he hadn't had it. Would the new administration be so accommodating? He didn't know the answer.

But he felt the pressing need to find out.

CHAPTER SIX

THE DOOR TO the bathroom was ajar, and from his vantage point just outside in the hallway, Bill Moyers could see the President of the United States sitting on the toilet reading that morning's *Washington Post*. It was a familiar scene for Johnson's young assistant. He was about to clear his throat and call out to his boss when he heard the famously booming voice instead call out to him first. "Moyers, you see this thing about Churchill?" the voice bellowed.

"Um...yes, Mr. President. Saw it," Moyers responded. "It's item one on your briefing today." The young assistant continued to hover near the entrance to the bathroom as he listened to the sound of the pages of the newspaper rustling in the President's hands.

"You think the old dinosaur is down for the count?" Johnson asked, still poring over the front page of the *Post*, focusing on the details of the story about the British giant's final hours.

Moyers peeked in, watching Johnson's face for clues to his mood—always a challenge. "It certainly looks that way," he replied cautiously.

"Well, when it happens, it will be the biggest news since VE Day!" Johnson barked, returning his attention to the text of the newspaper. Moyers thought, not for the first time, that the murder of Kennedy might fit that bill, but he also knew his boss's blind spot where the late President was concerned. His job was to bring things back into focus before Johnson launched into one of his infamous tirades.

"I imagine every leader in the world is making plans to travel to London for what will likely be a funeral of epic proportions. You want me to start those wheels turning?" Moyers tried his best to steer Johnson to a more productive track.

"I suppose," Johnson thundered. "But it's not really what I want to be doing in the first days of my *own* damn term." He tossed the newspaper onto the floor beside him. "Hell, the old man could die right on the twentieth!"

Moyers winced at the thought and tried to head off his boss's train of thought before it went totally off track. "Mr. President, even if that's the case, nothing will get in the way of your celebration. It's going to be the biggest and best inauguration since Andrew Jackson."

Johnson grabbed the newspaper again and stood up, balling it into his massive hand. "I'd rather be compared to FDR, boy," he snapped.

Moyers took this in stride. He was used to his boss's outbursts after spending years at his side. "Of course, Mr. President," he replied in a respectful but deferential voice. "But consider this: the passing of a giant like Churchill will give you a chance to be front and center on the world stage. You know your history, sir—that means political capital here at home. Everyone who's anyone will be there, and you'll be able to work your magic on them one at a time."

The President smiled, both at the thought and that his young assistant was so good at kissing ass and not forgetting who the boss was. Job security. "Well, get busy," he instructed, zipping his pants and fastening his belt. "But I don't want to be gone a minute longer than I have to. Didn't we just make a big deal about Churchill's birthday?"

Moyers sensed that Johnson was already looking for ways to avoid the visit to London he would surely have to make. "Yes, sir, his 90th. You sent a message and gifts. It was well reported in the British press."

"Yeah, but not much over here. The editors probably think Kennedy would've done better," LBJ said, with a sigh.

The toilet flushed, much to the relief of Bill Moyers, who moved his hand to his face to obscure his disgust. Moyers had worked for Johnson when he was Senate Majority leader and followed him to the White House when he became Vice President. He knew him well enough to know that there was more than a small chance of a meltdown between now and inauguration day if Johnson worked himself into a frenzy about the funeral of the century overshadowing his own moment in the limelight.

THE PRESIDENT OF the United States emerged from the bathroom while Bill Moyers patiently reviewed the morning's agenda. There was the latest report from the CIA Director John McCone about Vietnam. Johnson had been steadily increasing America's commitment in Southeast Asia, mainly through McCone's agency and other covert operations. Even after the Gulf of Tonkin incident the previous summer, Johnson was adamant about keeping the full scope of activities hidden from the public, and even from Congress. McCone was deeply uneasy about this approach and had already made up his mind to resign from the post Kennedy had appointed him to within the next few months.

As they moved toward the Oval Office, Moyers shifted the conversation to details of the upcoming inauguration. "Looks like the weather should cooperate, sir. Much better than four years ago." Lyndon frowned at his aide's mention of that anniversary. "It's going to be about forty degrees and cloudy, but no more snow after today. Just the inch or so on the ground now."

"Uh-huh, how about people? Anybody got the balls to predict how many will show?"

"Well, sir, all indications are that you'll be addressing the largest inauguration crowd ever assembled. Bigger than even Eisenhower's."

"Well, we'll see about that. Got my speech ready?"

"Yes, Mr. President, the latest draft is already waiting on your desk."

"Good—you get that boy wonder Bob Hardesty involved?"

"Yes, he gave it a thorough review and made some recommendations."

"Well, Billy boy, I want your fingerprints on it too. And like I told Hardesty, I want a short speech. Short and to the point. None of that flowery Sorenson shit, either. Real words for real people. Stand up. Speak up. Shut up. That's what my pappy always said to the preacher. You've got to write it so that the woman who cleans the building across the street can understand it."

"I agree, sir. I think you're going to like what you see," Moyers replied, nodding. The two entered the President's office. When LBJ was seated at his desk, Moyers said, "There's one other thing I want to bring to your attention, sir."

"Fire away, and then get out so I can get some work done. And send in Reedy."

"I will, sir. Now, that one thing is this: the British Ambassador is asking for a private meeting with you this morning. Very short notice. It's not really an official request, but something he wants to talk with you about personally."

"Ormsby-Gore, right?"

"Yes, David Ormsby-Gore. He was appointed by MacMillan back in '61."

"I remember. He was Kennedy's pal. He and Jack went way back to when old Joe Kennedy was over there before the war. Kennedy even lobbied for his appointment. Odd thing, I thought at the time."

"Yes, the Ambassador spent a lot of time with President Kennedy; they traveled together some. Word has it that he's not been the same since Dallas. Depressed, grieving, and such."

"What's he want to talk about?"

"No clue, sir. But he's insistent. Says it's very important that he speak to you, and he emphasizes that it needs to be a personal and private meeting."

"Okay, give him ten minutes this morning, but stay close. Now get out. I want to read this masterpiece of a speech you and your egghead friends have written for me."

CHAPTER SEVEN

"IT'S NOT THE White House, but it'll do in a pinch," Winston Churchill said. A soft cloud of gray curled from the long cigar he had just lit, and he and his wife Clementine surveyed the elegant suite of rooms in the British Embassy in Washington, D.C. The setting was undeniably grand, yet it lacked the historical weight of the President's residence.

Clemmie was pleased with the accommodations. It was, she thought, a place where she might feel quite at home. Their luggage and other belongings were already carefully positioned around the space, lending an ordered coziness to the rooms. She gave Winston a knowing smile, then poured them both a drink. "Well, President Truman doesn't know you as well as Franklin did," she replied. Her tone was gentle but pointed, a reminder of the different circumstances they faced in this new era.

"Of course, of course, I understand that. But you weren't with me back in '41, just after the Japanese attacked Pearl Harbor and dragged the Americans into a war we had been fighting for more than two years," Winston said, his voice tinged with the nostalgia of old war stories. "He was such a gracious host. Did I tell you that he saw me in all my glory once?"

"He what?" Clementine feigned shock, though she knew well the tales of Franklin and Winston's improbable friendship.

"Oh, yes, he wheeled around a corner as I was walking from my bath back to the bedroom."

She smiled tolerantly, "Oh, Winston, you and your childish fascination with being naked."

"I told him that Her Majesty's Prime Minister has nothing to hide from the President of the United States."

"Of course you did. Always with the wit."

"That was, of course, before my heart episode," he mused thoughtfully. "It's simply remarkable that the news of the attack during that Christmas visit never got out. That would've ended at least my part of the Grand Alliance."

"Well, it's obvious God had a plan for you, Winston, and He wasn't quite ready to meet you yet," she said. Her words were soft, full of love and a touch of irony. Then she walked across the room with a grace that belied her age, kissed her husband on the forehead, and handed him his glass.

Winston Churchill gazed for a long moment at Clementine. It was a look of gratitude and affection, as though he were looking over the top of eyeglasses he wasn't wearing. He smiled, briefly letting his serious demeanor drop. Then he examined the room once more, as if taking a mental inventory. "Actually, I think this will be more comfortable for you while I'm away in Missouri with the President," he said.

"And Randolph will be here tomorrow to help me see you off. I don't think it would be fair to unleash your son on the White House help," she replied, her voice teasing with the hint of truth.

They laughed, a shared moment that reminded them of the many challenges they had faced together.

"You're right, indeed, my love. But I do wish you'd consider going with me. This speech may create quite a stir," he urged, the prospect of the speech sparking a youthful light in his eyes.

"Yes, Winston, I've read it. Iron Curtain, and all that. But aren't you taking a tiger by the tail? Mr. Stalin may not be amused. And you may be putting President Truman in a tight spot. You'll likely get your stir."

"Well, that, I think, is the point, isn't it?"

Clemmie rolled her eyes, a gesture that mixed affection with exasperation. "Yes, of course, there must always be a point."

"I was thinking the other day about how I have now lived twenty-five years longer than my father did. I'm an old man. But not dead yet. I know this one speech in a small American town may seem an unlikely platform to mount yet another political comeback, but I'm determined to try." He ran his fingers through his thinning hair and laughed lightly, as if trying to convince himself as well as her.

"Of course you'll come back, Winston. You always do. Never surrender, remember that? But before you get on that train to the middle of nowhere, we need to reply to the cable about the house in Kensington."

"I know, Clemmie, but I'm finding it hard to make such a decision. It's a lot of money," he said with a sigh, though the real burden seemed to be the decision itself.

"Winston! You exasperate me. Since when has money, especially spending it, been any sort of problem for you? Lord Camrose and his friends have made us financially comfortable for the first time in our lives, and the money you'll earn for your book about the war will actually make us wealthy for the first time in our lives."

She sat down and looked at him expectantly.

"Yes, yes, and the fact that we can still stay at Chartwell as part of the trust's agreement, and that for just 350 pounds annually—well, that was a wonderful act of generosity."

"Not just to us, Winston, but to the country when Chartwell is given to the National Trust after we've passed on."

Churchill looked at his wife and smiled broadly, aware now that she had planned this entire line of discussion. "You're right, of course. No more worries about the butcher bill and whether or not the help is drinking my whisky. I'm beginning to climb out of the pit, Clemmie. The crossing on the Queen Elizabeth was refreshing, as were the days in Miami and Cuba. But I still feel the black dog barking at moments. That's why I've worked so hard on this speech. Dealing with a great issue is good therapy."

"I know, dear. I know you're getting better. But we do need to act soon if we want the house."

"All right, Clemmie, send the cable. Make the offer. But make sure we'll be able to annex the section next door. We'll need more space there. Of that, I'm certain."

"We're going to love the home, Winston. I hated Chartwell for many years, but I've grown to love it. I know you're going to grow to love our new home in London."

Winston smiled at her, and they clinked glasses.

WINSTON LEONARD SPENCER-CHURCHILL was born on November 30, 1874, at Blenheim, a palatial country house—one of the largest in the country—long associated with his illustrious ancestors. His mother, Jennie Jerome, hailed from America, while his father, Randolph, was a sometimes-successful politician whose career and life were cruelly abbreviated, partly owing to mental deterioration brought on by syphilis.

Winston had grown up amidst the opulence and privilege that the world of British aristocracy could afford him. He was pampered and spoiled by indulgent members of the household staff who functioned as surrogate parents. While most accounts describe him at times as an unhappy boy suffering from parental neglect, he cultivated an active imagination, fervently nourished by voracious reading habits and a propensity for audacious dreams. What he seemed to miss in familial warmth he made up for with an abundance of ambition.

Following an active and eventful, though brief, military service, he was elected to Parliament in 1900. During the First World War, he served famously as First Lord of the Admiralty, afterward reinventing himself politically and forsaking the Liberal Party for the Tories. Churchill spent much of the 1930s in political exile, considered by many as a man like his own father—possessing a once promising career, missing the ultimate mark, and falling grievously short.

Then a fellow named Hitler ascended to power in Germany.

Churchill's countrymen, particularly members of Parliament, had little appetite for another massive conflict, the painful memories of the last war still raw in their minds. Winston was often a solitary voice as he warned about Germany's potential for unchecked aggression. Events and history proved him right, and eventually he answered the call of King and Country, becoming Prime Minister of Great Britain on May 10, 1940, as the relentless Nazi war machine trampled Belgium and France beneath its iron boots.

The new Prime Minister's visage soon became the most iconic image of the era, and his voice became its resounding soundtrack. Churchill's passionate eloquence tapped deeply into the indomitable spirit of a battered population. His wartime leadership became the stuff of legend. And when the war in Europe concluded in May of 1945, he stood at what appeared to be a political summit.

But several weeks later, his party suffered a devastating defeat in the national elections, and Churchill was given what he called "the royal order of the boot." In the political wilderness once more,

Churchill still had one major comeback in him. And it began in March of 1946, in the homeland of his mother, in an improbable place—a wee town called Fulton, situated in President Truman's home state of Missouri.

There, in a gymnasium packed to the rafters, and following the President's glowing introduction, Churchill delivered a speech that sent shock waves around the world. It was officially titled, "The Sinews of Peace." But that identifier was quickly overshadowed by two resonant words.

In a moment that was historically electric, Churchill introduced the idiom that immediately entered the geo-political lexicon. *Iron Curtain.* An evocative, powerful metaphor, that would endure for decades to characterize a long and tense standoff between the Soviets and the West. A conflict that history came to know as the Cold War.

A line could be drawn from the significance of those words to the eventual and surprising return of the Tories, sweeping once more into power, with Winston back in charge. But by the time he returned to Number 10, the incomparably strong and resilient man who had so capably guided the realm through its darkest challenges was clearly a diminished version of himself.

Churchill often seemed weary, and he frequently took to working from his bedroom. By 1955, he had little choice but to resign again, this time due to failing health. That exit from office came with a finality and sense of sorrow absent when the voters turned him out ten years earlier.

Having surrendered the post and immense pressures of Prime Minister for the last time, he remained a presence in the House of Commons. Though he lingered on those parliamentary back benches, his poor health—and the emotional propensity for depression that had haunted him since youth—deepened his bouts of melancholy. He would sit alone at his desk, pondering his own inescapable mortality. The world was moving on, he brooded, passing him by. It was unrecognizable from the one he had known as a younger man.

Back then, when Britannia ruled the waves, the mighty sun never set on the glorious empire. Now, to Winston's profound sadness, there was hardly an Empire to speak of, and his beloved nation was experiencing a revolution of manners and morals. It was around this time that he told one of his secretaries, "I have worked very hard all my life, and I have achieved a great deal, in the end to achieve nothing."

He emphasized that final word: *"Nothing."*

CHAPTER EIGHT

A FEW MINUTES past ten o'clock, David Ormsby-Gore, the British Ambassador to the United States, entered the Oval Office. The scene was familiar yet strange, marked by the absence of a man who had been his close friend and the presence of a man who was *not* his friend. President Lyndon Johnson sat behind the stately desk, deeply engrossed in a document, seemingly oblivious to the world around him. Juanita Roberts, the President's efficient yet often flustered personal secretary, hesitated at interrupting the powerful man she worked for. She cleared her throat softly before she spoke. "Mr. President? Sir?"

Johnson raised his head with a start, appearing genuinely taken aback. "What is it, Juanita?"

"Your appointment's here. The British Ambassador."

Ormsby-Gore stood back and took in the scene, registering yet again how much things had changed in such a short time. A month earlier, he wouldn't have even needed an appointment to meet the

American President. The ease of the old days had vanished, replaced by formality and protocol. He used to stroll in unannounced, trading jovial pleasantries.

But that casual intimacy had been swept away by more than just the change of administration. There was a new sheriff in town. A sometimes-crude cowboy from Texas had replaced the urbane and articulate statesman from Massachusetts.

On the drive over from the embassy to the White House, he had succumbed to a torrent of memories, his thoughts clouded by nostalgia and longing. He thought of how he and Jack Kennedy had seemed like twin souls. But as he knew too well, history is a relentless force that defies expectation. It swept them up, and then it cruelly cast Kennedy aside. Ormsby-Gore brought himself back to the present as Johnson rubbed his eyes wearily and began to rise from his chair.

"Mr. Ambassador," Johnson said in his Southern drawl, "so great to see you. What can I do for you today?" He gestured for Ormsby-Gore to take a seat in a plush chair across from his desk.

"Mr. President, I'm very grateful for this meeting. Thank you for your time, which I well know is quite precious," said Ormsby-Gore, as he sensed the distance between his own words and his true feelings.

Johnson gave a nod and crossed his arms in a way that suggested both impatience and curiosity. "I know you loved President Kennedy like a brother, and I continue to grieve with you over his loss. Every time I come into this office, I have a sense of duty inspired by that great man." His words flowed with deliberate formality.

Johnson had a talent for dramatic gestures that bordered on the insincere. Many felt they could see through his rhetoric, sensing that his real emotions did not match the words he professed. But he knew that the power of words lay in their ability to persuade, to disarm, to manipulate. It was an art he practiced with great zeal.

"I'm touched by those sentiments. You are a great President and will lead this country with vision and strength for many years to come. One of the greatest contributions my late friend made to this country was when he chose you to run with him in 1960."

"Thank you, Mr. Ambassador. That's kind of you to say," Johnson replied with a mix of surprise and faint pleasure. There was something unexpectedly genuine in his reaction, as if the praise had struck a chord.

"Mr. President, I'm sure you know that Mr. Churchill is near death. The information I have is that he will, indeed, pass on to his reward sometime over the next few days. We are, of course, following a plan that has been in place for many years—the old bulldog has scared us a few times. Winston's a man of history. His passing will end an era."

"I agree. He's a great man."

"Indeed. But I did not ask for this time to rehearse all of Sir Winston's exploits. Rather, I wanted to talk with you personally and off the record about something that has come to my attention."

"I'm listening."

"Well, Mr. President, first off, you need to know what I'm about to share didn't come my way through, shall we say, 'official' channels. Nor am I here in my role as Ambassador. I know this sounds rather odd, but I need you to know this." Ormsby-Gore knew he was being deliberately vague, but there was no help for it. His pulse quickened as he awaited a response. Would Johnson dismiss his words as paranoia or be shrewd enough to see the bigger picture?

Johnson nodded affirmatively, while his eyes grew narrow, almost squinting, a characteristic mannerism. He knew not to jump in too soon. Sometimes the best way to get people to pour out their souls was to keep quiet and let the silence do its work. He said nothing.

Ormsby-Gore continued nervously, "Thank you, sir, for understanding. Here's what I know: I've picked up on some talk—what your intelligence people might call 'chatter'—emanating from certain quarters, that when the great man passes, his funeral might become the stage or backdrop for some kind of incident."

He paused, choosing words with caution. He felt the weight of responsibility on his shoulders. He was about to lay a heavy burden at the feet of a man who might simply fling it back at him.

"Incident?"

The question hung in the air between them. It was not too late to back away, but he braced himself to forge on. He couldn't help but feel the ghost of his old friend hovering nearby, a constant reminder of how things used to be.

"Yes, well, I know I'm being, shall we say, cryptic, but please bear with me."

Bearing with *anyone* was not Lyndon Johnson's strong point. But he resisted the urge to interrupt his guest.

"Because of my position, I must distance myself from reacting to mere gossip or incomplete information. Our embassy—any embassy, for that matter—is a breeding ground for such things. It's just that because of what we've seen in the past, there are some things worth considering with much more than the proverbial grain of salt. And my information comes from a similar source as some of the things I was hearing in the aftermath of President Kennedy's tragic death," he said.

Ormsby-Gore had not intended to speak of Jack, but his friend's memory loomed large. He paused, as if trying to gird his emotions. In reality, he had been hearing things even *before* Jack was killed. But that was to remain the Ambassador's sad and dark secret.

Johnson stared at his guest stone-faced. The mention of Kennedy brought to the surface memories he had worked hard to suppress. He was not sure if he resented the intrusion or welcomed it.

Ormsby-Gore resumed by saying, "It's the Soviets. It seems that there may be hardliners in the Kremlin who have designs on Western Europe and would love any opportunity to take action."

"Opportunity? What the hell are you talking about, Mr. Ambassador? Break it down to the nut gut."

Ormsby-Gore was not familiar with that colorful expression, one that Johnson was particularly fond of using, but he had heard enough of the President's blunt vernacular to grasp its meaning. Ormsby-Gore understood that the man had no tolerance for ambiguity. The President wanted the bottom line, expressed as clearly as possible.

"Of course, well, what I'm talking about—the nut gut as you call it—is the fact that while leaders from around the world are in London to pay their respects to Mr. Churchill, it would be a great time for some dramatic incident, even attack, that would create the kind of chaos that could become a smokescreen—or cover, as you might say here in America—for aggressive action."

Johnson's eyes narrowed again. "You mean a military move?"

"It's certainly possible."

"Do you think they have such a plan?" Johnson asked.

"Mr. President, I don't know if you know much about my background, but I have dealt with the Soviets for many years," Ormsby-Gore said. Johnson and the world had no idea just *how* true that was. "They want the world, but they don't want to fight a world war. If they can move swiftly to effectively neutralize any opposition, they'd love to turn all of Europe into their playground." The Ambassador paused briefly and added, "They can count, Mr. President, and they know they outnumber us."

Johnson grunted, then countered, "Khrushchev was deposed last fall, and we don't have solid information about what is happening in the Kremlin." Johnson had personally been grateful for the timing of that odd and surprising news out of Moscow the previous October. It had helped him bury a potentially embarrassing news item that had just broken, one having to do with one of Johnson's trusted aides being arrested on a "morals" charge in the middle of a political campaign. Khrushchev being ousted trumped Walter Jenkins sucking a man's cock in a Washington men's room, as Johnson sometimes described the episode in private.

Ormsby-Gore looked at the President and said, "I may be able to help you there, Mr. President. My sense is those in charge are more hardline than Khrushchev. These are the men who wanted to go to war over Cuba, a war they were confident they could win." He needed Lyndon Johnson to know that the stakes were much higher than even the Campaign of '64.

"Even nuclear war?" Johnson asked incredulously.

"Yes, at least a *tactical* nuclear war. They were ready to annihilate American troops on the beaches had there been an invasion in 1962."

"My God," said Johnson in disbelief.

"I believe they're waiting for a moment to bring their global vision to pass. And the gathering of more than 100 heads of state in one big room, well, such an opportunity may prove too hard to resist." Ormsby-Gore was now speaking almost as if he were thinking out loud, adding pieces to his expanding scenario.

"Yes, but there'd be international outrage—certainly the United Nations would oppose them," said Johnson.

"Of course they would, if—that's the key word—if Soviet fingerprints were clearly on whatever sparked such a scenario."

"What do you mean?" By this time Lyndon Johnson was completely engaged in what he now saw as much more than a perfunctory meeting with a high-ranking diplomat. What began as a courtesy meeting with a former Kennedy intimate was now a matter of global consequence. The mere hint of the Soviets embarking on a potentially history-altering gambit was not something he could take lightly. He knew, from experience, that the slightest international misstep could spell political disaster for him on the home front.

"Suppose something catastrophic should happen, something that, say, killed or disabled seventy-five world leaders. And what if such an event were made to look like the work of one of many possible terrorist groups, for example—and just an example here, mind you—the IRA?"

The implications sank in rapidly. Ormsby-Gore was delicately suggesting something almost unthinkable—that the Soviets might orchestrate a massive strike against Western leaders and pin it on someone else. Johnson absorbed the notion with a sense of both dread and intrigue.

"You saying they'd make it look like some kind of Irish terrorist job?"

"What I'm suggesting, Mr. President, is that they're quite good at misdirection and more than capable of using the IRA without the IRA ever knowing why they were doing it." Ormsby-Gore was aware that the CIA had a file as thick as a London fog on the Irish Republican Army's activities, especially since they had killed more than a dozen American tourists in London with a car bomb five years earlier.

"This is very serious, Mr. Ambassador. I need to look into this," Johnson replied, raking his fingers through his hair as the wheels in his mind began to turn. The stakes of ignoring such a warning were too high, and he knew that political fallout would reach him even if this intelligence was just a false alarm. He quickly weighed the balance between the risks of action and inaction. It did not take him long to decide.

"Of course. But, sir, please leave me and my government out of it," Ormsby-Gore said, firmly but with a tone that was at once diplomatic and insistent. "Prime Minister Wilson is not someone to talk to about this. He is unschooled in such things and—please never quote me on this—he's not completely trustworthy with information." The Ambassador also had good reason to believe that Wilson was a die-hard sympathizer with Soviet Russia.

Johnson nodded, as if to indicate that he appreciated the complexity and subtlety of his guest's position. The President knew, from personal experience, how delicate it was to deal with political rivals at home, and this was surely an even more sensitive situation. *Either way*, thought Johnson, *this is bigger than just a former Prime Minister in poor health.*

"Okay, David—may I call you David?" asked Johnson in a tone that attempted to convey more sincerity than many of his political opponents had ever experienced.

"By all means, Mr. President."

"How about over here, our intelligence services—what about them? You were around President Kennedy a lot and have a sense about this, I'd imagine."

"Indeed, sir, I do. Frankly, I wouldn't take this through the official channels but rather find a way to look into it behind the scenes. Maybe someone who knows how the intelligence world works, but who isn't working these days for the government. Maybe someone like Allen Dulles. I've always held him in high esteem, even when Jack, er, President Kennedy fired him."

"Well, you know I put Dulles on that Warren Commission. Good idea. I'll run all this by him," said Johnson, giving voice to the first piece of a plan that was already formulating in his mind. "And I promise, I'll leave your name out of it."

"I'd be ever so grateful, sir. I'm going to be resigning soon and going home, and I'd rather do so quietly. I just felt like I needed to step up and share what I know, or at least think I know, with you, Mr. President," Ormsby-Gore said.

THE MOMENT DAVID Ormsby-Gore cleared the Oval-Office door, Lyndon Johnson reached for the telephone and ripped it from its cradle. In an outburst that filled the room, he barked, "Moyers, get me Allen Dulles!" His eyes flickered with intensity. If there was any truth to what the Ambassador had said, the stakes were unfathomable. No time to lose.

Everything else could wait.

Dulles was the one man who knew the Soviets well enough to anticipate their moves. A dead Churchill and a chaotic funeral were not going to become a Soviet gift from God on Johnson's watch.

"I'll have him on the line in a minute or so, sir," Moyers replied.

"Not on the phone, you jackass! Get him *here* within the hour."

Johnson knew Dulles didn't have much to do these days except write his memoirs, so if Moyers was worth half his salt, he'd have the old spook in the White House pronto.

"Yes sir!" Moyer replied.

CHAPTER NINE

THE SON OF an Anglican Bishop, Sir Roger Hollis was, at first glance, an unassuming type of man, his demeanor as unobtrusive as his voice was soft-spoken. Everything about him seemed steeped in conservatism, from his choice of ties to the understated way he conducted himself professionally *and* personally. This deliberately cultivated affectation made him seem innocuous even when those around him would have been wise to glance his way *twice*.

Throughout that earlier meeting in the Cabinet Room at Number 10, he, in his role as Director General of the Security Service—informally known as MI5—had taken notes. The discussion was intense at times. But Hollis remained quietly at his place, a presence so subdued it bordered on spectral. He had only been asked one minor security question about St Paul's Cathedral.

Which was fine with him.

Hollis preferred to work in the shadows. Not just because of the nature of his job and the agency he oversaw, but because he was a man with secrets beyond the "official" ones he was sworn to keep. What no one in that Cabinet Room that day knew, not the Prime Minister nor anyone else, was that in the late 1920s, while working as a journalist in Shanghai, China, Roger Hollis had been recruited by Soviet Intelligence.

There had been some suspicion, rumors circulating like poison through the veins of Whitehall, but serious scrutiny would only come later when a subsequent investigation would nearly wreck the agency entirely. And suspicions would persist for decades after his death, when it was too late to reverse the damage he'd caused.

As a spy codenamed *Elli.*

LIKE OTHER YOUNG men of his station and background, often ones with deep familial ties to the old British Empire, Roger Hollis had viewed communism through the lens of idealism during his student years. Many of his contemporaries in similar circumstances, young men who would go on to be exposed for aiding the communist cause, shared this outlook. While still at university, and later during his years abroad as an aspiring journalist, Hollis's progressive leanings made him attractive to the Soviets.

Idealistically inclined youths regarded the spread of communist ideology as the most potent countermeasure to the rise of fascism, which was ominously expanding its influence across Europe in the form of Mussolini's Italy, Hitler's Germany, and Franco's Spain. The grim specter of nationalism, married with authoritarian rule, was enslaving entire populations and, as many supposed, would continue its advance virtually unchecked.

It was a landscape ripe for exploitation by the Soviets, who understood how to leverage such alignments. What seemed to these young Britons a heroic struggle had, in fact, been masterfully orchestrated as part of a grand espionage scheme emanating from Stalin's inner circle. The plot, decades in the making, was to cultivate and mobilize a fifth column within Britain.

In keeping with a scheme as subversive as it was ambitious, Stalin's plan revolved around the recruitment and cultivation of young British men who possessed the qualities necessary to ascend the social and political ladders of power. Their aristocratic backgrounds and generational pedigrees virtually assured their eventual acceptance into the highest circles of British society, allowing them to gain the very access to sensitive information that Stalin craved.

Meanwhile, their sympathies toward communism motivated them to work secretly in service of the Soviet cause. It was only later, when the story of Soviet infiltration became too large for the public to ignore, that the term "mole" would publicly emerge to describe these deeply embedded spies—and the source of this remarkably apt description would be none other than a celebrated novel from the British tradition of espionage fiction that described the hunt for an embedded agent who was one of three suspects—*tinker, tailor,* or *soldier.*

The British establishment would be shaken to its very core by the exposure of three real-life spies, and by the early 1960s, the stories of their betrayals had already begun to seep deeply into the cultural consciousness and narrative. The cases of Donald MacLean, Guy Burgess, and Harold "Kim" Philby, sent shockwaves through the corridors of power and respectability.

SIR ROGER WAS a survivor, if nothing else. In fact, his Knighthood, awarded by a Conservative government in 1960, was meant as a routine honorific in keeping with his position as Director General of the Security Service. He viewed it as an ironic testament to the intricate web he had spun over decades.

Because he stood uniquely poised to know just about everything happening in the realm of politics, state policy, and intelligence matters in the United Kingdom, he had managed to shield himself from the same disastrous fates that had befallen other comrades in espionage. But his mask of British respectability had come perilously close to being torn away just two years earlier, when MI6 zeroed in on Harold "Kim" Philby, who was then living and operating out of Beirut.

KIM PHILBY AND Roger Hollis had known each other for many years. They had started as sympathetic leftists at Oxford and Cambridge, young idealists swept into the tide of history and the grip of Soviet Intelligence. They grew to become friends as they navigated the perilous but prestigious ladders of the British intelligence community—Philby at MI6 and Hollis at MI5.

Together they formed, albeit briefly, a dynamic duo of Soviet espionage.

Then, in a shocking turn, the wheels came off for Philby when Donald MacLean and Guy Burgess defected abruptly to the Soviet Union in May 1951. Suspicion settled quickly and heavily upon Philby as the so-called "third man," a Soviet operative who had tipped off MacLean about an investigation closing in on him. After that, despite never being formally charged with a crime, Philby became a pariah to the British intelligence establishment.

In January of 1963, a mutual connection, Nicholas Elliott, was dispatched to Beirut to confront Philby head-on about his treacherous past. Hollis sweated it out in London, keeping a painfully close watch on the situation, fully aware that Philby's confirmed exposure as a traitor could very well spell disaster for him as well.

But Kim managed to flee to Moscow just before the hammer could come down, and it was at that moment that Roger entered into damage control mode, something he was remarkably adept at, expertly deflecting any potentially dangerous scrutiny that might have otherwise come in his direction.

The infamous "Profumo Affair" came along soon after Philby's notorious escape. It proved to be yet another embarrassing fiasco for the British government, and yet another episode of sensational scandal involving Soviet espionage. John Profumo, serving as the 46-year-old Secretary for War in Prime Minister Harold MacMillan's cabinet, became entangled in a sordid and politically disastrous fling with a 19-year-old model named Christine Keeler.

Most explosively, Keeler was also sharing her affections with Yevgeny Ivanov, who was not just a Soviet Naval Attaché but also a cunning spy. It was a sensational story of sex, power, and betrayal, one that had simmered out of public view for a couple of years before bursting into full flame in mid-1963. The drama threatened to bring down the Conservative government. Prime Minister Harold MacMillan resigned in October of that year, citing "health reasons" as the official cause.

But most suspected there was more to the story.

Hollis, with his finger always on the pulse of scandal, knew every sordid detail. Nothing in the world of espionage and high politics escaped his attention. He was acutely aware of the affair's potential connection to President Kennedy, a speculative link that hadn't yet made its way into the public consciousness. You see, Miss Keeler was friends with a couple of the American President's party girls, women who had been in the company of JFK on more than one occasion. But the President's fateful trip to Dallas ended any possible linkage.

HOLLIS LOOKED THE part of a college professor, more donnish than dashing, and was often described as round-shouldered with somewhat owlish spectacles. His rounded shoulders were the result of a spinal defect that progressed throughout his life and gave him a decidedly academic air. It was the reason he stooped slightly whenever he walked, although some privately joked it was due to the heavy burden of his secrets.

As he approached his sixtieth birthday, Hollis was well-established as the head of the British version of America's FBI. This meant he was uniquely positioned to alert the Soviets about British affairs and plans. And it allowed him to influence the British government on behalf of the system to which he owed his first loyalty. The notes Hollis had been taking that day in the Cabinet Room would, therefore, serve a dual purpose.

As did most everything else in Hollis's complicated life.

SEVERAL HOURS AFTER that meeting at 10 Downing Street on January 15, Hollis had dined by himself at The Savoy Grill—something of a ritual for him, his comfortable stand-in for interpersonal fellowship. He had three vodka martinis along with his usual grilled Chateaubriand with pommes soufflés and read the *Times* with great interest, paying particular attention to the political section.

After ordering dessert, he made his way to the men's room, walking slow and stiff, the way a much older man might. The attendant on duty was a man named Alex. No one had ever noticed that Alex was on duty anytime the director dined at the Savoy. It was a regular occurrence. Not that they were close, mind you. Hollis didn't even know Alex's last name. Or his real name, for that matter. He was simply Hollis's connection to his Soviet friends.

The director entered a stall and pulled an envelope from the inside pocket of his Savile Row suit jacket. He wedged it in behind the toilet tank, knowing that Alex would be retrieving it before anyone else used the stall. His business done, the director flushed the toilet, exited the stall, and washed his hands with great care, almost as if he was scrubbing something away.

Alex handed him a towel.

Before leaving the men's room, the director handed Alex a crisp new five-pound note and said, "Don't spend it all in one place, my good chap." The words confirmed to Alex that something had been left in the stall for him, and that he was to pass it along as soon as possible. How Alex actually did that was none of Hollis's concern.

"Very kind, sir," Alex replied, "but please allow me to give you some change." Alex then handed Hollis a one-pound note. This was also code, meaning that Alex had something for him in return. Hollis tucked it into his pocket. Per the protocol, he removed a folded piece of paper that had been concealed beneath a stack of freshly laundered towels and then left the room.

He returned to his table, where a dish of iced peach Melba was waiting for him. That also was part of the ritual. But the head of MI5 skipped the dessert, something that he didn't often do, and quickly left the restaurant. He found a phone booth in the hotel's elegant and expansive lobby. He entered and sat down, closing its door behind him.

He picked up the telephone and placed a call.

CHAPTER TEN

MICHAEL AND MOLLY Wheelan had dedicated themselves to Soviet intelligence for nearly three decades, their commitment unwavering despite upheavals and betrayals. Their son, Sean, at just twenty-four, had also been drawn into the effort, representing a new generation in the cause. He was in London at the time, living and working under the guise of a devoted office assistant while continuing the legacy of espionage that had become the family business.

Michael's journey into the world of subterfuge began at Oxford, from which he emerged with both an education and a cause. It was in the years leading up to World War II that the seeds of communism were sown deeply within him.

The recruitment of spies at Cambridge University was indeed more pronounced, and the fruits of that labor more plentiful, but Oxford was not without its own Soviet influence. The tentacles of the Kremlin reached those dreaming spires, extending their seductive promises into its classrooms and common rooms.

Michael was one of those young men within their reach, a recruit of singular promise and potential. He was recognized for his zeal and intellect, an individual clever enough to insinuate himself into the movement to liberate Northern Ireland from British rule. This cause was tailor-made for Soviet exploitation, a cultural and political struggle with which they could align, fan the flames, and ultimately control.

Michael's fervent combination of Marxist ideology and nationalistic yearning to set Northern Ireland free from British domination rendered him particularly susceptible to recruitment by the NKVD, the ominous progenitor to the infamous KGB. The Soviets saw him as ideal for their purposes.

His handler, a shadowy figure known to him only by the code name "Viktor," was the one who drew Michael in. It was Viktor who introduced him to Molly McNally, the vibrant daughter of a Belfast newspaperman. Molly was already aligned with the cause, a young woman steeped in communist ideas and eager to take action.

Their union, both personal and political, was the Soviet strategy brought to life. The Wheelans were products of the Soviet ability to marry discontent and dissatisfaction to anger and oppression, transforming grievances into revolutionary kindling.

They were not unique.

The Soviets repeated this game plan in their efforts worldwide, exploiting similar struggles at every opportunity, from Asia to Latin America to South Africa and beyond.

BIRMINGHAM, THE CITY where Michael now engineered his life, was an industrial powerhouse, with its factories and furnaces echoing the labor movement's fiery rhetoric. Although Michael considered himself truly Irish, his life's chapters were largely penned in this city. His parents had relocated there in the 1920s, departing the small coastal town of Port Stewart in Northern Ireland.

The senior Wheelan had taken up residence at the University of Birmingham after earning his doctorate at Queens University in Belfast, securing a position on the faculty to teach history and philosophy. Michael's upbringing was marked by comfort and love, a tranquil home life that stood in stark contrast to the path he would later tread.

His father's intellectual pursuits and his mother's nurturing hand crafted a childhood environment that was oddly serene for someone who would become involved in the dangerous and clandestine world of espionage. Most spies, after all, were motivated by deep-seated grievances or a quest to redeem family reputations—but Michael's path diverged from this pattern.

The years leading up to World War II were unparalleled. A global economic crisis had paved the way for the rise of fascism, and it was the war against this political plague—in places like Germany, Italy, and Spain—that attracted innocent yet passionate young men like Michael to the leftist "Popular Front." This so-called front was nothing more than an elaborate facade, orchestrated by the Comintern.

The Communist International.

This brainchild of Vladimir Lenin was a strategic vehicle to overthrow capitalism and promote communism, but it waxed and waned. When Joseph Stalin rose to propel its third iteration, his agenda of global revolution captured Michael's imagination and exploited his idealism. Despite his upbringing, he became a fervent believer that revolution could affect meaningful change from within.

A SHOCKING TURN of events rattled even the most committed leftists. The non-aggression pact the Soviet Union signed with the Nazis in 1939 opened the eyes of many students in Britain who had flirted dangerously with the promise of communism. This unthinkable alliance was a betrayal, bewildering and disillusioning idealists who had seen the Soviet Union as a bastion against tyranny. For many of them, this was the breaking point; their curiosity had overstepped its bounds, and they turned away from the works of Marx and Engels, their ideological journey ending abruptly amidst confusion and a sense of loss.

But not Michael.

He was among the few who remained unwavering in loyalty to Moscow. During the years of World War II, and the turbulent times that followed, he was deeply engaged in the secretive activities of the Irish Republican Army (IRA). His participation appeared zealous, yet his real devotion transcended the Irish struggle. The deepest allegiance in his heart was always reserved for the directives from Moscow.

As the tides of the Cold War shifted global alliances once more, his new primary Soviet contact, Yuri, pushed him in new directions. There was always a larger vision, a broader strategy at play. By the late 1950s, Michael was directed to take a seemingly mundane job at Newman Brothers Coffin Works, a prestigious establishment on Fleet Street in Birmingham.

It was puzzling at first, this insistence by Yuri. But with characteristic Soviet foresight, Yuri orchestrated his employment through discreet contacts within a local trade union. The effort was all part of a meticulously constructed Soviet plan, one that demanded patience and precision, placing operatives where and when they would matter most. The Russians were known to execute such plans with a willingness to let them simmer for years, even decades, as they did with Michael.

INTELLIGENCE FROM THEIR sources in Britain indicated that for the eventual state funeral of Winston Churchill, a large, elaborate casket would be commissioned at Newman Brothers. Michael's position there, thus, became a linchpin in a potentially daring operation. A coffin had indeed been built. With Churchill's final days approaching, only finishing touches were required—a specialty of Newman Brothers.

Michael's role was straightforward in its description yet profound in its implication. He was to ensure that certain "materials" were concealed within the coffin before it left for London. While he had not been informed of the exact nature of the materials, his instincts and experience surely gave him an educated insight. Yuri indicated the materials would be provided when the time was right. So Michael waited, continuing his work at Newman's, all the while scrutinizing the papers, his eyes glued to reports of Churchill's lingering battle with mortality.

Tension peaked when, during a week saturated with ominous news from London about the great leader's deteriorating condition, Yuri made a clandestine visit to Molly at their modest home in Birmingham, a humble abode in keeping with their unassuming life but filled with covert significance. Michael was at work, and the timing was impeccably calculated.

Yuri arrived with a large satchel, notably secure and mysterious in its appearance. He was clear in his instructions: Michael needed to follow the directives within the case as soon as possible. The satchel was locked, and no key was given as he slipped away, leaving Molly with anticipation and concern.

Around the same time that Yuri was delivering the satchel to Molly, Michael was making his way back to work after an extended lunch at the nearby pub. He had downed two whiskeys and a pint of Guinness, then lingered for a while, reading the midday paper and smoking a cigarette.

The large headlines in the *Daily Telegraph* all told the same story: Churchill had suffered a massive stroke and was now in grave condition. One story speculated that when the inevitable occurred, there would be a public funeral in London on a scale never before seen in Great Britain. This was followed by some punditry about the failures of Churchill's last years as prime minister, especially the dissolution of the British Empire.

Michael smirked at that. Britain's retreat from its colonial possessions in Africa and the Middle East, not to mention its humiliation in the Suez Crisis, was seen by more than a few as a victory for the Soviets. They were on the rise as England was on the decline.

He paid for his drinks and put the paper under his arm. Pushing open the pub's heavy door, he stepped outside and buttoned up his coat against the cold. He was less than a hundred yards from the mortuary when he noticed a woman walking toward him. She appeared to be in her late thirties, about his age, and was wearing over-sized sunglasses, which was odd, since there was very little sun at that moment.

As she drew closer, he saw that she had a simple scarf on her head, a gray trench coat on her thin body, and plain, flat shoes on her feet. *Eastern Europe? Could she be someone Yuri sent from London? Or from Moscow?* He didn't recall ever seeing her before. One thing was certain: she wasn't dressed like any native of Birmingham.

She met Michael's gaze for a moment but said nothing. Instead, she reached into her coat, pulled out a small envelope, and handed it to him. Then she walked off, crossed St. Paul's Square, and disappeared down a narrow street. Michael eyed the envelope suspiciously, as if it might explode in his hands.

KGB agents in Europe were being picked off with increasing frequency by the CIA and its allies, and he worried he might be next. *Is this a set-up?* He stood on the corner and, after watching the woman shrink into the distance, sat down on a bench by the side of the road. He looked at the name, Newman Brothers, etched in white on the mortuary's large front window.

Michael kept his eyes on the window as he carefully opened the envelope. It contained a small brass key and a typewritten message.

The note was in code, and Michael knew immediately what it meant. It was confirmation that Yuri had delivered something important to his home.

The hands on the clock seemed frozen as the afternoon stretched interminably at the Newman Brothers, testing Michael's patience with each passing minute. The anticipation was almost unbearable. He could not fully concentrate on his duties, especially when twice he overheard snippets of conversation about Churchill's declining condition.

One of his supervisors mentioned to a secretary that they should be ready for instructions at any moment for the special order to be delivered to London. "Could be today," the boss speculated. "Or tomorrow. Or whenever the old fellow finally decides to make it official." Michael, attempting to appear nonchalant, shuffled a stack of papers and feigned interest in them as his heart began to beat noticeably faster. He dared not make eye contact or linger, lest his anxiety betray him.

IT WAS NEARLY seven-thirty when Michael finally arrived at their flat on the west side of Birmingham. Molly was already waiting by the door when he entered. She had heard him coming up the stairs and was anxious to share her news. Michael smiled when he noticed the aroma filling the apartment.

Corned beef and cabbage.

Molly only made it on special occasions. And this occasion, he knew, was going to be special indeed. They both looked as if they might burst, brimming with excitement about recent developments. He leaned down and kissed Molly on the cheek, and she grabbed his hand and led him down the hall to their small bedroom. The meal would have to wait for a bit, trumped by a shared eagerness to uncover and exchange information.

He watched expectantly as she retrieved the satchel from under the bed. "Yuri came a few hours ago and left this. But it's locked, love," she said with a slight frown. "And the man didn't leave a key. Any idea what's inside?"

Michael let out a knowing laugh. "No bother, Molly dear," he said. "I had a visitor of me own today. Right about lunchtime. And you'll never guess what she gave me."

He was already savoring the moment as her eyes widened.

"A key?"

"'Tis indeed," he answered. He held it up, dangling it in the air for her to see. He opened the case right away and they stared at the contents for a long moment and then looked at each other in puzzlement.

"What do you suppose it is?" she asked.

"I think," Michael said, "that I should read this note."

CHAPTER ELEVEN

A SINGLE PAGE was sitting on top of the items packed neatly in the case. Michael reached for it, realizing immediately that it was actually three pages—a set of instructions. His growing excitement was confirmed as he scanned pages quickly. Molly sat beside him on the bed. "Well?" she asked, anxiously.

He cleared his throat and read the first page. It began with a description of the materials. "Semtex, plastic explosive, 18 ounces" was listed as the main item. Then there were two items that looked as though they might be cameras, or radios—one larger, one smaller. The instructions that followed were straightforward.

Michael's mind raced. He had read about the new development in explosives—particularly the creation of a pliable and stable plastic material out of Czechoslovakia, and he assumed this was what he had now received from his Soviet masters.

"So what is it you're to do with all this, Michael?"

Michael continued reading for another moment before answering. "Simple, my beautiful flower," he said, his voice trembling slightly as he spoke. "I'm to hide explosives and a detonator in the casket reserved for Mr. Churchill. Then we're to travel to London and deliver the remote detonator to someone. Yuri will make sure we know whom and when. Then we'll watch what happens when his coffin explodes in the church as his funeral service is underway."

Molly gasped, covering her mouth with her hand. She was all but speechless. She had no love for Churchill or anything he stood for, and she hated the British establishment as much as Michael did. He had long been the enemy of everything she held dear. But such an act would not only destroy his remains—it would kill many, many others in the church.

"But so many will die," she whispered.

"Apparently, that's the plan," Michael said, his mind swirling as he processed the implications. "Our people know that the room will be filled with world leaders and it's clear that they have a grand plan."

"My—oh, my," Molly said. "I need a whiskey."

"Let's have a glass of Tullamore Dew and toast the success of our operation."

"I was thinking more of steadying me nerves," she said with a faltering smile.

They were silent as they poured their drinks and clinked glasses, each downing the liquid in a single swallow. Michael lit a cigarette as Molly returned to the kitchen and placed dinner on the table. They were both quiet as they ate, still absorbing the details of the plot and what success would mean. It was an audacious plan, as big as any they had been involved with in their three decades of working for the Soviets.

Still, Michael could sense Molly's doubt.

She knew, as did Michael, that this was not about liberation for Ireland, but rather about a massive statement by the Russians. It was not the first time the Soviets had asked them to betray the cause of Irish freedom for the greater advancement of global revolution. In Michael's mind, it was all part of the same struggle, and that had always made it easier to justify.

But Molly looked somber.

"What's troubling you, Molly? We've been waiting for this for a long time," he said gently.

"I know," she said, "It's just...it's so big."

"It's going to be one for all the sons and daughters of Ireland, and Yuri promised us great things for our part in it. Don't worry. It'll be over and done soon and we'll be on to the next chapter."

"I suppose, I suppose." She rose. "I need another whiskey."

Michael rose as well and went to the case to examine the contents once more. He reread the instructions as he ate more of the corned beef and cabbage and tried to reassure his wife. He saw that she was still rattled and reminded himself that not many had her resolve. In the end, he decided to cut Molly some slack.

Michael spent much of the evening thinking about how to accomplish his assigned task. He decided to go back to Newman Brothers in the middle of the night to get everything done. He had a key to the place, although the owner never knew it. His handler had obtained it for him. He had never used it—had never had the occasion to.

But it would come in handy on this night.

SHORTLY BEFORE TWO a.m., Michael entered the darkened building on Fleet Street. It was eerily quiet inside, the kind of quiet you could feel. He moved quickly to the area where the casket reserved for Mr. Churchill was being stored. Michael needed to hide the materials in such a way that they would be impossible to discover. It was crucial that they remain hidden, and he had developed a plan during his post-supper meditations for exactly how to accomplish this. His mind raced as he thought of finally completing the mission, the years of waiting now reduced to just a few moments.

He opened the casket and, using a small torch he had brought, examined it from head to foot. His examination revealed more than he had expected. He felt around the foot of the rectangular box, reasoning it was the best place to conceal the explosive materials. *People never look at a dead man's feet*, he thought. He pulled some of the fabric away from the foot of the box, revealing foam cushioning customary in caskets. It was much more pliable than the plastic explosive he was working with, but he was sure he could make it work.

The fabric came loose more easily than he expected, and he continued to pull it away until nearly half of the box was exposed—the half that would remain shut, even during a public ceremony. Michael was surprised, and a little disappointed, by something he found beneath the fabric and foam. It shouldn't have surprised him because of his experience with caskets, but it did.

There was *metal* where there should have been only wood.

He quickly realized the casket had been lined with lead. He had heard of that, to be sure—many people believed the lining would protect the loved one's remains from the elements—or at least delay the impact of water and bugs and such. But Michael was fairly certain the people he worked for had not anticipated the presence of metal. He wondered how it would affect the power of an explosion.

He noticed the lead had been applied in sections, with clear seams where each part of the casket had been covered. He wondered if he could somehow pull up a couple of the sections without doing any noticeable damage to the precious box. Using a tool from a nearby workbench, he found a spot at the intersection of the casket wall and floor and probed it. He pulled at the thick metal lining, peeling it back. It was almost like tin foil, only thicker. Before he got too anxious, a perfect solution hit him.

Michael spent the better part of the next thirty minutes carefully—very carefully—removing two sections of the metal lining from the floor of the casket. He then went to the satchel provided by his handlers, and after he cleared off a section of the workbench, he removed some of the plastic explosive from its wrapping and began to mold it. Within a few minutes, he had created a flat pie-crust-like section, which he then spread on the casket floor.

He repeated the process several times.

He removed two additional sections of the lead lining to make all the materials fit. Nothing was left over, which meant he was carrying out his instructions precisely. If anything, he thought the casket had ample space to allow for more. It was a big box for a big man. Then he pondered where to put the small receiver—one linked to another device. The idea was that the explosive could only be detonated remotely, but the person pushing the button had to be within 100 feet. The receiver would start a clock, counting down toward detonation, Michael assumed, giving the person activating the device time to move a safe distance away.

Michael decided to put the receiver in the left corner of the casket, and he inserted four wires directly into the plastic explosive. He wasn't worried about it detonating, at least not yet. The companion device to the receiver was back at his house, miles away.

He smiled with satisfaction as he replaced the foam and the fabric and made sure the inside of the casket was once again in pristine condition. He gathered the scraps around him and put the lead sheets in his satchel. Then he took the extra step of policing the area more thoroughly to make sure there was no hint anyone had disturbed anything.

Michael was back home a little after five o'clock that morning. He put the satchel on the floor near the bed and quietly crawled under the covers next to Molly. She rolled over and smiled at him.

"Everything is set," he told her.

Their part was over—but for the trip to London and passing off of the detonator. They were both relieved and more than a little aroused. Something about the excitement and even possible danger worked as an aphrodisiac. He got an erection with their first kiss, and they made love with the passion of their early years.

And then they did it again before drifting off to sleep.

CHAPTER TWELVE

Washington, D.C.

THE SUMMONS FROM Bill Moyers had set Allen Dulles into near-frenetic motion. As he drove to the White House, his car winding through the familiar streets, he found his thoughts drifting back through time. It was only the second time President Johnson had sought him out, and the thrill of being summoned back to the heart of power was a balm to old wounds.

Standing once again on the precipice of influence, he could not help but reflect on the previous administration and the bitterly stinging exile he had endured after the Bay of Pigs disaster. Kennedy had treated him like a relic, a dinosaur from another era, and unceremoniously shown him the door. Allen had seethed with resentment then, convinced that the young President—so lauded, so full of his own vigor—would never allow the mission to collapse under its own weight.

Surely, Allen had believed, despite all the public denials and strategic hesitations, Kennedy would relent and send American troops to save the young and hopelessly outmatched Cuban insurgents who were dying on that desolate beach in the spring of '61. It was unfathomable to him that a leader would countenance such an ignoble failure.

The dismissal had been a staggering blow. Being fired by a man who was still a child when Dulles was already enmeshed in the art of international diplomacy was more than humiliating. Yet now, the thought of the bitter irony of recent turns of fate brought a thin smile to his lips, a wry acknowledgment of how quickly fortunes could change in Washington.

First, Johnson had extended a somewhat unexpected olive branch by asking Dulles to be part of the small, elite group tasked with conducting the "official" investigation into President Kennedy's assassination. The shadow of that dark day in Dallas still loomed over the nation, and the invitation to steer the search for truth, even if symbolic, was a reaffirmation of his stature and a nod to his enduring relevance.

Now, as he navigated through the gates of the White House, his mind wandered further back, drawn down the avenues of memory that seemed to greet him at every turn. How could it possibly be that nearly six years had passed since his older brother, John Foster Dulles, had succumbed to the inexorable march of cancer? They had been titans in the world of foreign policy, a commanding duo during the Eisenhower years. Though the malignancy had ravaged John's body, he had steadfastly maintained his duties as Secretary of State, serving with an indomitable spirit that Allen still deeply admired.

Those days had been nothing short of monumental—Allen presiding over the clandestine maneuvers of the CIA while his brother shaped the world stage from the State Department. Together, they had been an unstoppable force, their influence dominating the capital, their names synonymous with American power abroad. The Dulles brothers, preacher's kids from the obscure reaches of Watertown, New York, had once indeed owned the city.

But so much had changed.

He was once more an outsider on the periphery of the corridors where history was made. Yet this summons from Johnson held a tantalizing promise. Perhaps the President had another mission for him, something significant that could restore him to the center of the action. The thought was electrifying.

He brought the car to a stop and made his way into the West Wing.

BILL MOYERS HAD managed to produce Allen Dulles within the hour, just as President Johnson had angrily insisted. The young assistant beamed with satisfaction as he watched the former CIA director walk through the door of the Oval Office. Moyers noted with some pride that when Allen arrived, he had nearly two full minutes left to spare, yet he decided not to mention that fact to Johnson.

He knew better than to risk the President's wrath.

Johnson sat at his desk, ignoring the towering piles of paperwork that threatened to consume his every waking moment. The demands of the Presidency were countless and absolute, and LBJ poured himself into his role with ferocious determination, but right now he had just one priority—this meeting with Dulles.

Dulles looked the part of a man who had seen enough history to fill several lifetimes. His once smooth and carefully barbered hair showed signs of age, receding and gray. His skin had taken on a ruddy and weathered complexion. He sported a small mustache, and his sharp, blue eyes twinkled behind a pair of rimless glasses, which served to accentuate the keenness of his gaze.

He wore a gray herringbone jacket paired with black slacks. It was a look he had cultivated over the years, each article meticulously chosen and worn with the effortless dignity of an experienced man. His age showed, but his stride did not. He approached the

President's desk with alacrity, the gait of a man still firmly in command of his faculties despite the weight of his years.

"Good morning, Mr. President," Dulles said as he reached the imposing Presidential desk.

"Allen, welcome," Johnson replied with a smile that seemed to stretch the width of his face. "Thanks for stopping by on such short notice."

"My pleasure, Mr. President, always glad to be of help—but I'm curious as to what this is about?"

"We'll get there, my friend," Johnson said, leaning back in his chair and making himself comfortable. "What's your poison?"

Dulles took a moment to consult his watch. He noted that it was precisely seven minutes past eleven o'clock in the morning. With a chuckle, he said, "Well, it's five o'clock somewhere, I suppose. I'm fine with what you're having."

"Great," Johnson replied as he grabbed his telephone and barked instructions into it. "Bring two glasses of Cutty, two fingers each, for me and the director, and add water and ice." Johnson was well known for playing games when it came to this sort of thing. In this instance, it meant to make his own drink weaker—more water than scotch—a trick LBJ was fond of using at times like this. Always looking for an advantage. In less than a minute, a steward brought the drinks. After a brisk nod from Johnson, he quickly left the room.

"Allen, you and the boys did a great job on the Warren Commission thing. I know some have been critical, but you were thorough and fair. Most of all, you helped to put the whole thing behind us, and I know that helped me in the election," Johnson said, lifting his glass and admiring it for a moment before taking a sip.

"Thank you, sir. I feel that we did the job we were asked to do," Dulles replied, lighting his ever-present pipe. It was a distinct mark of his self-confidence that he did not bother to ask the President's permission to smoke. Dulles knew the Warren Commission was more about political theater than real fact-finding. He also knew his role was primarily to protect his former agency, as well as the one watched over by Mr. Hoover. As far as Dulles was concerned, the mission was accomplished. But many details were deliberately left out of the voluminous Warren Commission record.

"You up for another assignment?" Johnson asked, watching Dulles's reaction carefully.

"Always honored to serve my country and my President."

"Well, this one is more up your alley, Allen. But it's one that you're going to have to handle pretty much on your own—at least at first." Johnson studied Dulles with an intensity that belied his casual tone, gauging the director's reaction.

"All right...how can I help?" Dulles asked, blowing a thick plume of smoke as he spoke.

Lyndon Johnson leaned back in his chair, watching Allen Dulles with a calculating eye. He began to share the contents of the conversation he'd had with David Ormsby-Gore. A threat so serious and potentially explosive that he wanted to entrust it to no one but his most seasoned spy. He warned his guest that the information was to be handled with utmost discretion and urgency. Nothing could leak.

Nothing at all.

CHAPTER THIRTEEN

JOHNSON WAS COUNTING on Dulles to find out, and quickly, if the threat was as real as the British Ambassador seemed to fear. Johnson's voice was calm but carried a gravity that conveyed how seriously he was taking the matter. "You don't seem surprised by what I'm telling you here, Allen," the President observed, noting the unflappable demeanor of the master spy who sat before him.

"I wish I could tell you what you're telling me is surprising. But I can't, Mr. President," Dulles replied, thoughtfully puffing on his pipe. The smoke curled around him, meeting the air with a lazy defiance. "I've caught wind of something like this more than a few times—back when I was Director, and even since."

"Lately?" Johnson pressed, sensing there was more Dulles knew.

The veteran intelligence man exhaled a plume of smoke, leaned forward slightly, and stated, "Has McCone ever briefed you about the Soviet defector we've been working with since late '61—Anatoly Golitsyn?"

Johnson furrowed his brow, trying to recall, but came up empty. "Not that I recall. Who the hell is he? What's his story?"

"Well, sir, it's a long and complicated one," Dulles began, tapping the bowl of his pipe thoughtfully. "He came out through

Helsinki, brought his wife and daughter with him. High-up KGB official. Now, mind you, this all happened after my watch ended, after your predecessor let me go. But I've maintained close contact with many in the agency, as you might imagine."

"And as I hope," interjected Johnson, with a nod of approval. "Allen, we need you in the loop, just like I needed to keep Hoover over at the FBI. You men know where the bodies are buried. Or should be buried," he added with a slight, conspiratorial smile.

Dulles chuckled softly, a sound that conveyed his appreciation for Johnson's pragmatism. He continued, "Well, some of my friends in the agency set up a meeting between me and this Golitsyn fellow. They brought him to my house and then we met a couple of other times after that. Something he said made me think that our 'friends' in the Kremlin have some pretty grand plans."

"What kind of plans?" Johnson asked as he quickly leaned forward, crossing his arms over the desk.

"For one thing, Golitsyn believes that Harold Wilson, the British Prime Minister, is a Soviet agent."

Johnson's reaction was visceral, a reflex of disbelief and shock. "What the hell?" he barked, his voice echoing off the walls.

"I know, I know, it sounds far-fetched, but this defector says he was in a position to know about plans. He told us there were plans to make sure those sympathetic to Soviet aims would rise to power. So when that British Labor leader Hugh Gaitskell died, it was really murder made to look like natural causes to pave the way for Wilson. And you may recall, the reason Labor was elected in the first place had to do with that spy scandal back in '63—the Profumo thing."

"Yeah, Jack was watching that one closely and sweating it out. There were some connections over here. I think one of his girlfriends was connected."

"Indeed, that's why his brother had that East German girl, Ellen Rometsch, deported so quickly."

"I remember," Johnson said.

Dulles leaned back in his chair and paused, watching Johnson's silent concentration. The President seemed caught in a web of his thoughts, contemplating the political intrigue and espionage swirling around them.

Finally, the former CIA director broke the stillness and pressed forward, "The problem is, sir, we don't have any fool-proof way to confirm this. Not yet, at least. But the defector has been reliable in other areas." Dulles tapped his pipe lightly, letting the President digest his words before continuing. "You know Angleton?"

"Who?" Johnson asked, his curiosity piqued.

"James Jesus Angleton, Langley's head of counterintelligence."

"I've heard of him but never met him."

"Well, Jim Angleton is convinced Golitsyn is the real deal. He even tried to sound a warning to his counterparts in England, at MI5 and MI6, but I don't know what came of it." Dulles hesitated, offering Johnson a moment to catch up to his fast-paced summation. "Angleton also believes, and this is based on Golitsyn's intel too, that the Brits are compromised by a high-level Soviet mole." Dulles let the bombshell hang in the air, allowing its weight to settle.

Johnson's eyes widened.

"You mean like Philby?" the President asked, evidently alarmed.

"Yes. And it gets worse, Mr. President. There's some indication that we might have the same sort of problem brewing on this side of the Atlantic."

"Shit, Allen. Are you telling me there's a commie spy in the CIA?" Johnson's face was flushed with sudden, angry color.

"I'm not outright saying that. But the Soviets have been trying for years to get to that point. They've got a strategy, and they're sticking to it. The tricky part is, another Russian came to us recently. He goes by the name Nosenko."

"What's his angle?" Johnson demanded, his patience thinning.

"He claims Golitsyn is playing us. Says Golitsyn is a double agent still working for the Kremlin. Now Nosenko's story challenges and undermines almost everything we've gotten from Golitsyn."

Johnson exhaled loudly, finally releasing his pent-up frustration, and downed the watery scotch left in his glass. "Damn it all to hell, Allen. Which one of these sons-of-bitches is telling the truth?"

"Depends on who you ask, Mr. President."

"Well, Allen, I'm asking *you*," Johnson shot back, his voice sharp with urgency.

"I understand, sir," Dulles replied respectfully. "My instincts tell me Golitsyn is on the level and that this Nosenko fellow has been sent to throw a wrench in the works. But I must be frank with you, Mr. President, there are many over at Langley who see it differently."

"Well, I trust *your* instincts, Allen. You just need to help me get this sorted out—and be damn careful who you talk to about anything I just told you."

"I'll do my best, sir. Give me twenty-four hours, and I'll get back to you. I'll be beyond discreet; you have my word."

THE FORMER DIRECTOR of the CIA possessed a gift for recall that was both astonishing and precise. It had served him well in a life of strategy and intrigue. He was sure the latest warning about Soviet infiltration meant more than its face value. For instance, he recollected, with vivid clarity, the intricate development of a Pentagon operation back in '57 known as DROPSHOT.

It was nothing less than a full-scale war plan, detailing how NATO and the United States would respond if the Soviets made an aggressive move against Western Europe. Even while critics dismissed talk of Soviet infiltration as conspiracy or paranoia, Dulles knew that such a scenario was far from incredible.

The groundwork for DROPSHOT was well in place, he presumed, designed to be activated and mobilized on short notice if circumstances dictated. The first order of business for Dulles was to discreetly verify whether the plans were still current, ensuring that someone should get word to the right parties. The impending convergence of world leaders on London would necessitate not only meticulous security measures on-site, but also readiness and vigilance on the part of American and NATO forces. Dulles contemplated who could be trusted with this delicate intelligence.

One individual who came to mind was Air Force General Curtis LeMay. It was true that LeMay's aggressive recommendations had found little favor with the Kennedy team, but he was a man who had a clear understanding of military action against communist threats. He had been vocal in his opinion that Kennedy had handled the Cuban Missile Crisis with dangerous appeasement.

There were rumblings that LeMay, increasingly frustrated with Johnson and his Secretary of Defense, Robert McNamara, might soon retire. Perhaps, Dulles reasoned, LeMay would be willing to help him with this matter. Though never personally close, the two shared the experience of the Cold War, where they had stood shoulder to shoulder against Soviet encroachment.

Dulles arranged to meet the general at an apartment he kept in Georgetown for precisely such clandestine purposes. Upon LeMay's arrival, and after they exchanged brief pleasantries, Dulles laid out the full extent of what he had learned from Johnson. Despite the gravity of the information, none of it caught the hawkish LeMay by surprise. His distrust of the Russians was absolute and unwavering. He kept his ear to the ground and was always alert to rumblings, rumors, and any whispers of unusual activity.

LeMay suggested that the Soviets would indeed be committed to such bold moves and encouraged Dulles to find an operative to send to London. This needed to be someone not only versed in espionage but also skilled in navigating the complex web of international intrigue, a person adept at unearthing secrets and discerning truths amidst a labyrinth of deception.

The advice echoed in Dulles's thoughts. He silently considered the name that had almost eluded him before. *Yes*, he mused, *I know just the man.* Surprised it took this long for him to come to mind, he inwardly marveled at the forces converging at this critical juncture.

MEANWHILE, LEMAY MOVED quickly to reach out to Edward Landsdale, another general with the Air Force who had honed his skills with the Office of Strategic Services during World War II. Landsdale was back in Washington momentarily before a return to Vietnam, but LeMay thought this would be of great interest to him.

A man of significant experience and proven acumen, Landsdale had shown a masterful understanding of psychological warfare and political maneuvering. Dulles felt confident that both Landsdale and LeMay could be key players in uncovering the truth behind the alarming intelligence the British had shared.

Together, they mapped out a plan to leave no stone unturned, committed to finding hard evidence to validate what some would surely call a far-fetched plot. They were seasoned men, well acquainted with the nuances of both discretion and bold action, now joining forces to pick up the scent and follow a trail they hoped would lead to irrefutable proof of Soviet duplicity.

They *wanted* it to be true.

They were driven by a deeply held belief that the expected confrontation between America, its NATO allies, and the Soviet Union was inevitable. They meant to be ready for that day and resolved to do all in their power to see the Soviets decisively defeated and driven back to the borders that preceded the spread of communism in the aftermath of World War II.

Once Dulles briefed both generals on the agent he had in mind to send to London, they were all in agreement about the wisdom of that choice, and they moved quickly to set the plan in motion.

CHAPTER FOURTEEN

WHEN HE RETURNED to his office, Dulles moved quickly. Another man his age might have been tempted to slow his pace, absorb the quiet hum of activity around him, and savor the feeling of being back in familiar surroundings. But Allen Dulles was not another man, and his sense of urgency propelled him through the door.

He peeled off his coat and hat, affixing them to their familiar hooks, then made a direct line for a beautiful painting that always captured his eye. The subject of the piece was Bern, Switzerland's Old City, where a younger version of himself had been steeped in intrigue, a town that held a special place in his repertoire of career highlights.

Allen was a dedicated spymaster, one who could always be counted on to relive an episode or two of previous adventures. The veteran intelligence officer allowed himself a thin, reflective smile as he eyed the cityscape on the wall. It inevitably conjured fond memories of his cloak-and-dagger existence as Wild Bill Donovan's operative during the Second World War. He had represented the Office of Strategic Services (OSS) with distinction, keeping close tabs on Nazi activities while residing at a sparse but functional address on 23 Herrengasse.

But even those days paled in comparison to the tumultuous events of 1917, during the earlier global conflict, when he was serving in America's delegation in the same Swiss city. There was a particular event from that time, one that represented both a spectacular opportunity and a heartrending misstep that had haunted him through the years since.

On an unremarkable Sunday in April of that year, he was alone in his poorly lit office. A telephone rang, breaking the stillness, and a voice on the other end asked insistently to speak with someone in an official capacity. The man's English was poor, and the accent was thick and foreign.

"I'm sorry, but there is no one here to help you right now," Dulles said that day, certain the call had been nothing more than a nuisance.

"But I have a matter of historical significance to discuss," the caller pleaded.

"Let me take your name, and I will have someone call you tomorrow."

"This is Lenin. Pity. Tomorrow will be too late."

Years later, Dulles would tell the story when teaching young and aspiring spies the merits of listening to a source, no matter how insignificant it seemed. At the time of that fateful call, Vladimir Lenin was on a remarkable journey from Germany to St. Petersburg. He was preparing to spark a revolutionary blaze, and he was doing so with the help of the Germans, who hoped to push Russia out of the protracted and bloody war. They had found a willing partner in the man who would soon rise to power as the dictator of Russia.

Dulles always wondered if the ill-fated telephone conversation had been Lenin's attempt to reach out to another potential ally, to see if the Americans were interested in making their own deal, given their still tentative entry into The Great War that very month.

Now here he was, decades later, still finding himself involved in matters of extraordinary consequence. Officially out of office, no longer the Director of the Central Intelligence Agency, but still formidable, he had been called upon by the President of the United States to investigate a conspiracy of staggering proportions. To do so, he would need the help of people he could trust, operatives who knew how the world of espionage truly worked.

He moved the portrait aside and began working the combination on the safe hidden behind it, his fingers moving deftly. Within moments, he was rummaging through a heap of papers. He did not stop until he found what he was hunting for.

There you are, old friend. Now let's see if you can help me.

It was a small blue notebook, unassuming in its appearance but critical in its contents. In it, he had catalogued, among other things, an invaluable collection of names and contact information for old allies, those still active in the agency he had once commanded. He flipped through the well-thumbed pages, moving quickly and efficiently until a name seemed to leap from a page.

Dulles smiled.

Rome
January 19, 1965

HARVEY ELTON KING had nothing but contempt for Rome. His disdain ran deep, not because of the city's inherent traits, but for the circumstances that stranded him there. To him, the ancient city, with its monumental history, was a constant reminder of his spectacular fall from grace. The impressive fountains and piazzas held little allure, their beauty overshadowed by a sense of humiliation that suffused his every thought. Although he was not of the Catholic persuasion, he bore no disdain for the religion. Rather, he loathed the *place.* His own personal and professional Siberia. His St. Helena. A bitter postseason banishment. A place of disgraceful, ignominious exile from which he feared he might never return.

Once upon a time, the name Harvey King reverberated within the secretive halls of American intelligence as that of a living legend, a master of clandestine operations who could bend history to his will. Some still regarded him that way, and he himself certainly harbored no doubts about his greatness. But his star had fallen with those whose opinions held weight in the post-Dulles world of intelligence.

Men like John McCone.

The latest Director of the CIA had been appointed by President Kennedy after the none-too-gentle ousting of Allen Dulles. It happened in the aftermath of what the newspapers and pundits quickly dubbed the Bay of Pigs *fiasco*. To King's credit, he had managed to weather the storm of dismissals and forced retirements when Dulles had been swept out of power in 1961.

But it was another, even more perilous, Caribbean episode that had finally been his downfall, one that turned out more favorably for the so-called good guys but left King in the crosshairs of the President's inner circle. While the world heaved a collective sigh of relief, applauding Kennedy for pulling the world back from the brink of nuclear war, the secret dealings that had brokered peace left no place for men like Harvey King.

Behind closed doors, significant transformations were underway, hidden from the public eye. American policy toward Cuba shifted dramatically when the President whispered assurances to Khrushchev—among them a solemn promise that America would not invade Cuba.

But there was one glaring problem. King and a wide array of conspirators had other plans in mind. Plans that involved CIA operatives, exiled Cubans in Miami, and even members of the mafia. They were concertedly gearing up to eliminate Fidel Castro and transport Cuba back to its pre-revolution state. Free. Profitable.

So while JFK and Soviet leaders breathed relief, life on the ground remained volatile. Harvey was outraged when Bobby

Kennedy ordered him to abandon ship. A vehement argument ensued, with voices raised and tempers hot. King remembered the clash vividly. He had imbibed a bit too much strong drink before that crucial meeting and let loose a stream of choice words for the Attorney General, sealing his fate in the most undiplomatic fashion imaginable. His next stop was inevitable.

Exile—Siberia by way of the Mediterranean.

"MR. KING, THERE'S a call from Washington," came a woman's voice from a small speaker on the desk. She spoke in a tone that was professional yet tinged with a hint of impatience, as if she had been instructed to deliver the message multiple times before. The line crackled slightly, tethered to the old-fashioned phone by a single, loose wire.

It was nearly six o'clock in the evening in Rome, and Harvey King was busy nursing his fifth scotch of the day, the first having been poured promptly at noon. He eyed the glass in his hand with a mixture of satisfaction and resignation. He was a man of habit and seldom left the CIA's Rome office before seven o'clock, or his seventh drink—whichever came first.

As he sat behind his cluttered desk, a map of Cuba defiantly pinned to the wall behind him, he reached for the phone. It took him a couple of tries before managing to punch the button for line two. "King here," he said, his voice booming into the empty office. "Who's calling?"

"Relax, Harvey. It's Allen."

"Allen who?" King asked, then let out an explosive laugh that filled the room like a burst of gunfire. "Ha! 'Course I know who it is. Been a long time, Sport. To what do I owe a phone call from the world's most famous spook?"

"Cut the shit, King." Dulles' voice was sharp, the words tight. "I'm sure you've been hitting the sauce all day, but I need you to be sober as a judge right now. I've got something serious for you. Can you get your ass on a plane back to Washington tonight? I need you here as soon as possible."

There was a pause as King considered the urgency in Dulles' voice.

He leaned back in his chair, a sly smile playing across his lips. "What the hell you talking about, Dulles? What's so important that I need to drop everything and wing it home? Lyndon putting you back in charge of The Company because you did such a good job whitewashing the Kennedy thing in that Warren Report?"

Ignoring the dig, Dulles pressed on, his voice now carrying an edge of authority. "Now, Harvey, I know you have a tough time listening to anyone. But you'd better listen to me right now. This may be your big break out of the shithouse. Bobby Kennedy's in the Senate now, and the President has confidence in my judgment. He's given me an assignment. A big one. One that may save the world as we know it. Yes, that big. And I need you for it. So put the cork in the bottle. Take a shower. Pack a clean shirt. There's a TWA flight from Rome to Idlewild that leaves in two hours." He paused, then added deliberately, "Make sure you're on it. Then take a train to Union Station here in DC. I'll send someone to pick you up and bring you over."

His curiosity now piqued, King lowered the glass of scotch to the table and leaned forward. "Over where?"

"The White House," Dulles replied, the words landing with the weight of a bombshell.

Then he hung up.

CHAPTER FIFTEEN

HARVEY KING SAT at his desk, stupefied by disbelief. He moved the telephone from his ear, staring at it as if it were some alien apparatus delivering a message from another world. Incredulity turned to a wide grin, and he shook his head in glee. "Son of a bitch!" he almost shouted. He tossed the receiver back into the cradle and jumped up from his chair with a vigor that had been missing for months, the old fire suddenly rekindled in his eyes.

The White House.

The very thought sent a jolt of adrenaline coursing through him, far more potent than the liquor he'd been slugging all day. He fished through the clutter on his desk, pushing papers aside and sending them fluttering to the floor. Maps, memos, old photographs. He found what he was after—his passport, hidden beneath a stack of reports that had gone ignored for weeks. He snatched it up and stuffed it into his jacket pocket, then he turned his attention to the small suitcase that had been serving as a makeshift table in the corner of the room.

He opened it and flung its contents to the floor—a half-empty bottle of scotch, a wrinkled shirt, some outdated underwear. Dulles wanted him there yesterday, and there was no time to waste. The words echoed in his mind: *This may be your big break out of the shithouse.* Within a very few minutes, his suitcase was sparsely packed and he'd left the office, his mind racing. He hailed a cab and told the driver, "Aeroporto di Roma il più velocemente possibile!"

Harvey King got to Leonardo Da Vinci Airport in a panic, and he was the last person to board the TWA flight bound for New York. He settled into his seat and barely had time to catch his breath before the cabin doors closed and announced their departure from the gate. He cursed under his breath about having been given such short notice, then took a few more deep breaths, smiling as he thought about his old boss.

Dulles had put him back in the game.

He stretched his arms and legs, a hopeful sense of optimism flushing through his body as the plane began its ascent. Later, after dinner, just as he was putting a twirl of pasta in his mouth, a thought struck him with the force of a lightning bolt. January twentieth—the very next day. It was the day of Lyndon Johnson's inauguration. The more he thought about it, the more curious he became.

If the information Dulles had told him was so urgent, why on earth would those running The Company wait until the last minute to bring him back to Washington? Was it because they knew something might happen during the inauguration? If that was the case, why were they sending him to the White House? These questions started to unravel his relaxed mood, making him edgy and nervous.

Just then, an attractive stewardess strolled by, interrupting his thoughts. "Mr. Williams, would you care for a drink after dinner? Cognac, maybe?" she asked, using the name he always traveled under and giving him a captivating smile. He replied, "Thanks, gorgeous, but I think I'll pass." He smiled at the thought of passing up anything having to do with alcohol.

Harvey King sober. What a crazy-ass idea.

He reached for the newspaper that had been given to him just before the plane took off. It was the European edition of the *Herald Tribune.* As he flipped through it, he noticed something odd. Almost every story from page one to about halfway through the paper had something to do with the impending demise of Winston Churchill. Harvey King raised his eyebrows in even greater curiosity as he thumbed through the paper.

On the front page, only a couple of paragraphs were dedicated to the plans for Johnson's inauguration. King was fascinated by both stories. He had no idea that they were very much intertwined. But he wasn't stupid, and he started to think through the possibilities. The man who imagines himself to be a legend likes to think this way—especially when no one else does. He was dizzy with the things that were spinning around in his mind as the big airplane made its way across the Atlantic.

The crazy old bastard said this could be my big break, he thought.

IMMEDIATELY AFTER HE had hung up from his call to Harvey King in Rome, Dulles drove the short distance from his home in Georgetown to a considerably larger home across the Potomac in Arlington, Virginia. He parked in the driveway and walked quietly up toward the side of the house and made his way back to the greenhouse that he knew so well.

It was there that he found the man he was looking for. A man he regarded as an ally, even as a friend, but someone he never quite understood. Thin, even frail, with thick glasses and a perennial cigarette that he was always lighting while another still had life, James Jesus Angleton was precisely where Dulles expected him to be.

Surrounded by orchids.

"Good to see you, as always, Allen," Angleton said, bending over a beautiful white orchid with a small gardening tool in his left hand.

"You're looking good, Jim. The flowers are beautiful. You have a gift."

"They're a gift to me, Allen. They comfort my mind." He paused and looked up. "What can I do for you? You're not one to make social calls."

"Guilty as charged, Jim. We have a situation. The President called me in. Off the record. McCone's not to know."

For the first time, Angleton put the small tool down, and lit yet another cigarette. His interest was piqued. "Understood. How can I help?"

"I want your read on our cousins across the pond. Who can we trust over there?"

The thin man thought for a moment, measuring his words. "As far as I'm concerned, that fish stinks from the head. I've tried to warn my sources over there about Harold Wilson," he said. "I'm convinced he's a KGB plant."

"I'm aware of your thoughts on that, Jim. I'm also aware of your position on the real defector and double agent, even though most in the agency think differently." He was referring to Golitsyn and Nosenko, the two defectors who had divided opinion in the intelligence community.

Dulles was being careful not to offend.

"What do you want from me, Allen?" Angleton asked with a note of irritation.

"I want your read on MI5. Who can we trust there if we need something?"

"Roger Hollis is also a KGB agent," Angleton replied firmly, dark eyes hidden behind lenses as thick as his suspicions.

"Jim, surely you don't think everyone over there works for Moscow?"

"Of course not, Allen. But MI5 is compromised from the top down."

"The President's convinced there may be an attack on the horizon in conjunction with Churchill's funeral when all the world leaders will be in London," Dulles said, pausing, letting it sink in. "In fact, he's so persuaded of this, I'm guessing he'll be staying home and skip the big event."

Angleton looked genuinely surprised. It was hard to catch him off guard. "From where has Lyndon obtained this information?"

"I'm not at liberty—"

"Allen, you know me better than that."

Dulles sighed before answering, "It comes from the British Ambassador, but Johnson swore me to secrecy about that."

"Understood," Angleton said. He looked away for a moment and was quiet, calculating, pondering what was not being said. "And I believe the Ambassador has *unusually* good contacts in Moscow," he added, letting the words hang in the air for a moment.

Dulles, unsure what to make of the comment, continued on. "I'm sending Harvey King over to sniff around."

"He's a good man. Anything I can do?"

"Yes, Jim. When the time comes, I may need you to contact someone you trust at MI5."

"I'll be ready and waiting, my friend. Could you pass me those shears?"

CHAPTER SIXTEEN

LYNDON JOHNSON'S SPEECH was one of the shortest inaugural addresses on record. It took him just twenty-two minutes to share approximately 1,500 words. Applause slowed him down a bit. He counted eleven sustained interruptions; a fact he mentioned several times to numerous people throughout the day. And there was indeed a record-breaking crowd on hand. It was a Texas-sized affair from start to finish.

He told his fellow Americans: "Our enemies have always made the same mistake. In my lifetime— in Depression and War—they have awaited our defeat. Each time, from the secret places of the American heart, came forth the faith they could not see or that they could not even imagine. It brought us victory. And it will again."

They were words with a deeper meaning at the time, as only he and a few other men knew. As he spoke, he hoped the investigation he had set in motion was bearing fruit. Those thoughts preoccupied

Mr. Johnson as he watched the parade that day and danced with Ladybird at several Inaugural Balls later that evening.

Johnson knew that at a little after midnight he would be meeting with Allen Dulles and another man unknown to him. All under the radar and off the record, of course. Few would ever know about the meeting. But it would be one of the most important of the tall Texan's presidency.

Washington, D.C.
January 21, 1965

ALL PRESIDENTS PUT their unique fingerprints on the decor of the most famous office in the world, and Johnson had removed nearly everything having to do with his predecessor. The storied Resolute Desk was out, replaced with the desk LBJ had used as Majority Leader. The navy-themed decor was replaced by something akin to mid-century *cowboy*. There was, however, one remnant from the days of Camelot.

JFK's *rocking chair*.

Kennedy had liked it because of his bad back, but Johnson kept it simply because it was comfortable, especially after having some cushy tan pads added to the seat, back, and arms. A man who breathed action, he loved to sit and rock while his guests sat and sometimes squirmed on the sofas.

Johnson was seated in that rocking chair shortly before one a.m., face to face with two enigmatic men who sat across from him on a long sofa. One of the men was Allen Dulles, who had helped build the CIA into one of the most powerful and secretive institutions in the American government. The other man was someone Johnson had never met in person, though his reputation preceded him.

Harvey King was as colorful as he was mysterious. He was rumored to be one of the inspirations for Ian Fleming's fictional creation, James Bond. LBJ was genuinely proud to make the acquaintance of a man who had been whisked away from his covert work in Europe—a form of exile imposed by the Kennedy brothers—and brought inconspicuously back to Washington for reasons known to only a very few insiders.

While King might indeed have supplied Ian Fleming with some raw material for his famous spy novels, he bore no resemblance whatsoever to Sean Connery, Roger Moore, or any of the other suave and chiseled actors who would eventually bring the Bond character to life in decades to come. King was significantly overweight, notably balding, and typically dressed in a rumpled manner that suggested he had neither the time nor the inclination to pay heed to convention or propriety.

He was a hard-drinking, hard-charging, and hardheaded man who many believed was more of a loose cannon than a company man. He was much like the proverbial bull in a China shop—and in his case, he seemed to take that China shop with him wherever he went.

Despite his less-than-polished appearance, Harvey King had been at the epicenter of some of the CIA's most important and daring covert operations over the previous decade. His involvement spanned a dizzying array of clandestine missions, from a successful coup in Guatemala, to the construction of a tunnel beneath the Soviet sector in Berlin (infamously nicknamed "Harvey's Hole"), to his more recent and highly personal engagement as the point man for both Kennedy brothers in their deeply rooted and nearly obsessive desire to see Fidel Castro not only removed from power, but entirely removed from the face of the earth.

He had established himself as an expert in *counter*intelligence, where his early instincts about Soviet moles and American traitors had made him a singularly valuable asset as well as an unpredictable ally. King had been, perhaps, the first American intelligence officer to suspect Kim Philby of being a Soviet spy.

Philby had been on King's radar as early as 1951, though it had taken the rest of the American and British intelligence forces another dozen years to catch on to the man's duplicitous activities. Only after a dramatic defection one stormy night in January of 1963—from his refuge in Lebanon to a freighter bound for Odessa—did suspicion against Philby finally crystallize as the traitor fled toward his ultimate destination: the seat of Soviet power in Moscow, Russia.

Once a living legend, King had never lacked for admirers in the shadowy world of espionage. However, he had seen his star plummet in recent years. His resumed presence in Washington was a matter of considerable consequence, and though he was jet-lagged and weary, he was ready to prove that he was anything but a relic from the past.

He had consumed no liquor aboard the plane, but he'd remedied that oversight by nursing a series of J&B scotches over ice on the train. So much for his attempt at sobriety. But by the time of their meeting, the President himself had managed to put away more than his fair share of Cutty Sark. Neither man was close to drunk, but they were sufficiently lubricated to become animated about the one thing they had in enthusiastic solidarity.

An undiluted aversion for all things *Kennedy.*

King was not usually one to kiss ass, but he was tired of taking up space in the proverbial doghouse and decided to use his hatred of Bobby Kennedy as a means to find favor with the President. LBJ's loathing of the newly minted Senator from New York was no state secret, after all.

As for Allen Dulles, he was amused as he watched the back-and-forth Camelot-bashing between Johnson and King. He found it fascinating that on a day of such great triumph for the President—the triumph of all triumphs—the man could so flagrantly indulge in pettiness that was far beneath the dignity of his celebrated office. Dulles relit his pipe more than once as the two men aired it out.

Finally, and with their vital rapport established, they got around to the point of the meeting. "Allen, I assume you briefed our friend here about what we might be dealing with," Johnson said.

"Yes, Mr. President," Dulles replied. "Harvey's up to speed and ready to fly to London later today."

"Great!" an eager LBJ responded. "We need to get to the bottom of this. How do you propose to proceed?" Both men turned toward King, silently awaiting his response.

"WELL, I HAVE a few old friends who are former MI6, Mr. President. They're tied in there, as I still am with Langley. Once a spook, always a spook," King said with a smirk that played across his lips. He leaned forward, his eyes sharp and calculating despite his weary demeanor. "If there's something to this, there must be chatter. I'll find out if anything is on their radar."

King paused, casting a quick glance at Dulles before continuing. "Allen here mentioned your source talked about the possibility of some kind of operation made to look like the IRA was behind it. Well, for one thing, bombs are their signature. I'd like to get the plans for Churchill's funeral even before the old man buys the farm. That way, I can try to figure out the weak spots."

The Oval Office was dimly lit, the shadows playing across the walls, the hush of history filling the room as if it were a co-conspirator in the clandestine exchange. The only interruption was the faint ticking of a clock, each second amplifying the significance of their secretive meeting. Johnson regarded Harvey with a look of grim determination, his tall frame leaning back in the rocking chair.

"The devil, Mr. President," Dulles interjected, his voice calm and measured, "is in the details, as we know. We need to get ahold of the official state plans for the funeral. Do you think your source—

and we respect that you are guarding his identity—is in a position to get his hands on that information?" His pipe smoke lingered in the air, adding to the room's conspiratorial ambiance.

President Johnson nodded. "I wouldn't be a bit surprised. I'll see what I can do before you leave today," he said.

"One more thing, Mr. President," Dulles added cautiously, knowing the complexity of what he was about to propose. "We need to get Harvey to London without leaving a trail. Just want you to know we are going to bend some rules along the way." His tone was respectful but also indicated a business-as-usual attitude toward operating in the gray areas if it served the mission.

"Hell, break the damn things. I couldn't care less," Johnson replied without hesitation, a slight drawl underscoring his irreverence for the bureaucratic constraints that could impede their efforts. His eyes shone with a mix of defiance and determination. "Just make sure nothing tracks back to this office."

"Understood," Dulles replied, gratified by the President's no-nonsense approach. "I have access to a private aircraft owned by one of the companies I work with. We're going to send along with Harvey another man I trust, someone who can help him along."

"Fine," Johnson said, holding out his hands with the palms facing out. "Just don't give me too many details. I don't need 'em. I just need you men to help us avoid fucking World War III." The gravity of his words was softened by his crude manner.

Dulles hesitated—he wanted to test the waters on a particularly sensitive subject. "Mr. President...there's one more thing."

"Uh huh," Johnson said, expecting the question and bracing for the implications of his answer.

"I'm hoping you're not going to Mr. Churchill's funeral when the time comes. It could be very dangerous, and if the unthinkable happens, we need a leader who can lead. Frankly, I don't think our new Vice President is up to the job."

"Damn straight. Hubert can't wipe his own ass," Johnson said with the bluntness that was his trademark, a coarse humor lacing his otherwise serious assessment. "I hated putting him on the ticket. The guy talks too much and says nothing. I guess I could send *him* to England, but the idiot would probably embarrass us."

Dulles smiled, knowing that Johnson's disdain for Humphrey was as genuine as it was strategic. "Well, sir, you'll have many options when the time comes. Right now, we'll leave you to get some rest. Harvey will be ready to fly this evening. And congratulations on your Inauguration, Mr. President!"

"Thank you, Gentlemen. I'll work on getting those funeral plans to you as soon as possible," Johnson said. "I guess I could make an official request or something from their embassy."

He picked up the phone and barked into it. "Moyers, get a hold of Dean Rusk over at State. Have him contact the British Embassy and see if they have any advance details about a funeral for Mr. Churchill."

"Certainly, sir."

"And I need it ten minutes ago."

Bill Moyers called Rusk, who in turn called over to the British Embassy, and within two hours a copy of a report called "Operation Hope Not—Preparations for the Funeral of Sir Winston Leonard Spencer-Churchill" was on Johnson's desk. Moyers told the President that the delivery of the document to the White House had been personally facilitated by Ambassador Ormsby-Gore.

LBJ smiled slightly at that bit of information. He spent about thirty minutes reading through the impressive and thorough plan and was surprised that the funeral details for Churchill had been in development for so long. It was certainly going to be an epic event—one for the history books and not to be missed. Johnson then tasked Moyers with handing the materials off to Allen Dulles, who made sure that Harvey King had the file to read during his flight across the Atlantic.

CHAPTER SEVENTEEN

London

TRAVELING ACROSS THE Atlantic with Harvey King was the man who had been handpicked by Dulles. The mission required maximum finesse and discretion, and for that, Dulles chose a semi-retired intelligence operative named Tiernan Brogan. Known for his resourcefulness and undying commitment, Brogan was short, stocky, and sported a round face with a fiery red mane.

He was of Irish stock and had infiltrated the IRA for British intelligence during the early stages of the Border Campaign, an effort against conspirators in Northern Ireland. Although the campaign had concluded, Brogan's involvement left him with numerous contacts and more than a few scars from those turbulent days. Both he and King placed their bets on those connections proving valuable to their mission.

After sustaining serious injuries in Belfast, Brogan shifted his base of operations to America. He formalized his long-standing relationship with the CIA, developing it into a lucrative contract role. But Brogan's ties to London never fully relaxed. He had become a trusted, albeit unofficial, conduit for sensitive information flowing between the two nations' intelligence services.

His personal life had suffered as a result. Brogan was a divorced man, though not bitterly so. The marriage had lasted just under a year, and his ex-wife claimed, without malice, that he was a bigamist—married to his work. It was an accusation Brogan didn't even try to deny.

THEIR AIRCRAFT WAS a cutting-edge Learjet 23—the first of its class ever built. It had only recently been delivered to its shadowy owners. The purchasers were a company with clandestine connections to the United Fruit Company, a powerful conglomerate with vast interests stretching across Central and South America.

The Dulles brothers, Allen and the now-deceased John Foster, shared a complicated and enduring relationship with that company. This long-standing bond was woven from threads of financial ambition, political power, intricate intrigue, and indeed, a touch of espionage known only to a few.

As the jet pierced through the winter sky, Brogan and King went over the materials from Operation Hope Not. They each anticipated the dramatic funeral plans would be a superb and tempting target for those plotting mass mayhem. Still, neither was sure the source Johnson and Dulles had relied upon was correct, or even if the source wasn't some sort of plant. It wouldn't be the first time.

And it sure wouldn't be the last.

UPON ARRIVAL IN London, the two men chartered a car to the Dorchester Hotel on Park Lane, not far from Hyde Park. On the drive, they discussed their options. Harvey King made a comment about how cold the damn place was. Although the temperature in

London rarely fell to subfreezing levels, the damp air was a menacing chill that drilled through the heaviest wool overcoats worn by even the heartiest of souls.

Brogan replied, "Aye, but it's not Belfast."

They dumped their bags and immediately split up. Brogan visited many of the haunts where he knew the likes of the IRA were apt to go—and the likes of British intelligence were not. He was on the hunt for chatter. Brogan was convinced that if there was something going on that involved men who wanted so keenly to strike at the crown, his old pals would know.

King, meanwhile, set up camp near Hyde Park Gate and watched from the shadows over the next couple of days as two men who he had noticed hanging out near the Churchill home seemed to be replaced by two others, so similar in appearance that they could have been twins. All were dressed in dark, inexpensive-looking suits, and all wore their hats in that certain way that screamed Eastern Bloc—and more likely than that, Soviet. Harvey King's gut told him so.

And his gut was rarely wrong.

After all, when it came to suspicion of the Soviets, King's gut had been right about Kim Philby, it had been right about that tunnel in Berlin, and King's gut had been right about the Bay of Pigs. And while others often speculated that King had the grace of a bull, he consistently and reliably trusted his gut as he would a sixth sense. He was, however, a little surprised where the men went—or at least, how they got there.

They hailed cabs in a most pedestrian manner, without any concern about who might be watching them, and traveled straight to the Soviet Embassy. He followed them. *This is too damn easy*, he thought to himself. Not only did there seem to be no concern on the part of the men about being followed, but there also appeared to be no British agents around at all. *Damn careless*, he thought, chalking up the complete lack of surveillance to what he considered typical laxity on the part of British intelligence services.

He hadn't had much regard for them—or trust—since Philby. Even after King had warned them back in 1951, they had kept the man in the loop until he defected to Moscow. Watching the Russians move about without concern for anyone tracking them further convinced King that when it came to the Soviets, the British had a monumental blind spot. One as wide as the Thames.

Maybe Harold Wilson is a commie, after all.

CHAPTER EIGHTEEN

FIVE THOUSAND MILES away, a man sat in a sparsely furnished apartment in an old part of the city and consulted his time piece. The flat was drafty and depressing, but it was also discreet. His handlers had seen to that. As he looked at the watch on his wrist, he decided that the day had progressed far enough to warrant the first dram of what would surely be many.

He walked the short distance from the living room to the kitchen, where he reached into a cabinet for a bottle of vodka. He frowned. He preferred scotch. Vodka was so cliche, especially in Moscow. He muttered to himself, though no one was around to hear it, "Better than n-n-nothing, I suppose."

He poured about an inch of the clear liquid into a simple water glass and drank it in one practiced swallow. Then he poured another and made his way back over to the only comfortable piece of furniture in the entire flat—a large chair with an ottoman. He sat down, took another sip, and picked up a newspaper.

Harold Adrian Russell Philby, known to friends and former friends alike as "Kim," wondered if the clouds that seemed to be always hovering above him these days were beginning to dissipate. It was properly British, he thought, how a drink and a bit of newsprint could make the world seem less bleak. The paper was the Sunday edition of the *Times* of London, a publication he once wrote for. He'd received it earlier in the day, which was unusual. It usually didn't make its way to him until Monday or Tuesday of the next week.

He wondered if the unexpected, early delivery was a message in and of itself. He dared to hope it was. He was ready to be trusted again, ready to re-enter the game. He had worked for and thought about Moscow for so long, but now that he was actually there it felt like a cage—like a dream gone wrong. The life of a hero, the life he believed was his due, had eluded him since his defection more than two years earlier.

He'd been addicted to the drug of deceit for most of his adult life, spying for the Soviet Union since his college days at Cambridge, having been recruited along with three other men: Guy Burgess, Donald MacLean, and Anthony Blunt. Blunt had confessed to MI-5 in 1964, exchanging his treachery for a promise of immunity and anonymity. But Burgess and MacLean had been in Moscow since 1951.

Philby had helped them get there. He knew that this increased his stature in the eyes of those that mattered, but it also put him under suspicion as "the third man" in what became known as the Cambridge spy ring. Kim managed to deflect and deny the accusations effectively for more than a decade before going over to the other side.

By early 1963, he was under scrutiny again. He was living in Beirut, Lebanon and working as a journalist for a couple of London publications—The Observer and Economist. He was married and had two children. But when it became clear that he was about to be exposed as a traitor, he fled—leaving his wife and children, not to mention the Queen and country, behind.

His dream was to live out his final years as a hero in Russia. He wanted to become a full-fledged officer in the KGB, to be recognized as the savior of Soviet secrets. He wanted to be the man who put the final nail in the coffin of capitalism. This was a lot to want, he realized. And he wondered if it would ever happen.

His old friend Guy Burgess had been something of a rock star in Moscow, and the knowledge of it weighed heavily on Kim, like an iron anchor dragging under the currents of his own despair. Burgess had quickly become a darling of the Soviet establishment, living the life of a celebrated renegade. It stung that he had been featured on the cover of *Life Magazine*, no less, a few years earlier.

Philby, however, seemed to be barely a footnote, a shadow of a memory in the minds of the very men he had risked everything for. He wondered if they had already washed their hands of a man they once considered invaluable. Maybe that explained why he looked forward so much to the London newspaper—to each of its dog-eared pages. It offered him a threadbare but treasured connection to the past, to the place he had left behind.

The few ties he still managed to maintain were frayed to the point of snapping. His fifty-third birthday had come and gone a few weeks earlier, and he had marked it with the same sense of solitude that infused the rest of his life in Moscow. Alone. A few of his supposed "friends" had sent him a bottle of single-malt Scotch, a gesture both felicitous and cruel, given the thirst it sparked in him. It was meant as a gift, but it was really a reminder of things he had lost. Kim had tried to make it last—to be judicious and sparing in his indulgence.

He used every ounce of his self-control to slow himself down, but the bottle was empty by the end of its second day with him. He kept the empty for sentimental reasons. *Scotch*, he thought bitterly as he stared at it. *The sound of English. The Times of London.* These were the strings that tied him to who he once was. But those strings were slowly unraveling, and he knew they might also be the strings that made him little more than a puppet to the Russians. He was already suspect. That much was clear. He sipped the vodka as he turned the pages, still wondering if the early delivery was a sign. *Will they let me back in the game?*

HIS TWO YEARS in Moscow had been filled with disappointment. What he imagined would be a victory march had turned into something more like a death sentence, with boredom, suspicion, and loneliness his primary prison guards. Every day seemed longer than the one before. Then, one afternoon in late 1964, an official car had appeared at his building, and he was whisked off to a clandestine meeting with a small group of powerful men at a large estate on the outskirts of the city.

That day, Kim Philby was briefed about something big—so big that he could hardly breathe until he returned to his apartment, a place that suddenly seemed less like a prison—and he was beyond excited to finally be included. After so long in the wilderness, it was proof to him that he was trusted. It was confirmation that he was valued.

But since that one meeting, months had gone by without further contact from the group. Months of dreadful inactivity. Months of watching the hands of his watch crawl slowly forward and hoping that every tick would bring a change in his fortune. He began to despair of ever hearing from them again. The silence was the worst of all, more punishing than any condemnation.

Until today.

As he turned the pages of his precious newspaper and sipped his vodka—by now his fourth glass—he came across a personal note that had been inserted between pages six and seven of the main section. It was in English and said: *"Comrade Philby: Be ready at eight o'clock tomorrow morning. A car will pick you up in front of your building. Please pack a bag for several days."*

Kim Philby's heart raced.

CHAPTER NINETEEN

TIERNAN BROGAN'S EXHAUSTIVE tour of London's Irish pubs in search of familiar faces had produced little more than mild morning-after hangovers after two nights of effort. He had seen many old friends, and he'd jotted down some notes, but it seemed to him that none had delivered more than empty glasses and old tales.

He decided to revisit the Tipperary. During his undercover days with the MI5, he'd spent much time there, feigning allegiance to the cause, and he hoped now to encounter a few more friends from the not-too-distant past—when he'd gone by another name—who might give him more to report to King.

Brogan eased into the pub's bustling warmth and settled at a table in a shadowed corner. From there, he could observe with discretion. His first order was a pint of Smithwick's, and he nursed it slowly as he surveyed the other patrons. A few faces he recognized, but none that mattered.

He pulled out his notes and read through them all and realized that he had gleaned more than he thought. There was a repeated theme. Many seemed to know about *something*, but no one seemed to be doing it. This was distinctly odd.

He tucked his notebook back into his pocket and sat thoughtfully staring at the pint in his hands. None of his old IRA cronies were the type to sit back when a row was in the making—but not one of them seemed to be actively involved. Decidedly odd. He sighed deeply, suddenly, and looked around as though coming up out of deep water.

A striking woman seated a few tables away caught his eye. Her expression indicated she had already noticed him, and his initial impulse was to shift his gaze and avoid encouraging any advance. A slight hesitation followed, as something about her stirred a memory.

Do I know her?

A few minutes ticked by, and it finally clicked. Her name remained elusive, but he recalled she had played a role during The Border Campaign. Not a frontline fighter, but as part of the wider support team, coordinating efforts from behind the scenes.

What's she doing in London?

Before he could act on this new line of thinking, she stood, picked up a pair of full glasses, and walked toward him with the hint of a smile. She had a vibrant, contagious energy about her, and as she neared, he was struck by how stunning she was. Her red hair shone a shade or two brighter than his own.

"Fancy another drink, love?" she teased, extending one of the glasses toward him.

"Why, yes, thank you," he replied, accepting it with a nod.

"You don't remember me, darlin', do ya?" Her tone was playful, but there was an edge to her words that suggested she already knew the answer.

"Sure an' I do, but I just can't place it," he admitted, still hoping for the name to emerge from the fog of memory.

"Belfast. You're Sean Walsh. I'm Kaitlyn Dorcey." She winked, using the name Brogan had adopted when he infiltrated the IRA.

"Of course, now I remember. May I say, you're looking splendid, Miss Dorcey?"

"Why, thank you, Sean. You're not so bad yourself. What has you in London?"

Thinking quickly, he responded with a smile, "Just waiting for something exciting to come my way. Looks like I picked the right place to wait."

"That you did, Sean. That you did."

Brogan was skeptical that he would learn much from the enchanting Miss Dorcey that night, but he was pleasantly surprised. Their time at the Tipperary stretched into the late hours, a playful yet intense game of cat-and-mouse that both seemed to enjoy. Conversation flowed as easily as the drinks, and they transitioned from ale to Jameson's. He was thankful for his ability to hold his liquor, a skill honed over years, since she could certainly hold hers. At one point, he wondered if perhaps he was being played rather than doing the playing, but he shook off the thought. She seemed off duty, genuinely savoring the evening.

Just as he began to let down his guard, she abruptly drained her drink and announced, "Well, Mr. Walsh, it's been lovely, but I must go. I may be back here tomorrow evening, though. If you're lucky." She sealed her words with a passionate kiss that left him momentarily breathless. Then she turned and walked away, red hair aflame in the crowded room.

He hesitated for a moment, then decided to follow her—from a distance. She navigated two blocks, her pace steady, then climbed a set of stairs to a flat. He watched as lights flickered on behind a set of curtains, only to dim after a few minutes. For a brief moment, he considered staking the place out for the night, but that felt unnecessary and possibly risky. Besides, he needed to brief King on what he'd learned so far. Satisfied he had not been noticed, he returned to the small, cramped room he and Harvey were sharing at the Dorchester.

KING WAS ALREADY in their room, sprawled in a chair with a glass in hand, frowning. He sat up when Brogan entered and gestured at the bottle. Shaking his head, Tiernan sat on the bed and pulled off his shoes. "Fair worn these out, I have," he said as he dropped the second one. "And even an Irishman has a limit to the liquid he can hold, though the spirit takes up less space than water."

"Had a wee dram or two, have you?" asked King with a grin.

"Dunnamany."

"Anything to show for it?"

Brogan sat a moment before responding. He nodded his head once, decidedly. "My old pals are dropping hints about something big about to happen, but it's all winks and nods and "big"—bigger than anything for decades. And nobody's *doin'* anything. They're not recruiting or gathering supplies or...or...doin' anything," he repeated. "Something's on, but they're waiting for it, not pulling it themselves."

King opened his mouth to respond, but Brogan wasn't finished. "It's unnatural."

That surprised a laugh out of King, but he was serious again almost at once. "Yeah, the intel we were given was no rumor. There's definitely a major operation in the works, and the Soviets are firmly involved."

He shared what he'd learned by trailing the Soviets. "It's obviously going to be triggered by Churchill's death. They're not praying for him out there in front of his house."

Brogan grinned at that thought and reached for the bottle after all.

"What I don't understand, though, is their vigil out there. If the event is to be during the funeral, and it must be—that's when all of the dignitaries will be gathered—why all the interest in the house?"

"Pretty maids?" Brogan suggested as he poured himself a drink, a quick and uncharacteristic smile flashing across his usually somber face.

"Not noticeably," King replied with another grin. "And I've seen them in Rochester Row, too, just standing around. What do you think of that?"

Brogan downed his drink in one gulp. "Looks like the bastards are staying true to the script Allen briefed us on. Want to know what I think, Harvey?"

King smiled. He liked this guy.

"I think it's just about time to kick some Soviet arse."

CHAPTER TWENTY

Moscow

THE MEN THAT Harvey King had followed were precisely what he had feared: determined and resourceful members of the KGB, the intelligence apparatus of the Soviet Union. More than mere agents, they belonged to the shadowy Department Thirteen within the First Directorate, known for its ruthlessness and audacity.

This infamous department had orchestrated some of the Soviet regime's most cunning and daring operations, from acts of sabotage that crippled industries to kidnappings that instilled fear in the hearts of political adversaries and dissenters.

In the bustling Soviet capital, the Presidium convened in near-constant sessions. These were the hardliners, the men who had deposed Khrushchev the previous October. They had seen to it that he was removed without warning and without ceremony, replaced by a new leader with whom they felt more aligned.

To them, Khrushchev had shown far too much willingness to compromise with the West. They believed his disarmament agreement with President Kennedy in 1963—built on goodwill in the wake of the Cuban Missile Crisis—had been a dangerous act of betrayal. They were convinced war with the West was inevitable, and they were determined to wage and win that war on their own terms.

Victory would require preparation and cunning. And it would require taking steps that Khrushchev had been unwilling to consider, steps that they had already embarked upon during the summer months. The men of the Presidium signed off on a new and daring scheme, one crafted in that very Department Thirteen in the First Directorate with consummate care and precision.

IT WAS A delegation from Department Thirteen that handled Kim Philby. They had to use an English-speaking translator to communicate with him, though Philby had worked to pick up the Russian language in the two years he'd been there, especially the specialized portions of it that related directly to his work with the Presidium.

"Comrade Philby, your report on British intelligence and security is most helpful," said Leonid Brezhnev, the newly elected figurehead of the Soviet Union's collective leadership. He was the Chairman of the group and the man who, along with his closest allies, had engineered Khrushchev's unceremonious dismissal. "As you well know, we have our assets positioned in London for when the moment for action comes."

Since his ascension, the image of him being approved as the new Chairman by committee had been carefully cultivated, a counterpoint to the perceived dictatorial ways of Khrushchev. He knew Nikita was well aware of his scheming, but under the collective system, there was little he could do about it.

"It was my p-p-privilege, Chairman Brezhnev," Philby said, nodding with appreciation as he did. He was especially satisfied with the acknowledgment that the evaluation he had prepared about

British security efforts had been received favorably. "I'm aware of those very assets, and I'm c-c-certainly willing to help with them in any way you and the committee s-see fit," he added with a bit more confidence.

The room went quiet until another man spoke up. "One vital question we have is about the Americans. You did not deal with this in your report." This came from Alexei Kosygin, who held the title of Premier and was second to Brezhnev in the hierarchy.

Philby was caught off guard. The new plan was primarily focused on Europe and Philby's deep knowledge of the relationships and fault lines between the Continental powers and Great Britain. The fact that they were pressing him about the Americans was something he should have anticipated but had not. Until now, all of his interactions with the group had been cordial and even friendly. He had never been pushed or tested like this.

Momentarily flustered, he hastily gathered his thoughts and ventured a cautious reply. He tried to fight off his stutter, which became painfully pronounced when he was under stress. "My ap-p-pologies, Premier K-Kosygin. My instructions about the report I was to p-p-prepare did not include anything about the Americ-c-cans. I can write up something on that for you."

Brezhnev interrupted before Philby could say more. "Comrade Philby, there is no need to prepare a written report. Please, just tell us your opinions, if you have them, about President Johnson. We know it has been many years since you lived in the United States, and we do not expect you to be able to provide significant intelligence there. We also know your proud journey to our great nation has created a very tense situation between British security and the American CIA."

"Yes, I s-s-suppose it has," Philby replied.

"Comrade Semichastny, do you have any questions on this matter for our friend?"

"Certainly, Comrade Chairman," Semichastny replied, and then he picked up a paper and seemed to read from it as he addressed Philby. Vladimir Semichastny had been the Chairman of the Committee for State Security for the past few years, though he had no previous intelligence experience. In fact, he had no track record for expository reports, planning, or strategic operations, which had made it easier for Brezhnev to place him in a position of such power.

He was in the role purely because he was Brezhnev's political ally and had been a useful accomplice to him during the final phase of the Khrushchev coup. "Comrade Philby, we have reports that this man, Angleton, from the American CIA has been trying to convince some in British Intelligence that there is a highly placed Soviet agent in what they call MI5. Are you aware of this?"

"Yes, Comrade Semichastny"—Philby was surprised and elated by his success with the security man's name—"I'm aware of this, and I know Mr. Angleton, very well. We were once very c-c-close friends. I believe J-J-J-Jim has been heavily influenced by this m-m-man, Golitsyn." *Ugh,* Philby thought, and squirmed with embarrassment.

"That is correct," Semichastny replied. "We have sent our own man, Nosenko, to try to convince the Americans that he is, in fact, the real defector and this *mudak,* Golitsyn, is a double agent. Early indications are that there is now much confusion about this inside the American intelligence community. My question to you is, will this man, Angleton, be convinced? Or will he be a problem?"

Philby reflected for a moment.

It was not the first time he had encountered such direct questions about Angleton. They had once been so close that they shared the term "cousins" to refer to relationships between the international agencies they represented. He had not expected Angleton's deep suspicion of him and the defection, but he should have. Eventually, he replied to Semichastny's careful questioning. "I wish I c-could assure you that Angleton will be no problem, but I know him too well. He will c-continue his mole hunt and should not b-b-be underestimated."

Brezhnev then said, "Let us discuss KOBA and the need to proceed at once," he said to those assembled. "If we succeed, Johnson and Angleton will be irrelevant."

THE AMBITIOUS PLOT had been given the codename "KOBA," a reference to Josef Stalin's early revolutionary name. It was an appropriately bold choice given that the plan was nothing less than a blueprint for ultimate Soviet conquest, fulfilling the unfinished dreams of both Lenin and Stalin for total domination across Europe, including a decisive incursion into Great Britain.

KOBA's audacity lay in its *simplicity*.

The masterstroke was to begin with a single catastrophic event. They would strike an unprecedented blow with a calculated act of political terror that would leave the world aghast and leaderless. In the chaos and confusion that followed the sudden and simultaneous deaths of numerous global leaders, long-dormant agents provocateur—operatives who had infiltrated their targets over the course of many years—would launch an orchestrated wave of precision bombings and assassinations.

Collaborators within leftist groups would fan the flames of unrest, transforming the streets of Europe into arenas of dissent and upheaval. Political demonstrations would erupt with fierce intensity, directed against the very governments of Western Europe that were paralyzed by the London catastrophe.

This manufactured chaos was designed to create a window of vulnerability and a rare historical opportunity, one into which the Red Army would march with unstoppable force. The Soviets had ninety motor rifle divisions at the ready, each one standing by for immediate deployment. These were bolstered by fifty divisions of tanks, a formidable war machine prepared to roll over any opposition.

Seven divisions of elite airborne troops completed the grim picture.

The plan called for a swift and annihilating air assault on NATO positions, to be immediately followed by the massive insertion of airborne divisions behind enemy lines. Then, with everything in place, they would flood the continent with millions of troops. The tanks were primed to smash through defenses while the airborne forces sowed confusion and disorder.

The objective was brutally clear: complete military control of all of Continental Europe within the breathtakingly short span of thirty days. The tactical aspects of this grand design were orchestrated by the experienced hand of Defense Minister Andrei Grechko, who had meticulously prepared for the assault. But the spark, the bold stroke that would ignite the Soviet Union's great victory, had come from a different source.

Years before KOBA was even drafted, a keen and calculating strategist within the KGB had envisaged a scheme to capitalize on the inevitable death of Winston Churchill. This man, Yuri Andropov, was young and fiercely ambitious, and he had long seen the aging Churchill as the ultimate symbol of capitalist defiance, a thorn in the Soviet flank ever since the Russian Revolution.

Though Churchill and Stalin had been forced into a wartime alliance during The Great Patriotic War, as World War II was known in the Soviet Union, Stalin had harbored deep mistrust toward his British counterpart. He even authorized an assassination attempt on Churchill at a small college in America after the war. The plan was scrubbed at the last minute, but Stalin's desire to eliminate Churchill never waned—not even in death. He was incensed that Churchill had coined the phrase "Iron Curtain," a term he desperately wanted to eliminate from history.

The plan to rid the world of Churchill once and for all was passed on as part of KOBA. Agents were embedded within the Irish Republican Army, an organization that had shown some sympathy towards Marxist-Leninist ideology. A man, his wife, and later their grown son became the plan's primary operatives, each carefully placed and meticulously prepared to execute their roles when the time came.

Now, as the Presidium met in Moscow and agents reported regularly from London, it was almost time. The Soviet leadership, especially the hardliners who had orchestrated Khrushchev's fall from power, were fully aligned. KOBA was in motion, and when the moment came, the Soviets would be ready to act with precision and overwhelming force.

"YOUR CAR WILL be ready in a few moments, Comrade," Brezhnev said, dismissing the others with a wave of his hand. As the men stood to leave, he gestured to Philby and said, "While we wait, I'd like a private word with you." Brezhnev led the British defector to a small office with a single desk and a few chairs. He shut the door and they sat next to each other. "We have a job for you connected with the plan codename KOBA."

"You d-d-do?" Philby asked, surprised. He scolded himself inwardly for stuttering.

"Yes, Comrade. With your extensive experience in the British Security Services, you are a valuable asset to us. We're sending you to London tonight."

Kim Philby was shocked. "London? You can't be serious!" he protested.

The chairman stared coldly at Philby. "I'm very serious. You must know that I'm not one for tricks or jokes."

"How? What will I do?" Philby asked. He was both intrigued and anxious to hear more.

Brezhnev calmly explained, "You'll be disguised with a full beard and a change in hairstyle. Your cover name is William Henderson. You are a broker dealing in rare books and art who travels frequently. We've booked a room in that name at The Savoy. We'll furnish you currency in pounds, and you'll have a contact at the hotel. You will know him as 'Alex'—he is an attendant in the men's room there."

"How long have you been planning this?" Philby asked, amazed at the audacity and detail Brezhnev offered.

"Since well before your extraction from Beirut." Brezhnev leaned forward, his fingers steepled knowingly. "Our plan is for you to monitor MI6, as well as the American CIA during KOBA."

"But surely MI5 will discover me. I'm c-certain they monitor the movements at the S-S-Soviet Embassy as they did before I left," Philby said. He was anxious to understand the risk.

"Indeed, they do. In fact, the head of MI5 knows you're coming."

"That doesn't sound very s-s-safe." Philby worried this was an embellishment to encourage him.

"Nothing to be bothered about. You and Mr. Roger Hollis have much in common," Brezhnev said with a sinister smile. His eyes bore into Philby's with a piercing sincerity.

Philby paused, grasped the meaning, and instantly cracked a small smile. Brezhnev smiled back, and both men were soon laughing. Kim Philby was delighted at the thought that he would soon be going home. And he was even more delighted with the idea of a suite with all the amenities at The Savoy.

He stood up to leave the meeting, his mind brimming with possibilities. Thoughts of London flooded back: dreary days in the rain-soaked city, clandestine meetings in dark pubs, familiar faces that might be horrified—or worse, thrilled—to see him again. The plane ride was long enough for him to prepare, to strategize, and to savor the triumph this assignment represented. He would return as a different man, literally and figuratively.

Back in the thick of it—back to being important.

CHAPTER TWENTY-ONE

London

EARLY THE NEXT morning, while darkness still lay heavily over the city, Brogan made his way back to Kaitlyn's flat. He positioned himself half a block away, rubbing his hands against the cold as he waited. Kaitlyn emerged a little before eight o'clock, her steps hurried and determined.

He tailed her discreetly as she moved through the streets, eventually stopping in front of an unremarkable building. It bore all the signs of a failed business, perhaps abandoned. Kaitlyn knocked on a side door, which promptly opened. She disappeared swiftly inside, the door closing behind her.

Over the next several minutes, he watched as five men entered the building, none of them in any particular hurry. He noted their casual dress and speculated that they were operatives of some kind, likely IRA, though a couple of them had features that seemed more Eastern European. He contemplated his next course of action, weighing options with the precision of an old hand.

Then he noticed the approach of two additional men, this pair strikingly different. They wore suits. Brogan watched as they entered the building. It was then he spotted another figure moving toward him at a deliberate pace less than a block away.

Harvey King.

HARVEY AND TIERNAN put their heads together and Tiernan quickly told Harvey he'd followed an IRA agent there this morning. Harvey had been following two Soviet agents. "Nine people, two women and seven men—at least two of them, possibly four or five—Soviets," Harvey said. "I have a feeling this is no ordinary IRA operation." Tiernan grunted agreement.

They silently positioned themselves in the shadows, their eyes fixed on the building and their minds busy.

Meanwhile, in the back room of the empty shop, the well-dressed Soviet operative who called himself Erik was speaking with deceptive fervor, "As members of the Polish Underground press, our part has been to publish *Samizdat* materials—prohibited pamphlets, newspapers, and other such things the Soviets call subversive." His eyes gleamed as though with delight. "And they *are. We* are. Just as you are. We're here to offer the IRA a chance to unite with us in a grand collaboration."

His companion spoke with feigned conviction, "There is a chance to show the world the hypocrisy of the Soviets *and* of the British Crown. A chance to embarrass them in a way that reverberates across the globe." He paused to gauge his audience. The operatives had persuaded their IRA friends to undertake a joint venture—one cleverly designed to reflect badly on the Soviet Union and England. But they had to make sure it never occurred to any of them that the blame for whatever was about to happen would fall directly at the feet of the IRA.

A case of misdirection.

"The entire world will be watching," another added, sensing their growing interest. His voice rang out, "You cannot miss this chance to make history," playing to their passions and aspirations with his own. For in his mind as he spoke, he saw the bomb go up in an event of monumental importance that would shake the foundations of the world order. And while the dust was settling, and before any fires could be extinguished, the leadership vacuum created by the deaths of dozens of world leaders would be exploited to the Soviets' advantage. Western Europe would fall into the hands of the Communists virtually overnight. And no one, not even the Americans, would be able to intervene.

Kaitlyn and her IRA friends were not privy to this grand design, or even what form the "joint venture" was to take, but the genuine exultation in his voice moved them They wanted to be part of something that would strike at the very core of British life. And the disruption of Churchill's funeral fit their needs perfectly. It was poetry to their ears. They were repulsed by the media attention lavished upon the dying former Prime Minister. "It will be good to be finally rid of the old sot," they said amongst themselves.

Michael Wheelan opened his satchel, retrieved a small device, and placed it with care on a table in the center of the room. "A push of this button, when one is near enough to the casket, will start the clock," he said with an air of authority. "There is a five-minute timer. That's as far as I can take you. I imagine one of you will be handling this part of the operation."

One of the Soviet agents spoke up confidently. "Yes, yes. This is already taken care of. We have someone who will be well positioned to take care of this." He looked around reassuringly and saw no hesitation.

OUTSIDE AND UNABLE to see or hear what was going on inside the building, Brogan and King discussed theories grounded in years of experience. They considered getting closer to learn more but decided against it. Caution took precedence.

Finally, they observed Kaitlyn leaving, casually but with a hint of purpose in her step. They waited a few minutes longer and then saw others trickling out of the building in pairs, spreading in different directions, cautious yet with looks of triumph on their faces. Brogan and King decided they had seen enough for now and made their way back to their hotel, anxious to compare notes and make sense of that morning's work.

SEVERAL HOURS LATER, an Antonov An-24 aircraft, operating under the auspices of the Soviet airline Aeroflot, descended through overcast skies and touched down at London Airport. Aboard the aircraft were forty-four souls, some eyeing one another with the wariness of strangers sharing a confined space. Among them, was a man with a recently acquired beard and wearing an expression of jubilant triumph that seemed at odds with the winter morning.

William Henderson walked briskly past the customs officers. Immigrating into a country he had long betrayed, he cleared with almost absurd ease, as if the British had forgotten or forgiven. A car was waiting for him at the curb, its engine idling impatiently. He was whisked through the grey streets of a city preparing to mourn its greatest statesman. His destination was the imposing Soviet Embassy, a bastion of Communism in the midst of Capitalism.

His return to London was an act of extraordinary daring, and he was greeted with the reverence reserved for one of their most audacious and successful operatives. Three residents who knew the true identity of the bearded man welcomed him with open arms. To them, Kim Philby was nothing short of a celebrity hero, a man who had betrayed king and country and lived to tell the tale. And in a room away from prying eyes, the two Soviet operatives who had briefed Kaitlyn and the IRA earlier that day went over their plans in far greater detail for the second time.

CHAPTER TWENTY-TWO

THE CHURCHILL VIGIL lasted a full week as anticipation gripped the world. During that span, the people of London gathered at the statesman's home in a surprisingly orderly but unyielding throng. The crowd seldom dipped below several hundred, even in the middle of the night, clinging to slender lamplight on the street's edge or huddling under umbrellas when the weather worsened. This was, after all, London in January, and icy rain swept through on most days. Some had thermoses of hot tea to ward off the winter chill.

The headlines communicated Churchill's deteriorating condition each day striving to convey the same ominous truth with fresh urgency—SIR WINSTON LOSING GROUND, CONDITION OF SIR WINSTON WORSENS, CHURCHILL CLINGING TO LIFE. It seemed as if the world was holding its breath, pausing in its natural momentum, waiting for history to turn this profound page.

News outlets from around the globe gave prominent placement to the story of Churchill's illness, some running continuous updates that chronicled and forecast each dip and rise in his vitals.

Morning radio programs from Tokyo to Rio began with the latest from London. Major magazines dispatched writers to prepare his obituary.

Meanwhile, another story emanating from the American capital captured the interest of many Churchill devotees. A proposed statue of the former Prime Minister, planned to stand against the divide between the British Embassy and American soil, looked certain to include a detail that had initially provoked fierce opposition.

For a time, it had appeared that Churchill would be forever bronze and *cigar-less*, but a decisive vote among committee members secured the familiar oral appendage. Despite some misgivings, they had ultimately decided to honor his likeness as the world remembered him: a statesman whose cigar was as notable a feature as his bowler hat.

THE WEEK SAW a torrent of messages from world leaders. Lyndon Johnson sent a heartfelt communication from Washington. "We are all very sorry for your illness and we are praying for a rapid and complete recovery. All of us continue to look to you for wise counsel and judgment." Former President Eisenhower's telegram from Gettysburg reflected a deep and personal sorrow: "Mrs. Eisenhower and I are deeply distressed to learn that our old friend has been stricken with another illness." Charles De Gaulle cabled from France, describing his "feeling of shock" at the news of Churchill's decline.

Across the globe, the planners in various capitals had begun to discuss the possibility of attending a solemn event. Travel and logistical arrangements were being drawn up, and aides were instructed to prepare for the likelihood of journeys to London in the very near future.

Somewhere in all this activity, the public utterances of Labor Party leaders captured the attention of political observers. Teachers in Great Britain who had been on the verge of a strike over a pay dispute declared their intention to walk off their jobs "at a more suitable time." It was a collective expression of solidarity with Churchill—the Tory. They did not wish their work stoppage to distract the country in advance of the passing of an era. That unions would bow to Churchill's illness and adjust their plans accordingly was an unexpected gesture that took some observers by surprise.

In the Soviet Union, the reaction was predictably colder and dismissive—even bitter. Radio reports in Moscow were clipped and sparse, often allowing days to pass without a single update. The newspapers there were more direct in their estimation of the Briton's fate and made little effort to hide their official disdain.

The Soviet defense paper *Krasnaya Zvezda* carried language that described Churchill as the *godfather* of the Cold War and accused him of poisoning international relations from the moment of his infamous "Iron Curtain" speech in 1946. The paper said it would take generations to undo the damage of the Churchill years and suggested that history was about to close the book on a troublesome, imperial man. Soviet statements emitted none of the warmth that accompanied those emanating from elsewhere in the world. Even in his final days, the ailing Prime Minister retained a capacity to stir passions east of the curtain.

The anticipation of his death became so intense that some World War veterans who had served under him spoke of the old days as they gathered. For others, it seemed too much to bear. Crowds slowly thinned during the middle part of the week as Lady Churchill's requests for privacy became more urgent. Even the most determined curiosity seekers began to respect her wishes, doubting that the man himself would emerge from the house again.

By Thursday, January 21, word spread that Churchill was coming to the end of his life. Dr. Moran, who had been attending to him, told reporters that the legendary statesman was at a low point, indicating that his condition had taken a dire turn. Meanwhile, the

Archbishop of Canterbury, Michael Ramsey, informed a congregation that the great man was indeed approaching death.

By this time, the situation outside had been transformed dramatically. The crowds that once gathered day and night had dispersed at Lady Churchill's request, leaving behind only the silent testimony of snow, freshly fallen and undisturbed, that covered the narrow dead-end street that had so recently been clogged by onlookers.

THOUGH THE BUSTLING presence of curious masses had vanished, the area around the home was not entirely deserted. Edmund Murray and the other three officers maintained their steadfast vigil, standing guard. The task now seemed to be more an act of honor than one of protection, their presence a quiet homage rather than a security measure. Even the press, which had been hovering near the doorstep, had moved back a block or so. This was something Mrs. Churchill deeply appreciated.

Anthony Montague Brown, one of Churchill's devoted secretaries, had been the bearer of Lady Churchill's appeal for privacy. He walked over to where the reporters were now gathered and read a message of gratitude: "I would like to thank you for the speed with which you complied with Lady Churchill's request. She was very touched. She has been feeling the strain." The journalists received the message with gestures that were almost like bows, expressions of respect that were rare in their line of work.

The Friday news brought more reports of Churchill's failing condition. Yet there was a stir of sorts when the home directly *behind* 28 Hyde Park Gate caught fire. Even then, the response was subdued. Three fire engines rushed to the scene, but in a move mirroring the respect shown by those outside the home, they arrived *without* sounding sirens or bells, a testament to the profound silence enveloping the neighborhood.

Later that same Friday, an unexpected moment of joy punctuated the gloom. Lady Churchill was called to the telephone for news that brought a rare smile to her face—the first in what seemed an eternity. Her grandson, Winston, was on the line, eager to share the birth of their third great-grandchild, a boy delivered at Westminster Hospital. He was premature but, according to Winston's exuberant report, was doing quite well. Minnie, the boy's mother, was also in fine health.

Clementine shared the joyous news with everyone in the house, a brief but bright interruption to the somber mood. She then went into her husband's room and whispered these happy details in his ear. However, the great man, though still breathing, was likely unaware of the blessed event.

CHAPTER TWENTY-THREE

Kensington

THE CASKET WAS immaculate, a polished mahogany masterpiece lined with sumptuous silk. It made its way from Birmingham to London with solemnity, borne by a gleaming Rolls Royce hearse that moved reverently through the damp streets. As it arrived at J.H. Kenyon Ltd, the Westminster funeral home with a historic reputation, the words on the placard outside—"Funeral Directors for the Royal Household"—seemed to take on a new significance.

The following day would mark the anniversary of Churchill's father's death, a poignant echo that stirred memories of an enigmatic prophecy. It was a prediction made by Winston himself, some twelve years before—that he would meet his end on that same fateful date.

Could it be that Churchill was mustering his legendary endurance, clinging to life with resolute strength, and willing his frail body to hold on until prophecy became truth? Was it possible that the iron will that had defied armies and altered history was now fixing its determination on the page of a calendar and the hands of a ticking clock?

As others in the house slept fitfully late into the night, Clementine kept a solitary vigil. Just after one a.m., she visited Winston's room. She entered the dimly lit space quietly, not wishing to disturb the fragile peace. Pausing at his bedside, she tenderly took hold of his hand. The quiet in the room was profound, the air heavy with anticipation and unspoken words. After a few moments of sharing in that silence, she returned reluctantly to her own bed.

UPON WAKING AT dawn, Clementine sensed a shift. When she returned to Winston's room at about seven that morning, she beheld a change. Its unmistakable mark was there, written in the pallor of his skin and in the weight of his breathing. The realization struck her with the force of a finality she had long refused to accept. The time had come. She moved quickly and calmly to summon the family.

The house came alive with muted urgency.

Randolph arrived first, hurried and flustered, the expression on his face one of pained comprehension. He was accompanied by his son, Winston, who bore a resolute demeanor that belied his youth. They joined Mary, ever the stoic, and Sarah in the drawing room. Clementine was there as well, composed but clearly burdened by the weight of her foreknowledge. She held court as the matriarch, gathering her family in what was now the final hours of their great patriarch's life.

After a few minutes, the doctors, Lord Moran and Lord Brain, the neurologist, entered the room. The pronouncements of these learned men had been frequent that week, and now they were present to give the ultimate one. A nurse, keenly aware of the decorum and the gravity required, placed a tray of steaming coffee on a small table. The cups remained untouched as the minutes drew on and silence prevailed. Some in the room stood, while others sat and fidgeted with their hands, pensively eyeing the clock as its hands crept toward the hour of destiny.

Then, just before eight a.m., Roy Howells, Winston's devoted valet, appeared in the doorway., his face grave. The words he spoke were unnecessary, for they all knew what was to be said. Yet when he cleared his throat and announced, "I think you had all better come in," it still felt immense.

They formed a quiet procession, a line of family and friends that stretched the length of the hallway and into the room where the great man lay. One by one, they approached his bedside. Some knelt immediately, reverence overpowering them before they could even think. Others leaned in and whispered words, hoping against hope that their voices might reach him in those final instants on the mortal side of eternity.

Eventually, all those gathered knelt, an act of collective supplication and surrender. All eyes turned to the motionless figure on the bed as a clock in the distance began to chime. The echo of its eighth stroke still lingered in the air as he drew his last breath.

He was gone.

CHAPTER TWENTY-FOUR

Washington. D.C.

AN HOUR OR so after nightfall on the day Winston Churchill took his last breath, President Lyndon Baines Johnson orchestrated an intricate charade. Summoning a select group of reporters to his private bedroom at the White House, he staged this spectacle with precision, mindful of its dramatic purpose and effect.

He had vanished from the public eye the day before, sequestered within the corridors of the Presidential mansion and conspicuously absent from the Oval Office. A whispering campaign had gained momentum, echoing through Washington's press circles: the President was ailing. This was a stark contrast to the robust image LBJ had confidently displayed to the American people just days prior during the inaugural pomp and ceremony.

By Saturday, the President had already started to lay the groundwork for his ruse. He engaged Rear Admiral George Burkley, his personal physician, in a protracted discussion. Johnson's instructions to Burkley were clear—and calculated. He wanted the Admiral to loop in the rest of the White House medical staff, but he summoned Burkley to the Oval Office, where he could look him straight in the eye as he explained his plan.

"Now, Doc, I can't go into a lot of detail," Johnson said, leaning in close. "But it's important that I have a good excuse to be absent from a certain big funeral over in England, when the time comes."

Burkley had listened intently, his demeanor professional. "I've been following the news, sir, and it looks like he doesn't have much time," he replied, referring to Churchill. "I'd say maybe another twenty-four hours at most." He was caught off guard by Johnson's request, though he did not let it show.

"I'm sure you're right," Johnson concurred. "So how are we going to play this? It can't be anything people would worry about—just enough to keep me off that airplane. Don't give me the plague or a heart problem. Last thing I need is folks starting to pay attention to Hubert."

Burkley nodded, comprehending at last the subtlety Johnson demanded. "Understood, sir. We could say you have a bad cold and cough. Your predecessor used that one effectively during the Cuban crisis in '62 when he had to rush back to Washington from Chicago."

The Kennedy reference was like a barb.

Johnson hated the reminder that he had inherited Burkley—and so much else—from JFK. But then he checked himself. He remembered that Burkley had guarded Kennedy's medical *secrets* with fierce loyalty, including the one about Addison's Disease.

That had always been a thorn in Johnson's side. He had known for years that Jack Kennedy suffered from the hormonal disorder and that it could potentially be fatal. He had tried to expose it during the heated race for the nomination in 1960. But Kennedy's strategic denials had somehow sufficed for the press, and the issue had receded from the national conversation.

Johnson's suspicions had been unequivocally confirmed on that fateful day in Dallas when Burkley, now standing before him, had instructed the emergency room staff desperately trying to save

Kennedy's life to administer steroids because the President indeed had Addison's. Johnson knew that was the real reason why the Kennedy camp had been so insistent that no post-mortem be conducted in Dallas. Those secrets, like countless others, had been buried along with Kennedy at Arlington National Cemetery.

So Johnson knew he could rely on Burkley's discretion.

He cut through the tension with a bark, "You just look out for me like you did for him and we'll be fine."

"Yes, sir. What I recommend is we stick with the bad cold diagnosis," Burkley reiterated. "It's vague enough to be believable, but convincing people will require some effort on your part, Mr. President."

"You give me the cold and I'll sell it like nobody's business," Johnson declared. "I'll put on a show that'd make old John Wayne proud. You got any of that Vicks stuff? The salve? Gimme plenty of that. Not a smell in the world that says cold better than that God-awful scent."

"Great idea. I'll fetch some straight away."

Burkley made sure he was the only medical officer initially aware of the plan, although his assistant, Navy Captain James Young, and a New York throat specialist, Dr. W.J. Gould, would soon be involved in the case, as well. In fact, all three doctors were present when the seven reporters arrived in the President's bedroom Sunday evening. Johnson put on a spectacle worthy of Broadway's finest theatrics—sprawled in bed, his hair astray, while coughing violently. The cloying aroma of menthol suffused every corner of the antique-furnished room.

Speaking in labored tones, barely more than a whisper, Johnson addressed the journalists. "Fellas, my medical people are advising against a trip to London for Mr. Churchill's funeral, and I want you to know I fought 'em on it, but Lady Bird agrees, and she's the boss."

"How do you feel, Mr. President?" inquired one of the reporters, his pen poised over a notebook.

"Well, not good. I guess I don't have the bouncy feeling I usually have," came Johnson's reply. He punctuated his words with a sudden, dramatic blow into a handkerchief, then allowed himself to sink back into the pillows.

A couple of the reporters exchanged furtive glances, each raising an eyebrow at the other as they fought to contain their amusement over the peculiar phrase. The scene was just as Johnson had planned, though; he knew these men had taken the bait.

In the lull that followed, Dr. Burkley interjected from his position near the corner of the room. "Um, gentlemen, the President is suffering from a very bad cold, and it's gone down into his chest. We need to watch it," he said, offering just the right amount of medical authority to give the set-up some credibility. "A lengthy airplane trip at this time would likely aggravate his condition."

The President, playing his part to the hilt, offered a weak nod in Burkley's direction. It was an acknowledgement, a subtle signal to the doctor that he had delivered his lines perfectly and that Johnson was grateful for the assist.

"Who will you send in your stead, sir?" questioned another reporter, his tone suggesting he was already composing the headline in his mind.

"Well, I'm going to send Dean Rusk and Earl Warren over there." Johnson's response was swift, suggesting he had considered the matter and made a firm decision.

"And Vice President Humphrey?" another reporter asked the obvious question with an air of anticipation.

"No, the Vice President won't be going either," was his surprising reply. The curt response seemed to close the door on the subject. The reporters didn't press him further.

When the bedside briefing concluded, the reporters gathered their belongings and shuffled out, whispering among themselves about the scene they had just witnessed. They soon exited the White

House, and the chilly January night greeted them with a gust of wind.

Three of them piled into one car, eager to compare notes.

When they were finally out of sight—and earshot—they could no longer contain themselves. Visions of headlines dancing in their heads, they erupted into a chorus of laughter over the President's choice of words and began crooning a parody of a recent number one hit song by the Righteous Brothers, the melody infectious and their adaptation mocking, yet gleeful.

"He's lost that bouncy feeling…whoa oh, that bouncy feeling…".

LYNDON JOHNSON UNDERSTOOD, perhaps better than anyone, that his explanation for staying behind while the world's leaders gathered overseas would be greeted with doubt, derision, and conjecture. *Let them ridicule*, he thought. *If America appears wary and unsteady, then so be it. This is the cost of security and survival.* It was a deliberate strategy.

Not an act of cowardice.

His resolve was firm—to remain out of harm's reach and prepared to react to any disaster. Should anything unthinkable occur, he knew he would be better positioned than the others to handle the fallout. He calculated his moves with precision and with a full sense of historical consequences. LBJ was uncertain as to whether the Soviets could achieve such a daring maneuver. But by staying away, he challenged them with a critical question: Would they risk obliterating the world if the United States would be unharmed?

THE SURPRISING ANNOUNCEMENT that Johnson would not attend the London ceremony was rushing through corridors of power in Moscow the following day, sending ripples of concern through the

Kremlin. The most ardent hardliners soon found themselves on the defensive. They faced anxious inquiries from several Presidium members who worried that the KOBA plan was either compromised or would possibly fail. How could they confidently execute it if the leader of their most formidable adversary decided that he would remain safe and sound, thousands of miles away?

Yet the bold voices that once dominated the Presidium rose to meet the challenge. They attacked the questions head-on, brushing them aside as the protests of timid men unwilling to seize destiny. The plot survived intact, and the firebrands who spearheaded it regained momentum. They thought they had accounted for everything. There was no hint that any of them considered the possibility that Johnson even knew of their scheme, let alone that his surprise decision was based on it.

Reports had reached them that the "package" was indeed prepared and that all was set to go. The casket would rest in the center of St. Paul's Cathedral, surrounded by a congregation that would include Prime Ministers, Presidents, Kings, and Queens. What the mourners would not know was that the casket would also contain enough explosive power to turn the funeral of one of the century's most iconic leaders into an unimaginable calamity.

CHAPTER TWENTY-FIVE

WITHIN HOURS OF the shocking assassination of the vibrant young American leader on November 22, 1963, plans for the funeral of John Fitzgerald Kennedy were being hastily assembled. There were no blueprints in place for the unthinkable. It was unchartered territory.

Late that very evening, Jacqueline Kennedy, having flown back to Washington from Dallas with the casket containing her slain husband, was consumed with grief but somehow supported by her unwavering sense of history. With dignified and ever-present grace, she gathered her thoughts and asked key members of the White House staff for a quick but thorough investigation into the funeral of Abraham Lincoln that had taken place nearly a century earlier under similar circumstances.

She wanted to use it as a model for her murdered husband's farewell.

IN MUCH THE same way that Jackie Kennedy modeled her husband's funeral on the funeral of Abraham Lincoln, an earlier funeral had influenced the plans for Winston Churchill's farewell. Back in 1898, England said goodbye to one of its other towering figures, William

Ewart Gladstone—the first time a funeral had become a global media event.

Gladstone had been a political heavyweight who cast an enormous shadow over his times. He served as Prime Minister on four separate occasions over nearly four decades. He was often referred to by the initials G.O.M. They stood for "Grand Old Man," though his contemporary and long-time political rival, Benjamin Disraeli, suggested the initials meant, "God's Only Mistake."

The parallels between Gladstone and Churchill were akin to those drawn between Kennedy and Lincoln, but for one noteworthy difference. Queen Victoria *detested* Mr. Gladstone for reasons personal and political. She believed he was a quarrelsome, cantankerous old man and frequently referred to him as "half mad." Around the royal court he was known as the man the Queen most loved to hate. Victoria ignored Gladstone in death as much as she despised him in life.

Victoria was silent on the matter of a State Funeral and only agreed when it became evident that Parliament overwhelmingly approved of the honor. Her eldest son, Albert Edward, the Prince of Wales (future King Edward VII) was greatly embarrassed by his mother's pettiness. He personally apologized to Gladstone's widow as she was leaving the funeral service at Westminster Abbey.

Things were refreshingly different when Winston Churchill died.

Queen Elizabeth II had great affection for him. Her recommendation for a full State Funeral made its way to the House of Commons within hours of his death. In keeping with Churchill's storied life, his funeral was to be dramatic and grand.

THE METICULOUSLY ORCHESTRATED plan long in the making—frequently updated and code-named Operation Hope Not—was set into motion. The British government began to release glimpses of the elaborate proceedings that would unfold over the next week, capturing the attention of a world in mourning.

It was announced that Churchill would lie in state in Westminster Hall, a place steeped in history and significance, from Wednesday through Friday. The enormous hall was 250 feet long. An architectural marvel from the Middle Ages, it was located adjacent to the House of Commons where Churchill had famously waged political battles.

The announcement recalled the similar honor given to Gladstone in 1898, when over a quarter of a million mourners filed past to pay their respects. This time, expectations were even higher. No one attempted to guess how many would follow suit for Churchill, but the number was sure to break all records.

On Saturday morning, the casket carrying the beloved statesman's body would be solemnly placed upon a military gun carriage for the journey to St. Paul's Cathedral for the funeral service. Following that, Churchill's body would travel to a pier near the Tower of London. From there, a barge was to convey the casket along the Thames toward the Festival Pier on the river's south side. This journey was designed to be in full view of the iconic Houses of Parliament.

From Festival Pier, the casket would then be transported to Waterloo Station, where it would be loaded onto a train expressly designated for the 70-mile journey to Blenheim Palace, the ancestral family home where Churchill had been born and would now be buried in a tranquil churchyard. There, he would join his father, Lord Randolph Churchill, and his American-born mother, Jennie Jerome. These, of course, were merely the skeletal outlines of the plan.

The true narrative lay in its exhaustive details.

AS THE WORLD focused on London, the magnitude of the event began to unfold. All the pomp and ceremony of the occasion would involve an extraordinary cast of thousands. Oversight of this massive undertaking fell to the Earl Marshal, a seasoned fifty-six-year-old noble named Bernard Fitzalan-Howard, the Sixteenth Duke of Norfolk.

A man of tradition who was known for meticulous attention, the Duke had proven himself an old hand at managing state spectacles, having presided over the coronations of King George VI in 1936 and Queen Elizabeth II in 1953. Given that his primary duty—indeed, his only duty—was to orchestrate these grand ceremonies, he spent years in careful preparation and watchful waiting, much like a military general poised in times of peace. Over the years, he had kept a discreet eye on Churchill's declining health, not with morbid intent, but driven by a genuine desire to be ready to give the great man the sendoff he merited, one that the entire nation would stand proudly behind.

From the very inception of Operation Hope Not, the Earl Marshal had been its guardian. He was also invested with a personal mission: to ensure that his nation and its long-standing traditions—traditions sometimes derided in the modern age—would, through civility and splendor, command respect and, in his hope, even rebuke those who embraced what he viewed as the unruly tide of cultural change.

Given that more than a hundred nations would dispatch official delegations, including many heads of state, he was acutely aware that his efforts would be intensely scrutinized and analyzed by several hundred million viewers across the globe.

Indeed—the eyes of the world would be on his masterpiece.

CHAPTER TWENTY-SIX

THE CAREFULLY PRESSED uniform that he wore bore the initials H.H.—for Harold Higgins, though those who worked alongside him just called him Harry. In just a few months, he had become known as one of the most diligent sextons among the many charged with the maintenance of the iconic church. His talents with tools and his knack for repair work quickly earned him a reputation as the go-to man for fixing just about anything in need of attention.

It wasn't long before he was considered someone who could be relied upon. But there was an aching truth that Harry alone understood, one that no wrench or screwdriver could fix. Nor was he able to divulge the true reason he had taken the job, a reason that was wrapped up in a story far removed from the Anglican rites daily surrounding him.

The most difficult aspect of his daily life was enduring the continuous pomp and ceremony of the Anglican services. It was not that Harry had an aversion to ritual itself; quite the contrary, he was steeped in a tradition rich with its own ceremonies. What weighed on him was the manner in which the British conducted their religious observances, which he found lamentably inferior to the practices he held dear.

Harry was an Irish Catholic through and through, his heart always beating in time with the Emerald Isle, and yet he was masquerading as a loyal servant of the Church of England, an institution not only foreign to him but one presided over by Her Majesty the Queen—the symbol of the very dominion he sought to undermine.

Despite these challenges, Harry accepted the assignment taking it all in stride, driven by the sense of duty that had always compelled him. When initially approached about the position at St. Paul's, it was not by an official emissary of the church. Instead, it was a contact from back home in Belfast. A man with whom Harry shared a history going back to childhood, when both served as altar boys. They had remained fast friends through the years, both committed to the grand vision of liberating Belfast and all of Northern Ireland from British rule.

As men now in their forties, their resolve had not waned.

Harry had never shied away from getting his hands dirty for the cause, repeatedly managing to evade the ever-watchful eyes of the authorities. His presence at St. Paul's was still a mystery to him, but wherever he was needed, Harry would be there. He understood that the mission was larger than his curiosity. So he waited, knowing that sooner or later he would learn his purpose.

Then, today, from out of the blue, a message came to him in the most unexpected way. Tucked between the pages of his morning newspaper, he discovered a note slipped in with precision and meant only for his eyes. He smiled as he read the familiar handwriting: *"Harry Dear: A few of us are getting together tonight at the Tipperary for a pint, please join us. Seven o'clock. There is much to talk about. I miss you. Love, KAITLYN."*

The sight of her name sent a cascade of memories washing over his mind. He had known her for what felt like a lifetime. He was hopelessly in love with the fiery redhead whose spirit matched her striking hair. She had a habit of appearing and disappearing from his life according to her own whims, yet he relished every moment she chose to share with him.

Her presence was electrifying, and though he suspected he was a mere pawn in her games more often than not, Harry didn't care. Life was always better when she was in the room. He couldn't shake the feeling that her invitation had something to do with his assignment. *Does she have news about why I'm at St. Paul's?*

Or perhaps she had other plans entirely—plans that involved him in ways more *personal.* The anticipation was both thrilling and unsettling as the hours crept by that day. He could hardly wait to see her, to hear her voice, and to finally learn what was meant by "much to talk about."

HARRY FOUND HIS way to the pub about ten minutes past seven, eager and expectant despite his tardiness. The radio stations had been reporting non-stop that the old trout, Churchill, had finally died. He had two things to celebrate now. As he entered the bustling but quieter than usual room, his eyes quickly settled on Kaitlyn, who was seated at a table in the far corner with a man and a woman. Her fiery red hair was unmistakable even in the dim corner. She looked up just as he walked over, a wide smile spreading across her face, her eyes bright and welcoming. They were already well into their second drink—maybe their third—and their smiling camaraderie suggested a reunion of old friends.

"Harry Higgins! It's been far too long, darlin'. Please, meet me friends, Michael and Molly Wheelan. They're in London on holiday for a few days." The lilt in her voice was unmistakably Irish but also filled with mischief.

"You don't say?" Harry replied, concealing his surprise and perhaps a tinge of disappointment at not having her to himself. He promptly excused himself and went to order a pint at the bar, taking a moment to think about this unexpected turn and its possible implications. When he returned with his drink, he joined them at the table and asked, "Where you from, Michael?"

"Birmingham," answered Michael, his accent resonating with British inflection.

Harry struggled to maintain a polite demeanor, concealing a frown he knew was almost involuntary. He hoped he was being successful in masking his true feelings as he said, "Oh yes, that's a wonderful city."

At that moment, Tiernan Brogan walked into the pub. He'd stopped by the Tipperary the past two nights in hopes of catching up with Kaitlyn, but she hadn't shown. Tonight was different.

"Over here, Sean," Kaitlyn called across the room and their eyes met. She gestured vigorously for him to come over. "Grab a pint and join us," she added with a coquettish grin.

"Don't mind if I do." He made his way to the bar and was back in a moment, ale in hand.

"Once around again," said Kaitlyn, her words merry and spontaneous as she resumed the introductions. "This is my friend from back when. Name's Sean Walsh. And Sean, these fine folks be Michael and Molly Wheelan. And that's Harry Higgins."

Brogan immediately thought Michael looked vaguely familiar and did a subtle double take. Wheelan didn't appear to notice, nor did any of the others, but Brogan's memory was sharp. After a few minutes, it came to him: he recognized the name from an old operation and knew he was dealing with more than a mere tourist from Birmingham. Curious, he observed Michael with renewed interest, wondering how everything connected.

Conversation turned lively as drink after drink was downed, the talk all the while carefully avoiding any subjects of real significance—except for Churchill's death which they were quietly celebrating. Harry was on edge, trying to discern if this was a social call or something more. He noticed Kaitlyn's sly glances, and he wondered if she was playing her usual games or signaling something else entirely. His mind raced through possibilities, but with Kaitlyn, it was always hard to be sure.

After another round, Kaitlyn abruptly declared that she had to be going, cutting through the camaraderie with her usual lack of subtlety. "Sorry to leave you like this, but I've other business tonight." The party broke up just like that. Harry, Michael, and Molly left at the same time after saying hurried goodbyes. They were hardly out the door before walking briskly in the same direction. It was clear to Brogan that they weren't merely headed back to their flats. They were going someplace *together.*

And in a hurry.

Brogan watched for a moment, calculating his next move, before setting off after them. He knew he had to be careful following Harry, or *whoever* he was. The man's real identity was uncertain, but his associations were becoming clearer. After a series of rapid turns, Brogan confirmed a growing suspicion. Their destination was the building he and Harvey King had been watching earlier in the day.

The four of them went inside.

Brogan waited for a few minutes, weighing whether to follow them in or regroup with Harvey. The speed with which they were moving told him everything he needed to know. He turned and headed back to the hotel and briefed Harvey King on the evening's events, from the unexpected meeting with the Wheelans to the hurried trek to the IRA safe house.

"What does this Wheelan guy do in Birmingham?" Harvey asked, keen to understand the sudden flurry of activity.

"Don't know, but should be easy enough to find out," Brogan replied, already anticipating his next move. "I've got an old contact at MI5 who keeps files on IRA types. I'm sure this Wheelan is connected." He picked up the phone, making the call as he reached into his coat pocket for a cigarette.

A few minutes later, just as Brogan was about to light another cigarette, the phone rang back. The contact was ready with the requested information. As he listened intently to the voice on the phone, Harvey King watched the blood drain from Tiernan Brogan's face. What he heard was beyond anything he had expected.

"Son of a bitch!" Brogan exclaimed, nearly dropping the receiver.

"What's up?" Harvey asked with urgency, sensing the sudden shift.

"Grab your coat. We need to head to Birmingham right now!" Brogan replied, already moving to the door with a mixture of haste and intent.

MEANWHILE, HARRY HIGGINS was back at his small flat not far from St. Paul's Cathedral. He removed a small device from his pocket and placed it in a tiny space beneath a loose floorboard in one corner. He now knew why they had wanted him to get the job at the famous Anglican Church.

And he was ready to carry out his assignment.

CHAPTER TWENTY-SEVEN

THE TRAIN DEPARTED from London's Euston Station shortly after eleven pm. Its destination was Birmingham's New Street Station, and it was on schedule to arrive around one-thirty. The night was cool, and the dimly lit passenger car in which Harvey King and Tiernan Brogan sat was less than half full. They had chosen seats at a comfortable distance from the other travelers, hoping to keep their conversation far from any prying ears.

"Okay, Sport," King said, "here's what we have. There's chatter in DC about some potential plot and incident having to do with Winnie's funeral. They've picked up enough noise back there to make them nervous. And now we have some clown with IRA ties who just happens to be in London on the day Churchill dies though he's from Birmingham and is working at the very factory where Churchill's jumbo casket was built?"

"Outfitted, actually. The casket was built somewhere else—not sure where," Brogan corrected. "This company, Newman Brothers, is famous for decking out caskets for the rich and famous. They're known for their fancy brass fittings and shit like that. At least, that's what my contact at Five said," he added.

"Too much of a fucking coincidence not to mean something," King said.

"I agree," Brogan replied, his thoughts spinning toward the sinister possibilities. This was more than a mere chance alignment; it was a pattern forming around them—too intricate to ignore. He considered his next question carefully. "What's the plan once we get to Birmingham? It'll be almost two."

"That's the best time to work in the shadows, Sport," King said, his confidence unshakable. "The question is, do we check out their home, or do we go straight to the casket factory?"

Brogan weighed the options. Time was of the essence. "I say we check out the factory. If something's been fooled with, that's where the clues would be. Especially this time of night."

"Factory it is, then."

They sped through the sprawling blackness of the English countryside, the train a bullet in the night. Brogan stared out into the vast dark. *An attack at the state funeral for Winston Churchill? The media circus will be global.* He glanced at King, who was dozing off, then returned to the landscape whizzing by.

The train pulled into New Street Station at 1:24 a.m. The few passengers who disembarked were met with the damp chill and rising fog of a Birmingham winter night. King and Brogan charged up the steps and across Station Street.

"Fleet Street is five blocks that way," said Brogan as they rounded the corner.

They kept to the shadows as they made their way toward the factory. Brogan thought through the work ahead of them—something he had done a dozen times since leaving London. Worst case scenario—they don't spot anything unusual and have to check the Wheelan house as well. Best case—they find evidence that someone has already planted something explosive in the casket, though he couldn't quite figure how they expected to get it past the security sweep, and they are back on the train before breakfast.

They kept up their brisk pace, barely breaking stride as they weaved around a couple lingering down the street. Brogan's breath formed small clouds as they approached the corner of Fleet Street. He could see the outline of the building ahead of them.

"The place is shut for the night," said King. "No one around. Our lucky night."

The building stood silent and dark as the two investigators eyed it furtively from across the empty street. The night was grim, the kind that Londoners say breeds ghosts and criminals. A quick glance confirmed that the scene was just right for what they had in mind.

"Looks pretty straightforward to me. Let's find a side door and go in. It's been a while since I did a covert entry. It'll be fun," King said.

Brogan eyed him with a mixture of respect and disbelief. He couldn't quite figure out this American who seemed to thrive on intrigue but appeared so cavalier about it. King's reputation as an ace spy preceded him, yet his manner was often more like a mischievous boy intent on causing trouble. Brogan wasn't sure exactly what to make of him, but he knew better than to question the man's instincts. He nodded his assent, and they moved quickly and quietly across the street.

King picked the lock on a side door. They were in the building swiftly and took out their flashlights as they made their way through a tangle of dim, narrow corridors. "Look for anything with Wheelan's name or initials. Or any clue as to where the big man's casket was worked on," King said in a low voice. "Try to find a room or area that looks like where they put stuff together."

They broke off in different directions to cover more ground. The building seemed a labyrinth, each corner they turned revealing more workshops and areas filled with shadowy old equipment—tools of a macabre trade. They had been in the facility about ten minutes, and were about thirty feet apart, when Brogan suddenly called out. "Over here!"

King was there in a flash, and they beamed their lights over a large workshop area. At one end was a workstation with Wheelan's name scrawled on a sign. Excited by the find, they dug through the drawers of the workbench and went through papers in the desk. They were deliberate, though made sure to put everything back exactly as it had been. The last thing they wanted was to alert anyone that they had been there. But after a spirited search, nothing incriminating turned up.

"Hard to know what you're looking for when you don't know what you're looking for, huh, Harvey?" Brogan said.

King didn't respond.

He was on his hands and knees and uncharacteristically silent. Brogan went over to him and trained his light at the floor where King was hovering. The Yank was rubbing something between his fingers.

"What is it?" Brogan asked as he stooped down to take a look.

"Not sure," the veteran spy said in a whisper. "But I'll tell you what I think it *might* be. It feels and looks like a few small shavings of plastic explosive."

"Holy hell!" Brogan exclaimed.

"Well put, my Irish friend," King said, his voice now filled with grim satisfaction. "This Wheelan fool may have planted a bomb in Winston's big box!"

"I think it might be time to tell someone and get some help with this thing," Brogan said, still stunned by the magnitude of their find and its implications.

"You're right, Sport. But who can we trust? This thing has conspiracy written all over it. And Dulles told me to trust no one."

AT THAT MOMENT, Harvey King and Tiernan Brogan had no clue just how true Dulles's caveat had been. They could not have had even the slightest suspicion that when Tiernan called his trusted contact at MI5 for some background on Michael Wheelan, that one simple request would set off alarm bells at the highest levels of that agency. Nor could they have known that, within the hour, the ripple effect had put some dangerous bad guys on their back trail.

As the two Americans made their way out of Newman Brothers in the dark of the night, they came face-to-face with three ominous-looking figures in the shadows. King quickly surmised they were not representing the local constable. They weren't even British. He saw them for what they were because he had dealt with the likes of them more times than he could count over the years.

Russians.

One man spoke up and said, "We would like to talk with you. Please come with us. We mean you no harm." But Harvey King sensed the lie. The trio was there to learn what, if anything, he and Brogan knew. Thinking quickly, King calculated only two possible outcomes—kill or be killed.

He grabbed his gun and fired three shots with great poise and precision, dropping all three men in less than two seconds. As the savage sound of the shots rang through the night air, Brogan leaped back and fell to the ground for cover. "What the hell, King? You might tell a guy what you're going to do. Now we'll have the authorities on our case," he protested.

"Not a chance, Sport. Let's get the hell out of here."

"How can you be sure they weren't just company security?"

"I have a nose for Commies, Brogan. I can smell the fuckin' bastards. And when I get the chance, I kill 'em, before they can kill me. I just saved your ass. You're welcome."

Brogan still didn't know whether to trust King's instincts, but he couldn't deny the man's nerve. As they made their escape, each second felt like a lifetime. They could hear the distant wail of sirens but were on a train bound for London before the police even got to Fleet Street.

LESS THAN AN hour later, word came down from Scotland Yard that the events that night at Newman Brothers were a matter of national security and to be kept out of the newspapers. Once agents arrived from London, all evidence in the case, including the lifeless bodies, was turned over to MI5. No questions asked. The order was authoritative and unambiguous. Official Secrets Act and all.

Under normal conditions, the killing of three men near where Churchill's casket was adorned should have been big news, at least one would think. But the story would never see the light of day.

CHAPTER TWENTY-EIGHT

THE TRAIN BEARING Harvey King and Tiernan Brogan hurtled toward Euston Station in London, its arrival anticipated for a few minutes after six o'clock Monday morning. Settled in their seats, they pored over newspaper articles announcing the death of Winston Churchill and detailing the elaborate arrangements for the statesman's funeral, absorbing all the information they could. Less than a day had passed since the great man's death, and the nation seemed to stand still, gripped in mourning and anticipation.

The two men had a lengthy discussion about their next course of action, aware that they were navigating blind and essentially on their own. With no one to call upon for assistance, it fell squarely on their shoulders to unravel the web of events swirling around them.

But King had made a series of notes culled from the materials about Operation Hope Not during the flight across the Atlantic. Those cryptic jottings were now crammed inside a well-worn leather notebook clutched tightly in his jacket pocket. One particular detail, something that seemed oddly out of place to King at the time, pertained to the handling of Churchill's remains. The body would be embalmed at his home and would not leave there until transferred to Westminster for the official lying-in-state.

"But he can't be taken to Westminster until the House of Commons votes on it?" King queried, fully aware that Brogan possessed greater insight into British customs and procedures than any American possibly could.

"Correct," confirmed Brogan, his voice steady with certainty. "And the paper says that the House will meet in special session later this morning. They'll likely vote on it and then adjourn for the entire week."

"So where's the fancy casket now?" King pressed, urgency lacing his words.

"Your guess is as good as mine," Brogan conceded, the frustration evident in his reply. "Probably at some London mortuary."

"I didn't see anything in the newspaper about that, did you?" King asked, his mind racing.

"No," came the succinct response.

"Well, if that casket *has* been tampered with in any way..." King began, the wheels of suspicion turning.

"You mean if explosive materials have been put in there?" Brogan inquired, knowing well the implications.

"Of course I mean that, jackass!" King snapped, feeling the weight of their mission. He quickly checked his tone and apologized. "Sorry, Sport. I'm tired."

"We both are. You sure you don't remember reading about a mortuary in that report you read on the plane?" Brogan asked.

"Doesn't click," King replied. "You're the expert over here. Wouldn't they use a special place for this? Like what they'd use for the royal family or some duke or duchess or whoever the hell else might be better than the rest of us mere mortals?" The words were barely out of his mouth when he slapped a hand to his forehead. "Idiot," he exclaimed. "Of course!"

Brogan looked at him blankly for a moment, then they both said at the same time, "Kenyon!"

"In Rochester Row," King added. "How could I have been so blind?" He shook his head.

"I have even less excuse," Brogan said, disgust in his voice. "I remember from when George the Sixth died and Queen Mary a year later, back in the early '50s. I was in college. That's the place. Funeral directors to the Royals, and all that."

"Well, great, now we know. When we hit town, we'll check it out. If the casket is there, no telling when it will head over to Churchill's home," King said, already planning their next steps. "Once he's tucked away in that big box, we'll *never* get a look inside."

ROGER HOLLIS HAD personally plucked Sean Welling from a new class of recruits to work by his side as one of his trusted assistants less than a year after the bright young man had first joined MI5. He had been watching him, quietly, since very soon after his arrival.

An Oxford graduate with first-class academic honors in European history, Welling had distinguished himself quickly as a tireless worker—one who appeared more dedicated than many who had come to the Security Service with much more experience. And he was someone with whom the director took a special pleasure in talking, often with great animation and always in private. They spoke at work and even after hours on many occasions.

This raised a few eyebrows, and there were plenty of whispers that perhaps the director and his young assistant were enjoying a relationship that went beyond that of coworkers. They were. But not in a way anyone would have guessed.

In fact, in many ways, Welling had been *created* by Roger Hollis.

The file under Welling's name in the official records at Leconfield House on Curzon Street was extensive, and it told a rather fascinating story about Mr. Welling. He had been born out of wedlock in Hastings. His mother, in an act of desperation or selfishness or both, had given him up when he was only four months old. He was passed around from home to home until a childless couple in Yorkshire, Clive and Elizabeth Welling, adopted him, giving him a family and future.

Mr. Welling was a teacher, and Mrs. Welling a kindly woman who hired out for domestic work. Young Sean went to live with them when he was just shy of his third birthday. He grew up surrounded by love. He was a good student and eventually earned admission to Oxford, where he distinguished himself as a bit of a scholar.

He was later recruited into the Security Service, where he, like cream rising to the top, soon found himself moving in heady circles. But he did so in a way that seemed to bother no one. He was friendly, humble, likable, and dedicated. The director took a special interest in such a bright lad.

And it was all a *lie*.

Sean Welling was really Sean *Wheelan*, the only son of Soviet spies Michael and Molly from Birmingham. He had been groomed for the cause and committed himself to the Soviets before he was out of primary school. Long before he left Birmingham to study at Oxford, his British-raised legend and new identity were firmly established and fully developed. There was little chance that anyone would have any reason to dig very deeply into the records to find the truth about a teenage boy just starting advanced university study.

But if anyone had been of a mind to dig deep enough, they might have learned that the real Clive and Elizabeth Welling, along with their infant son Sean, had died during a German bombing raid in the Poplar section of London in 1941, and they had no relatives or family members left.

It was all too easy to exploit.

One of the very first letters Sean received when he got to Oxford University was from Roger Hollis. Three sentences long, it said congratulations as well as anything could have: "If you wish to be of true use, you will expect us when you least expect us. Do not fail us. Timing is everything." If anyone else had read it, the letter would have seemed like nonsense.

But Sean knew *exactly* what it meant.

ON THE DAY following the death of Sir Winston Churchill, Sean Welling awoke to a day imbued with both gravity and peril. He arrived at Leconfield House, the venerable headquarters of MI5, well before the break of dawn.

With a sense of purpose that burned as intensely as the cold January chill, he settled into his post just outside Director Roger Hollis's office a little before six. The work that lay ahead was daunting and multifaceted, possessing layers of both official duties and clandestine endeavors that required deft management and careful execution. It was the latter that consumed the young man's thoughts as he sipped a cup of coffee, laden with heavy cream and even heavier doses of sugar.

His mind wandered to the clandestine meeting with his parents—his real parents, Soviet agents Michael and Molly Wheelan—a few hours earlier. They had gathered away from prying eyes to discuss their audacious mission. They spoke in hushed tones, leaving some details deliberately unsaid, the anticipation was palpable.

Sean, Michael, and Molly understood with an unspoken certainty that they stood on the brink of something monumental. The very magnitude of their ambition, nurtured for decades, fueled their spirits. A lifetime of patient labor and subterfuge, waiting for the opportune moment, seemed finally to be culminating in an event of unprecedented significance. A vast and historical success appeared within their grasp, a triumph for the cause that had demanded the depths of their loyalty and resolve.

Sean's strategic position within MI5 allowed him to monitor the ebb and flow of sensitive information. He also had a couple of men in key positions to be eyes and ears for him. He shuddered to think how easily his man might have missed hearing that phone conversation about Michael Wheelan. Sean had been swift to act upon the information, but the revelation that Brogan and his associate were aware of Michael's existence had been alarming.

The abrupt silence from the three operatives sent to Birmingham had been worrying as well, and their deaths complicated matters. Yet Sean had managed to suppress any immediate fallout, leveraging his influential station to maintain control. An authoritative missive from Hollis's personal assistant was enough to quell any burgeoning rumors and keep the truth obscured.

The intricate balance of deception remained delicately poised, though for how long was uncertain. Sean knew that the knot of concerns must be reported to Roger Hollis without delay. This daunting task would demand both tact and composure, for he was keenly aware that the Director, a man not renowned for his patience or leniency, would regard the unfolding situation with considerable vexation.

As the clock ticked towards six-thirty, the office was yet to stir with the full bustle of activity that would surely come. Sean anticipated that Hollis would arrive momentarily, setting the day's direction with his usual authoritarian presence. He began to compose in his mind the most judicious way to present the complications that had arisen, bracing himself for the displeasure he was certain to face.

The key was to convey the gravity without revealing the full extent of their predicament, a delicate feat that required a precise use of half-truths and omissions. Sean sat at his desk, appearing to be the model of diligence and efficiency, while beneath the surface, he was a maelstrom of urgency and clandestine resolve.

CHAPTER TWENTY-NINE

KING AND BROGAN finished breakfast at the hotel cafe around six thirty. The sleepless night seemed to have little effect on them. They appeared alert and energized, ready to plot their next course of action. After polishing off his food, Brogan unfolded the *Daily Mail* and laid it on the table between them.

It confirmed what they pretty much knew to be fact. The firm of J.H. Kenyon Funeral Directors in Westminster was indeed handling the Churchill arrangements. If there had been any lingering doubts that the casket was being kept there, the article put them to rest. It also indicated that the casket would be delivered to St. Paul's on Tuesday morning. This gave the men the rest of the day and night to figure out a way to access it and find out if it contained explosive materials.

They weighed their options. Was there time for a trip out to Kenyon? Could they break into the building and check things out? And if not, was there anyone they could count on to work with them? Asking about Michael Wheelan had clearly tipped off someone to put the now-dead Russians on their trail.

Brogan wiped his lips with a napkin and sipped his coffee. He still couldn't figure out how a call to MI5 had triggered Soviet operatives. He said as much to his American counterpart.

"Moles," King remarked.

"Moles?"

"Yeah, moles. Both the Brits and the Americans have that problem," King said. He looked like a teacher explaining something very basic to a student. "The Russkies have worked on this for decades, Sport. You think Philby, MacLean, and Burgess were all they had?"

"Obviously *you* don't," Brogan said.

"Damn straight." King leaned back in his chair. "In fact, there are some people in the CIA who think the top man in your government is a KGB plant."

"You mean the Prime Minister?" Brogan asked incredulously.

"That's exactly what I mean," King answered. "This fish stinks from the head down. We can't trust anyone official over here." He flicked an inch of ash to the floor.

Brogan considered that possibility.

"How about *unofficial?*"

"Going to have to give me more than that, Sport." King said.

"Well, look at this little tidbit in the paper," Brogan said. He folded it a couple of times and handed it to King with a brief article in the center. The headline read: FORMER BODYGUARD RECALLS CHURCHILL'S COURAGE.

King took a moment to read the short piece. "Oh yeah, Walter Thompson wrote that book about his time with Churchill," King said. "My ex-wife and I watched him on *To Tell the Truth* a couple of years ago. He was old Winnie's personal bodyguard back in the war. Saved the old man's life several times, to hear him tell it. Retired Scotland Yard man. Must be at least 75 by now."

"He loved Churchill," Brogan answered. "If he knew what we knew, he might move heaven and earth, and even hell, to get to the bottom of it. And he's absolutely *unofficial*. He'd know how to open doors, or even kick 'em down if needed."

"So how do we find old Mr. Thompson?" King asked.

"Well, the article mentioned a London flat, so it shouldn't be too hard. Besides, it's the only lead we have. We should leg it."

"What?"

"Leg it. You know, run for it."

"Why don't you just speak English, Sport?"

They left the cafe and headed out into the chilly London morning. On the street, they found a vendor selling papers and bought a handful of them. The articles were mostly the same as the ones they had read on the train: Churchill's death, the funeral plans, the expected crush of mourners and dignitaries. They went back to their room and scanned the stories to see if anything new might give them a clue. Brogan didn't think there was much of a chance they would find anything they didn't already know. King agreed with him. But at this point they couldn't rule out anything or anyone. As far as they could see, the article about Walter Thompson was still the best to go on. He was an unofficial source and might be able to get to the bottom of things.

They hailed a cab and set out. First stop was Kenyon, just to be sure. Then on to find Mr. Thompson's flat, and fast. They had no time to lose and were certain that anyone else who might be working for Soviet interests—knowingly or not—would be equally determined to track down the casket before it was delivered to Churchill's home.

IN A MIDDLE-CLASS neighborhood in St. John's Wood, Walter Thompson was nearly finished dressing. He was an early riser and had been up for hours. In the immediate aftermath of Churchill's death, the press had called him. He thought they would be back in touch, but the phone had been silent. Not that it much mattered. He wouldn't have been able to say much more than he had. And there was little chance that the coverage could outstrip his own knowledge or satisfy the appetite he had for hearing all the details.

The elderly former lawman adjusted his tie and puttered around his flat. A small television set was in one corner, across the room from a comfortable chair. He walked over, turned it on, and sat down to watch. Thompson hoped the networks would get around to using more of the interview he had given a day earlier.

He looked for something on all of the stations, but none had made any mention of his comments. *Probably holding it for a special program.* At least, that's what he kept telling himself. No doubt there would be interest in his revelation that he had saved the great man's life so many times that Sir Winston had called him a "bodyguard unto death."

Mary, Thompson's wife of more than 50 years, knew there would be no way to pry Thompson away from the television. She fussed a bit about having the solemn newscasts interrupt their regular routines, but not much. She was soon as engrossed in the programs as her husband was. She contented herself with needlework and the respectful silence that occasionally crept into the room.

The Thompsons lived in a second-floor flat near Wellington and Circus Roads. It was not a fancy place, but it was comfortable and neat. The kind of place you might expect a retired policeman and his wife to have after several decades of service. Framed pictures of the family lined the wall. There was a wedding photo, a couple of school snaps of their son, then later ones of him as a proud young officer, then a father.

Images of Winston Churchill were interspersed among them.

MARY THOMPSON BROUGHT a steaming cup of tea to her husband, who sat resolutely in his armchair, eyes fixed on the flickering images from the screen. The former lawman watched the news in silence as memories of the past paraded by. He had spent the night dozing in that very chair, his conservative business suit still crisp and unwrinkled as though he had not even moved.

The death of his former boss had left him with profound grief, and he clung to the hope that more reporters would seek his thoughts following the earlier interview he had given, a session that seemed cathartic. Yet no new inquiries had come, and his hopes were slipping away when a sudden knock on the door echoed through the flat.

Walter broke his gaze from the television and looked toward his wife. "Mary dear," he said, his voice a blend of anticipation and weariness. "Let me head to the back for a moment and wash my face. Let in whoever it is and tell them that I'll be right out."

"Of course, my love," she said gently, moving towards the door. She opened it to find two men standing there, their presence a curious blend of urgency and hesitance. "Yes?" she asked.

"Mrs. Thompson, we're sorry to bother you so early, but we'd love to have a word with your husband."

"Certainly, and what newspaper are you with?" she inquired, a trace of skepticism in her polite tone.

The two exchanged quick glances. "Newspaper, um, yes, we're with the *Times*," one said, his uncertainty giving way to a more confident nod.

"The devil you say?" Mary replied, her surprise mixed with a bit of amusement. "Well, please come in. I'll fetch Mr. Thompson. Can I offer a cup of tea?"

Brogan responded with practiced British charm. "Yes, that'd be lovely. Many thanks, Mrs. Thompson."

As she headed to the kitchen, Walter Thompson emerged from the back room. He straightened his tie and greeted his visitors with a robust handshake. "Mrs. Thompson says you gentlemen are from the *Times.* Mighty fine. I'm happy to talk to you about Mr. Churchill. And please let me sign copies of my book for you."

"Very kind of you," Brogan replied, careful not to reveal their true agenda too hastily. "You served Mr. Churchill during the war?"

"Actually, I did two tours of duty with him. Back in the 1920s, then, yes, during the war. He was a demanding boss."

"There are stories that you saved his life," Brogan continued, pressing just enough to keep the conversation aligned with their mission.

"Many times. I've written about it all in my book," Thompson stated, his pride softened by the nostalgia of the years between.

"Yes, of course," Brogan answered, his patience measured, while King, less restrained by formality, shifted his posture with mounting impatience.

Just as Mary prepared to bring the tea into the room, King decided to abandon the pretense. His voice was firm yet respectful. "Mr. Thompson, we have great respect for you and your work, but we are not journalists. We've been sent here by the President of the United States."

The room fell silent. Mary's shock manifested in the clattering of an empty teacup onto the carpet.

Walter Thompson paused, his expression unreadable as he absorbed the revelation. Then, with an inquisitive calm, he inquired, "To what do I owe this kind of visit and honor on this particular day?"

Brogan knew his next words would have to strike a delicate balance between urgency and discretion. "Well, sir, we've been sent to Great Britain to investigate a possible plot involving Mr. Churchill."

His face first registering disbelief, then amusement, Thompson replied. "Well, I suppose you men have heard the news. Churchill is gone. He is now out of any danger from this world. I suppose he is in a summit meeting with his Maker right about now," Thompson said as he retrieved the teacup.

"Of course, we know he's dead, Thompson," King replied, curtly. Then he caught himself. "Sorry, sir. My partner and I didn't get much sleep last night."

"I know how you feel. I understand. Please proceed and tell me how I can help you and President Johnson."

"Recently, someone in the British government told President Johnson that Mr. Churchill's funeral might become the backdrop for exploitation on the part of the Soviet Union," King said.

"How so?"

"We're not at liberty to talk about the details, but our investigation has led us to believe that there's a measure of credibility to this possibility."

"What can you tell me?"

King fielded this question. "Just this. I left three Russian thugs dead in a doorway in Birmingham a few hours ago."

"What the devil were you doing all the way over there—and what does that have to do with the late Prime Minister?"

"We paid a visit to the establishment where Mr. Churchill's casket was prepared, and we found evidence that leads us to believe what President Johnson told us may be very true," King replied.

"And this evidence?"

"Let's just say, that it's possible that the casket in which Mr. Churchill's body is to be placed in a few hours contains explosive materials."

CHAPTER THIRTY

HARRY HYLTON-FOSTER HAD watched over the British House of Commons for nearly five years, guiding with a steady and unflappable hand. His tenure was marked by dedication to protocol, appreciation for the dramatic flair that defined the tumultuous arena of parliamentary debate, and profound enjoyment of his prestigious role.

Supported by members from both sides of the political aisle, as was the tradition for most individuals who had occupied the venerable seat, Hylton-Foster's position was considered firm and beyond challenge despite the perennial unpredictability that characterized British political life.

The Speaker was approaching his sixty-fifth birthday, and he often found himself reflecting on the passage of time. *Churchill was my age when he first became Prime Minister,* he mused with a mixture of reverence and introspection. In his modest anteroom, a space so proximate to the House floor that he could often hear the fervent debates when he sheltered there, he examined his image in the full-length mirror. *I'm planning to retire in a few months, after a full career. Yet old Winnie reinvented himself at my age and changed the world. What a man!*

His thoughts followed a familiar path as he considered how Churchill had been catapulted to the forefront of British leadership and world history at an age when most men looked to rest. *Is there something left for me after Speaker?* He put the thought aside for the time.

Today's session demanded his full attention.

The quiet filtering from the next room as he completed his preparations was almost eerie. The chamber was most often filled with raucous clatter, shouting, and the gavel's commanding call for order. On any typical day, the unusual silence might have prompted him to wonder if he would enter the chamber to find it empty.

Today, however, he anticipated even the aisles and galleries would be overflowing. As he surveyed his polished appearance in the mirror's reflection—white shirt and bands, black coat draping a black gown beneath, stockings neatly pulled up and buckled shoes securely fastened—he prepared himself both physically and mentally, steeling himself for the historic announcement he was to deliver.

The Speaker reached for the final adornment that would complete the ceremonial attire identifying him with this venerable duty—the imposing full-bottomed wig. It had become a familiar part of his ritual, the weight and texture reassuringly constant amid the vagaries of politics. He placed it on his head, adjusting its long curls for a moment until it sat perfectly.

Hylton-Foster took a deep breath to calm his fluttering nerves and glanced over at the clock on the wall. It was nearly half-past two, precisely the moment he had planned to enter and commence the session. With determined steps, he made his way toward his elevated and commanding seat.

All stood as he took his place.

The atmosphere, though somber, was charged with anticipation. The Commons was indeed packed, with every Member in attendance and visitors filling the galleries to capacity. The usual banter had given way to a heavy silence. As he scanned the room, Hylton-Foster's attention immediately focused on one man positioned with resolve and readiness. "Mr. Prime Minister," the Speaker's authoritative voice rang out, introducing the moment.

Harold Wilson took a few deliberate steps toward the podium. "Mr. Speaker, I have a message to the House of Commons from Her Majesty the Queen." He spoke with the gravity the occasion demanded. The chamber remained frozen in anticipation of what was to come.

Wilson approached the Speaker's elevated chair and handed the ornate document to Hylton-Foster, who accepted it with the composed formality befitting the transfer of such an important communication. The significance of the message rested heavily in his hands as he adjusted his eyeglasses and began to read its contents with the clear, respectful tone that the magnitude of the moment required:

> *"From Her Majesty the Queen: I know that it will be the wish of all my people that the loss which we have sustained by the death of the Right Honourable Sir Winston Churchill, KG, should be met in the most fitting manner and that they should have an opportunity of expressing their sorrow at the loss and their veneration of the memory of that outstanding man who in war and peace served his country unfailingly for more than fifty years and in the hours of our greatest danger was the inspiring leader who strengthened and supported us all. Confident that I can rely upon the support of my faithful Commons and upon their liberality in making suitable provision for the proper discharge of our debt of gratitude and tribute of national sorrow, I have directed that Sir Winston's body shall lie in state in Westminster Hall and that thereafter the Funeral*

*Service shall be held in the Cathedral Church of St. Paul.' –
ELIZABETH REGINA."*

Hylton-Foster's voice carried the weight of history, and as he finished, an echo of silence hovered over the room. Every face in the chamber reflected a profound acknowledgment of what had been said and what it signified. The decorum of this ancient tradition and the sudden sense of time's inexorable march were etched into the somber expressions. Here was the confirmation of Churchill's passing and the nation's intent to honor him with the full breadth of its gratitude and pomp.

As if choreographed to capture the significance of the moment, many Members had already donned mourning, anticipating the news, their black attire a stark visual representation of grief. Hylton-Foster took a moment to absorb the echoes of history and duty reverberating within him as the chamber sat quietly.

PRIME MINISTER WILSON stood once more. He paused, letting the moment sink in, and then began to read the words he had meticulously crafted over the past several days. The address had been written to honor both the man who had dominated the past century and the nation that still revered him, each word deliberately chosen to signify the depth of national sentiment.

"I beg to move," Wilson articulated, reverence resonating in his tone, "that an humble address be presented to Her Majesty humbly to thank Her Majesty for having given directions for the body of the Rt. Hon. Sir Winston Churchill, K.G., to lie in state in Westminster Hall and for the funeral service to be held in the Cathedral Church of St. Paul and assuring Her Majesty of our cordial aid and concurrence in these measures for expressing the affection and admiration in which the memory of this great man is held by this House and all Her Majesty's faithful subjects. In accepting this

Motion, this House, and, by virtue of its representation in this House, the nation, collectively and reverently will be paying its tribute to a great statesman, a great Parliamentarian, a great leader of this country—"

CHAPTER THIRTY-ONE

THE GLOW OF the television cast shadows in the Thompsons' London flat as Prime Minister Harold Wilson carried on with his lengthy address. The air in the small living room was thick with anticipation, as Mary Thompson deftly refilled the teacups and listened attentively to the urgent exchange.

Her husband had become an unexpected asset in an unfolding conspiracy. King leaned forward with urgency, his eyes intent as he pressed the former bodyguard about his connections to Churchill's inner circle. Time was slipping through their fingers, and any misstep could cause their perilous plan to unravel like so much thread.

"Yes, I know people on his staff," Thompson confirmed, a glint of pride in his eye at still being relevant to such daring schemes. "His chief guard is Ed Murray. He's on loan from Scotland Yard, just like I was back in the day." He was quick to assert his still-sharp acumen to these younger men of intrigue, as if to prove that such treacherous waters were his natural habitat.

King pressed further. "What we need is someone who can get us into Kenyon's Mortuary, and it must be discreet. Do you understand?" The question hung heavily in the air.

Thompson raised an eyebrow at the challenge. "Yes, of course I understand. I'm old, not daft," he replied. "You youngsters wouldn't even know 'RADAR' if not for Churchill. I was there when we approved the project! It was one of the many ways that great man saved the nation and the world." There was both reminiscence and reproach in his voice.

King nodded, aware that their fate was tied to Thompson's ability to navigate this delicate terrain. "No argument here, Thompson. We mean no disrespect," he assured.

The old man raised his palms in a gesture of reassurance, as if accepting their apology and the enormity of what lay ahead with equal ease. "I'm also not a sensitive old man. You have a job to do. I want to help. You want me to talk to Detective Sergeant Murray about this?" His voice was a lifeline, offering hope that their audacious and possibly dangerous mission might indeed be possible.

Brogan, who had been listening intently, joined the conversation with an air of seriousness. "The issue is that we already know someone from MI5 is trying to stop us. It stands to reason those same people have contacts at Scotland Yard." The conspiratorial undertones were unmistakable

"Likely," Thompson conceded. "But not Murray. No one can be around Churchill for so long without loyalty and discretion." His confidence in Murray's steadfastness was the gamble they needed to take.

"How would you contact him?" King asked, the question as much a plea as a plan.

"Simple," Thompson said with a grave assurance. "I'd head over to the house to pay my respects. Mrs. Churchill never liked me much, but she knows how much her husband did. I'll find a way to talk with Murray alone and see if we can get a look at the casket. I'll get it done." There was a weight of certainty in his voice.

MEANWHILE, HAROLD WILSON was nearing the end of his historic speech in the House of Commons. The Prime Minister looked across the rows of seated Members. "We meet today in this moment of tribute; of spontaneous sympathy this House feels for Lady Churchill and all the members of his family. We are conscious only that the tempestuous years are over; the years of appraisal are yet to come. It is a moment for the heartfelt tribute that this House, of all places, desires to pay in an atmosphere of quiet."

Wilson paused, the chamber now as dramatic as his words. History loomed large. Wilson continued, his voice rising again and evoking not only Winston Churchill's life but the seismic events through which he had so prodigiously led:

> *"For now the noise of hooves thundering across the veldt; the clamour of the hustings in a score of contests; the shots in Sidney Street, the angry guns of Gallipoli, of Flanders, of Coronel and the Falkland Islands; the sullen feet of marching men in Tonymandy; the urgent warnings of the Nazi threat; the whine of the sirens and the dawn bombardment of the Normandy beaches—all these now are silent. There is a stillness. And in that stillness, echoes and memories. To each whose life has been touched by Winston Churchill, to each his memory. And as those memories are told and retold, as the world pours in its tributes, as world leaders announce their intention, in this jet age, of coming to join in this vast assembly to pay honour and respect to his memory, we in this House treasure one thought, and it was a thought some of us felt it right to express in the Parliamentary tributes on his retirement. Each one of us recalls some little incident—many of us, as in my own case, a kind action, graced with the courtesy of a past generation and going far beyond the normal calls of Parliamentary comradeship. Each of us has his own memory, for in the*

*tumultuous diapason of a world's tributes, all of us here at
least know the epitaph he would have chosen for himself:
'He was a good House of Commons man.'"*

The room was uncharacteristically silent as Harold Wilson
stepped back and took his seat. The House then became a platform
for British eloquence. For the next hour or so, several prominent
members weighed in about Winston Churchill. Members from every
political persuasion spoke from their hearts about the man who had
dominated world history for so long.

One of the last speakers that day seemed to sum it all up for
everyone. He was a "back-bencher" named R.H. Turton. Churchill
himself, though remembered for so many great deeds, had spent a
great deal of time in his political career riding the back benches of
the House. So Turton's words, as well as the fact that it was someone
like him sharing them, were powerful:

*"Sir Winston Churchill loved this House. Your freshest
memory of him, Mr. Speaker, will be of him rising from
that seat below the Gangway, reluctantly accepting the
support of two honorable Members, tottering to the Bar of
the House and there making his bow to you, Mr. Speaker,
and to Parliament, which he loved. As this afternoon we
sadly leave this Chamber and pass under the Churchill
Arch, we will recollect that that arch was left by him
untouched and un-repaired to remind Parliament of the
fury the Nazis unleashed against this nation and this
Parliament. To many of us in future that battered and
chipped relic of the former Chamber will be a permanent
memorial to the man who loved democratic freedom, who
revered our Parliamentary procedure and who in the
judgment of all was the greatest Member that Parliament,
in all its 700 years, has ever known."*

Soon thereafter, the question was called and agreed to unanimously. What had been assumed was now official. The grand farewell for Sir Winston Leonard Spencer Churchill would be of the highest order.

A full state funeral.

CHAPTER THIRTY-TWO

MORE THAN AN hour had passed since he met with King and Brogan, and Walter Thompson was now winding his way through a modest crowd gathered near Hyde Park Gate. He paced himself as he approached number 28, breathing in the crisp air. His every footstep heightened his anticipation. It had been several years since he had last visited the residence. His return today was like stepping back not only into history but into a legacy that still pulsed with life. There was one face he hoped to see above all others, and his spirits lifted when the door swung open to reveal just the person he had hoped for.

"Thompson! So nice of you to call. Please come in," said Edmund Murray with genuine warmth.

"I thought to call first but then decided to just pop over this way. Sorry if this is an intrusion."

"Not at all. Is it not like old times? Would you like to speak to Mrs. Churchill?"

"Oh, well, yes—to pay my respects and that sort of thing. But the real purpose of my visit is to speak with you, old chap."

"Me? What the devil for?"

"Well, can we find a quiet spot? I'll fill you in. I think there is information you need to know. Urgent information."

Murray raised an eyebrow, momentarily hesitant. "Okay, Thompson. Let's talk first. Then I'll take you to the family," he said. He led Thompson through a labyrinth of hallways, each filled with memories of historical magnitude, and then down a narrow stairway to a basement office that appeared well-used and functional. "We can talk here."

"Excellent. Thank you so much for this courtesy," Thompson replied as he took a seat.

"Well, you have me curious, I'll say that," Murray said, pacing slightly as he waited for Thompson to begin.

"I understand. Let me make a start. I was paid a visit a bit ago by two men who said they had been sent by the American President."

"Lyndon Johnson?" Murray's eyes widened with surprise.

"I think they only have the one President, so yes, that's the bloke."

Murray replied, "We just got word from Ambassador Bruce that President Johnson is very ill and will not be attending Sir Winston's funeral."

Thompson pondered the weight of Murray's words. They seemed to fit the larger puzzle. Then he continued, "Well, that would certainly make sense in light of what his emissaries shared with me."

"Why you?" Murray pressed, skepticism lacing his voice. "If they have a message for this family, they should send it through official channels. I'm sorry, but this makes no sense at all."

"I suppose it doesn't. And that's about to get worse."

BROGAN WAITED IN their room several minutes. He called the hotel operator and asked if there were any messages. There were not. Then he made his way to the elevator when King failed to appear. He found his companion in the lobby bar. He sidled up next to his partner and gave a knowing nod.

They had a long, crucial night ahead, and Brogan was not about to let alcohol play the spoiler. Once Thompson arrived, there would be much to discuss. The implications of their mission had already grown large and ominous, and it was necessary to have a clear picture of what Winston Churchill's staff knew or suspected.

"Your finest ginger ale, Sport," said King, with a playful grin.

"No hard stuff?" Brogan prodded, though he was more relieved than concerned.

"Hey, we're on a case," King replied, waving off the implication. "You can get shit-faced if you want, but as for me, it's soft drinks until we get to the bottom of this thing."

Reluctant to let his guard down, even for an instant, Brogan motioned to the bartender. "I'll have what my American friend is having." The barman set down a pair of drinks, and Brogan continued: "Thompson must be in tight with the family if he's getting this kind of face time. Either that or he's overplaying what we gave him. Think he'll get Murray to bite?"

They paused and watched the television flicker with reports of the historic event they were sent to influence. Reports poured in from dignitaries around the globe. It seemed as if all the world was on its way to London. Brogan wondered aloud which unseen hands were pulling at the strings. "We need to add more troops to this show. We're outnumbered."

"We've been burned, Sport," King said, leaning in as if to avoid any stray ears. "Someone knows we are hot on this trail. Most likely they have eyes either on or in that funeral home." His tone carried both disappointment and determination, indicating he wasn't ready to admit defeat.

"How are we going to get in?" Brogan inquired, knowing that King may already have warped together some unconventional plan.

"I don't think we are," King replied with a rueful grin.

"Who, then?" Brogan pressed, hoping for an answer that made sense of their dilemma.

"How about Thompson?" King suggested, the idea as daring as it was reckless.

"He's old and not all that steady. I'm not sure he's up to it," Brogan countered with skepticism. The thought of involving the aging Thompson in such a risky task seemed dubious.

"Listen, Brogan. The man spent decades in harm's way to protect Churchill. I think the adrenalin alone will take a quarter-century off the old guy's clock—at least for enough time to get the job done." King's voice brimmed with confidence, painting Thompson as a man of resilience and undying commitment.

"Maybe so," Brogan conceded. "But will he do it?" His voice was tinged with doubt, reflecting a lingering uncertainty about convincing Thompson.

"Of course he will. He'll see it as his duty. I know his type." King's certainty was unshakeable, as if he had already seen the outcome unfold in his mind. The conversation paused for a moment, each man considering the implications if Thompson were to refuse.

A SHORT WHILE later, Walter Thompson made his way into the bustling bar at the Dorchester. The retired lawman removed his hat, found a corner table, and then glanced about his surroundings as he settled in. The atmosphere hummed with the low murmur of conversations, clinking glasses, and the soft notes of a jazz piano.

Behind the gleaming bar, Harvey King glanced up, catching Thompson's reflection in a well-placed mirror. He signaled to Brogan, and the two of them moved with purpose toward Thompson. They reached the older man's table just as he was getting comfortable.

"Mr. Murray will lend his support to our investigation," Thompson announced as the two men sat down. His voice carried a note of pride, perhaps a renewed sense of belonging to a world of intrigue and danger that he once knew so well.

"What I figured," King said as he eased himself into the chair next to Thompson. He gestured toward Brogan. "But the redhead here had his doubts about your chances."

"Have a drink, Mr. Thompson?" Brogan asked, ignoring King's jab as he pulled up a seat.

"Nothing for me, thank you. I'm back on duty," Thompson responded with a broad smile. The expression was one of satisfaction, perhaps a flicker of his old spirit coming to the fore.

"Indeed you are," Brogan replied, returning the smile. He suspected that the retired detective was relishing this return to service.

"How shall we proceed?" Thompson inquired, leaning forward, his interest piqued.

Harvey's reply was swift and direct. "Well, there is no 'we' on this one."

"I don't understand," Thompson said. He searched their expressions, readying himself for whatever complex twist this case might present.

"We're burned, Thompson," Harvey explained. "At least me and the redhead here. Can't go anywhere near that funeral joint."

Thompson grimaced slightly at the American use of the word "joint," a slight jolt to his British sensibilities. Yet he chose to overlook it, pressing on to the matter at hand. "Are you saying this is a solo operation?"

"That's exactly what we're saying, old man," King affirmed. His voice carried the weight of necessity, and his eyes locked on Thompson, assessing the man's resolve.

"Well, you might start by not calling me old," Thompson retorted with a hint of bravado. One could almost see the decades melt away as the thrill of the chase reignited within him. "Apparently, I'm the only operative you have."

King and Brogan exchanged an amused glance and raised their glasses in Thompson's direction. He had no drink of his own, but he picked up his hat from the table, put it on his head, and tipped it to them in a gesture that was both humorous and defiant.

"So you need to square it with this Murray guy. I think the best plan is for you to do your examination of the casket sometime tonight," King suggested. He leaned back, confident in Thompson's ability to execute the task.

"I'll set it up, Mr. King. Let's say about half-past nine," Thompson planned aloud. "That should be late enough to avoid too much attention yet give us enough time to figure out what to do if there is a bomb in that box."

"Won't look like a bomb, per se," King advised. "What you'll be looking for is some plastic explosive. It's like putty and can be worked into just about any shape."

"I'm familiar with it," Thompson nodded. The man had seen his share of wartime plots and sabotage; tinkering with dynamite was not new to him.

"Good. Now, it's obviously hidden out of sight. Maybe in the lining," King mused, as if mentally reconstructing how the explosive might be concealed.

Thompson considered this. "I know the casket is lined with lead."

"It is?" Brogan's surprise was apparent. The use of such material seemed an unexpected detail.

"Yes. That's been long planned," Thompson stated. "Protects the remains from the elements down through the years."

"Is that lining inside the wood?" King asked, his investigator's curiosity prompting him to visualize every element.

"Not likely. I'd say it was an insert, like veneer," Thompson replied, recalling specifics with the precision of a man who was used to remembering details.

King thought this over. "I'll bet you a new hat the funny putty is in between that lead lining and the wood. I'd look there first." He gave Thompson a calculated look. "You'll need some tools."

"Oh yes. I have some fine tools," Thompson said, almost with nostalgia. "They've been in storage."

Walter Thompson lingered at the Dorchester bar for another fifteen minutes. Harvey King had asked him about the old days, when the lawman was still guarding Churchill. Soon Thompson was in the middle of an animated story. "Just a day or so after Mr. Churchill became Prime Minister—this would be May 1940—he decided, against my advice, to travel to Paris to meet with Paul Reynaud. The French were on the brink of catastrophe and the old man wanted to persuade them to fight on. I remember that the boss turned to me at one point and said, 'Give me your gun, Thompson. You never know what will happen. I do not intend to be taken alive,'" the lawman said with a bit of a chuckle.

"Would he have done it? Would he have taken his own life?" Brogan asked.

"Not bloody likely. He might have taken a bullet from another gun, though. I'm sure, however, if he did die like that, he would've taken quite a few of the enemy with him to the other side."

"Fascinating," Brogan said.

A wide smile came to Thompson's face.

"What?" King asked.

"I was just remembering what happened when we did finally meet the French Prime Minister."

"Do tell."

"Well, Reynaud was in the company of his mistress—some Countess such and such. He had sent his family out of the city and toward the coast for safety. This tart suddenly lunged at Mr.

Churchill with a knife in hand! I grabbed the knife from her and shoved her away."

"Incredible," Brogan said.

"Indeed. Might have been the shortest British Premiership in history. And we wouldn't be here making our big plans today," Thompson said. He then pulled out his watch and said, "Well, gentlemen, I need to be on my way. Where shall we meet up after I'm finished with the assignment—here?"

King replied, "No. Too public. Let's rendezvous at your flat—say about eleven?"

"Splendid. I shall see you both then. Wish me luck."

"God speed, Mr. Thompson," Brogan said. Thompson gave the duo another tip of the hat and made his way to the exit.

CHAPTER THIRTY-THREE

"ABOUT DONE, HARVEY?" Brogan asked, only to see the sudden alarm in his colleague's face. He quickly grew uneasy. "What is it?" he asked.

King's voice was tense. "We have company. Look at the mirror behind the bar to your left. You should be able to see a couple of ugly-ass fellows."

Brogan followed King's instructions, and with a casual glance, he saw precisely what his companion had warned him about. Two men with a distinctly brutish demeanor were making a concerted survey of the room. He had no doubts about who they were.

Finally, their unwanted guests settled in at a table on the far side of the room, almost directly across from them. King acted swiftly, sliding his chair slightly to the left and gesturing for Brogan to do the same, quietly maneuvering them both out of the direct sightline of their watchful visitors.

"I'd bet my left nut they are friends of the gentlemen we met in Birmingham," King said.

"Well, we can't sit here for long. If we can see them, they can see us. We need to move."

"I agree, Sport. We can't go back up to the room—it's probably blown, too."

"I'm listening. You're the boss here, Harvey."

"Gee, thanks." King paused, calculating their next move. Finally, he said, "Here's the plan. Whatever happens, meet me at The Criterion in Piccadilly in one hour."

"Okay, got it. But how do we get from here to there?"

"Need a diversion. Then we run like hell."

"What kind of diversion?"

"We'll split up. You go out the side door, I'll head out the front. Now, I want you to get up and walk slowly toward this end of the bar. The toilets are out that door."

"Okay—"

"When you get near the bar, fling that glass of yours down toward the middle of that big mirror. Then hightail it out the door. I'll watch the bad guys and plan my exit accordingly."

"I'm sure they'll be following me."

"Better for me," King said with a broad smile. "After all, you're younger and faster."

Brogan stood up slowly, trying to maintain calm as he moved. With his back to the bad guys, he shuffled over toward the bar. He looked once more at King just before turning and flinging his glass—actually a sturdy mug—into the air. It hit the mirror and shattered it in a split second.

Panic erupted.

Cries of surprise filled the room as patrons ducked or turned to see what had happened. The two visitors leaped from their chairs, eyes trained on Brogan as they ran toward him. But Brogan was out the door in a flash, disappearing into the corridor. It was clear that the bad guys were thrown off guard, momentarily caught in the confusion. King seized the opportunity to disappear. He bolted from his seat and moved swiftly through the main entrance, vanishing out onto the street.

Meanwhile, Brogan was moving at a full sprint. He turned a corner and, on impulse, entered the lady's privy, which was, fortunately, unoccupied. He stood as still as his pounding heart would allow, straining to listen for the footsteps of his pursuers. Three long minutes later, the coast was clear. He let out a quick breath, composed himself, and made his way out a back exit of the hotel and into a narrow alley behind the hotel.

AS BROGAN AND King were bolting from the *Dorchester*, taking separate paths and navigating the frenetic London streets, Sean Welling sat absently tapping a pencil at his desk in headquarters. A sudden and unexpected ring of the telephone broke his trance. He picked up the receiver, identifying himself.

"H-h-hello," came the reply, the voice on the line wavering and hesitant. "I'm c-calling from the Savoy to confirm the director's dinner reservation for six thirty this evening."

For several seconds, Welling sat puzzled, furrowing his brows, as he tried to reconcile the mysterious information with the director's planned itinerary. No such meeting was scheduled for that evening. A realization dawned on him. This was *code*.

"Oh, er, yes—that is confirmed. The director will be there."

"Wonderful," the voice concluded, and the line went dead.

Welling leaned back, a serious look crossing his face. He drew a contemplative breath before standing and taking several brisk steps toward the Director's office. He gave one solid knock, and an authoritative voice responded from the other side.

"Very sorry to bother you, Director. But you just got a call from the Savoy confirming your dinner there tonight."

"Tonight?" Roger Hollis said. He appeared bemused as he spoke through a half-open door. "I don't recall—"

"Yes, Director. You remember—six thirty?" Welling gently interrupted, his eyes glinting to communicate the call's significance.

"Ah yes," Hollis replied, a knowing look spreading across his seasoned face, his demeanor transformed by sudden comprehension. "Did the caller identify himself?"

"No, Director—he did not. Sounded nervous, though—almost like he had a stutter."

"A stutter, you say?" Hollis murmured as he seemed to drift away in thought, his mind spinning out the implications.

"Sir?" Welling pressed, eager for further instructions.

"Well, thank you, Sean. That's all for now." Hollis waved him off, his posture one of a man pondering complex scenarios.

Sean closed the door, deep in thought. Something was brewing; that much was sure.

Thoughts racing, he wondered who was behind it and what the game plan was. *Complicated business,* he thought to himself. *Complicated and dangerous.* He allowed himself a grim smile. *Of course, it always is.*

AT FIVE PAST three, and a minute or so after their scheduled reunion time, Tiernan Brogan finally showed up at the splendid and crowded Criterion Restaurant. He had lost his tail—at least for the moment. He immediately spied Harvey King seated at the bar, looking calm and in command of the situation. He crossed the room to join him.

As Brogan situated himself on the stool next to his American accomplice, he noticed that the spy, who had been drinking ginger ale at their last meeting, had now switched to something considerably stronger. "Gotta keep a clear head, Harvey," Brogan remarked. He gave a small, knowing laugh. "Better take it easy on the hard stuff."

"Mind your own damn business," replied King with a smile, betraying more amusement than annoyance. "We got plenty of time.

Nothing but time until eleven. So I figure I can take a break. Join me?"

"Just one, I suppose. What're you drinking?" Brogan asked, a note of interest in his voice now.

"Irish, in honor of my partner," King answered, lifting his glass in a mock toast. He signaled the barkeep with a small gesture. "Barkeep, please bring my friend a glass of this fine whiskey—what do you call it?"

"Tullamore Dew," the barkeep replied. "Coming right up."

Brogan's eyes glinted as he watched the drink being poured. "You had me checked out all the way down to my whiskey—do I have that right?"

"You're quick, Sport. Real quick," King said with admiration. Then he winked at Brogan, relishing the bond they had formed so quickly in the line of danger. It was a far cry from the days when he felt he could trust nobody.

"How are we going to get back into our room at the *Dorchester*?" Brogan asked as he took a cautious sip.

"We're not," King replied, shrugging off the concern like a jacket he no longer needed to wear.

"What about our things?" Brogan raised a practical question, leaning in as if to get a more detailed answer.

"What do you have there that can't be replaced in thirty minutes at *Selfridges*?" King countered, his voice full of the swagger that was so distinctly American. "We left nothing of value in the room—certainly nothing that would be of any interest to anyone snooping around. That's the beauty of traveling light. I got my gun and my notes. We'll pick up anything else we need later and maybe we can persuade Thompson to let us flop at his flat."

"Whatever you say. Now what?"

"Let's find a way to call Dulles. We're overdue to check in. He's probably pissing blood by now," King said, his tone flipping from casual to urgent and back again in an instant.

"Need a secure line," Brogan warned, his voice lowering a notch as he spoke.

"Hell, we just need to speak in generalities. Dulles knows the drill. We can use any old phone. No matter who listens, they'll never figure out what we're talking about." King took a deeper sip this time, savoring both the drink and the easy adaptability of his plans.

Brogan finished the last of his drink, feeling the comfort of both the whiskey and King's plan settle into him. "So who do you think is after us now?"

"Hell, I wouldn't be surprised if it's every bastard in London," King said with a grin. "I was hoping to draw the Russians out, but I didn't know they'd show up this quick. Stands to reason there'd be one or two locals, just to cover their asses."

Brogan placed his glass on the bar with a small thud.

King said, "We could just sit here and see who shows up," a challenging light in his eyes. They both assumed nothing would happen until later, but they also knew nothing ever went as planned.

Brogan nodded with reluctant agreement. Then he said, "You ready to get moving?"

King stood up with deliberate leisure, as if the urgency of their escape to Piccadilly was already a distant memory. He drained his glass and paid the tab. "Remember, we got plenty of time, Sport."

Brogan watched as his partner kept his cool and his pace, following him out of the beautiful building and down Regent Street.

KIM PHILBY WAS elated to return to the city he knew so well. He relished the simple thrill of breathing the London air, and his lavish suite at the Savoy was a bittersweet reminder of everything he had been forced to abandon in the name of duplicity.

Yet now, here he was, and it pleased him greatly. His two long years marooned in Moscow had been an exercise in endurance and adaptation, exposing him to the full weight of the Soviet machine.

They had been eye-opening, challenging all previous conceptions of the might and unwieldy trust of the empire he served. *How marvelous*, he mused, *that my Soviet handlers put such faith in me.* He allowed himself a rare smile of amusement at what he perceived to be paradoxical trust from his masters.

What Philby could not perceive, ironically, was that his masters actually had *little* faith in him. They had assigned two covert operatives to shadow his every move, ensuring he did not deviate from his prescribed path. Despite his vaunted reputation as a master spy who prided himself on his instincts and ability to detect danger, Kim was oblivious to the presence of his watchful shadows.

His official instructions were clipped and concise—*remain in your suite unless specified otherwise.* He was to await further orders and to venture out only for necessary meetings at the embassy. But Philby was never one to slavishly adhere to rules, especially when they clipped the wings of his newfound freedom. He was determined to make the most of his venture back to his beloved England and to savor every cherished moment in case the Soviets yanked him back to the bleakness of Moscow at a moment's notice.

Not long after making the call to Sean Welling, Kim took the first opportunity to flout his orders. He ventured downstairs to the hotel's renowned American Bar. It was explicitly off limits. His Soviet masters had ordered him in no uncertain terms to steer clear, not only of public view, but also of temptation in the form of alcohol.

But Philby had always regarded himself as something of a maverick, unwilling to bend to directives that did not suit his personal tastes. He checked his disguise, complete with a false beard and glasses, and entered the bar with a practiced nonchalance. He took a seat at the far end, already savoring his small act of rebellion.

"What can I get you, guv'nor?" the barkeep asked, eyeing him with polite curiosity.

"Thank you, my g-good man," Kim replied, "Black Label please. A double."

He drank contentedly, immersed in the taste and nostalgia of his first drink back in London. Even here, his instincts failed him. He never noticed the two men at the other end of the bar, men who would have seemed conspicuous if he had cared to look beyond his self-satisfaction. If he had scrutinized them from behind his disguise, he might have found it curious—or perhaps not—that they were drinking *vodka*.

FROM A TELEPHONE booth a block away from the Criterion, Harvey King murmured into the receiver, his eyes scanning the street and ears on the listen for any unusual noises. Nothing. Just the sound of his own breath and his rapid, low words. "Yes sir. We've pretty much confirmed things," he said, after a pause.

He glanced out the cloudy phone box window as a black cab pulled up in front of the restaurant. A large man with an overcoat and the evening tabloids got out and walked toward the Criterion's entrance. King kept his eye on him until he was inside and then returned his attention to the street.

"As bad as we thought?" Allen Dulles asked, his voice crackling over the transatlantic line.

"It's starting to look that way. But we'll know more later tonight."

"How much later?"

Harvey paused for a moment, struck a match, and lit a cigarette. He took a long drag and smiled at his ability to rattle the usually calm director. "Eleven o'clock or so here—six your time."

"All right then. Find a way to call me."

"Copy that." The line went dead.

CHAPTER THIRTY-FOUR

MARY HEARD HER husband enter their flat and called out a cheerful hello from the kitchen. Silence was the only response. Somewhat puzzled, Mary turned her attention away from her preparations and walked out to the living room. Her husband, Walter, appeared momentarily, emerging with a distracted air from the cramped room he used as his office. She barely had time to register his presence before he headed straight for the front door, a small satchel clutched purposefully in his left hand.

Curious, Mary watched as he turned left towards the storage area just outside their door. There he hesitated, reached into his pocket, and withdrew a key to unlock one of the locker-type doors. She returned to her kitchen work with questions lingering in her mind. Walter's furtive demeanor was at once familiar, recalling memories from years past, and a feeling of déjà vu settled in her stomach like a stone. Her imagination was running wild, and she resolved to find out exactly what was going on.

Mary set her jaw and left the kitchen once more, keeping her footfalls light as she approached. She felt a twinge of guilt for what almost seemed like spying on her own husband. When she peeked furtively around the corner, she saw Walter carefully placing several items into the small satchel.

"Something for a rainy day, dear?" she called out, deciding to break the secrecy.

Walter was startled, but he quickly composed himself. "I need some tools for an assignment," he explained, his voice casual but tinged with a hint of the old excitement she remembered. He closed the locker door with a decisive clank.

"I'd imagine this has much to do with those two men who visited us," Mary surmised.

"Yes, but it's not something I can talk about. All very hush-hush." He met her gaze, his face a blend of anticipation and apology.

"Haven't heard that phrase for years. Used to hear it all the time when you worked for Mr. Churchill." She wore a knowing expression, recalling the countless times similar scenes had played out during the war.

"When *we* worked for Mr. Churchill," he corrected her, a rare smile forming at the corners of his mouth.

Mary smiled in return, a myriad of memories flashing through her mind. "Yes, of course. *We* worked for him. But I just typed his endless letters. You saved his life."

"And I'm about to do it again, my dear Mary," he declared, his eyes alight with purpose. She saw in his expression the young man he once was, the man to whom danger was an unspoken ally.

"The devil you say. And how might one go about saving the life of a dead man?" Mary asked, her tone half-joking and half-concerned at the implications of his mission.

"For starters, Mary, we can help make sure this dead man doesn't lead to many more dead men." Walter's voice was earnest, conveying both gravity and urgency. She realized he meant every word.

DINNER AT THE Savoy Grill was a ritual that Roger Hollis typically relished, a comforting pause in the midst of his otherwise clandestine business. This evening, however, his presence in the opulent dining room was born of necessity rather than leisure. He made a point to insist only on a simple bowl of chicken soup, dismissing the wine steward with an air of urgency.

Hollis's demeanor was that of a man with much on his mind, a man who could be called away at any moment from even the most extravagant of tables. His customary civility was absent. As the waiter departed, Hollis took the opportunity to briefly leave his table. His gait, usually so deliberate, was quick as he walked to the men's room.

The attendant Alex, a familiar face, stood ready to offer his usual courtesy.

Hollis washed his hands and palmed a five-pound note into the young man's hand. "Very kind of you, sir. Please let me give you some change," Alex said obligingly, offering a one-pound note in return. The exchange was swift, practiced, with Hollis also retrieving a small stack of towels. Tucked between two towels was a slip of paper, which bore the simple, yet provocative, instruction: "Room 312."

The Director returned to his table, though his mind was now elsewhere. He ate about half of his soup, each spoonful consumed mechanically, without savor or appreciation. Hollis signaled for his bill and left sufficient funds to settle his account, along with an ample tip. "I forgot an important meeting, sorry to leave so abruptly," he said to the waiter. He walked out of the restaurant and purchased an evening paper at the newsstand in the hotel lobby.

Before he took his next steps, Hollis looked around, his keen eyes conducting an inventory of faces and possible observers. Convinced he was unobserved, he slipped into the lift. "Third floor, please," he told the attendant. The ascent was marked by a quiet anticipation, one that was hardly dispelled even as Hollis stepped out into the corridor.

Kim Philby, now minus the comic disguise of a fake beard and mustache, greeted Roger Hollis with an almost theatrical grin. The ease and familiarity were genuine, despite the passage of years and the magnitude of their shared treacheries. Though Philby had lived in exile since his betrayal had been uncovered, he appeared unchanged, even vibrant. Hollis, who was seven years older, returned the smile.

"R-roger, you old son of a b-bitch, so nice to see you," Philby said with a cadence that was both jocular and charged with insinuation.

"Color me surprised, Kim. Never thought I'd see the likes of you again—at least not in *London*," Hollis replied, a subtle undercurrent of admiration in his voice. The distance that had once separated them vanished almost immediately as they laughed, the sound echoing off the hotel room's walls with an air of incredulity.

"I'm drinking Black Label; can I fix you one, old fellow?" asked Philby, already in motion with the bottle.

"Please, yes, thank you. But I must ask two things of you."

"Fire away," Kim said, pouring the drink with a nonchalance that belied the importance of their meeting.

"First, what the hell are *you* doing here? And second, what the hell are you doing *here?*" Hollis asked, a note of disbelief mingling with his genuine curiosity.

The question led to a moment of silence, one that seemed to fill the room with the consequence of the risk. "Simple, Mr. Director. I'm on official b-b-business for our friends," Philby replied, a mischievous lilt in his voice as he delivered the drink.

"I gather that. But what is it that requires such risk?"

Philby leaned back, taking pleasure in the magnitude of what he was about to reveal. "Simply the most bold and visionary thing our friends have ever contemplated," he said, his words carefully chosen. "It's a vision that Comrade Stalin first had, and one that, even after his death, was kept alive for the right moment."

"And that moment has arrived?" Hollis asked, probing with the cautiousness of someone who was all too aware of the implications.

Philby gave a knowing smile. "I think you already know the answer to that, Roger. Please don't be coy," he said, his delivery both teasing and certain. He smiled and took a long pull from his glass. "You're not in the dark. I'm aware that you've been in the loop for a while. This is no time for games. We go back too far."

"Indeed we do, Kim," Hollis said, taking only a conservative sip of his drink, as though rationing it for a long conversation. "I was thinking today about our old friend Gouzenko."

Philby seemed momentarily taken aback at the mention of this old, nearly forgotten name, but he recovered quickly, warming to the memory. "Ah yes, Canada," he said, a distant look coming over his face.

"You sent me on that mission back in '46. He was naming names and causing so much trouble for our friends. That was when you were on track to become the head of MI6," Hollis said, reminding Kim of a time when their futures seemed assured.

"Yes. It's true. Can you imagine? I should be the head of MI6 now. That was always the plan. And it would have happened, but for that awful wreck of a man, Burgess," Philby responded, his voice tinged with bitterness and the recognition of how differently their careers had unfolded.

"I heard he died a while back. Did you ever get a chance to visit with him in Moscow?" Hollis asked, the question at once innocuous and loaded.

"Why would I have wanted to do a thing like that? The man ruined my life. He wanted me to visit him when he was dying—his liver, you know—but I refused," Philby replied, his anger repressed but palpable.

"I'm sorry," Hollis said, his voice carrying an air of unstated allegiance to the past they shared.

"He did leave his library to me," Philby continued after a pause, his tone slightly mollified by the thought. "A few weeks after his demise, several boxes appeared at my doorstep. The man had great taste in books, got to give him that. Six collector's edition copies of *Middlemarch*, can you imagine it?"

"What's life like in Moscow?" Hollis asked, genuinely curious about the exile his companion had endured.

"Bloody boring," Philby replied reflexively. Then he caught himself, remembering the necessity of optimism in the face of such loss. "It's a remarkable p-place, though," he amended.

"But you miss England, don't you?" Hollis said, sensing the unspoken longing in Philby's eyes.

"I suppose that's true. But it's all so much water under London Bridge, old fellow," Philby said, his voice dismissive but not entirely convincing. He studied Hollis with renewed intensity, as though gauging how much had changed since their last encounter.

"I can't stay all that long, so please tell me what you need to tell me," Hollis said, knowing that they had achieved the necessary level of candor to discuss what truly mattered.

"Certainly. Well, it's called KOBA...."

CHAPTER THIRTY-FIVE

AT PRECISELY NINE o'clock that evening, an unlikely pair made their way along a dimly lit alley in Marylebone, approaching the side door of a stately building. The door was marked "Office." Walter Thompson, former bodyguard to Britain's most storied prime minister, walked briskly alongside an active-duty member of Scotland Yard, Edmund Murray.

The purpose of their clandestine visit to this venue was clear to them as they navigated puddles glistening under the dim streetlamps. It was nothing short of a mission to foil a conspiracy involving the desecration of the body of Winston Churchill.

"Thank you so much, Murray, for agreeing to help with this business at such a late hour," Thompson said. The weight of the satchel in his hand seemed to lend extra urgency to his steps.

"Not at all. We share something powerful in common—a love for the Churchill family, and I'd sure hate to see something so sinister as what you are suggesting happen to them at such a time," Murray replied. As they neared the door, Thompson knocked, though he appeared uncertain, and spoke quietly before any response came. "My dear chap, since you are on active duty and I'm an old relic from the past, best you take the lead with the people here," he said.

"You're a living legend and you know it," Murray replied, just as a young man opened the door with an eager look on his face. "Good evening," Murray said without missing a beat. "I'm from Scotland Yard, and my partner here and I are representing the Churchill family. We need to have access to the casket and to your moving plans."

"Oh yes—please come in," the young man said, showing none of the caution one might have expected. "I'm Winston Fleming, and it's pretty much just me and a cleaning crew here right now, but for the officers in the front who are keeping watch until morning."

"Winston, is it?" Murray asked, as if the name were a password.

"Yes, sir. I was born on May 11, 1940, the day after Mr. Churchill became Prime Minister. Now I gets to be a little part of history, I guess."

"Indeed you do, young man," said Thompson with a knowing smile.

Fleming's eyes trained on Thompson with growing recognition. Charmed by the presence of what was clearly a celebrity figure to him, he said with unfeigned enthusiasm, "You're the bloke who guarded Churchill all those years! Saw you on television. I pretty much watch and read everything about Churchill, seeing as I was named for him, and all."

Thompson nodded, slightly embarrassed yet pleased at the recognition. "Yes, young man. I'm Walter Thompson," he said.

"So the family brought you out of retirement to help with security!" Fleming exclaimed, more a statement than a question, as he buzzed with excitement.

"Yes, something like that. We need to have access to the casket for about a half hour. Could you direct us to the room?" The urgency in Thompson's voice was palpable, but he maintained a courteous demeanor.

"Follow me. Right this way," Fleming said. He led them through a series of shadowy corridors, the sound of their shoes echoing on the polished floors, before stopping outside an unlabeled room. Thompson and Murray entered. Fleming returned to his post.

Along the walls of the room were massive black and white photographs showing Churchill's many facets of life—the young soldier in India, the fearless writer announcing his candidacy for parliament, the commanding Prime Minister flash-lit to fierce purpose by a *Life Magazine* photographer.

"Great God, this is something." Murray said, unable to keep from exhibiting surprise.

"There it is," Thompson said, as his eyes landed the casket resting upon an old eight-foot table.

"Best be quick," Murray replied.

FROM THEIR HIDDEN vantage point high above the street, Harvey King and Tiernan Brogan had watched Thompson and Murray approach the side door of the Kenyon funeral establishment. The streets were quiet and their view unobstructed from the rooftop perch. It was a convenient spot, just half a block away and close enough to watch the drama unfold, while keeping just out of the range of trouble.

The good position had an added, unexpected benefit—they could keep an eye on both ends of the block thanks to a large mirror they had found and propped up on an old bucket. That enabled them to monitor the area around the corner of the building.

Murray and Thompson were just inside the door when Brogan saw a reflection of two figures in the mirror. He tapped King on the shoulder and pointed. King turned to see what his partner was talking about. "Here," King said as he fumbled to retrieve a small pair of binoculars from his coat pocket. King passed the glasses to Brogan. "You won't believe this," he said. "Take a look."

"Bloody hell," Brogan replied. "That's them."

A minute later the two men across the street from the funeral home looked up at the roof where King and Brogan were perched. They ducked out of sight but kept using the mirror to track the activities across the street.

"Doesn't matter if they see us," King said. "We got the high ground and they know it. They're the ones who'd better watch their asses."

Harvey then speculated out loud on the significance of their presence. "Are they looking for us, or are they looking for something else?" King asked.

"They've been watching this place since the day we arrived, haven't they? And now they've seen Murray and Thompson." He handed the binoculars back to King, who quickly focused them on the pair now standing near the Kenyon building.

"We've got to make sure they don't interfere. Murray and Thompson need to get out of there in one piece and without anyone reporting to the Soviets that they've been here," King said.

"There's got to be a way to take them out without killing them," Brogan said.

King shook his head and looked at Brogan like a wise old man looks at an innocent child. He adjusted the binoculars and watched the two men cross the street. "You should know by now, Sport. There's always only *one* way."

"Always?" Brogan asked. "Always only one way?"

"Bad guys who do bad things are always better off dead," King replied.

Brogan said, "I guess they won't be following anyone if they're pushing up daisies. But it's still not my cup of tea."

"Well, maybe you should put some of that Tullamore shit in your tea, Sport."

WITH THE DOOR securely closed behind them, Thompson and Murray didn't waste a single moment. After a quick glance to make sure they were not disturbed, they carefully opened the casket, pausing for a brief moment to reflect on its beauty and import. The body of the man they had both served so loyally for so long would soon be placed inside. It gave them chills to think that it could be blown to bits. Thompson pulled gently at the fabric covering the inside of the casket. He started at the head with a certain degree of caution but found nothing.

Murray offered, "If I were to hide something, it wouldn't be by the head—but rather by the feet. No one looks there."

"Good thought," Thompson replied. He then began to pull at the fabric at the foot of the inside of the casket, exposing a small device as he did so.

"What do you make of this?" he asked, handing the item to Murray with some degree of concern.

"Looks like a timer or trigger of some sort."

"Indeed it does. And where there's a trigger, there's bound to be something to trigger," Thompson said. He began working on the floor of the box without hesitation. "Reach into that satchel and find something I can use to peel back some of this lead flooring."

Murray rummaged through the case and soon found a putty knife. He handed it to Thompson.

Thompson began working on the corner of the lead lining with resolve. After a few minutes of prying, he put the tool down and pulled at the flooring. "Rolls back like the top of a sardine can!"

"What's under it?"

"Looks like mud or putty of some sort. I suppose it's that plastic the American was talking about."

"How much is there?"

Thompson kept pulling on the veneer. "Looks like it goes back about halfway."

"Will it come up?"

"Appears to pull right up," Thompson said. He began to hand pieces of the dangerous explosive to Murray. He said, "There is some plastic wrap in the satchel. Let's secure this material."

Within a few minutes, all of the explosive material had been removed from the casket and wrapped. Thompson replaced the lead and pressed it down, then began to put the lining back in place.

CHAPTER THIRTY-SIX

KING AND BROGAN had climbed down the back side of the building and circled around behind the two Soviet agents. "Okay, Sport," King whispered. "You take the guy on the left. I'll get the big guy. We're using blades, old boy," he continued, handing a knife to Brogan. "No need to draw attention or a crowd."

With catlike stealth, they approached the men from the rear and could hear them speaking in Russian. King attacked a split second before Brogan, but neither victim had a chance to scream or do anything to defend themselves. They plunged their weapons into the men with surgical precision, then dragged the lifeless bodies around a corner where they threw them down an unlit stairwell. Brogan saw a tarp nearby and flung it down the stairs, where it blanketed the dead Russians. They hoped the bodies would not be discovered until well after daybreak.

Which was still hours away.

"OUR WORK HERE is done," Murray said with a sense of satisfaction as he closed the lid of the casket. "I'll get the light. You carry the satchel as you were when we came in."

"Yes, of course, since I'm the one who looks like the hired hand," Thompson replied.

They made their way back to the station where young Winston Fleming was deeply engrossed in a book. He barely noticed the men.

"Interesting reading?" Murray asked, trying to break the ice and bring the youth's attention to their return.

"Yes, it is, sir! In fact, while you were in the room with the casket, I realized that I had a copy of Mr. Thompson's book in my office. Mr. Thompson, your stories are fascinating!" Fleming said enthusiastically.

"Why, thank you, young man," Thompson replied, impressed with the lad's energy. "Would you like me to sign your book?"

"Well, I don't want to take advantage, but I was going to ask if you'd do just that. It would be an honor," he said, his voice filled with excitement.

"Not a problem." Thompson took the book from Fleming's eager hands, smiling as he flipped to the inside cover, where he wrote a heartfelt note: *"To Winston Fleming, a wonderful young man named after a great man. – All the Best, Walter Thompson."*

Winston Fleming teared up as he read the inscription, genuinely touched by the gesture. He never asked, or even wondered, about what might be in the satchel Walter Thompson was carrying.

"Thank you so much, Mr. Thompson. I can't tell you how much this means to me," Fleming said, holding the book as if it were a treasure.

"Not at all, young fellow. It's the least I could do for someone so dedicated to a great man's legacy. Keep reading those stories," Thompson replied warmly.

THOMPSON AND MURRAY moved briskly down the dimly lit street, filled with the knowledge that their mission had been successful, but also that they were not yet in the clear. The chill of the night air seemed to sharpen their senses as they turned the corner and suddenly stopped in their tracks.

Less than half a block away, they saw two familiar figures striding quickly toward them. The men were unmistakable in their determined gait—Harvey King and Tiernan Brogan, who had obviously been waiting for them to emerge. "Friends of yours?" Murray asked Thompson with a note of surprise, his eyes not leaving the approaching figures.

"Indeed they are," Thompson replied with a knowing smile. "They're the men sent by President Johnson." He looked back toward Murray to gauge his reaction.

By now, all four men were face to face, standing under the harsh glow of a streetlamp. King, with his characteristic urgency, spoke up first. "We need to get you men out of here," he said. "Had some company. Friends of the same bastards we met in Birmingham."

Murray's curiosity was piqued. "Where are they?"

Harvey King grinned, the corners of his mouth twisting with a sense of satisfaction. "They're sleeping," he said cryptically. He turned his attention back to Thompson. "Who's this man, Thompson?"

"This is Mr. Edmund Murray of Scotland Yard. He's been taking care of Mr. Churchill for many years."

Tiernan Brogan interjected with a teasing tone. "Oh, so you took Thompson's old job," he said, throwing an almost playful glance at Murray.

Murray showed a twinge of annoyance but answered with composure. "Yes. Something like that."

Harvey was impatient to know more. "What's the situation, Walter? Is it as bad as we feared?"

"Well, Mr. King," Thompson responded, visibly relieved to share the burden, "it's as you said. We found enough explosive to level a city block. We have it all right in here." He raised the satchel slightly to emphasize the gravity of the contents.

"Then that means we're still at risk," King said, looking over his shoulder as if expecting an ambush.

"Best we get the hell out of here," Brogan said, urgency in his voice. "A lot of bad people out and about."

They moved as a unit, with Thompson and Murray flanking the satchel and King and Brogan watching both the front and back. The streets were empty but for a few stray cats and the occasional vagrant. They turned corner after corner, the sound of their footsteps echoing off the brick-faced buildings around them.

Almost on cue, the uncomfortable silence was broken by the screech of a car tire in the distance. The noise seemed to light a fire under them as they quickened their pace toward the nearest station. They knew that the longer they stayed in the area, the greater the risk they faced. When they reached the station, it was as if a collective breath was released, but only briefly.

THEY ARRIVED AT Walter Thompson's flat shortly after eleven o'clock. Exhaustion had etched dark rings under their eyes, but urgency kept them moving. Meanwhile, Edmund Murray returned to Hyde Park Gate.

Mary was waiting up for her husband, an embroidered blanket draped over her lap. Her eyes widened with mild surprise at the unexpected entourage, but she quickly entered full hostess mode. "My, oh my, what a pleasant surprise," she exclaimed, smoothing the creases from her skirt. "My husband didn't tell me he was bringing young Americans for supper!" She observed the strain on their faces and set to dispel some of it. "I've made a late meal for Mr. Thompson, but there's plenty. Will you men be staying for a bit?"

Harvey King glanced wistfully toward the kitchen. "Well, that's mighty fine of you, Mrs. Thompson. We'd love something to eat.

But we have to leave soon thereafter. We need to find a new hotel. Had some trouble at the *Dorchester.*"

Mary's eyebrows arched inquisitively. She looked over at Walter. He nodded as if to confirm the seriousness of the situation without dwelling on it further. "I wouldn't hear of it. You'll stay right here for the night," she said emphatically, her tone leaving no room for argument. "It's far too late to be hunting a room."

"Are you sure?" Brogan asked, though his voice carried an undertone of relief.

"Of course, I am. You fine gentlemen represent the President of the United States. What kind of harridan would I be if I didn't help you?"

The men exchanged quick, grateful glances, and King turned back to Mary with genuine appreciation in his voice. "Thank you kindly. We accept," not bothering to ask what harridan meant.

"Walter, speaking of the President, I need to place a call to one of his men," King added as an afterthought. "Might I use your telephone? You'll be reimbursed for the call. "

THOMPSON CAREFULLY CLOSED the door, leaving Harvey King undisturbed in the small and dimly lit room he used as an office. On the second ring, the gravelly voice of Allen Dulles came on the line.

Using the codename he and Dulles had settled on long ago for covert operations, King began his report. "This is Little Harry. Problem confirmed and neutralized," he said, his voice calm but carrying a note of urgency.

"That's great news, Little Harry. Were there any challenges?" Dulles replied. His voice was steady, but there was also a discernible note of relief in his words.

"Two. But both are under wraps. I think we need to round up some others. Could use a few more hands," King responded, hinting at the complex network of involvements that still needed to be addressed.

"Yes, of course. Recommendations?" Dulles inquired, assuredly expecting King to have some expert insights on how to proceed.

"I'd start with a mutual friend who works with us closely and build it out from there." King's suggestion left no doubt as to who he meant.

"Ah, yes. Consider it done. I'll have some boots on the ground to meet up with you in less than twenty-four hours." Dulles swiftly agreed, already orchestrating the deployment of men with precision and foresight.

"Roger that. Little Harry signing off," King said, concluding the conversation with the satisfaction of a man who knew the matter was in competent hands.

"Good luck, my friend." The words were simple but genuine, illustrating the deep bond and mutual reliance between the two men in this high-stakes affair. Dulles was already thinking several steps ahead.

CHAPTER THIRTY-SEVEN

WASTING NO TIME at all, Dulles promptly dialed another number. "Hunt, this is Allen. I need you at my office in two hours. And I need you to bring four trustworthy friends." Dulles spoke with the authority of a man used to being obeyed without question.

"Absolutely, Allen. What's up?" came the immediate response. Hunt's tone was eager and free from hesitation, emblematic of someone well-accustomed to such urgent summons.

"I'll brief you at the office. Oh, and make sure you and your friends pack bags. You're going on a trip." Dulles gave the instructions with the clarity of someone who expected thorough preparedness for extensive and uncertain tasks ahead.

"Might I at least ask for how long?" Hunt queried, knowing well that the answer would be indefinite.

"Long as it takes, Howard." Dulles finished the call and sat for a moment, his mind already racing with the next moves in this intricate and clandestine game.

Dulles emerged from his study and made his way down the hallway, lost in thought but certain of his next moves. Hunt was assembling a crack team; soon they would be over the Atlantic. Dulles knew that Johnson would want to be briefed as soon as possible, even if it meant interrupting the President's evening meal for this urgent intelligence.

He grabbed his coat and hat and hurried out the door to his Cadillac. The streets of Washington were quieter than usual for a Sunday afternoon as he guided the car through Georgetown and along the familiar route he had traveled countless times before. He was at the White House within minutes. Though it was not yet six p.m., the sky was an inky black with the chill of January all around.

Despite not having called ahead, Dulles had no difficulty passing through the gate. His face was well known to many of the men who worked at 1600 Pennsylvania Avenue, a recognition that stretched back to his time as President Eisenhower's closest confidant in matters of espionage. Now, as then, the urgency of his business was self-evident.

Once inside the West Wing, he approached a slender young man at a reception desk who seemed startled by the unexpected appearance of such a distinguished figure. "Please ring the residence and have someone tell the President that I need to see him immediately about a matter of great urgency," Dulles instructed with a tone that brooked no dissent.

"But sir—the President is having dinner with the first lady," the young man stammered, clearly uncomfortable with breaching such a domestic setting.

"I'm aware it's suppertime, young man," Dulles said, his voice carrying the weight of authority and a touch of impatience. "You know who I am, right?"

"Yes, Mr. Dulles, but I—"

"But nothing. You just do as I say. The consequences are on me."

The young man frowned, but the severity of Dulles's demand left no room for argument. He picked up the telephone and relayed the message exactly as he had been told. Soon, Dulles was being ushered into the dining room on the second floor of the residence. President Johnson and Lady Bird were just finishing their meal.

"Oh, I'm so sorry, Mrs. Johnson—didn't mean to interrupt your meal," Dulles said with a perfunctory politeness, seeing the First Lady get up from the table and begin gathering dishes as he entered.

Lady Bird turned and said with a forgiving smile, "It's fine, Mr. Dulles."

"Allen, come right in. Don't mind Bird—she has work to do. I imagine you have some news from our friends across the ocean. Am I right?" Johnson said, clearly in good spirits as he gestured for Dulles to take a seat.

"Yes, I got a call from Harvey King a bit ago. He confirmed the whole thing. They dug enough plastic explosive out of the big casket to blow up a city block. But they got it all. And we think no one is the wiser."

"You mean, the Russians still think the bomb is intact?"

"Yes, sir."

"Son of a bitch. Aren't they going to shit their commie pants when they wait for a big boom that never comes," Johnson said, grinning like a triumphant cat.

"Which brings me to another point."

"Yes?"

"I think we need to send a few more hands over there as soon as possible to round up the people who've plotted such a horrific thing. We've got the upper hand, sir. This could be a huge intelligence and operational victory for our side."

"Do you have someone have in mind?"

"I'd like to send Howard Hunt. In fact, he's assembling a small team to meet at my office in about an hour. I can have them in

England, completely off the record and under the radar, by this time tomorrow, if not before."

"You trust this Hunt fellow?"

"Completely, sir. He worked with us in the Bay of Pigs thing and is discreet as hell."

"Well, that Bay of Pigs thing was a clusterfuck, Allen. You know that."

"Yes, of course. But I also know there was much more to that story than what meets the eye."

"I suppose. You spooks and your wilderness of mirrors bullshit. Just don't drag this administration down through any fucking looking glass, you hear me?"

"Yes, of course. I'll keep it clean and covert. But I think we're going to learn a lot about our enemies over the next few days. Churchill's funeral service is scheduled for Saturday. They plan for it to be interrupted by terror. We now know that's not going to happen. But we'd sure as hell like to scare the hell out of them for once."

"Go to it. When you go out, have that boy bring me a double Cutty."

LESS THAN AN hour after Johnson asked for the scotch at the White House, Howard Hunt and his men arrived at Dulles's office on K Street. The old spy chief was waiting for them, leaning back in his chair behind a large wooden desk and puffing on his pipe. Five chairs were lined up, ready for the group. *No time to waste*, Hunt thought. He appreciated that. He had rounded up four of the most reliable associates he could find on short notice, all of them men with a history of "unofficial" business—missions that never officially existed.

At Hunt's side were Ferguson Matthews, Frank Sturgis, Howard Perlstein, and James McCord, each man as tightly wound with anticipation as Hunt himself. They were all experts in covert operations and had been around long enough to know the stakes were seldom low.

When he saw them, Dulles laid his pipe in a small ashtray on the desk. "You boys ready for an adventure?" he asked. There was a twinkle in his eye, the kind they all recognized.

Hunt nodded and replied with confidence. "I can assure you, Allen, these men are the best of the best."

"Or at least the best available on short notice on a cold-as-hell January night," Dulles quipped.

There was laughter, short but genuine. "That could be true, too, sir," Hunt said, smiling at how quickly he had managed to bring them together.

Dulles motioned for everyone to sit. His voice turned serious, the kind of serious those men understood.

"Find a seat, and I'll bring you up to speed," Dulles said. "I'm sending you to England—unofficially—to help fix a problem for us. I want you to know the President of the United States is aware of your mission, but he can never be connected to it. It's off the books, boys. Understand?"

There was a collective, "Yes, sir."

"Howard, how'd you round up this crew so quickly?" Dulles asked. "You men work together before?"

"Yes, Allen. These men are experienced operatives. We last worked together on that Mongoose thing down in Florida. Before— well...you know," Hunt said, sheepishly.

"Yes, Hunt. I know. We all know." Dulles stood, satisfied with the answer. "Excellent. Now you men head over to Davis Field in Manassas. I've got a DC-3 fueled and ready for you. Crew of two. You'll fly into a small airport about thirty miles northeast of London. A colleague of mine will meet you there and get you to the city, where you'll meet up with the leader of this mission. Harvey King."

The men looked at one another.

The mention of King's name stirred them. They all knew King's reputation. If he was involved, it meant their mission was both critical and dangerous—real 007 stuff. They were chosen for their ability to handle both. The meeting wrapped up quickly. There was no time to linger at the office. In less than an hour, the team was heading out of Washington in a gray sedan. Conversations in the car were clipped and intense.

"Harvey King." McCord said with a wide grin. "I'll be damned. This is big."

AT DAVIS FIELD, a small private airport in Manassas, the DC-3 was waiting for them as Dulles had promised. It was not a new aircraft, but it was reliable, and it was theirs for the night. The crew, which included a young but competent pilot and his much older co-pilot, was already on board.

"Well, here we go, boys," Hunt said as they climbed the steps up into the large propeller plane. "Let's see if we can defuse this thing before anyone knows we were even there."

They settled into the cargo area, which was sparsely outfitted but sufficient for operatives accustomed to working under less-than-luxurious conditions. The seating was hardly comfortable, but they settled in for the long flight. They were all glad to be in the thick of a high-stakes mission, even with the prospect of a cramped and chilly night. The plane lumbered down the runway with its telltale growl and began to reach for the skies.

About ten minutes after takeoff, the co-pilot, a fellow named Clark Williams, came back to the cargo area. He said, "Okay boys, this bird is equipped with an extra tank of fuel, but we're going to have to make a couple of quick stops to get over—one in St John's and the other in Iceland. We're on a tight schedule, so no more than fifteen minutes at each spot. You can get off and stretch your legs, but you want to avoid being noticed."

"Thank you, Clark. How long to St. John's?"

The co-pilot looked at his watch. "I figure we'll be there in a little less than five hours. So get some shut eye. I don't know what you men will be doing in England, but I suspect you won't be sleeping much once you get there."

"You heard him," Hunt said. He wadded up his trench coat to use as a pillow.

CHAPTER THIRTY-EIGHT

London
January 26, 1965

AT ABOUT THE same time the team en route to England stopped to refuel in Newfoundland, Harvey King, Tiernan Brogan, and Walter Thompson were sitting at the table in the Thompsons' modest flat. The first glimmers of morning light crept through the floral curtains. Mary Thompson served them a fine full-English breakfast.

Before them was a hearty feast. Fried eggs, grilled tomatoes, fried mushrooms, bacon, sausage, baked beans, and thickly sliced toast slathered with butter. Brewing tea filled the air with a comforting aroma that mingled with the smell of the feast. Harvey, a man renowned for his robust appetite, was almost beside himself with anticipation as he surveyed the bounty.

He grabbed his fork, barely able to contain his eagerness.

"Walter, you're one lucky lawman," King exclaimed. "She cooks like this for you every morning?"

"Not every morning, but once a week or so," Thompson replied with a smile, his voice brimming with pride. "Most mornings it's just porridge and tea. But nothing is too good for men representing the President of the United States."

"Hell, I may need a nap after breakfast," King groaned playfully, looking at the food with eyes bigger than his stomach.

Mary chuckled as she poured tea. "I always tell my husband what my mother told my father. Eat breakfast like a king, lunch like a prince, and dinner like a pauper. This is why my Walter is in such great shape for his age," she said, casting an affectionate glance at her husband.

"You must be on to something. This looks delicious," Brogan said, ready to dig in.

"How many men are coming from the States?" Thompson asked.

"I believe it's five, but not sure. I do know the leader of the group," King said, speaking between bites. "He's an old pal of mine in the business. A fellow named Howard Hunt. He's top shelf and knows how to run an operation and manage a team."

"When do you expect these men? Where will they stay?" Mary asked. Her voice was a mixture of concern and curiosity.

"I'm sure we can find some arrangements for them," King replied, rubbing his jaw. "They won't be here until close to noon. Long flight on a slow plane."

Mary nodded, a thoughtful expression crossing her face. "I was talking to Walter last night about this. One of our neighbors, Mrs. Shelby, is on holiday in Greece right now. She'll be gone a month. I have her key. I look in on her cat every day. She has a nice flat—bigger than ours, actually. Now, if your boys can behave themselves—and if they don't mind a grumpy old cat—I'm sure her place would work for them for a couple of days. Nothing long term, mind you."

King paused, touched by the generous offer. "That's very generous," he said sincerely. "I can assure you we don't plan to stay around long. Once our work is done, we'll be out of your hair."

"Fine, then. I'll prepare it all for five guests," Mary replied decisively. "But all the meeting, eating and drinking, will be done in this flat."

"Whatever you say, Ma'am," King replied, his voice filled with gratitude. The men resumed their breakfast, finishing every last bite as if savoring one final indulgence before duty called.

AFTER BREAKFAST, THE three men retreated to the cozy living room, its simple comfort providing a backdrop to what promised to be a tense planning session. Floors creaked slightly under their footsteps as Harvey, Tiernan, and Walter settled into the space, each man finding a seat amidst the clutter of papers and books.

"Well, 007, what's next?" Brogan asked after a short pause.

"That depends," the older man replied, stroking his chin thoughtfully. "First thing to know is if the bodies of our two friends have been discovered yet."

"No tellin'," Brogan said. "But why were they there, anyway? You think maybe they were following Walter and Murray, or just casing the funeral home on their own?"

"Big difference between those two scenarios," King said. "If they were following our guys, then yeah, the Soviets would know they were onto something. They'd be expecting their boys to check in, and once they didn't, the alarm would go off for sure. But I think it's more likely that they had just gone back to watching Kenyon's, then saw Walter and Murray going in, which would have the same effect either way. If they were just at the funeral home routinely, then the bodies being found would only be a red flag if they think we already know what's going on."

"Not much of a difference, then," Brogan replied.

"A hell of a difference! If they were just observing and not following, they wouldn't have had enough time to report back before lights out. Our lead would be a lot longer."

Brogan asked, "But when the bodies *are* found, won't that alert the Soviets that there was activity at the funeral home?"

"Yes," King said slowly. "But we can hope the casket has its occupant before that happens—and is long gone from the funeral home. Not likely anyone will disturb it then."

Walter Thompson weighed in. "Let's think this through," he said. "If they found the bodies before the casket went out, wouldn't they pull the plug on the whole operation?"

"They might," King replied, cautiously. "But even if they did, within a matter of hours, everything we need to confirm what they're up to will already be in place. They'll have to watch and wait to see if what they've planned actually comes off."

"So, you and this Hunt fellow have some history?" Brogan asked, changing the subject.

Walter Thompson listened as Harvey King warmed to the new line of conversation.

"I should say so," King replied. "We worked together on an operation south of the border back in '54."

"Guatemala?" Brogan pressed. "It's a pretty well-known story in our ranks."

"And a successful one," King said. "It's what we should've done in Cuba in '61 at the Bay of Pigs. Hunt was in that one, too. Eisenhower was willing to do what needed to be done. Kennedy didn't have the stones to finish what Ike started. He was a lot more profile than courage, frankly."

"I heard he was working on something big for Cuba before he was assassinated."

"Yeah. He and brother Bobby really wanted to off Castro. Even roped the mob into the effort."

"Think that's what got him killed?"

Thompson was listening to this with great interest, missing the old days in harm's way. "For what it's worth, he could've learned a lot from my old boss," he interrupted.

King nodded. "Actually, Jack had great admiration for Mr. Churchill," he replied. "But he was more of a politician than a real leader of men. I think he died because he left too many missions unfinished."

"Care to elaborate?" Brogan asked King, whose expression turned strangely serious.

Harvey was lost in thought for a moment, like a man with a painful secret to tell. But he caught himself. "No. Not at all. Water under the bridge. I just hope Johnson learns from his predecessor's mistakes."

Thompson remarked, "Well, the fact you two gentlemen are here—with more on the way—seems to speak powerfully to that point."

King was silent for a moment, conscious of the weariness in his own voice. The past indeed cast a long shadow over the work that lay ahead. "I suppose so," he said. "But this Vietnam business could be tricky for him."

Brogan remarked, "My guess is, if you pull this operation off, Harvey, the Cold War will get a little hotter and all bets will be off."

The conversation had taken a sobering turn, and Thompson was the first to break the growing silence.

"You fellas will have to tell me more about Hunt," Thompson said. "Sounds like a real character."

King chuckled. "Oh, he's a character, all right. But I'll let you find out for yourself when he gets here. Maybe before we put him to work in that borrowed flat, we can dust off a bottle of Scotch and get a few more war stories out in the open. He knows a lot of them, and I have a hunch you'll be hearing a lot from our other partners."

"I suppose I should be thankful Mary can handle all this hospitality," Thompson said.

"You have a good thing going, Walter," King said. "Mary's a real treasure."

"Thanks for a wonderful breakfast, Walter," Brogan said. "We'll see you in a few."

"Good luck," Thompson said. "I'll not be far if you run into any trouble."

King and Brogan took their leave, filled with a new sense of purpose. Thompson, meanwhile, remained in the flat, catching his breath and readying himself for the next round.

THE BUZZER ON the desk sounded loudly, startling Roger Hollis from his reverie. The noise was a constant irritation—made worse by the knowledge it usually meant trouble of some kind. He pushed the button, "Yes, Sean?"

"Might I have a moment with you, Director?"

"Of course. Come right in."

Sean Welling was standing in front of Hollis an instant later. Roger could read in his body language what his words soon confirmed. "Sir, we have a bit of a problem."

"I'm listening," the Director replied, suppressing a grimace.

"Two of our friends seem to be missing."

"Missing?" Hollis asked sharply, his voice betraying more emotion than he wanted it to.

"Indeed. They haven't checked in for several hours. Some other friends are conducting a search, but because of what happened to the men in Birmingham, there is obvious concern."

"Concern?" Hollis repeated.

"Yes, Director, at the highest levels," Sean confirmed, making a point to lock eyes with the MI5 chief.

Fear crossed Hollis's face. "I see. Thanks, Sean. Please keep me posted."

"Very good, sir. I will."

Sean turned and began to leave the office, but Roger called out, "Sean, is there a way you could arrange another meeting with our friend at the *Savoy*?"

"Certainly, sir. I'll set it up. Lunch today?"

"Yes. But let him know we'll eat in his room. And please tell him that it's urgent," Hollis said.

"IT'S A MANHUNT now, Brogan," King said. "We need to go back to that building and follow the bad guys wherever they go. We should operate on the assumption they have no clue that their bomb has been neutralized."

Brogan replied, "Think the target is Westminster? That's where the body is going today. According to the paper, the public viewing will start early tomorrow morning."

King answered. "No. I think the target is St Paul's on Saturday. That's what our intel suggests. The attack was supposed to be designed to kill some major players on the world stage. Take 'em out so the commies can gobble up Europe. No bigwigs will be all in one place until the funeral service itself. So that's the place we need to check out," King replied, showing the impatience of a man anxious for the fight.

"Think they have someone on the inside there?"

"I sure as hell would," King snapped.

"Well, that scenario buys us some time. We'll have reinforcements tonight."

"And let's make sure we use the next few hours wisely. Once they're here, we need to know where to send the cavalry."

CHAPTER THIRTY-NINE

Paris

IT HAD BEEN several months since Henri Girard had been contacted by his handler, and he was long overdue for a meeting. Generally, the man he knew simply as "Peter" gave Henri about forty-eight hours' advance notice. But the person Peter had used a few hours earlier—the one with the enchanting female voice—was clear, "Yes, he will meet you for coffee at the usual place in two hours."

Now, Girard waited at one of many similar-looking places along the famous boulevard. The Champs-Élysées was now a bold, beautiful, and busy thoroughfare. Quite a contrast from the war years when few people, and fewer automobiles, were moving about.

Henri was mildly curious as he sipped his espresso. His jet-black hair was slicked down close to his scalp, and his pencil-thin mustache was heavily waxed. He was wearing a dark business suit, complete with a starched white shirt adorned by cufflinks bearing the NATO logo. After he had finished reading the first few pages of *Le Monde*, he looked up and saw Peter approaching.

They shook hands and ordered coffee—Henri's third cup.

"Thank you for meeting on such short notice, my friend," Peter began. "There's a matter of great importance I need to share with you."

"Of course," Henri replied. "I have some time. I took a few hours of time off from the office."

"Ah yes, the office. This is what our people are interested in. The time is fast approaching for a moment of great importance."

"Intriguing. What can you tell me?"

"Of course, you know that our friends have a propensity for compartmentalization."

"Yes, yes. I'm well aware. I've been working with them for more than twenty years, you know."

"Certainly. I know your file very well. We have an important assignment for you as part of a great plan that will change the course of France, Europe, and the world."

At that, Henri took a sip of his coffee and carefully folded his newspaper. "I'm listening."

"You are aware of Mr. Churchill's death and the upcoming funeral in London?"

"Yes, of course. About half this newspaper is about this," Henri said, pointing emphatically at the folded copy of *Le Monde*. "But our friends have no great affection for the infamous anti-Bolshevik. How does his death translate into some kind of master plan?"

"It's called KOBA." Peter filled Henri in on the basic details of the plan.

Henri was impressed, but a bit skeptical. "And where do I fit into this?" he asked.

"Simple, my friend. We need you to activate your old skills and eliminate your boss, Manlio Brosio—the Secretary General of NATO."

"My, oh my—that *is* quite a plan. And how do you propose I pull this off? He's surrounded by several layers of security."

"We leave the details to you. But it would be best if his death looked like an accident at first, so as not to hint of a conspiracy. We want our enemies to be off-balance and distracted at the crucial moment."

"Anything else?"

"Yes. Please find a way to give us the most recent details about NATO troop placements."

"Good God, Peter. You want me to climb the Eiffel Tower while I'm at it?"

Peter smiled and lit a cigarette. "No need for that. There will be plenty of time for such things once the Soviet Army controls this decadent city."

"What about De Gaulle? Any plans for him?"

"Were you not listening, Henri?"

"I don't follow."

"He will die with so many others when that church is destroyed right in the middle of long-winded eulogies about Churchill's pathetic life. Think of it as Stalin's revenge."

The broad implications of what Peter had said left Henri Girard momentarily stunned and unable to produce a reply. And Henri, a man used to navigating the dangerous waters of espionage and political intrigue, felt a twinge of uncertainty. It was a massive undertaking, a conspiracy that would reverberate throughout the Western world, and he was only fully now realizing the gravity of his involvement. He paused to gather his thoughts, trying to reconcile his instincts for self-preservation with the allure of being part of such a monumental event.

"Stalin's revenge," he said at last, nodding slowly as if granting his own assent.

Peter leaned back in his chair, reassured by Henri's reaction. He sipped his coffee and let the silence linger, knowing that his words had effectively captured Henri's imagination. "Nothing like a Hollywood ending," he said with understated satisfaction. The lightness in Peter's voice belied the severity of the scheme, but both men knew the stakes were as high as they could be.

As Peter lit another cigarette, the smoke spiraled lazily upward, mirroring the precarious nature of the situation they were discussing, Henri seemed to regain some of his composure. Despite the perilous nature of the assignment, he was still an operative of considerable skill and experience. "When will I have what I need?" he asked, signaling his acceptance and readiness to proceed.

"When the time is right, you'll know," Peter replied, exhaling a thin line of smoke. He was confident that Henri understood the cryptic message hidden in his words; it was only a matter of days before everything would be set into motion. The timing, as always, was crucial, and Peter knew that Henri's patience would be tested as plans unfolded.

Henri folded his arms, his expression thoughtful yet tinged with apprehension. Would he be able to turn his years of careful, often tedious work into the coup de grace that his comrades now demanded? "So there is nothing more?" he asked, letting a hint of tension seep into his voice.

"More than enough to keep you busy," Peter replied with a smile. He stubbed out his cigarette and finished his coffee. It was obvious Peter had absolute faith in the eventual outcome, an assurance that both comforted and troubled Henri.

Moments later, Peter stood to leave, extending a hand to Henri with an air of finality. "We will be in touch," he promised. "Until then, be careful. There is much riding on this."

They shook hands, and Peter walked briskly out the door, quickly blending into the crowd of people on the busy boulevard. Henri watched him go, feeling a mixture of anticipation and dread. He had been entangled in numerous schemes before, but this was of an entirely different magnitude. The implications were staggering, and as he sat back down at the small café table, he wondered just how deeply the plan would entangle him.

Henri ordered another coffee and unfolded *Le Monde*, pretending to lose himself in its pages while his mind raced. Each sip from his cup felt like a small act of defiance against the enormity of what he had just agreed to. With mounting anxiety, he read and reread the stories about Churchill's funeral preparations, searching for details about the world leaders and dignitaries who would be in attendance—De Gaulle, Johnson, Adenauer, King Olav of Norway, King Frederik of Denmark, and so many others. Just how many would die, he wondered, at this unprecedented occasion?

The Champs-Élysées remained busy around him, full of life, motion, and sound. He tried to let its comforting bustle soothe his nerves. His resolve hardened. He would be a part of history. He left a tip and carelessly tossed the unfolded newspaper on the table. Moving with an unhurried but determined stride, he made his way to the avenue, consumed now by the tremendous stakes of the operation and the delicate roles he would be called upon to play.

London

THE ORDER FROM room service at the Savoy, consisting of two bacon sandwiches and a bottle of Johnnie Walker Black Label was waiting on the table when Roger Hollis knocked impatiently on the door. Five minutes early, if the clock was to be trusted. Kim Philby finished a drink and answered the door, greeting his guest with a devilish grin.

"Late enough in the day for you yet, old man?"

A deep breath and a weary smile preceded Hollis's answer. "Nothing for me, Kim. Except maybe some tea."

"Way ahead of you," Philby said. "Right there on the table."

The two men ate and talked. The sandwiches were excellent, and the conversation was even more delicious to the two conspirators.

"Two of our friends haven't been heard from for several hours. I'm concerned about what it means."

Philby raised a brow, but didn't interrupt. To him, a few hours seemed trivial. But Roger was the cautious type. "Where were these 'friends' supposed to be?" he asked.

"Last we knew, they were keeping an eye on the Kenyon building." Hollis lowered his voice, as if someone might overhear.

"Ah yes, the favorite of the royals," Philby said with casual disdain.

"That's where the casket is right now," Hollis said. "A bit later today, it'll be taken to Churchill's home at Hyde Park Gate. From that point, the body will be in it, and there will be no access."

"So I'd imagine you're concerned the package may not be all that secure?" Philby did not stop eating, his demeanor cool and indifferent.

"Yes, and I need you to communicate that to our friends. Please make sure they understand that we have no confirmation the secret has been discovered. But they should know."

Philby looked across the table, eyes gleaming with amusement behind the fog of cigarette smoke. "All r-right, R-roger," he said, exaggerating his stutter for effect. "I'll pass the information along and l-let you know the reply." He took a large bite from his sandwich and smiled. "I've missed food like this. Nothing like it in Moscow." He poured himself another drink, leaving the tea untouched for Hollis. "Of course, you know I'd rather be there."

Hollis glanced nervously at the door, then back at Philby. He lowered the edge of resignation in his voice. "I wouldn't be so sure about that. You'll be dead or jailed for life if you set foot there again. I think your dear friends have written you off for good."

Philby leaned in like a schoolboy about to tell a secret. "Were that true, I'd be the f-f-first to know. No, my friend, I'm back and fully in the game here."

Hollis was getting used to Philby's brand of sarcasm, but there was still something unnerving about his flippant attitude. After all, this was about more than a missing package.

"What can you tell me about KOBA?" Hollis asked with an edge of insistence in his voice. "Are we all systems go?"

Philby took his time before answering. He poured more whisky, pushed his empty sandwich plate aside, and lit another cigarette.

"Yes, we are all systems go!" he said with a loud laugh as if they were two kids preparing some schoolyard prank. "And this is just the beginning. London will mark the greatest act of terrorism in history. The funeral will be like no other."

CHAPTER FORTY

THE BLACK ROLLS ROYCE hearse, gleaming like polished onyx, pulled up to the service door at Kenyon Funeral Directors on that gray and somber Tuesday afternoon. It was a little past three when the hearse arrived, precisely on time according to the careful plans laid out by authorities. The timing of this event had not been disclosed to the public, as officials deemed it best to avoid significant crowds and the inevitable congestion of London traffic.

The air felt heavy with secrecy and sacred duty. Despite the efforts to maintain discretion, however, news had indeed spread through whispered networks. Several hundred curious and somber Londoners had already gathered, waiting for the better part of the afternoon.

Largely hidden from the onlookers, a small team of men worked quickly to load the large, lead-lined casket into the back of the vehicle. Even in their haste, they took every care, knowing the casket carried the monumental weight of more than simply its occupant. Once it was securely fastened by heavy braces, the back door of the hearse closed.

A single car from Scotland Yard led the small procession as it pulled out from the lot. The stately hearse fell in behind the escort.

The vehicles turned left and circled around the building. When the small convoy finally came into the view of the waiting crowd, several people began to move toward the motorcade. But they were quickly motioned back by the driver of the first car. The hearse and its escort turned right onto a narrow street, passing an unassuming brick building and its nondescript stairwell.

That particular stairwell was the temporary resting place of the two "missing" Russian operatives—so close yet so hidden.

HARVEY KING AND Tiernan Brogan were among the many gathered outside Kenyon's at that hour. They had returned to the scene to ensure the dead bodies remained undiscovered. As the hearse pulled away and the spectacle of the casket's removal faded, the crowd thinned in short order. If the operatives were found now, it would be disastrous. Walter Thompson had arranged for King and Brogan to have a vehicle and cleared sufficient space in his basement freezer. It was just large enough to store the bodies until they could be permanently disposed of.

Once the coast was clear, Brogan cautiously maneuvered down the steps into the shadowy stairwell where the bodies lay. Hidden beneath a hastily arranged cloth, the corpses now seemed starkly exposed without the commotion of the crowd to mask them. He glanced around nervously as he stripped the covering away and rewrapped it around the first man. King had driven the vehicle up so close to the stairwell that it blocked nearly all view from the street. Brogan worked with urgency, lifting the bodies by himself and transferring them quickly from the concrete steps into the back of the vehicle.

As he slammed the back door shut, King said, "These fine gentlemen are going to have to stay back there until dark, Sport. Then we can put 'em on ice."

Brogan climbed over the gearshift and contorted his body to drop into the passenger seat. The thought of driving around London with dead Russians in the back didn't sit well with him. But he shrugged and said, "You're the boss."

THE BLACK HEARSE turned into South Kensington, winding its way past the iconic red brick buildings that characterized the area near 28 Hyde Park Gate. Despite the effort to conceal when the casket would be brought to the house, the news had leaked out and spread like wildfire.

Nearly a thousand spectators had gathered. They were held back by a light police presence, but none of them rushed forward, neither toward the hearse nor the house. Indeed, it was quite the opposite—the crowd respectfully maintained its distance, creating a silent pathway for the vehicle to proceed and park directly in front of the townhouse.

Several men, all known to the family, stepped forward to off-load the casket. Because it was lead lined, it required tremendous effort to lift, but the pallbearers were determined. They took slow, careful steps toward the front entrance of the home, moving in unison. A hush fell over the crowd, broken only by murmurs and whispers of condolence, words like "God bless him" and "Farewell, Winston." The men made their way up the narrow staircase.

Edmund Murray opened the door.

Once inside, they carried the casket to the rear of the house and into the bedroom where Winston Churchill had breathed his last. The interior was thick with emotion and history. The great man's body lay waiting, dressed in the full military uniform of his youth.

Three family friends carefully lifted him, their eyes heavy with the weight of duty and loss, and placed him in the casket. Clementine Churchill stood nearby, her normally composed and resilient form overwhelmed by the occasion. She was inconsolable, weeping as her husband disappeared into the coffin.

"How long before we must leave?" she asked the man who seemed to be leading the operation, her voice trembling yet composed.

"We don't plan to move him until it is well past dark, ma'am," the man replied with respect. "We'll be out of your way in a minute or two, that I promise. And if you need anything from us, please don't hesitate to ask. We're here to serve you and honor your wonderful husband. There likely wouldn't be much left of England were it not for him."

"Will you and your men be escorting him to Westminster Hall?" Clementine inquired.

"No, ma'am. A military honor guard will be here for that later on," he replied. His voice was steady, but his eyes, like those of the others present, were moist with tears.

FOR THE NEXT several hours, Clementine stayed in the room, lost in thought, each moment sinking deeper into a pool of memories. Members of the family and close friends took turns sitting with her. They were quiet at first, but soon it became a gathering of remembrance, a private tribute that was as personal as it was profound. As daylight faded, they shared stories of Churchill's life, from his turbulent early years to his unyielding leadership during the war—his triumphs to his defeats.

They spoke in hushed tones, their words painting a vibrant picture of the man they all loved. They wondered aloud how his loss might affect a nation that had been so accustomed to his presence and guidance.

About half past six, there was a stirring outside. The honor guard from the Royal Navy had arrived. Clementine watched with tearful eyes, yet with unmistakable pride, as the casket was closed.

Several more family members had arrived by that time. Randolph Churchill stood close to his mother. Diana and Mary were on either side of her. Many of the grandchildren were present, too. Lady Churchill embraced them all and then turned her attention back to the men who were preparing to move the casket.

The casket was again lifted by the family friends and taken through the house toward the front door. As it made its way outside, a slight drizzle began to fall from the gray London sky. The crowd remained eerily quiet. The line stretched two blocks, from 28 Hyde Park Gate to the entrance of Kensington Road.

The men placed the casket gently in the back of the hearse which was now flying the insignia of Buckingham Palace. It slowly pulled away from the curb and made its way toward what would be Winston Churchill's home for the next few days.

Westminster Hall.

There were eight cars in the procession. Three of them carried members of Churchill's family. They rode along Knightsbridge, past military personnel who lined the roads. The vehicles proceeded down Constitution Hill, the lights of London twinkling amid the fog and mist of the late evening. They moved past the gates of Buckingham Palace, then to Westminster, where the next leg of the journey would begin. The entire drive took barely five minutes because all traffic in the area was stopped.

Once inside New Palace Yard, eight Grenadier Guards stood ready to carry the casket into the Great Hall, led by an officer with a drawn sword, his every step synchronized with the dignified march of the guards. Clementine Churchill walked behind the casket along with her children and grandchildren.

The casket was placed on an enormous catafalque draped in black velvet with braided silver edges. The catafalque measured forty feet long, seventeen feet wide, and seven feet tall. A Union Jack flag was draped over the coffin. Dr. Michael Ramsey, the

Archbishop of Canterbury, received the casket with the gravity the occasion deserved and offered a brief prayer in Churchill's memory.

Five officers took up their watch positions.

After a few minutes, Lady Churchill and the rest of the family returned to their vehicles for the short ride back to Hyde Park Gate. Westminster Hall remained empty for the night, except for the vigilant guards. They served throughout the night—and week—in twenty-minute shifts.

CHAPTER FORTY-ONE

London
January 27, 1965

IT WAS MORNING when the DC-3 landed at Stapleford Aerodrome, a small airfield just northeast of London. After the aircraft taxied to a halt beside a partially dilapidated hangar, the men exited and were greeted by a chill that cut through their clothes. Awaiting them was an older man with a white beard, smoking the last inch of a cigar.

"Welcome, Gents!" he said, his voice thick with a Scottish lilt. "Name's Lithgow, Blair Lithgow. I hail from up north—a wee place we call Scotland. Mr. Dulles and I have an arrangement, so here I am. Your host for the next few days. Exciting they shall be, am I right?"

Hunt examined the man. "I can't say for sure, Mr. Lithgow," he replied for the group. "But we have a job to do which just may raise our blood pressure a point or two."

"Of that I'm sure, Mr. Hunt. Now, do you men need to visit the privy before we make the trip over to London? Your chariot awaits," Lithgow said, pointing to a gray panel truck parked nearby.

Lithgow took to the road as if it were a speedway, despite the early morning fog that reduced visibility to a few yards. Hunt winced as Lithgow narrowly avoided a collision with a coal delivery lorry. The pace did not relent as they traversed the countryside, the truck rattling every bone in their bodies. Two of Hunt's men— McCord and Perlstein—were soon clutching their stomachs, their faces pale and their distress unmistakable.

Forty-five minutes later, the truck screeched to a halt in front of Walter Thompson's modest brick building. A few minutes later, Harvey King gathered Hunt and his team around a large table. In a low voice, he briefed Hunt and his men about the latest developments. Then he told them to get some shut eye.

Mary Thompson was both gracious and stern as she led the new arrivals to the vacationing Mrs. Shelby's flat. She gave the men a few ground rules. "No eating over here. And please pick up after yourselves, gentlemen. We don't want to leave a mess."

"Yes, ma'am," Hunt said.

To a man, they were asleep within five minutes.

Washington, D.C.

PRESIDENT LYNDON JOHNSON sipped his third cup of coffee while sitting behind his desk in the Oval Office. He had been awake for much of the night, coughing and pacing the floor, and the caffeine was more necessity than indulgence. The desk was the same one he had used for years as a Senator and later as Vice President, dark and massive.

There were two telephones on his desk. One was a simple rotary model, its black casing and heavy receiver starkly utilitarian, suited to a man who valued function over form. The other was a special creation with six buttons and an attached speaker device, an apparatus uniquely engineered to Johnson's specifications. With characteristic impatience, Johnson forcefully punched one of the six buttons.

Bill Moyers came on the speaker almost instantly, "Yes, Mr. President?"

"Get in here," Johnson barked.

The young aide was through the Oval Office door in a handful of seconds, appearing as if he had sprinted the entire distance from his office. As he walked briskly toward the President's desk, he noticed that Johnson's televisions were, as usual, all on. The President, a man obsessed with both telephones and television for their immediate conveyance of power and information, had requested a specially built cabinet with three monitors; he had insisted on being able to watch all three networks—ABC, CBS, and NBC.

Simultaneously.

Johnson's voracious appetite for information and opinion, whether favorable or damning, meant that the screens were seldom dark. Moyers also observed that his boss was not dressed in his customary suit and tie but was still clad in his pajamas and a large, lavish silk robe, with comfortable slippers adorning his lanky feet.

"What can I do for you, Mr. President?" Moyers asked, his tone respectful yet informal. "How are you feeling, sir?"

Johnson's eyes were glued to the screens, and he ignored the preamble of small talk. "Did you see Hugh Downs's interview of Richard Nixon on that *Today* show?" he demanded.

"Sorry, sir. Don't have a television in my office," Moyers replied.

"Gotta fix that, Billy boy," Johnson retorted with a mixture of irritation and urgency. "Dick Nixon," he said, mockingly accenting the first name, "had the gall to criticize me for not going to the Churchill funeral. Says a common cold is no reason to miss it. That Churchill and the Brits went through hell to keep the world safe for democracy and all that shit. Kennedy was right about him. He's a cheap bastard."

Johnson's voice was a blend of disdain and exasperation, and his Texas drawl elongated the consonants in a way that gave them a biting twist. The mention of Kennedy brought a shadow briefly across his face. He resented that the ghost of the dead President still haunted the corridors of power and the expectations of the nation.

Moyers listened carefully, aware that his boss was fishing for affirmation as much as he was issuing a declaration. Trying to read the President's mood, he ventured a question: "Are you rethinking your decision, Sir?"

"Hell, no!" Johnson replied almost before the sentence was out of Moyers's mouth. "I'm still sick. In fact, I'm not even sitting here in this office at this moment. I'm in bed with a raging fever. Got that?"

"Of course, sir." Moyers was cautious yet clear. This was familiar territory, and the young aide knew how to navigate it. He watched Johnson's face closely as the President began to squint. It was his "tell"—the way aides knew he was about to either explode or ask something uncomfortable. "The world knows you aren't going—that's a done deal."

"You'd better be right," the President said, the intonation a mix of grudging agreement and paternal warning. Johnson reached for another sip of coffee, as if it were a final concession to the state of affairs. "You go back to that office of yours and have someone find you a television, you hear?"

"Yes, Mr. President. I will."

Moyers turned to leave, aware that his presence was no longer required or wanted. As he closed the door behind him, Johnson sank back into his chair and looked around the office, the seat of power he had spent his entire career angling to occupy.

He was the most powerful man in the world, yet he felt besieged by forces both seen and unseen—international chaos, domestic unrest, and the indelible legend of his martyred predecessor.

CHAPTER FORTY-TWO

London

HUNT AND HIS team squeezed around the table in Walter Thompson's flat. A hearty English breakfast awaited, a repeat of the meal that Harvey King and Tiernan had partaken of a day earlier, filling the air with the pleasant aroma of bacon and eggs. As plates were piled high and steaming cups passed hand to hand, lively conversation began to fill the room.

In this makeshift war room, each man was issued an assignment.

"We can't dismiss the possibility that the bad guys have plans for more than one bomb. And we're going to operate on the assumption they are none the wiser that we've removed the explosive shit from Churchill's casket. This should give us a big-ass advantage," King said, as he reached across the table for another piece of toast.

"Do we have a good read on all the official activities related to the funeral?" Hunt asked.

Brogan, who had been watching the others from the edge of the table, pulled a page from his coat pocket. "Yes. These things have been published widely," he said. He smoothed the paper out on the table with steady hands, then leaned in to scan it closely. "For example," he continued, "this morning at nine o'clock, people will start moving past the catafalque in Westminster Hall to pay respects. There are estimates that more than a quarter of a million people will do this between today and early Saturday. It'll be around the clock but for an hour each day when they'll halt the queue for the staff to spruce things up."

"Okay," King said, nodding as he considered the busy schedule. "So we need a couple of you guys to head over there this morning and check it all out—keep your eyes peeled for anything unusual. Tiernan—you should take one of these men with you. You know what some of the suspicious looking folks look like. We need to split up, since we're the only ones who could recognize any of the faces in the crowd."

"Fine, but I'd also like to check out St. Paul's," Brogan replied, raising a point that seemed to catch Hunt a bit off guard.

"Why? Nothing happening there until Saturday," Hunt interrupted, puzzled. "At least that's what I thought I read in the paper."

Brogan fixed a knowing look on Hunt and said, "I'm well aware of that, Howard. But you see, I imagine if they had been—and for all we know, still are—planning something big at the funeral service itself, they have someone on the inside."

"Of course," Hunt said, chastised. The realization of what Brogan implied struck him hard. "That would certainly follow."

"Well, you see, I've seen some faces. There's this lady I know from some of my hush-hush work when I was undercover for Five. She knows me as Sean Walsh from the IRA."

"How well does she know you?" Frank Sturgis asked, speaking up for the first time with a suggestive question that drew some throaty laughs from the other men.

"Well, um, we had our moments back in the day," Brogan replied, feeling a twinge of shame for embellishing things. Back in those days, any relationship with the red-haired beauty had existed only in his fantasies.

"Bet you did, old boy," King said with a hard slap on the back, causing Brogan to momentarily lose his breath.

Brogan composed himself and continued. "Her name's Kaitlyn Dorcey. I saw her the other night at a pub with an interesting crew."

King added, "That's right. And that led us to Birmingham and to clues that led us to the bomb in the box. What're you thinking, Brogan?"

"Just one of the blokes there. His face is imprinted on my brain. He was quiet, almost afraid, when I met him. It was just a brief thing, but something in my gut says that guy is in this thing up to his eyeballs. All I'm saying is I'd like to check both Westminster Hall and St. Paul's to see if this Higgins fellow is anywhere around."

"Okay, Sport. How about you head to St. Paul's first—let me and a couple of these guys head over to Westminster Hall. Take Hunt with you," King instructed, confident that Brogan knew what he was doing.

"Sounds like a plan," Brogan agreed, relieved to have his instincts trusted.

"Great. Let's head out in a few. Not all at once. Stagger it. We don't have a fucking parade permit. Watch your backs. Tradecraft, men. Tradecraft.

Walter, you come with us to Westminster."

"Splendid. Now, do you men have weapons?" Thompson queried.

The Americans chuckled. Hunt spoke for them "One of the benefits of flying below the radar, sir. We've brought our arsenal with us," he said, moving his suit jacket aside to reveal a gun.

Harvey added, "There's a pub called McRory's 'round the corner from St. Paul's. Let's meet up there half-past eleven."

Two of the Americans looked at their watches and realized they were still set to Eastern Time back home. They made the leap five hours forward, rechecked the time, and began to make quick work of settling the last of their gear.

Minutes ticked by as each team organized and reviewed their game plan, ensuring all the crucial points were covered. Brogan and Hunt headed off first. A couple of minutes later, the rest of the team left in pairs, looking like tourists trying to blend into the crowd. They made their way through the city with precision, ever cautious that they weren't being followed.

Time was on their side for the moment. As hundreds of thousands of citizens flocked to the streets to mourn their deceased leader, it would have been easy for someone to spot them. They took care to avoid that.

THE DAY BEGAN bleak, angry clouds spitting a few brief showers just long enough to scatter those who'd forgotten to bring umbrellas. Then the skies cleared. Both teams were in place at Westminster Hall and St. Paul's. They felt confident that they had their bases covered as they took their positions.

King and Thompson that at Westminster Hall the line ebbed and swayed like a massive living thing. When the doors closed, the line would thin. When they reopened, the serpent-like formation quickly gathered length. They had never seen anything like it.

It was a full day before Winston Churchill's casket would make its way through the city, but the people were determined. They stood strong in the defiant British spirit the great leader had inspired during the darkest days of war. Braving both cold and a relentless mist, they remained in a steadfast line for the opportunity to file past the catafalque and pay their last heartfelt respects.

Among those braving the elements was Adam Wilkinson, an RAF veteran who had flown Spitfires during the Battle of Britain.

With him was his young son Paul, and the two sat close together on a rain-soaked blanket, wrapped in their heavy coats. Adam often regaled the boy with tales of heroics during the war, always most fondly telling him about the day Churchill himself had visited the squadron.

On this night, the boy's eager questions were more about that day than about the funeral they had traveled from Yorkshire to attend. They were set on being among the first to pass by Westminster Hall when the queue began to move.

"Tell me again what happened when Mr. Churchill came to see you, Father," Paul said, his voice full of eagerness.

Through a gentle smile, Adam replied, "I've told you this story so many times, I'm certain you know it by heart."

He reached into a wicker basket at his side and handed the boy a boiled egg his wife had sent along for breakfast. "Here, Paul. Your mother will ask if you've eaten. She'll have my head if I say no."

Paul took the egg and began to peel it, hands chilled from the damp air. "How long before we go in? How long before we see him?" Paul asked, shivering a bit in spite of himself.

Adam glanced at his watch, tilting it to shield it from the drizzle. "Less than twenty minutes now. Won't be long at all."

"So there's time for the story once more. Please, Father?"

"Fine. Let's see. It was back in August of 1940," Adam said, turning his mind to those intense days. "Hitler's air force was—"

"The Luftwaffe!" interrupted Paul, eager to show he had listened well.

"Yes, Son. The Luftwaffe," Adam continued with a knowing grin. "They were bombing the city nearly every single day. Even some of these grand buildings—Parliament itself included—were badly damaged."

"Were you flying every day?"

"Not every day. No, I was sometimes stationed in the Operations Room. Our squadron was assigned to help with the aerial defense of London, a very critical job," Adam explained, his voice touched by both pride and nostalgia. "I was in the Ops Room working with Number Eleven Group, making sure all the boys in the air had the best possible information about the enemy's movements."

"And that's where Mr. Churchill showed up? That's where you met him?"

"Yes, it is, Son. On the sixteenth of August, he walked straight into the room where we were working."

"Was he smoking that big cigar?" Paul asked.

Adam chuckled. "He had it in his mouth. But, you know, he never lit it the entire time he spent with us."

"What did he say to you?" Paul asked, his eyes wide with curiosity.

"He asked me what my role was. And then, he shook my hand and said the nation owed me and all those in the room so much."

"But he said more, right? He said that famous thing. The one we read about at school. Wasn't it to you first, before the whole country heard it on the BBC?"

"Yes, indeed."

"Please say it again, Father."

"Well, Son, I'm sure you know it better than I do at this point," Adam said, pulling the boy closer against the chill. "Let me hear you recite those famous words."

"All right, Father. 'Never in the field of human conflict was so much owed by so many to so few.'"

"Perfect!" Adam replied, genuinely impressed. "Word for word."

"You know what I was just thinking?"

"I haven't the slightest clue, my dear boy."

"You could almost say it like this: 'Never in the field of human conflict was so much owed by so many to one man.'"

Adam smiled, a tear forming as he processed his son's perceptiveness. "I'm proud of you, Son. You are absolutely correct."

The father and son sat quietly for a moment, reflecting on the story as the drizzle stopped falling. In just a few short minutes, the line began to move forward and carried them along with it, slowly but surely approaching St. Stephen's Porch and the South Steps. They were among the first of the tens of thousands who would enter the Great Hall that day to pay their respects to the man whose voice and courage had given his nation the will to prevail against seemingly insurmountable odds.

CHAPTER FORTY-THREE

AS THE LINE stretched out slowly, mourners shuffled patiently along the sidewalk toward the public entrance at Westminster Hall. Harvey, Walter, and the Americans scrutinized the queue meticulously from multiple positions. They assessed the behavior and demeanor of those who waited. Despite their vigilance, nothing seemed suspicious, nor did they perceive any unusual movement that might suggest a clue.

The crowd, an immense and orderly gathering of thousands, consisted of quiet individuals steeped in contemplation. They all appeared to be people who had come to whisper a solitary word of gratitude to a man whose death marked the end of a monumental era.

King let out a sigh and sat down heavily on a bench across the road from the line of solemn mourners. His thoughts shifted to Brogan and Hunt, making him wonder how they were faring at their own station. He suspected they faced a similar situation.

In fact, at St. Paul's Cathedral, it *had* gone about the same for Brogan and Hunt. Nothing was particularly noteworthy or out of the ordinary—until that singular moment when they observed Harry Higgins rushing down the cathedral's iconic front steps. He moved briskly, his pace confident as he walked off purposefully down the block. Brogan and Hunt, recognizing an opportunity, trailed him at a discreet distance.

They watched as Higgins turned left at one corner and then, without hesitation, slipped into a small establishment. The sign above this establishment read: AITKEN & CO. BOOKS – NEW & USED – COLLECTIBLES.

"Well, I sure as hell can't go in there myself. Higgins knows my face. It'll have to be you this time, Hunt," Brogan remarked with a nod.

"On it," Hunt replied, determination in his voice. He crossed the street, approached the entrance, and pushed open the door. Inside, the sheer volume and variety of books on display astonished him. It was a collection far more extensive than anyone might imagine by merely glancing at the storefront's unassuming exterior.

An older man, with a refined and deliberate air, looked up from behind a counter cluttered with tomes. "Good day, sir. I'm Jonathan Aitken, the proprietor. How may I assist you today?" he inquired with keen politeness.

Thinking quickly to maintain his cover, Hunt responded, "Yes, thank you, Mr. Aitken. I'll tell you precisely what I'm in the market for. I'm looking for anything collectible by Dickens, if you have it. I am particularly interested in *A Tale of Two Cities.*"

"Well, my good man, you've come to the right place indeed. I rather think I know exactly where to find what you're seeking. Could I plead for patience? Allow me less than five minutes," the proprietor assured, eagerness in his voice.

"Of course. I'll just browse a bit while you do," Hunt replied, glancing around the room.

"Yes, that's great. Plenty of books for your browsing pleasure. Now, if you'll excuse me, I'll see to it," Aitken said as he exited the room, a sense of urgency in his step.

Hunt began to make his way through the aisles, shifting his focus from shelf to shelf as he searched for his true target. At last, he caught sight of Harry Higgins at the rear of the store, locked in an animated and intense conversation with a young man who couldn't have been more than twenty-five years of age though making every attempt to appear older. He was dressed in an immaculately tailored business suit, which he wore with an air of seriousness that seemed meant to impress.

Hunt observed for a moment, weighing his options, and finally decided to report back to Brogan. Just as Hunt headed towards the exit, he noticed the salesclerk returning, clutching three dusty volumes in his hands. Aitken seemed out of breath and visibly disappointed to see his customer departing so abruptly.

Hunt lingered by the shop window after he left, observing Higgins and the young man through the glass. They were still deep in conversation, with body language suggesting a relationship of tension and urgency. The young man gestured with his hands as if explaining something, or perhaps protesting, while Higgins stood with arms crossed, listening intently. It struck Hunt as a dynamic that warranted closer attention.

He walked over to the corner, where Brogan watched with anticipation, scanning the street to ensure that no one else was watching them.

"HE'S IN THERE talking to some younger fellow. There's something about their body language that makes me think that the guy in the suit is the one we should be concerned about," Hunt said to Brogan, with a sense of urgency that was only slightly tempered by the need to remain inconspicuous on the busy street.

"Think we should split up, then?" Brogan asked, gauging the situation and Hunt's reaction.

Hunt replied, "Well, the way I see it, we already know this Higgins fellow works at the church. No doubt he's the inside man for whatever they've planned. He probably has whatever remote device they would need to activate the bomb."

"Only there's no bomb. So he's not an immediate threat. You think the younger man is the boss?"

"Maybe not the big boss, but he's certainly your Mr. Higgins's boss. I say we let Higgins go back to St. Paul's and we both keep an eye on the new guy."

"Agreed," Brogan said, nodding as they watched the bookstore's entrance.

A moment later, Harry Higgins exited the bookstore and, without any hint of suspicion, walked away in the direction of St. Paul's. Hunt and Brogan waited, watching the distance between them and their new target. They remained vigilant, careful not to lose track of their quarry.

After about two minutes, the young man in the fine suit walked out the same door and got into a taxi. Hunt and Brogan got into one a few moments later and followed, their pulse quickening with the thrill and uncertainty of pursuit.

Apparently confident no one was watching, the passenger in the lead car did not direct his driver to do anything evasive. Instead, he traveled directly to his destination, one that became clear to the two men in the following car when they entered the city's Mayfair section. Brogan and Hunt were astonished when the lead car turned onto Curzon Street and then stopped in front of Leconfield House.

The headquarters of MI5.

"TELL YOU WHAT, Brogan. You take this taxi to the rendezvous spot back near St. Paul's. That pub, whatever the hell the name is."

"McRory's."

"If you say so. Head back there. I'll stay around here and watch. Tell Harvey to get his ass and his team over here. But discreetly. This thing just got a helluva lot more interesting."

"Not to mention more dangerous," Brogan said as Hunt got out of the car.

The thrill of discovery and the possibility of danger gnawed at Brogan as he relayed the instructions to the driver. The taxi maneuvered through the streets, retracing their earlier route, and Brogan found himself mulling over the day's rapid developments. What had initially seemed like a straightforward task of shadowing a low-level conspirator had quickly escalated into something far more intricate and perilous. The young man's visit to Leconfield House suggested a level of complication they hadn't anticipated, adding layers to the conspiracy that both baffled and concerned him.

Was the presence of the young man at MI5's headquarters indicative of infiltration at the highest level, or was it a clever misdirection meant to send Brogan and his team chasing shadows? The questions swirled in his mind as landmarks flashed by the taxi window. He knew Harvey wouldn't be pleased to learn that Hunt had stayed back alone and could already hear King's voice reprimanding him for letting Hunt take the more dangerous position. Yet, the instinct to gain more intelligence before regrouping had been too compelling to ignore. Brogan hoped that Hunt's keen sense of observation would yield important information.

The driver, sensing Brogan's urgency, spared no time, darting swiftly through the city's afternoon traffic. As the cab turned onto the street where McRory's stood, anticipation tightened in Brogan's chest. He had to get everyone back together and draw up a plan.

If nothing else, they had to protect the most obvious target, St. Paul's, and the massive crowd expected on the day of the funeral. But the unexpected twist of having this new player emerge from the very heart of British intelligence had sent them all back to the drawing board, forced to reconsider every assumption, to rethink every angle.

CHAPTER FORTY-FOUR

KING AND HIS crew were crowded around a table at McRory's, sipping pints, throwing the occasional dart, and fretting over the time. Brogan and Hunt were past due, and the Americans speculated on the reasons. It was unlike Hunt to be unaccounted for so long. Just as the first real notes of concern began to sound, Brogan came through the door and made straight for the group.

"About bloody time, Sport," King said. "Where the hell is Hunt?"

Brogan, working to catch his breath, answered, "You're not going to believe this one, old boy. Hunt's keeping his eyes on the headquarters of MI5."

"What the hell?" King reacted, nearly spilling his beer.

"You heard me. He's there now," Brogan said, enjoying the obvious surprise of his American friends. "We followed someone there."

"That Higgins fellow?" King asked.

"No," Brogan replied, "but we did see him."

"Where?" King demanded. His mind had already painted a picture of imminent danger somewhere else in the city.

"Coming out of St. Paul's. But that's not the point."

"Higgins at St. Paul's. Wouldn't that make him a great candidate as the inside man?" King pressed.

"Probably. But this thing likely goes much deeper. Now just stop asking questions and listen for a change, Harvey."

King took the rebuke in stride and said, "Okay, Sport. Fire away."

TWENTY MINUTES LATER, the entire team was in the vicinity of Leconfield House. They were positioned covertly in various places, but from each vantage point they could see each other, as well as the main door and two other doors to the building. With no better options, they decided to simply wait for the man in the suit to emerge once more and then follow him.

After about two hours, the young man appeared. Brogan alerted the team with visual hand signals. The members of the team broke up, with Hunt and Brogan taking the lead on foot and the others blending in with pedestrians in the area. The target walked down Curzon Street and over to St. James Park.

Once in the park, the man sat down on a bench next to a man and woman.

"Holy hell!" Brogan whisper yelled. "That's Michael and Molly Wheelan."

"Who?" Hunt asked.

"He's the man who works at the casket place in Birmingham—who likely put the explosive material in the casket."

"Holy shit," swore Howard Hunt under his breath, expressing the collective sentiment of the group.

This was a very real connection between at least one man at MI5 and a Soviet plot to kill world leaders. Harvey King and the team tried to figure a way to find out the identity and position of the young man they had seen with Michael and Molly Wheelman.

Despite his age, Walter Thompson had managed to keep up with them all. He spoke up now. "Mr. King, might I offer you and your team a suggestion?"

"Of course, Thompson. What're you thinking?" King responded in a deferential tone.

"Let me follow the fellow back to Five. I can come up with a reason to be visiting. Then I can do my best to find out who he is and what section he works for. I know my way around the place. Spent some time there in the old days. Still have a few friends there—much younger than I, mind you. But I'm confident I could leverage my name a bit and shake the tree to see what falls out."

"Anyone got a better idea?" King said as he looked at Hunt and Brogan.

Brogan spoke up. "Let's do it." They all nodded affirmation and kept their eyes on the three people on the bench about fifty yards away.

Finally, the young man hugged the woman and man and walked away. Harvey King motioned to Matthews and Perlstein to follow the couple. The rest of the team hung back while Walter Thompson fell in behind the young man. Thompson had good instincts and looked like any of a dozen other old men in the park.

Sure enough, the young man walked back to Leconfield House and straight in the front door. Thompson followed him. He was stopped before he got to the front door by a security man, who rudely said, "Excuse me, old man, might I ask who you are and what your business here might be?" The man put his hand on Thompson's lapel and pushed slightly.

"I'm Detective Sergeant Walter Thompson, and I represent the family of the late Sir Winston Churchill. I need to speak to the young man who just entered that door," he said, pointing with emphasis.

The security man hesitated, slowly recognizing Thompson. "Oh, very sorry, sir. I've read your book. So very sorry for your loss."

"Thank you. Now would you be so kind as to tell me the name of that young man who just went in? He treated me rather rudely a few moments ago, and I plan to register a complaint on behalf of Lady Churchill."

"Oh my, sir. I'm sure Mr. Welling didn't mean anything by it."

"Welling, you say?"

"Yes, Detective Sergeant, that's Sean Welling. He's a personal assistant to the director himself, Mr. Roger Hollis."

"Is he, indeed? Well, he needs to learn some manners. He's one arrogant arse of a young man."

"Would you like me to have any message passed along to him?"

Thompson paused, then brushed his left lapel dismissively with his right hand. "Well, I don't suppose it's all that important. I had no idea he was in such an important job. Must have a lot on his mind, what with all the people coming to town for my late boss's funeral and such. Let's leave it be for now. What's your name?"

"I'm Malcolm Brisbane."

"Well, Brisbane, you've been very helpful. I feel much better now. If you want, I'll come back by in a day or so and give you an inscribed copy of my book."

"That would be remarkable, Mr. Thompson. But I'll just bring my own copy and have it with me as long as it takes for you to get back."

"Have a good afternoon, Brisbane."

AROUND FOUR O'CLOCK, London time, the team—minus Matthews and Perlstein—was once again seated around the table at Thompson's flat. They were weary from the day's events, but their spirits were bolstered. It was time for tea, and Mary had prepared some wonderful items: cucumber sandwiches, smoked salmon with cream cheese, warm scones with clotted cream, preserves, and cake. The table was a comforting sight, laden with food, and the men found a degree of solace in the hospitality of their hosts.

"This is called Dundee cake, Gentlemen," Mary informed the men as she served the tea. "It's a Scottish fruit cake. Mr. Churchill loved it. It pairs very well with this fine Earl Grey tea. Twining's—same as Her Royal Highness drinks at this hour." The aromatic spread seemed to temporarily lift the seriousness of their mission.

"Thank you so much, Mrs. Thompson. You're going to spoil us and ruin us for America," King said. He picked up his cup and raised it. "Not sure if you're supposed to toast with tea, but here's to Walter and Mary Thompson, two wonderful hosts."

"Hear, hear," they all said, their voices rising in unison for the toast.

Walter then raised his cup, clearly feeling at ease among his American comrades. "Since we're toasting, here's to our American friends who have come to protect the honor of the late, great Winston Churchill." He had the look of a man reinvigorated by being back in the intelligence game.

"Well, I gotta tell you, Thompson, you're still a top-notch lawman and intelligence professional. That was a great bit of detective work getting Sean Welling's name for us," King replied, savoring his tea.

Brogan interrupted, setting his cup down with a snap, as if he had just made a breakthrough. "You know, it just struck me. I told you I knew the Wheelans from an operation some years ago, when I was working undercover in the IRA."

"Yeah, I remember. What of it?" King asked, curious where Brogan's train of thought was leading.

"Well, I'm almost certain they have a son, and by my guess, he'd be about the age of this Sean Welling fellow," Brogan replied, the significance of this revelation dawning on him.

"From Wheelan to Welling—that's not much of a leap," King mused. The room went quiet for a moment as they digested the implications of what Brogan had said.

Howard Hunt added, "This is adding up to a conspiracy of monumental proportions. King here knows that I write spy novels, and I can tell you that this is the stuff of an espionage classic."

"Let me get this straight—you're a spy novelist, and Harvey here is the real James Bond?" Brogan said with a smile, trying to introduce some levity into the situation.

"Hey, truth is stranger than fiction, Sport," King said. They all had a good laugh at that, a brief moment of camaraderie amid tension.

Thompson spoke up, and his voice carried a tone of deep concern. "Let me see if I have this right. You're saying that a personal assistant to the Director of MI5 is secretly the son of two members of the IRA?" His incredulity was palpable.

"It's worse than that, Thompson," King said. "These Wheelan people are part of a plot we believe was put together by the Russians. This would mean that they are really Soviet spies. And their work for the IRA is just an assignment from the communists." His words hung heavily in the air like the scent of the aromatic tea they were drinking.

"Good God!" Thompson said. "Mr. Churchill never did trust the Russians, all that riddle, puzzle, enigma thing. But this is almost too much to swallow." He shook his head in disbelief, grappling with the enormity of the situation.

"The Russians have been in the mole business for decades. It didn't start with Burgess and Philby—and it sure as hell didn't end there, Thompson," King said, his voice steady and grim.

Thompson said, "Maybe we should be taking a look at the director himself." Hunt and King exchanged a look, each silently acknowledging the gravity of Thompson's suggestion.

"Let's have some more of this great tea, Mrs. Thompson. I think your husband is on to something." King said. He helped himself to more Dundee cake, his mind racing with the consequences of their discoveries.

BY THE TIME their teatime meeting was over, the Americans and their British ally had come to some conclusions. Howard Hunt had committed to being the point man on the Roger Hollis angle, pressing Thompson to probe further into the MI5 chief's possible duplicity, while others on the team promised to work on a way to get at Michael and Molly Wheelan, as well as Harry Higgins.

They were increasingly confident that the bomb Thompson and Murray had taken out of play had been the main event in the grand Soviet scheme, but not yet absolutely certain. Their mission, though, was now clearly—and ominously—morphing into a hunt not just for explosives but also for intelligence, operatives, and moles.

Matthews and Perlstein showed up after the dishes had been cleared and cleaned, but Mary, being the perfect hostess, had saved their portions. As they dug in, they updated and briefed the rest of the team about their earlier surveillance of the Wheelan couple.

"When they left the park," Perlstein began, "they headed over to a pub called the Tipperary, where they met up with a lady."

This got Brogan's attention. "What'd she look like?"

"Easy on the eyes, that's for sure. Bright red hair—even brighter than your mop, Brogan. About five feet two, maybe. Gorgeous green eyes," Matthews answered.

"That'd be Kaitlyn Dorcey. She seems to be in the middle of this somehow."

Hunt added, "We're certain this Wheelan couple is working for the Soviets."

Matthews asked, "How about the redhead? Is there more that's *red* about her than just her hair?"

Brogan shook his head defiantly. "Not a chance. She's IRA through and through. No way she's a commie. Only politics for her have to do with kicking the Brits off the Emerald Isle."

"What makes you so sure?"

"Because I know her. Watched her work on operation after operation for the IRA; none of them could've possibly had anything to do with the Russians."

Harvey spoke up. "You may have a blind spot, Brogan. But then again, you may be right. I've been around a long time, and I know for a fact the Soviets love to use proxies. It wouldn't surprise me at all if that was the case here."

Hunt added. "I agree. After all, if they've planned some big bang to change the world, they'd sure want it to look like the work of someone other than them. Classic cover. Make it look like an IRA job, then exploit the fallout. Which makes me wonder if this Kaitlyn girl may be a weak link for us to exploit." He paused and looked over at the Irishman. "And by us, I mean you, Brogan."

All eyes were now on their ruddy colleague. "I imagine you're right. And if you are, then I know the last thing Miss Dorcey would want is to be used by anyone—especially the Soviets."

"Hey, Sport. You need to head over to that pub and see if she's there. Go work your Irish magic. You might just save her life."

Tiernan smiled. "Well, I guess I can suffer through a night with a beautiful woman for a good cause."

CHAPTER FORTY-FIVE

AS BROGAN SPRUCED up a bit and prepared to head over to the Tipperary, Hunt pulled King aside and said, "Harvey, think old Thompson here will mind me making another call to the States?"

"Dulles?"

"No. Angleton. I could catch him just before lunch in DC."

"Yeah, better catch him quick. After his usual dose of martinis, he'll be slow on the draw."

Harvey King went over to Walter Thompson and whispered into the older man's ear. Hunt watched as Thompson nodded. King looked over at Hunt and thumbed at the door to Thompson's small office.

Hunt went in and shut the door behind him. He placed the call, using a private number that connected directly to James Jesus Angleton's office. It rang four times, leaving Hunt just about to hang up, convinced that the wizard of counterintelligence had already departed for one of his favorite Georgetown haunts with some of the boys from the office. But on the fifth ring, Angleton answered. They quickly dispensed with the small talk.

"You know what I think about our friend Hollis, don't you Hunt?"

"Yes, Jim. I'm aware of your suspicions."

"More than suspicions. They're facts."

"Well, if so, then I can probably help you make an airtight case. I just need some help. Surely you have a file on the guy. Dig it out and help me with some patterns—the guy's habits. Stuff like that."

"Gladly, my friend. Hold the phone." Hunt could hear some noise. File drawers opening. Papers rustling. Footsteps. Then, after a couple of minutes, he heard something slam shut and Angleton was back on the phone. "Okay, here we go. We've had some eyes on the man here and there. Nothing official, mind you. More of an off-the-record kind of thing."

"Of course," Hunt said. He was well aware of the broad latitude Angleton tended to take. His superiors usually just left the man alone with his mysteries, conspiracies, and endless intelligence webs.

"I think your best bet is going to be over at the Savoy. It's always been a favorite haunt for Hollis. He drinks and dines there at least four times a week, according to my notes. Mostly alone, by the way. Doesn't seem to have many close friends. Sometimes in the company of a young staff member named Sean Welling."

"Got it," Hunt said. He resisted the urge to divulge what they had just learned about young Mr. Welling. "Thanks a million, Jim. I'll get back to you if I need more."

"My files can always use fresh material, Hunt," Angleton said.

Hunt opened the office door and stepped back into the room. King and Thompson were in close conversation, tapping their fingers on the large map of London that had been mounted on the wall opposite the windows and was now marked with thumbtacks and notes.

"Good news, boys," Hunt said. "Our man frequents the Savoy. Drinks, dines, the whole nine yards. Looks like we'll have no trouble finding him up close and personal." He smiled as they took in the news. "He's in the habit of dining alone," he added, his eyes flicking over to Brogan, "except when he's got that young fellow Welling in tow."

SHORTLY BEFORE EIGHT o'clock that Wednesday evening, Her Majesty, Queen Elizabeth, accompanied by her sister, Princess Margaret, and her husband, Prince Philip, the Duke of Edinburgh, entered Westminster Hall. With all the grandeur befitting their stations, they moved solemnly into the vast, echoing chamber where Winston Churchill lay in state.

The long line of mourners—which stretched for more than a mile, back across Lambeth Bridge—was halted as the royal party arrived. They had been moving slowly past Churchill's casket at the pace of about four thousand per hour all day long. They huddled against the cold, some tearful and others stoic, awaiting their turn to pay homage.

The queen and her party entered the vast room through the Star Court and the middle door across from the catafalque. They stood silently near the casket for a few minutes. Then they left through the same door, and the long line began moving once again.

TIERNAN BROGAN LOOKED the room over as he entered the Tipperary, but did not see Kaitlyn Dorcey. He went to the bar and ordered a pint. Then he walked over to a corner table, where he had a good view of everything. He nursed his drink, but before long had to get another. He was prepared to wait the length of three pints for her to appear. She came in just as he was approaching the bar for his third pint.

"Fancy meeting you here, Sean," Kaitlyn said as she met him at the bar.

"Kaitlyn!" he said with a big smile. "What a lovely surprise. Let me buy you a drink. What's your pleasure?"

She was flattered by his passionate greeting. "Well, if you leave the weak stuff behind, I'll join you in a Tullamore."

He called up the drinks and they made their way over to his table. They clinked glasses. His goal for the evening was to get her to somehow open up about the operation she was working on. But he couldn't help thinking about a different goal, too. Something more intimate.

He did his best to put that idea out of his mind, which was increasingly difficult as one drink led to another. He was impressed with her tolerance. Yes, Tiernan was Irish through and through, complete with an ability to drink prodigious amounts of liquor, but Kaitlyn's skills were on a whole other level.

Their conversation over the next few hours ricocheted from old missions, to life back in Belfast, to the reasons neither of them had married. Eventually, Brogan decided to bring up the elephant he wanted to bring into the room. "Quite the show this week here in London. Churchill's funeral and all."

Kaitlyn drained her glass and wiped her hand across her mouth. Then she gave the first sign that the alcohol was beginning to loosen her lips. "Yes, quite the show. And the best is yet to come," she said, a slight smile and gleam in her captivating green eyes.

Tiernan played dumb, attempting to draw her out. "Yes, I've been reading about it in the papers. The world is watching. Leaders from all over here. Quite a moment for our British 'friends,'" he said, emphasizing the last word with slight sarcasm.

"Oh, Sean, you can be so thick sometimes."

"How?"

"You go over there and get us two more glasses of this fine whiskey, and I'm going to tell you a story." Tiernan looked down at his glass. It was still half full. Kaitlyn grabbed it from him and finished his drink in a long swallow. "There," she said. "Now off with you, and be quick about it, Sean. It's not good to keep a girl waiting," she added, slightly slurring her words.

When Brogan got back to the table, he handed a glass to Kaitlyn. Then he raised his own, "To Kaitlyn Dorcey, the most beautiful girl in all of Ireland."

She smiled, "Why Sean, you bastard. You trying to charm me?"

"Is it working?"

She smiled again and winked. "We can talk about us, or we can talk about Sir Winston Churchill."

Brogan was momentarily torn between his mission and his passion. He quickly rationalized that the best way to get her to talk about her part in a great conspiracy was to continue to pursue her. So he replied, "Churchill who?"

"Good answer, Sean. But it's Churchill you're going to get, before you get me," she said.

"Um, well, okay...I...er," Brogan stammered.

"Why, Sean, you're blushing. Are you smitten?"

"I am. Have been, by the by, since we first worked together."

"Well, we shall get back to that. But these are days that are going to change our future. And I'm not talking about you getting all horned up."

"I'm fine, Kaitlyn. Been controlling me self for years," he said. They laughed. "Sounds like there's something you want to tell me."

"Well, it's a secret now, but soon the world will know."

"I don't follow."

Kaitlyn finished the new drink in front of her and looked around to make sure no one else was listening in. Then she said, "Sean, think of it. The great irony of something happening at the funeral of the great enemy of our cause."

"Something?"

"Some friends of mine are planning an incident at St. Paul's."

HOWARD HUNT SAT in the corner of the dimly lit American Bar, nursing the one drink he allowed himself for the evening. The glass was barely touched, its amber contents catching the light in a wayward prism as it sat ignored. He was determined to keep his senses sharp, his eyes ever searching the elegant space for the telltale presence of Roger Hollis.

The Savoy was exactly as James Angleton described in his overstuffed files—an old haunt of Hollis, where the director of MI5 was known to dine and drink with a solemn regularity. But this evening, Hollis was proving elusive. The plush carpets and muted chandeliers of the bar seemed to swallow time whole, and Hunt realized that over two hours had passed since he settled in with a view that afforded him every angle of both the bar and the entrance to the attached Grill Room.

Still no sign of the man.

Knowing that the elusive spymaster could be equally unpredictable, Hunt resigned himself to another fruitless night. He would finish his drink, he decided, and then head back to the flat. He took two small sips, feeling the liquid burn softly down his throat, when a man walked into the bar and settled in a spot about ten feet away.

Hunt's instincts, honed over years of fieldwork, immediately went on alert.

The man had a full silver beard, glasses, and hair to match. But something wasn't quite right. The color was inconsistent, and Hunt noticed a tinge of darker hair peeking out. He surmised that the man was wearing a wig. Then there were the glasses—large frames that reminded Hunt of some he used on occasion when undercover. He stared, taking in every detail, and would have wagered that a closer inspection would reveal the lenses had no prescription at all. Just for show. The man noticed Hunt's gaze and turned his back slightly. He ordered a drink in a stammering voice.

"Welcome back, Mr. Henderson. Same as last night?"

"M-m-mighty fine, my good man. Yes, p-please."

"That room number again, sir?"

"312."

Hunt felt a surge of excitement but kept it off his face. He made a careful mental note of the room number, and his thoughts raced.

The stammer.

The disguise.

The odds were that in his search for Hollis, he had stumbled onto something even bigger. He considered approaching the man to strike up a conversation but decided against the risk. Such a move might scare him off for good. His curiosity piqued and his mind spinning, Hunt left the bar without finishing his drink.

He knew he'd be back.

He headed out into the chilly night and down the Strand, hailing a black cab to Thompson's place, eager to check in with Harvey King and tell him of this new and unexpected lead. The driver took him across Lambeth Bridge, where Hunt noticed the lines of people still gathering. Their solemn purpose reminded him that time was short if they were going to do anything about the suspected plan. He hoped Brogan was having as much luck with Kaitlyn Dorcey as he was with his accidental quarry at the Savoy.

Turns out, Brogan was, indeed, getting very lucky.

KAITLYN LED BROGAN to her nearby flat, and Tiernan was keenly aware that she had decided either to reveal more details about the so-called Churchill incident or to fulfill a long-standing fantasy of his. He was willing to take either or both, in any order, and she announced her immediate intentions the moment the door was closed behind them. He would have expected nothing less of her. And that was one of the many things he liked about Kaitlyn Dorcey. She kissed him passionately in her small living room, and he smiled at the thought of telling the team all he was going through for this mission.

They made passionate love and drifted off to sleep.

Brogan got up about thirty minutes later and found some coffee in the kitchen, as well as a percolator. He turned on the stove and within a few minutes the aroma of coffee filled the small flat.

In a few minutes, Kaitlyn appeared in the doorway in his shirt, stretching and smiling at him.

"Sorry to wake you."

"No bother at all. How about we turn that pot off for now and head back to bed for another round if you're up to it?" Her eyes widened. "Oh, I see you are," she said with a wicked laugh.

The mission would have to wait a bit longer, as Tiernan Brogan took another one for the team.

CHAPTER FORTY-SIX

RAIN-SOAKED STREETS STRETCHED beneath Hunt as he returned to Thompson's flat, where a sense of urgency loomed like a gathering storm. Over the hum of dim lighting, he recounted to King the peculiar details from his evening at the hotel bar, where his encounter with an intriguing man—who sported an ill-fitting wig and had a pronounced stammer—stood out especially.

The man had not looked like the usual clandestine operative on a recon mission; he had kept to himself in an unusual way for someone under orders. Yet, the bartender had vouched for his frequent presence.

"You mean like a stutter?" King asked, skepticism lacing his words. "You sure it was a wig? The guy was in disguise?"

"As sure as I'm sitting here right now," Hunt said, his voice carrying the weight of conviction. "But the guy wasn't doing recon. Kept to himself. The bartender knew him from other nights. The man is staying in room 312."

Harvey King fell silent as he processed this revelation, lost in a tangle of thoughts that harked back to earlier, sharper days of espionage. Then, as if breaking the tension of his own musings, he spoke aloud, mostly to himself, "No. Couldn't be. There's no way they'd do that."

Hunt looked at him expectantly. "No way who would do what?"

"Well, this is a big Russian operation apparently, right?"

"Sure."

"And they have been in the spy and mole game big time for years. We've been talking about Hollis, right?"

"Yes. Where are you going with this?"

"Well, remember what I was talking about back in '51, and how Beetle Smith asked Jim and me to write up reports about a suspected mole?"

"Sure—Philby," Hunt replied. "I was wondering—that stutter. So you think that stuttering bastard in room 312 at the Savoy is Kim Philby?"

"I sure as hell think it's worth checking out," King continued, animated by this incredible possibility. "I mean, think about it. The Soviets extracted Philby from Lebanon, what, two years ago this month?"

"Yep. January '63."

"Well, most of us from the old days assumed that the commies had been grooming Philby to run MI6 one day. If he hadn't been discovered, hell, they might have moles running both MI5 and MI6 right now. Those guys play for keeps. And they take their time. Who knows, but what if this whole conspiracy with the bomb in the casket has been in the works for a decade or more? That's the way they do things."

"So somehow Philby was sent back to run it?" Hunt asked, his mind spinning with the implications.

"All speculation. But it's sure a hell of a theory," King said, warming to the idea. "The story I've heard is that good old Kim's been drinking and depressed in Moscow. But what if that's disinformation shit? What if he's back to exact revenge?"

"We need to call Dulles," Hunt said, rising with urgency that matched the ticking of a clandestine clock.

"And Angleton," King added, already reaching for the phone.

Paris

MANLIO BROSIO HAD been the Fourth General Secretary of NATO for less than a year, a post to which he was appointed in 1964, and where he had already started to make his mark. At sixty-eight years old, he possessed the energy and stamina of a man half his age, a trait that surprised many of his subordinates and colleagues across the organization. His background in law and diplomacy in his native Italy revealed him to be a skilled manager and negotiator who had deftly navigated the turbulent waters of post-war European politics.

Those who observed him noticed he was always impeccably dressed, his suits tailored to the lean frame of a man mindful of his appearance. His serious-looking face, marked by thin lips and a receding hairline, was rarely seen in anything but a composed expression, even during a crisis.

Brosio's calm demeanor and steady hand at the wheel of NATO endeared him to the many staff members who worked around him. They admired his dedication to the alliance between Western nations, appreciating his ability to remain focused and unflustered amid the mounting tensions of the Cold War.

Since his appointment, Brosio had come to rely more and more on his aide, Henri Girard, a man who had ingratiated himself as both indispensable and loyal. Girard's cluttered desk was only a short distance from Brosio's office door, symbolic of his proximity to the General Secretary and his inner workings.

What Brosio did not know was that his growing dependence on Girard had been cultivated with great intent and care. The assistant was now perfectly positioned to do the bidding of his true masters, the KGB and the Politboro, as they set their sights on undermining the very organization Brosio was tasked to lead. Girard's discreetly sharpened talents and calculated availability made him an ideal mole in the heart of NATO's operations.

A role that required both nerve and duplicity.

Henri was working late that Wednesday, sitting at his paper-strewn desk long after many of his colleagues had left for the evening. He had created busy work to justify the extra time at the office, knowing that his real mission was far different than the menial tasks he appeared to perform.

He was waiting for Brosio to leave for the night, aware that his boss was also inclined to long hours. Yet because Henri managed Brosio's calendar, he knew precisely when the General Secretary would be gone. Dinner plans had been made with the Italian Ambassador to France, an old friend of Brosio's. Henri knew the meal would stretch on for hours, providing him ample time to complete his covert job. Brosio left the office punctually, dressed in his usual fine attire, ready for a night of wine, food, and diplomatic conversation—an evening that his assistant was counting on.

As soon as Brosio departed for dinner, Girard sprang into action. He quickly entered his boss's office with a singular mission: to acquire up-to-date information on NATO troop placements and overall readiness. The General Secretary had trusted Girard implicitly, even with the combination to the safe hidden on the wall, behind a painting of a serene Tuscan landscape.

The Soviet agent knew exactly where to look for what he needed and wasted no time. He found a thick stack of files in the safe, documents brimming with the sensitive details Moscow eagerly sought. Using a small Minox camera, he took dozens of photographs, rapidly clicking off frames as he hurried through the files.

Though he didn't stop to read each page thoroughly, he was confident that any information kept in the secured compartment was current and highly relevant to his employers. After completing his task, he meticulously returned everything to its place and put the film in a small envelope. With evidence in hand, he left Brosio's office as undetected as he had entered.

Henri left the Palais de Chaillot moments later and wound his way through the Paris night, making a beeline for a small cafe not far from the Gare du Nord. In the busy establishment, he easily blended into the crowd, a lone man in a sea of travelers and Parisians enjoying their evening meals. There he met Peter, his Soviet handler, and quickly passed the envelope to him.

Girard stayed only long enough to enjoy a single espresso, avoiding any semblance of lingering that might arouse suspicion. Peter departed as quietly as his contact, taking the film back to a dark room in his apartment, where he developed the images with care and precision. Soon, the materials were copied, labeled, and on their way to Moscow.

As the city settled into its late-evening rhythm, the lights of Paris flickered in offices, cafes, and apartments. An ocean away, in Britain, another mission played out, though it moved at the hands of agents unaware of one another's existence. It was likewise calculated and deliberate, executed in the methodical style of those who felt history was on their side.

CHAPTER FORTY-SEVEN

London
January 28, 1965

KAITLYN DORCEY RETURNED from the kitchen with a tray steady in her hands. On it rested two simple cups of coffee accompanied by slices of bread thick with butter. It was a modest breakfast more befitting the lives of two lovers in hiding than of well-organized revolutionaries. She met Brogan's eyes with a teasing smile and said, "I haven't been food shopping for a while, love, but this should settle our insides a bit."

Brogan looked at her, his affection clear despite the dangerous game they were playing. "I'd rather have bread and butter with you than steak with anyone else," he assured her with a wink.

"Aren't you the charmer? Aiming for another go at it, are you?" she asked with a playful nod, curling next to him, her presence both warm and conspiratorial.

Brogan reached for a cup of coffee, a glint of mischief in his eye. "I think you wore me out, honey."

She raised an eyebrow, the cleverness of a seasoned activist shimmering beneath her playful facade. "Honey, he calls me," she said, her voice smartly challenging him, as if they were again in the thick of political debate.

"What would you prefer?" Brogan asked, maintaining his composure.

"It's fine. More bread?" Kaitlyn passed him a piece, crumbs falling onto the sheets like the details of their secret plots. Her casual demeanor was steadying, like a calm before a storm they both anticipated.

"Thanks. I was thinking while you were in the kitchen," Brogan said. "Thinking about what we talked about back at the pub. About something that might happen at the big funeral on Saturday."

Kaitlyn took a large bite of bread. Her words came through muffled but charged with the weight of conspiracy. "It'll sure make a noise."

Brogan probed further, wanting to know just how much she had been told. "What exactly is it that will make this noise?"

She took another sip of coffee, a calculated pause, then looked him squarely in the eye. "You sure you want to know? Might be better for you to just ignore what I said while you were getting me drunk so you could have your way with me."

"Getting *you* drunk? I couldn't keep up with you," Brogan retorted, lightness in his voice masking his determination to extract the truth of her involvement. "I think it was actually the other way around."

"You would!" Kaitlyn replied with a bright laugh that sliced through the tension. Then she paused, studying his face. "I'll tell you about it if you really want to know."

"I do. What's happening?"

She leaned in closer, the intimacy of her whisper seeming to amplify the seriousness of her revelation. "Some friends of ours have rigged things so that right in the middle of all the nice things being said about that old devil Churchill, there will be a loud explosion. Not a large one, mind you, but enough to get the notice of all the television cameras, not to mention everyone in the pews."

Brogan's mind raced. He knew the explosion had been designed to be much bigger than Kaitlyn was envisioning. But he didn't let on. "To what end?"

"To what end? Is that what you asked? To what end?"

"Sorry, honey—didn't mean to upset you. Of course, I understand it's designed to be a statement."

"Damn right."

"And will the IRA take the credit?"

"Of course. Why wouldn't we? Our feelings about Churchill and his imperialism are well known."

Brogan pushed for more, his curiosity genuine but shrouded in feigned carefreeness. "Well, I was just thinking—"

"About what?" she interrupted, the impatience of an unacknowledged collaborator creeping into her voice.

"Well, this is pretty big, isn't it? Everyone and their dog will know about it in minutes. Are you sure the Brits won't trace it back to us?"

Kaitlyn shot him a slightly offended look, as if to question his loyalty for even asking.

"Sorry," he said again. "I know you've got your bases covered. But can you blame me for being careful?"

She softened and leaned back, her smile returning. "No, I can't blame you, Sean. I guess I'd be worried too if I wasn't so bloody sure of myself. We've got it all sorted out. We'll be on our way to Dublin before the smoke even clears."

"Then I've got nothing to lose by sticking around, do I?" Brogan said with a grin.

He tried to mask his own doubt, even pretended for a moment that he wasn't ahead of her on the escape plans. The truth was he had his own ideas for an early exit—and a very different notion of just how big the explosion would be.

Arlington, Virginia

IT WAS LONG after dark in Arlington, Virginia when the black telephone in the small green house rang. James Jesus Angleton was again working on some of his prize orchids. They somehow reminded him of the intricate patterns of counterespionage, delicate and complex. Those closest to him were certain his love for the flowers was somehow connected to his obsessive work in a psychological sense, a metaphor for the layers of deception he unraveled.

The greenhouse was filled with shelves of the exotic plants, the blooms a riot of color in the dimly lit room. He put a small shearing tool down on a table and removed his gloves before he answered the telephone on the seventh ring.

"Yes?"

"Jim? It's King. I assume this is a secure line?"

"It is, Harvey. I'm in the greenhouse."

"You're going to turn into a damn orchid one of these days, old boy."

Ignoring the dig, Angleton asked, "What can I do for you, Harvey? Find out more about our friend at Five?"

"Not quite. But during our investigation we did stumble onto something that begs a second look."

"Why call now? Why not wait for more intel?"

"Well, it's just that if this is what we think it might be, it's something you'd particularly want to know about, Jim."

"Harvey, I'm a spy. You're a spy. But cut the cryptic shit. What the hell are you talking about?"

"There's a chance that an old friend of yours may be here in London. And you'll never guess who it is."

There was a brief pause and then Angleton said, "Philby."

"How'd you know?"

"I didn't. But you're a piss poor poker player. Besides, you said friend of mine, not friend of ours. So that narrowed it down. Tell me what you have."

King briefed Angleton in detail about Hunt's encounter with the mystery man. "What we need—and can't really get it over here; don't know who to trust—what we need is anything we have on a Brit named William Henderson. Probably a fake. But worth looking at."

"I'll check it. What's your plan going forward?"

"Well, I sure as hell can't check it out myself. Philby and I have some history, as you well know."

"Understood. How about Hunt? He's a good operative. Do he and Philby have any history?"

"Not a bit. They've never met."

"Then let him run with it. But I'd put another man there with him."

"Done. Do we have anyone else here in country—anyone we can trust?"

"I'll see what I can do. I know that we can't work through the official channels on this, so our station there in London needs to be kept in the dark," Angleton said.

King thought for a moment, then he said, "How about I call one of our old friends in Rome? Just saw him last week. We had dinner."

"You mean Romano?"

"Hell yes. Johnny Romano. He was prepared to do anything we needed back when the plan was to off Castro. I'm sure he can get us some muscle."

"I've no doubt that he can. But it needs to be discreet."

"Seriously? Hey, Jim, if there's any group that can keep a lid on things, it's the mob. And they're not bad at disposal either. We have the beginnings of a body count here."

"Okay, Harvey, make the call."

"Hell of a thing, Jim."

"Indeed."

"SOMETHING'S BEEN BOTHERING me for a few days," Tiernan Brogan said to Kaitlyn Dorcey. Initially hesitant, he now felt he had no time to delay. "And now that we've had this splendid time together, and you've told me what you've told me, it's bothering me even more." He searched her expression, seeking to read her reaction through the dim light of the room.

"What the devil are you talking about?" she asked, curiosity mingled with confusion. She pushed herself up, sitting straight in bed, and inadvertently spilled some of her coffee on the shirt she was wearing. "Sorry, love. I can wash this out in a bit. What's been bothering you?"

She seemed entirely unaware of the gravity of his thoughts.

He wanted to break the ice, but he knew he had to work the edges. "It has to do with some of the people you had with you the other night at the pub."

"Who?" she asked again, a slight edge to her voice.

"Michael and Molly Wheelan. I don't think you know everything about them."

Her tone and body language were noticeably defensive as she shot back, "I've known them for years, and their son, Sean, too. Whatever are you talking about?"

He forged ahead, determined to make her see the danger. "When I saw them—particularly him—the other night, he looked familiar, but I couldn't place him. Then it hit me. I recalled an operation over in Birmingham about four years ago. You weren't part of this one. But Michael was."

"I'm sure he's been involved in many things. What's your point?"

Brogan could see she had no idea the seriousness of what he was about to reveal. "Well, it's that I happened to observe him one night—totally by accident, mind you—talking with a man I knew to be an agent for the KGB."

"The Russians? What the hell was he doing talking to a Russian agent?" Her eyes widened, showing the first sign of doubt.

"I haven't a clue. But I followed him twice more over the next week—this time on purpose—and observed him talking to the same man. One time he handed the Russian a large envelope."

"That makes no sense."

"Of course it does. Haven't you ever been approached?" He looked at her intently, hoping she could connect the dots he was laying out.

"Approached? By whom?"

"By a Russian."

Her voice was tinged with incredulity as she replied, "Of course not! I've got nothing to do with those commie bastards. I'm an Irish patriot. My quarrel is with the crown."

"A true believer."

"That'd be me," she said, proudly. But there was a hint of uncertainty as well.

He nodded and continued. "Well, *I've* been approached. In fact, I was once approached by the same man I saw meeting regularly with Michael Wheelan. I told the guy to go to hell when I realized he was trying to turn me. But it looks like your friend Michael may have made a different choice."

"'Tis hard to believe, Sean. Michael's been a big part of the plan I just told you about. In fact, he's the one responsible for the device—the bomb." She paused, processing.

"You're missing my point, Kaitlyn."

"I'm not missing a damn thing, Sean," she said, angry. "My friend also works for the Russians. I get it."

"But do you get what it means? Who came up with the idea to put a bomb at St. Paul's?" Brogan asked. He was fishing, taking a risk.

Kaitlyn thought for a moment and then said, "Come to think of it, love, it was Michael Wheelan who started this whole thing. He brought me and the others in."

"Just as I suspected. And my gut tells me that Michael Wheelan got the idea from the Russians."

"But why?"

"I'll tell you why. Or better yet, let me ask you a question: what if the Russians are behind something bigger and are just using our IRA people to facilitate the plan?"

She listened and then said, resignedly, "And then blame it all on us."

"I think so. With all the world leaders in one room on Saturday, it's possible that this 'incident' you've worked on could turn out to be bigger. Much bigger."

"Deaths?"

"Think about it. What if the Russians want to kill off dozens of key world leaders at one time—De Gaulle, Wilson—the whole lot? And what if they want to blame it on the likes of you and your friends?"

"But why would they do such a thing?" Kaitlyn was beginning to buy in to Brogan's premise.

"I can think of a few reasons. Mainly, though, if they create an unstable world political environment of that magnitude, they could exploit it for their own purposes."

"Such as?"

"Such as an excuse for making a move on Western Europe. They've wanted to do that since the days of Stalin."

"Oh my God!" she said, standing up. She was trembling. "What have I done?" She turned to Brogan with wide eyes. "The bomb must be stopped!"

CHAPTER FORTY-EIGHT

Rome

GIOVANNI "JOHNNY" ROMANO wrote down the address Harvey King had given him and dropped the piece of paper on the desk. It was a symbol to him, a sign that something big was about to happen. He was smart enough to know he would be wise to involve himself— not just to help his old friend but to ensure a seat at the table, a place in whatever important things were about to unfold.

He got up from his chair and leaned into the hallway, his eyes narrowing with determination as he barked a hurried command. "Tony, get Vince and Dom—I want you guys on the next flight to London. Go to this address. Then call and tell me what the hell is going on!"

Moscow

MEANWHILE, OTHERS WERE calculating their own moves in a complex game of global chess. Their intelligence services had already intercepted reports of increased activity among American operatives in Europe. Although they would not know all the details for several days, the Russians were keenly aware that Harvey King's relocation was not business as usual.

Pots of steaming coffee and plates of assorted pastries filled the table as the breakfast meeting commenced in the cold yet imposing space of the Kremlin. It was a strategic Thursday morning, on the twenty-eighth of January, a moment primed for decision-making that could affect the world balance.

Leonid Brezhnev fixed his gaze on Vladimir Semichastny across the massive, plate-strewn table. "Comrade Semichastny, you have the materials from your agent in Paris?" he inquired with a voice that commanded the room. Gathered around him were pivotal figures of the Politburo and several calculated men from Department Thirteen in the First Directorate, all with an air of expectation as they awaited Semichastny's reply.

"Indeed, Comrade Chairman," came the assured response from the head of the KGB, his demeanor one of confidence and authority. "They tell quite a story."

Brezhnev pressed further. "Does this story have a happy ending?" His query was laden with the weight of expectation, his eyes scrutinizing Semichastny's every expression for the smallest flicker of doubt.

"Yes, it does," the director confirmed with a calm assurance. "It is clear from these documents that the nations of Western Europe, as well as the Americans, have made no unusual moves. There is no indication of any kind of NATO mobilization or even an increased level of readiness. It appears our enemies are sound asleep." Relief washed over some faces, a calculated anticipation visibly easing in the room as Brezhnev absorbed this favorable intelligence.

In a deliberate manner, choking the air with an aura of authority, Brezhnev lit a cigarette. Then, evoking the spirit and gesture of their late and fearsome leader, Josef Stalin, he stood and began to slowly clap his hands, a performance of calculated triumph. The sound of applause filled the cavernous room as everyone joined in, a symphony of loyalty and shared purpose. After a few moments, Brezhnev reclaimed his seat with a deliberate motion, and the others followed suit, their movements synchronized to the hierarchy that governed them.

Brezhnev continued with the air of a man in charge, "Now to the matter of our assets in London, what's the latest report from there, Comrade Semichastny?" His words stabbed through the fading echoes of applause and brought the room's attention back to a point of tension. The mention of London shifted the mood palpably, an undertone of unease rippling through the group. They steeled themselves for news that might disrupt the victorious aura that had just prevailed.

"Our men on site tell us that three of our agents have been killed, and two others have not been heard from for more than twenty-four hours," the KGB chief replied gravely.

The sudden shift in tone was as cold as the Moscow winter outside. Uncertainty tensed the room. "Who's responsible?" Brezhnev demanded, his voice cutting like a blade through the whispers of concern that now animated the group.

The director did not hesitate, though his words admitted to a troubling lack of clarity. "We believe there is some American presence and interest," he reported. The specter of American interference hung like a dark cloud over the assembly, casting a shadow over the plans they had felt certain of only moments before. The men exchanged glances filled with suspicion and a volatile mix of fear and resolve.

Brezhnev's mind turned once more to the larger picture. "Is this related to the fact that President Johnson will not be attending the service in that London cathedral?"

With measured precision, Semichastny responded, "No way to tell. The reports say he is sick. We have no one in a position to be able to verify this." His admission of uncertainty was haunting to the men, for it insinuated that the Americans might be craftier than anticipated.

The Chairman paused, weighed the risks and rewards, and then calmly demanded, "Your recommendation?" He leaned in towards Semichastny, eyes glinting with the sharpened edge of expectation and power.

The KGB director's voice resonated with conviction and assured intent. "Comrade Chairman, I believe we must move forward with this great visionary mission for Mother Russia and the Warsaw Pact nations. Our great cause is to liberate the remainder of the continent from the decadent grip of capitalism. I'm confident that if our enemies had any real suspicions, we would see a certain measure of military mobilization. They are indeed sound asleep." His words hung in the air, heavy with ambition and the sense of an historic inevitability, as all eyes in the room shifted from the Director of the KGB and back to the Chairman.

Brezhnev, a leader who understood the weight of his words and the momentous nature of their deeds, finally said, "I agree." He stood again, and this time the clapping was more resolute, its echoes a precursor to their bold intentions.

Their resolve was unshaken.

CHAPTER FORTY-NINE

Washington, D.C.

WHILE LADY CHURCHILL kept a solemn vigil within Westminster Hall during her husband's lying-in-state, across the Atlantic Ocean, a parallel commemoration occurred at Washington D.C.'s National Cathedral. A vast gathering of nearly three thousand mourners filled the grand space, while countless others joined through the screens of television sets and the crackling airwaves of radio.

They came to pay homage and to listen as Adlai Stevenson, the former two-time Democratic nominee for President and currently serving with distinction as the United States Ambassador to the United Nations, took the podium to deliver a eulogy that would resonate through history.

With the elegance and eloquence that had become his hallmark, Stevenson addressed those present and the millions beyond, each word a testament to the indomitable spirit of Churchill. The rhetoric rang with such clarity and brilliance that some might have imagined Churchill himself behind the words. For nearly thirty minutes, the audience was enraptured by his tribute, his voice weaving a tapestry of remembrance that honored the late leader's extraordinary journey. He dedicated his closing remarks to the essence of Churchill's being, his faith, and his enduring legacy.

Stevenson's finely wrought eulogy took a poignant turn as he reflected on Churchill's simple yet profound faith that underpinned his life and leadership:

"IN THE LAST analysis, all his zest and life and confidence sprang, I believe, not only from the rich endowment of his nature, but also from a profound and simple faith. In the prime of his powers, confronted with the apocalyptic risks of annihilation, he said serenely: 'I do not believe that God has despaired of his children.' In old age, as the honors and excitements faded, his resignation had a touching simplicity: 'Only faith in a life after death in a brighter world where dear ones will meet again—only that and the measured tramp of time can give consolation.'

"The aristocrat, the leader, the historian, the painter, the politician, the lord of language, the orator, the wit—yes, and the dedicated bricklayer—behind all of them was the man of simple faith, steadfast in defeat, generous in victory, resigned in age, trusting in a loving providence, and committing his achievements and his triumphs to a higher power.

"Like the patriarchs of old, he waited on God's judgment, and it could be said of him—as of the immortals that went before him— that God magnified him in the fear of his enemies and with his words he made prodigies to cease.'"

PRESIDENT JOHNSON HAD not attended, resolutely clinging to the excuse of his cold while overseeing the intelligence operation unfolding in England. In the seclusion of the Oval Office, he watched Stevenson's speech on television, Bill Moyers by his side, the strains of the broadcast echoing against the room's silence.

"Adlai might be a pansy-ass," Johnson remarked with the characteristic bluntness that masked his own insecurities, "but he can sure put the words together. How come my guys can't write me speeches that smart?"

His manner was gruff, but Moyers had long since learned to discern the low drumbeat of doubt that ran beneath his boss's bravado. With practiced skill, he set about the necessary work of managing Johnson's outsized ambitions and equally large uncertainties.

"Mr. President, Stevenson has nothing on you," Moyers replied smoothly. "Your inaugural address the other day was a masterpiece, delivered with impeccable timing and tone."

Johnson let Moyers' soothing words settle over him, but still, the gnawing sense of having been outmaneuvered persisted. "I suppose, Bill," he muttered, "but I can't help thinking I should be the one in that church speaking about Churchill. Damned Russians. I'll never forgive 'em for causing me to miss this moment."

The lament hung in the air—part self-pity, part indignant resolve—as Johnson wrestled with the significance of history playing out an ocean away without him.

"What's the latest from our guys over in England, if you don't mind me asking?"

"Dulles tells me that they've taken care of a bomb," Johnson replied with a careful cadence, "but they don't know if there might be more of 'em. I feel like hopping on Air Force One and hightailing it over there. I have half a mind to do it."

"Mr. President," Moyers said, choosing his next words with the precision of a practiced diplomat, "of course you should do whatever you think is best. But I do think there is potential danger there."

"Danger?" Johnson's voice rose, a note of suspicion sharpening his Texan drawl. "You think this is about me being a coward, Moyers? Is that what you think of your President?"

Horrified at the suggestion and the thought of his illness-stricken commander in harm's reach, Moyers replied quickly, intent on dispelling the notion before it could take root. "No, no, of course not, Mr. President. This is not about courage, it's about wisdom. It's about having a firm hand on the rudder if something happens that gives the Russians a chance to move on Europe. You, sir, may be the only thing standing between war and peace."

Johnson's imposing presence seemed to deflate as he absorbed the aide's rational entreaty. He stood for a moment in contemplative silence, poised between the impulse to act and the responsibility to restrain. Wordlessly, he took a sip from his ever-present glass of Cutty Sark before acknowledging the truth of Moyers' statement.

"Ah hell, Bill," he finally said, resignation weighing down the bravado. "I know that. It's just that it's a hell of a thing."

"I know it is, Mr. President. No doubt about it." Moyers let the moment linger, knowing it was one the President would not long indulge.

Motioning to switch off the television, Johnson gestured for Moyers to follow him to the next pressing matter, another meeting, another conference, anything to keep his mind away from what he could not control. As they retreated from the room, the great shadows of Washington's winter dusk began to stretch across the capital, the city's lights blinking alive against the deepening night.

London

SHORTLY AFTER NOON on Thursday, Howard Hunt slipped through the doors of the Savoy Hotel followed closely by Jim McCord. In the taxi on their way there, the two men had developed some hand signals for silent communication, anticipating a long and possibly tense day of watching and waiting for Roger Hollis.

The stakes were high, and both men were eager.

So Hunt was taken aback to find the MI5 director already in The Grill, comfortably settled with a sandwich and a pot of tea. The man appeared to be relaxing over lunch by himself, reading some papers from an oversized folder. It was a startling turn of events. McCord, instantly alert, was poised for the next move.

Hunt gestured toward the far wall where there was a bank of pay telephones. "Tell King that Hollis is here and that we're going to watch him for any possible contact with the man in room 312," Hunt instructed.

McCord nodded and walked briskly, careful not to draw the attention of those seated nearby. Hunt took a table by himself, one that offered a good view of Hollis. He watched the director through hooded eyes, making sure to appear as though he was engrossed in working the Times crossword puzzle. Snapping the paper sharply, he randomly filled in words with ink, adding a contrived look of concentration. The waiter filling his water glass glanced at the puzzle, clearly impressed.

Hunt's strategic nonchalance was rehearsed to perfection.

"Just a bowl of whatever soup you're serving today," Hunt said, his eyes never leaving the newspaper. By the time the soup arrived— split pea, to Hunt's chagrin—McCord had already left the telephones and was seated on the far side of the room. Hollis was still alone, still reading. The two men made eye contact, and Hunt wiped his mouth with a napkin, the signal communicating: "If he moves, you follow."

McCord understood.

He placed himself in position, ready to make the next move. His server brought a glass of ginger ale to his table. The drink was still fizzing when Hollis did a triple dab of his mouth with a folded napkin. He got up and walked away from his table. McCord let a few moments pass before trailing after him. From a distance, he watched Hollis enter the men's room. McCord hesitated, deciding not to follow him in. He hovered near the entrance, observing anyone else who might enter.

Less than a minute later, Hollis came out again and was making his way to a lift. McCord considered his options, making a split-second decision to try to catch the same elevator car. He barely made it, slipping in just as the doors were closing. He noticed that the operator pressed the button for the third floor, so McCord indicated it was his destination, as well. He forced a smile as Hollis cast a long, suspicious look at him. McCord fished through his pockets as if looking for something, keeping his head down and his expression blank.

He followed Hollis off the lift, pretending to head in the opposite direction from the one the director was taking. McCord heard a door open and then close behind him. He turned and quickly walked back the way Hollis had gone. His impeccable sense of hearing told him that the door Hollis used was on the left side of the hall and a few down from the lift. He looked at the numbers there and saw the room had to be either 310 or 312. The possibilities narrowed the situation to one conclusion.

Acting quickly, McCord took the lift back down to brief Howard Hunt.

"Has to be 312. That's the room our mystery man occupies," Hunt decided. "We'd better lay back and watch for a bit. If it's Philby's room, there's no way those KGB bastards would have him in a place like this without their own surveillance, so they gotta have some eyes 'round here somewhere. We need to be careful. You grab a paper and sit somewhere. I'll check in with King this time. Got a coin?"

McCord nodded and fished one out of his pocket and tossed it over. Then he picked up a copy of The Guardian as Hunt headed for the phones.

"Yep. Room 312. Something's up in that one, old boy," Hunt crowed when he finally reached King.

"You guys sit on this. Hang tight. I'll be by in a bit," King replied.

"You'd better stay out of view, Harvey. If it is Kim, he'll see you coming a mile away. You're hard to miss."

"Yeah well, I know a thing or two about tradecraft, Hunt. Don't worry about me. Just don't get blown yourself."

THE COLD AIR bit through Harvey King's coat as he walked up the Strand. The wind drove a persistent drizzle into his face, but he barely noticed. It was all coming together on this operation. He could feel it. He was more than ready to spend the day closing the net on Kim Philby.

The rain picked up, and King quickened his steps toward The Savoy. He was surprised to see Howard Hunt casually walking away from the hotel, toward him. He stopped and waited for Hunt to meet him. "What the hell, Hunt?" King asked. "Told you to stay put."

"I improvised—so sue me."

"This is my operation—"

"King," Hunt interrupted. "Would you shut your damn pie hole for once? Listen to me. Hollis left about ten minutes ago."

"Did you follow him?"

"I sent McCord with him. But that's not what you need to know. Just stop talking!"

"Okay, Hunt. No need to be a bastard about it."

Hunt's next words were golden. "Philby—or at least the guy we think might be him—is back in the bar."

"Now?"

"As we speak."

Harvey King thought for a moment. Timing was everything. After all these years, he didn't want to blow it. "Here's the plan, Sport," he said. "You go back to the bar and keep an eye on him. Meantime, I'll get into that room."

Hunt started to interrupt. King spoke over him, "But here's the deal. If he makes a move, you pick up the nearest house phone and ring room 312 once—just once. That'll give me time to scram."

"You got it," Hunt replied.

"Now you head back. I'll be thirty seconds behind you."

Howard Hunt turned and made his way back to the hotel.

Could it really be Philby? King asked himself. Had they finally run him to ground? They'd been so sure they had him in Beirut two years back, only to have him slip away. And now that bastard had the gall to be here? He was going to know for sure within the next few minutes. By the time Hunt reached the bar, King was through the front doors and on his way to the lifts, looking every bit the part of someone who belonged there.

He told the elevator operator, "Take me up to three."

The hallway on the third floor was vacant, except for a housekeeping cart. Harvey found room 312 and, using a device he kept in his pocket, picked the lock in a matter of seconds. Once inside, he poked around, careful not to disturb things. He saw several glasses scattered around the room but surmised the one on the table next to the bed would be the best bet to bear Kim Philby's prints—if indeed he were the occupant of the room. King was going to find out. He was certain of that. One way or another, he would see to it. Using his handkerchief, he wrapped the glass and then put it in his pocket.

Just then the telephone rang—once.

King made his way out of the room, down the hall, and past the elevators. He hid inside a deep doorway and waited. When the elevator arrived, he saw the mystery man exit and walk straight to room 312.

Kim Philby, you lying son of a bitch. We got you after all these years.

CHAPTER FIFTY

"PROBABLY GOING TO have to get our friend Detective Sergeant Murray to help with this one, Mr. King," Thompson said. He turned his gaze to the water glass now perched on his kitchen table. "I'm sure he knows someone who can run a trace on the prints, but he'll have to know what it's about. We can't keep him in the dark if we're to get anywhere with this mess."

"He's played ball with us so far, Thompson. I trust him not to make a hash of it," King replied with calm certainty.

"Yes, he has," Thompson acknowledged, still wary. "But we've yet to talk with him about a link to Hollis, MI5, and all that bloody rot. He might feel some need to speak to others higher up about our work in this matter." The risk loomed large in his mind—one misstep, and the repercussions could be disastrous.

King nodded slowly, absorbing the weight of Thompson's words. "Can't hurt to ask," he pressed, his urgency unmasked by a twitch of impatience.

"I suppose not," Thompson said, remaining cautious, his voice a blend of resolve and resignation. They both understood the delicacy of planting seeds of suspicion without revealing too much too soon. "Let me take this to him and see what he says. How do they say it on American television? I recall a phrase from my tour over there. Ah yes—stay tuned?"

King laughed, a moment of levity in an otherwise somber exchange. "Yeah. That's it. We're going to stay tuned, Thompson. Just hurry every chance you get." His smile fading, he added, "The sooner we confirm our suspicions about the man in room 312, the better."

Everything in King's gut pointed to a leak within the Service itself, but without proof, they were fumbling in the dark. The entire operation hinged on their next step, and the pressure to move quickly weighed heavily upon them. It was a delicate play, like setting mousetraps in shadows.

Mary came into the room. "Now, you fine gentlemen need to give me my kitchen if we're to have a proper tea. Off with you," she said with a gentle wave of her hand.

KAITLYN DORCEY SAT in the dim cacophony of the Tipperary pub, feeling a rare and unsettling sense of trepidation as she cradled a pint of Smithwick's in her hands. Normally composed and analytical, she found herself on edge, anxiously contemplating the implications of her recent conversations with Sean. His chilling revelations had left her with the grim certainty that Michael and Molly Wheelan were deeply embedded agents, working as part of an intricate Soviet espionage network.

In a decisive move, she had agreed to ring the pair at the modest building that they frequently used as a front and bait them with the pretense of urgent information. The plan was simple yet audacious: lure them to her flat under the guise of a private meeting and have Sean and Matthews ready to secure them upon arrival. Now, as she sat alone in the bustling establishment, she considered the profound ramifications of tonight's work and wondered how far the couple's betrayal extended.

Time felt suspended, every glance toward the door heightening her anticipation, when her quarry finally appeared. She had only about an inch of ale left in her glass when she saw the couple from Birmingham make their entrance. They scanned the room, then confidently walked over and joined her at the table. "I'll get us a drink, and another for you, Miss Dorcey," Michael offered, his tone as pleasant as ever, betraying no suspicion of her duplicity.

"No," Kaitlyn countered, her voice barely louder than a whisper. "Let's not talk here." Her eyes darted discreetly over her right shoulder, making sure they weren't attracting unwanted attention. "My flat is a block away. Besides, I have a proper drink there—a nice new bottle of Tullamore Dew."

"Sounds splendid," he replied. His nonchalance suggested he had no idea of the trap into which they were walking. The three of them left the crowded pub, stepping out into the cool night and moving quickly across the cobbled streets toward her flat, a sense of urgency veiled as discretion.

As soon as they were inside, the men hiding in the flat leaped into action, overpowering the couple before they had a chance to resist. Michael and Molly were seized with precision, their arms wrenched behind them and secured as Matthews swiftly tied them to separate chairs. The operation was executed flawlessly, and within two minutes, the room was silent except for the sound of restrained breathing. Michael and Molly struggled against their bindings, their eyes seething with anger and disbelief.

Ferguson Matthews pulled out two syringes filled with a potent sedative and calmly approached his captives. Before they could vocalize their outrage, he injected Michael and Molly in their necks with practiced ease. The chemical quickly took effect, their bodies slumping under the tranquilizing influence as they fought a losing battle against unconsciousness. Even in their groggy state, they glared at Kaitlyn, their expressions a mix of betrayal and contempt.

She returned their disdain with a cold, accusing stare of her own. "You bastard," she said, her voice filled with both anger and vindication. "Working for the Soviets all along! We're going to find out all the parts of the story you've forgotten to mention." Kaitlyn leaned over and slapped Michael's face, the impact sharp against the dull thud of his heavy breathing. Her fear and apprehension evaporated, replaced by a steady resolve.

Brogan and Matthews exchanged satisfied glances as the sedative did its work. They watched in silence until both Michael and Molly were slumped in their chairs, heads lolling to one side, and then began methodically searching the couple's pockets for anything that might offer additional insight into their covert operations.

Michael's jacket yielded a small notebook filled with what appeared to be coded entries, while Molly had tickets for a rail journey to Liverpool, presumably their next point of contact for a drop or rendezvous. Calm and efficient, Brogan secured these items before gesturing for Matthews to help double-check the ropes.

As the last knots were tightened, Brogan looked over at Kaitlyn with an expression of mixed gratitude and admiration. They all knew the risks she had taken, not just in luring the Wheelans into a trap but in implicating herself in an operation that could have gone awry in so many ways. She remained composed, her determination unshaken by the dramatic turn of events.

WALTER THOMPSON REACHED for his coat and exited the flat with confident determination. He was certain that transactions maintained in person, with no telephones being tapped or letters intercepted, were most secure in instances such as these. The matter was of great sensitivity and utmost urgency, and Murray was someone whom, over time, Thompson had grown to trust. The meeting was too important to be derailed by any carelessness.

He grabbed the glass in its protective covering, hailed a cab, and sped across town to meet the detective. As the taxi wound through the streets of London, every turn was marked with the city's familiar sights, but Thompson scarcely noticed. He was consumed by thoughts of the mystery man. If their suspicions were correct, this was a discovery that would shake the very bones of the British establishment.

The cab crossed the Thames, and he could see the imposing structure of Scotland Yard rising along the river. Thompson leaned forward and instructed the driver to pull over a block away, wanting to approach on foot to arouse less attention. He stepped out, paid the fare, and did not regret the tip—though generous for a Scot—as this was, after all, not coming from his own pocket. He walked briskly.

There would be value in catching Murray outside of the building.

THOMPSON SAW MURRAY standing on the pavement, looking both ways as if checking to see if Thompson was being followed. They met just outside Scotland Yard Headquarters. Murray looked up and gave him an uncertain nod.

"Whatever prints are on this glass may turn out to be quite revealing and important, Murray," Thompson said, handing him a small bag and lowering his voice in a manner characteristic of the conspiratorial nature of the exchange.

"All very cloak and dagger, Thompson. You turning into Sherlock Holmes?" Murray said, a smirk playing on his face, trying to keep the matter light against the heaviness of the situation. They laughed, but the camaraderie felt more to Thompson like an effort from Murray to conceal something deeper and more preoccupying.

"If our suspicions are correct, it will be important that this goes no further than you and him—at least for now. Understood?"

Thompson looked closely at Murray as though attempting to read his thoughts. He sensed that something weighed on the detective, some matter further pressing than the mystery of the fingerprints.

"You look down—something on your mind?" Thompson asked, now with a true curiosity.

"Yes, actually. I think it's time to put in my papers and retire," Murray said, almost too casually.

"The devil you say. Why would you retire now, at a time like this?" Thompson pressed, suspicious of the sudden declaration.

"It's time," Murray repeated with resignation. "I can't go back to normal police work after what I've been doing for so long. Surely you understand?"

"Indeed, I do. But retirement is not all it's cracked up to be, old boy," Thompson replied, trying to dissuade him. He wondered what new secret burdened the detective and made him seek the reassurances of domestic peace and an end to the dangers of his career.

"You and the Missus seem to get on quite well," Murray responded, though somewhat wistfully. "I owe my love some good years—never even been on a honeymoon. It's time."

"Well, the first thing is to get us those prints. After we learn who the mystery man is, you may want to stay on for another bit of time." Thompson leaned in, hoping to encourage Murray to see the matter through to its conclusion, whatever the risks involved.

Murray nodded, acknowledging the task at hand, and headed into the building. The hallways of Scotland Yard were familiar to him, yet today they felt stifling. With each step, he questioned not only his next actions but also his very future. Murray knew the importance of this mission and saw it now with a sense of foreboding finality.

He soon reached the area where his friend worked, and after a tense wait, he had the confirmation. He trembled as he read the name scrawled on the small slip of paper: Harold Russell Adrian Philby.

He was chilled to the bone.

"Good God!" he exclaimed to himself, in shock at the ramifications. He wasted no time, almost sprinting through the halls with the bag of evidence clutched tightly in his hand, his heart racing not only with disbelief but also with fear of what would come next. He left the building and headed straight for Walter Thompson's flat.

KAITLYN HAD SAT silent for the better part of an hour, which was quite unusual. Her waters were seldom, if ever, still. Brogan watched her as she stared out the dirty window of her flat, deep in thought and seemingly miles away, trying to make sense of it all. They'd subdued the Wheelans, and Matthews had gone to report, but the situation felt unfinished. He walked over to where she sat.

"Not like you to be so quiet, love. I know this is an awful lot to think through."

She turned to look up at him, her eyes full of doubt and troubled thoughts. "None of this makes any sense to me. I've worked with them before, you know. We've been friends. Betrayal hurts, Sean."

"I know. I know."

"I find me-self wondering if there are now other things I don't know."

"Other things?" he asked with a touch of uneasiness.

She nodded. "Yes. Who can I trust? Do I even know you, Sean? Have you been truthful with me all along?"

"Of course, I have. You're just shaken," Brogan said. "Give it some time. It's a lot to process."

"What are we to do now—just sit here and wait forever?"

"No. I'm waiting for word from the blokes I'm working with on this one."

"And about them, Sean. I may not be keen as mustard, but it's clear even to me that you're working with the Yanks. What are the Americans doing here, and how did you get to throw in your lot with the likes of them?"

"It's a long, complicated story." Brogan hesitated, not sure how much to tell her.

"Well, love," she said with a faint smile and a sparkle in her eye. "It appears we have some time on our hands."

"JIM, IT'S PHILBY, for sure. He's here in London and involved in all this Churchill funeral mess. Not sure what his role is, but it must be significant."

"Fascinating," Angleton said. He was at his desk and smoking another of his ever-present cigarettes. "What's your plan?"

"We're going to catch him in his room this evening—if we can."

"Now listen, Harvey. I want to be there for the briefing."

"I'm thinking more like interrogation, Jim."

"Whatever the case, I want you to hold him until I get there. I'm catching the afternoon flight to London. I'll need someone to pick me up at London Airport in the morning, your time."

"Roger that. I'll send a guy. By that time, we'll probably be set up in Philby's room at the hotel. By the way, our friend in Rome sent us three of his 'associates.' So we've got plenty of muscle for whatever we need."

"Great. Glad to hear it. Now, I'm going to book a room there under one of my legends—Marco Renaldi. We can move Philby to my room when I get there. Keep my plans from him. I can't wait to see the look on that lying bastard's face when he sees me."

CHAPTER FIFTY-ONE

HOWARD HUNT SPENT nearly the entirety of that Thursday evening at the Savoy, where he awaited yet another elusive appearance by Kim Philby. He cycled through the motions of a man with endless time to spare, reading a newspaper beneath the grand chandelier, and later, sitting tight-lipped with a drink in the bar.

He paused his mission long enough to consume a sandwich, before giving way again to the stately confines of the lobby. He maintained a regular pace, moving every thirty minutes from lounge to exit, always carrying the conspicuous signal: a folded newspaper. Each of these circuits was an indication for Harvey King, waiting strategically across the street, that the infamous spy had yet to make an entrance.

As the grand clock in the lobby ticked past eight, King observed Hunt emerge one more time, empty-handed this round. The signal was clear: Philby had landed. King found him in the bar—the treacherous figure unmistakable, despite the cumbersome wig and matching beard. A dark Sports jacket hung carelessly over Philby's frame, his light blue shirt unbuttoned at the top, projecting an image of casual defiance. Slinking like a predator who'd spotted prey, King navigated the sidewalk on swift feet and joined Hunt.

"Just sat down and ordered a drink," Hunt reported softly, eyes flicking toward Philby's table. "If his pattern holds, he'll have another, then back to the room. I give it fifteen minutes." His voice was low, almost lost beneath the din of hotel chatter. "I'll ring once from the house phone when he's on the move."

As they strolled through the lobby's elegant corridors, Hunt peeled off and angled toward the bar while King walked briskly toward the lift. Within five minutes, King was in position inside room 312, gun drawn, crouched slightly out of sight from the door, acutely attuned to the faintest sound.

True to expectations, the man in the sloppy disguise drained his second scotch and signed his tab with a flourish. Hunt shadowed him discreetly, and by the time Philby moved in the direction of the lift, Hunt was already at the house phone. "Ring room 312, please. But just the once," he instructed the operator with urgency. He watched Philby until the lift door shut on his figure, then rushed to the nearby stairway and ascended quickly to the third floor.

In room 312, King heard the single ring of the telephone and was on full alert. Only moments passed before he detected the key in the door. In the hallway, Hunt's gaze was locked on Philby as he slipped in behind him. Timing it with precision, he reached the room just as Philby entered and deftly caught the door before it closed and shut it behind himself.

"Hello, Kim," King said.

PHILBY WAS VISIBLY shaken. "W-what the hell?" he stammered, his voice cracking with shock. Almost simultaneously, Hunt appeared with a gun trained steadily at Philby's spine. "Harvey K-King—is that you?" Philby sputtered, trying to mask his fear with a nervous tremor in his voice.

"One and the same, Kim. And please meet a friend of mine, Howard Hunt." King's voice was laced with triumphant satisfaction.

Philby glanced over his shoulder, eyes calculating, then turned back to King. He drew himself up with a veneer of false bravado. "You old devil—what are you doing in London?" he asked, working to project a calm he did not feel. "You assigned here these days?"

"Cut the bullshit, Philby. The question is what are you doing in London these days?" King barked.

"Yes, old boy. I s-s-suppose it is." Philby's voice was uneven but still attempting a veneer of casual indifference.

He hesitated for a moment, gauging the men before him. "I'm mostly laying low these d-d-days," Philby finally replied, slowing his speech to steady his nerves. "Not a lot of action. Q-q-quiet, really. Picking up little j-jobs here and there." He looked from King to Hunt and back again. "Freelance work." He paused, seeing no sympathy in King's eyes. "You know. The usual." His wits began to return, and an insolent grin crept at the edges of his mouth. "I'm not the only one making a c-career comeback, I see."

King gave a snort of derision.

"I WAS DOING some freelance work, investigations and such, and this American approached me in Belfast about doing some work for his company. Small stuff. Surveillance. Photos. Men misbehaving," Brogan told Kaitlyn. He watched her closely, wondering how she would react now that he was finally opening up to her about such a dangerous chapter of his life.

"You're a bloody Peeping Tom? That's what you've been doing all these years?" she asked with a mischievous look in her eyes. There was something in her tone, a teasing lilt, that made Brogan feel more at ease with his confession, even as he feared how much to reveal.

"Much more dignified than all that," he tried to protest. "But eventually the same man, Harvey King approached me to help with a different kind of investigation."

"And you agreed?" It was clear in her expression that she wasn't finished with questions—not by a long shot.

"Not right away," he said. "But they were very persuasive—they made it clear that I'd have a problem with them and Five otherwise."

"What kind of problem?" she pressed.

"A lock the door and throw away the key problem," Brogan replied grimly. He'd worn his "Sean Walsh" persona for so long that he felt like he actually remembered the fear of that fictional coercion and how the thought of rotting away, forgotten by all, had persuaded him to agree to their terms.

"When was all this?"

"I started helping the 'company' last year," he confided, "but this current thing is only a couple of weeks old. They were working on a tip. Once they told me what it was they were looking for, I had misgivings. I mean, we all bloody hated Churchill, but the idea of the Russians using our cause as a cover for their power-hungry plans, well, that was too much. So I signed on." The words spilled out, a release that almost felt like betrayal even as they left his lips.

"I'm not sure what I would do in the same situation, but I surely understand, Sean. I feel better now. Are they asleep for a while?" she asked, nodding at the Wheelans. Her willingness to accept stunned him, a rush of relief mingled with the guilt that still gnawed at his insides.

"Michael and Molly won't wake until the middle of tomorrow. Why?"

"Gives us some time to make up. Come with me," she said, taking him by the hand and leading him to the bedroom.

Brogan felt a measure of guilt, but he pushed through it in anticipation of a night of pleasure. He did wonder though if he would ever be able to be completely honest with the girl he now loved very much.

TRUE TO HIS word, Jim Angleton was on a flight to London late that afternoon. He had left hastily from Dulles International Airport aboard the Pan Am Clipper, a sense of determination pulsing through him that felt more akin to his earlier days in the agency. Angleton was scheduled to arrive in London early—just after seven a.m. local time. *Plenty of time to catch up with events and take the old bastard by surprise,* he thought to himself.

His large satchel, heavy with the weight of several "Philby" files, was tucked securely at his feet. As the aircraft droned steadily over the Atlantic, he pored over the documents with a focus that bordered on obsession, making extensive notes for the upcoming interrogation he had so patiently anticipated. He had his own questions, of course, but he knew many others were still left unanswered from their earlier years.

Adrenalin drove him nearly as much as the strong coffee and the endless chain of cigarettes on which he puffed with resolve. Though he was a spy well-trained in being inconspicuous, he was rendered almost invisible by the mere presence of another passenger—a former President of the United States, seated several rows ahead of him—in First Class.

Once the plane touched down, it took Angleton no time at all to clear customs. The notoriously efficient master of infiltration now had only to wait for his luggage—a momentary lapse in the otherwise fluid progression of his journey. He was met outside the terminal by Howard Hunt, who filled him in on the details as they drove toward The Savoy.

Hunt assured Angleton that everything was going according to plan, and that Harvey King had scrupulously followed instructions, restraining himself from engaging Philby in any substantive dialogue. The old spy had been caught unawares, just as they had hoped.

He wasted no time in checking into room 408 at The Savoy, where he took a few minutes to freshen up before the phone rang.

"Welcome to London, my friend," came King's voice on the other end. "Ready for some company?"

"I've been ready for this since 1951, Harvey," Angleton replied with an air of steely anticipation. "Bring the prisoner to me."

King and Hunt led Philby discreetly up the back stairwell to the fourth floor of the grand hotel. They were careful to avoid any unwelcome eyes as they made their way along the dimly lit corridor, the gravity of their mission reflected in their cautious movements. They moved past the lift, leading their captive to room 408. King knocked twice on the door, a prearranged signal, and it immediately swung open to admit them.

"That cigarette smells vaguely familiar," Philby said, sniffing the reek of smoke that mingled with the stale air of the room. He twisted around and saw Angleton standing behind the door, poised with an expression that was both calculating and ironic. A broad grin split across Philby's face. "I'll be d-d-damned, if it isn't my old friend, J-J-Jim. How the hell are you, old man? Still s-smoking those wretched weeds?"

Angleton fixed his gaze upon Philby, studying him with an intensity that spoke volumes more than words ever could. He gave King a nod, instructing him to deposit Philby in the lone chair set conspicuously in the middle of the room. Finally, Angleton broke the silence. "It's been a long time, Kim. Too long. We have much catching up to do. Can we get you some water or tea?"

"I know it's quite early, but I'd love a scotch, if I m-might?" Philby replied with a jesting tone.

"Sorry, Kim. You're going to need a clear head."

"Jim," Philby said, dragging the name out with a laugh. "You remember those four martini lunches at Harvey's in Georgetown. We managed to s-s-survive those with our wits about us."

"That was a long time ago, Kim, though I'm sure I still can't keep up with you when it comes to the sauce." Angleton's body language, which had been stiff up until that moment, began to relax.

"We're going to have a long talk. If it goes well, we'll have that drink."

"Promise me two and you can fire away, old b-boy. I'm all yours."

CHAPTER FIFTY-TWO

THOUGH DWIGHT D. EISENHOWER had served two terms as President of the United States, he preferred to be called "General" Eisenhower after he handed over the reins of leadership and left behind the grandeur of the White House in January 1961 to quietly retire at his farm in Gettysburg, Pennsylvania. During his tenure, Eisenhower had been a remarkably popular President, and throughout the nation, he continued to be revered and cherished, a symbol of stability and strength.

The public's high esteem for him remained so unwavering that when his successor—young and charismatic John F. Kennedy—found himself ensnared in political controversies, particularly those concerning military and foreign policy, one of Kennedy's first strategies was to orchestrate a series of photo opportunities that highlighted him in consultation with the venerable Ike.

These were carefully crafted images, typically portraying the younger President listening intently to the seasoned statesman's sage and worldly insights. Once Kennedy was felled by an assassin's bullet, Lyndon Johnson followed suit and arranged for Ike to appear by his side in moments of political peril.

So it was nothing short of another inexplicable oversight on President Johnson's part that he didn't choose the General to serve as America's official representative at Sir Winston Churchill's funeral. After all, Eisenhower and the British wartime Prime Minister had cultivated a formidable partnership as they worked closely with each other, side by side, during the perilous years of what Eisenhower himself referred to as "The Great Crusade"—the massive and historic build-up to D-Day and the eventual and hard-earned liberation of Europe from the blight of Nazi tyranny. Their relationship had been one forged in the crucible of war, marked by mutual respect and a shared vision for peace, making Eisenhower a profoundly fitting choice to honor Churchill.

A few days before the funeral, Bill Moyers made a concerted effort to persuade the President to send Eisenhower to London. To Moyers, the decision was glaringly obvious and strategically sound. "It just makes sense, Mr. President," he earnestly told his boss, hoping to sway him with reason. "If not you, and if not the vice President, a former President is the obvious choice." He expected that Johnson would recognize the wisdom in his words, yet the President's response was swift and dismissive.

"Not going to do it, Bill. I have my reasons, and you're just going to have to take my word for it." Johnson's tone left little room for argument, and Moyers, though bewildered, had no inkling as to Johnson's real motives. Moyer suspected that his boss was withholding something significant, a deeper agenda perhaps, but he had learned through experience that it was futile—and potentially perilous—to press Johnson on such matters.

"Yes, Mr. President. So should I arrange for McNamara and Rusk to represent us?" Moyers asked, resigned to the President's decision but still puzzled by the logic behind it.

Johnson paused, contemplative, weighing the symbolic value of the delegation he intended to send. He knew that merely dispatching his Secretary of Defense and Secretary of State might be perceived as inadequate for such a momentous occasion. After a moment of careful consideration, he added a key figure to the list.

"Add Warren to the list. And tell the Chief Justice he'll be leading the delegation." The inclusion of Chief Justice Earl Warren was a calculated move, his presence would signal the importance the United States attached to honoring the memory of its ally.

But Eisenhower went to London anyway.

Despite the White House's quiet machinations and Johnson's security fears, Eisenhower made his way to London, determined to pay tribute to his old wartime partner. It was an unforeseen development in Johnson's careful planning, one that caught the President and his advisors by surprise. What they didn't know—at least not until the situation was entirely out of their control—was that the invitation to the funeral had come not from the American government, but directly from Her Majesty the Queen herself.

On behalf of the nation and honoring the requests of the Churchill family, the Queen extended the invitation to the former President, who accepted it with deep humility and resolve. Even the BBC, eager for his presence, had made special arrangements for Eisenhower—a key figure in Churchill's wartime strategy—to be involved with their extensive broadcast coverage of the funeral.

When Eisenhower, with characteristic thoroughness and adherence to protocol, informed Johnson of these plans, he did so expecting some resistance. The President was tempted to intervene, to caution Eisenhower against the trip. But he knew that any overt attempt to restrain this American icon might inadvertently endanger the very operation he was seeking to protect. Harvey King's covert mission required the utmost secrecy, and any unusual moves might expose the elaborate counterterrorism efforts in place.

Begrudgingly, Johnson decided against direct confrontation. Instead, he subtly indicated his apprehensions by alerting Dulles and ensuring a heightened state of security around Eisenhower's visit. Special instructions were relayed to the American embassy in

London, emphasizing the necessity for meticulous precautions for their illustrious visitor.

As a result, when the Pan Am Clipper carrying James Angleton touched down in London, several discreet agents disembarked alongside other passengers. They strategically positioned themselves near the tarmac, eyes scanning every detail, prepared to shadow the General's movements and intercept any potential threats. Their vigilance was evident as they kept watch over the bustling airport crowd, waiting for the moment the former President would emerge.

Finally, Eisenhower appeared at the top of the aircraft steps, a formidable figure in a dark topcoat and matching felt hat. He descended with a vitality and presence that belied his years, his legendary smile bright and unwavering. As he reached the bottom of the stairs, he was surrounded immediately by dignitaries and admirers. To them, he was not just the former President but the victorious and emblematic General, the hero of Normandy—even in this solemn context of mourning, the triumphant conqueror.

Amid the welcoming assembly on that brisk Thursday night stood David Bruce, the esteemed U.S. Ambassador to Great Britain. With the decorum and respect befitting the occasion, Bruce personally guided Eisenhower to a waiting car. They traversed London's iconic streets, the city abuzz with preparations for the grand funeral, until they arrived at the American Embassy. There, in anticipatory deference, a splendid room was set aside. The rest of the designated "official delegation," including McNamara, Rusk, and Warren, was not slated to arrive until the following day.

As the embassy staff bustled with preparation, Eisenhower expressed his appreciation to Ambassador Bruce. "Thank you so much, Mr. Ambassador," he remarked courteously as his luggage was delivered. "This is very kind of you. Now, I'd like to visit Westminster Hall first thing in the morning to pay my respects to my old friend." Eisenhower's tone was both nostalgic and firm, a reflection of his resolute intention to honor Churchill personally and promptly.

Bruce, acutely aware of Johnson's concerns, suspected that the President would prefer Eisenhower to maintain a low profile until the funeral itself. Thus, he approached the matter with gentle diplomacy. "Sir, I'm not sure that's the best thing," he advised cautiously. "The crowds are very large, and the logistics might be difficult." Bruce knew well the obstinacy of powerful men, yet he hoped that the General might reconsider or delay until the security situation was more manageable.

Eisenhower, however, was unwavering—his determination impervious to polite suggestion. He responded with good-natured defiance, reminding the Ambassador of his military stubbornness and independence. "Well, Mr. Ambassador, I'm sure you have a point," Eisenhower replied, his eyes twinkling. "But I'm going to pay my respects there even if I have to walk there all by myself." The statement was a clear assertion of his intentions and capabilities, a signal that he was accustomed to overcoming far greater logistical challenges.

"Understood, sir," came Bruce's resigned but respectful reply. He realized that Eisenhower's mind was set and that any further argument would be futile. "We'll take care of it. How about we leave here around eleven?" Bruce's acquiescence ensured that the logistics would indeed be sorted, and the promise of security measures would both satisfy Eisenhower's intent and Johnson's concerns.

"Splendid. And thank you, Mr. Ambassador," Eisenhower said, acknowledging Bruce's diplomatic compliance. "I'm well aware that President Johnson is concerned for my safety and has likely given all sorts of instructions about my security, but I'm an old hand at these things, as you know," he added, his expression a blend of gratitude and amusement. His renowned smile—the same optimistic and reassuring expression that calmed nations and troops alike—flashed across his face, signaling his contentment with the arrangements and his anticipation of the solemn duties ahead.

THE CROWDS WERE once again large that morning, and the line of mourners at Westminster Hall, a steady procession slowed as word spread that General Eisenhower had arrived to pay his respects. At first, there were only murmurs and a few pointing fingers. But soon the name was on many lips and was passed from hushed voice to hushed voice. Parents telling children who the General was and how important he had been to Winston Churchill and to the world they were inheriting.

Others, older people, reminisced quietly about the days when Eisenhower, along with Churchill, had been a daily part of their own lives and hopes. The formal procession paused as those who had already seen the casket tarried longer to look back at another piece of history.

Eisenhower removed his topcoat and hat as he entered the large room. Even this act seemed to captivate those around him. His two aides stayed back as he walked slowly and respectfully to within a few yards of the catafalque. He stood with his head bowed, a public man having a private moment, in silent reflection and prayer.

This moment was interrupted when another famous man from those war-torn years came and stood ten feet from the General. Charles De Gaulle. A new round of whispers swept the crowd: speculation as to whether they would acknowledge each other, memories of their roles defining the Free World, gossip about old tensions and rivalries.

The French President, a large, formal figure in his dark coat, stared directly ahead. The man who led the "Free French" during the war, and whose relationship with Churchill was stormy at best, did not bow. He stood at attention as his way of remembering and showing respect.

One man in the crowd whispered to his wife, "You remember what old Winnie said about that French bastard, right?"

She was horrified and shout-whispered back, "You keep your tongue!"

But the man continued, "He said, 'That De Gaulle thinks he's Joan of Arc, but I can't get my bloody Bishops to burn him!'"

"I'm warning you!" she scolded, looking around in embarrassment. Several people who overheard him smiled at the spat and at the memory of the famously caustic Churchill remarks. But their smiles were discreet, and their attention soon returned to the two great men, each communing in his own way with the memory of the third.

After several more minutes, the Eisenhower's aides approached. As he put his coat and hat back on, he stopped briefly to shake some of the outstretched hands that had gathered in the hall. He left soon after and returned to the American Embassy. It was there, a short time later, that he sprang a surprise on his host—one that was quickly reported back to Washington.

As he sat down to an early lunch with David Bruce, General Eisenhower looked especially pleased with himself. "I'm not actually going to attend the service at St. Paul's," he told the Ambassador.

"Sir?" Bruce asked, clearly caught off guard, unable to hide his surprise even in front of such a distinguished guest.

Eisenhower smiled, obviously enjoying the moment. "I'll be keeping out of the crowds and away from any fuss. I was keeping this news close to my chest, but people from the BBC have asked me to be in a studio with them throughout the day, offering commentary on the events. So rest assured and pass it along to President Johnson that I'll be safe and secure. Not to mention warm and dry."

Ambassador Bruce raised his glass of water. "A bit early for anything stronger, but this water will do. To President Eisenhower and the BBC."

Eisenhower smiled and raised his glass. Then he said, "This chicken salad is delicious. Sure wish Mamie was here."

CHAPTER FIFTY-THREE

"IN EXCHANGE FOR my s-s-safety, I can give you information about something b-big about to happen. Right here in London," Philby said. He paused deliberately, savoring the moment.

His words sent a charge through the room. Both Angleton and King knew precisely what Philby was alluding to. The Soviets had been planning a grand gesture, a shocking statement on British soil. But thanks to an informant, the Americans were already several steps ahead, and the plot was effectively neutralized. Philby's belief that he was dangling a priceless piece of intelligence was almost laughable, but it also presented both a challenge and a chance.

Angleton removed his glasses and rubbed his temples, looking across the shadowy room with a mix of astonishment and disbelief. Philby's audacious offer hung in the air, almost tangible. The man who had been at the center of an international espionage storm, who had slipped through the nets of MI6 and CIA to embrace the Soviet cause, was now proposing to switch sides again.

Harvey laughed, breaking the silence.

Angleton waved his hand dismissively, signaling Harvey to let it go. "No. I want to hear more," he insisted, his curiosity and professional instinct piqued. He knew there was risk, but he also sensed an opportunity—a potential goldmine of information.

"Okay, Kim," Angleton replied, as coolly as he could muster. "Let's say I'm willing to give you the benefit of the doubt. But first you'll need to tell me more about this big thing you think is about to happen. Something I can use. Right now." He leaned forward, watching as Philby shifted in his seat. The Brit was testing the waters, trying to play his trump card without giving away too much too soon.

"You Yanks b-b-believe you have it all figured out," Philby said, leaning back confidently. "But you're wrong. I know a lot. Enough t-to make you look like fools. And what I can tell you will have you shitting your p-pants."

Well?" Angleton pressed, hands steepled in front of him. He knew from experience the value of patience but was leaning toward impatience. "What exactly is it you know?"

The tension was momentarily broken by the loud chime of a clock from the hallway, a somber reminder of time passing. Outside, London was battening down for one of the most significant events in its modern history. The city would have been on high alert even without the threat of Soviet terrorism. Philby, however, had no idea that his precious information had been rendered worthless.

Angleton kept a steady gaze, making the Brit twist in his seat.

Philby said, "Your p-people will be dealing with the fallout for a long t-t-time. Then you'll need me because all hell is going to b-break loose!"

Angleton allowed himself a small smile, careful not to let Philby see the full expression of his amusement and triumph. He had desperately wanted to know if the Soviets thought their plan was still viable, and Philby's revelation—and his cluelessness—offered more certainty than he could have hoped for. Everything was going according to schedule.

The plot would be a complete dud.

"Not going to happen, Kim," he said at last, his voice hardening.

Philby pivoted, trying to recover, refusing to be dismissed so easily. "That's your American arrogance speaking. The Russians know you b-b-better than you think. I can make sure this really doesn't happen if you t-t-take me with you."

It was beginning to grate on Angleton, this endless British bluff. He had what he came for and was ready to be done with the charade. "You've got nothing, Kim."

Philby shook his head, frustration mingling with desperation. The bravado was fading, and Angleton could feel the sweat forming on that famous Philby brow. The American's icy demeanor was clearly getting to him. He shifted tactics again.

"Jim, I'm serious about defecting. I need to g-g-get out of here before it's too late. But more important, you need me to make sure you're safe."

Angleton stood up, his shadow looming over the Soviet spy. It was time to leave. He'd gotten everything he needed and more.

"We'll let you know," he said, and turned to go, "but don't hold your breath."

THE WEATHER WAS an enemy that Friday morning, showing no mercy to the crowds on the eve of Mr. Churchill's funeral. The skies were dark, and a biting wind drove sleet in all directions, but the people braved the cold and wet without complaint. Most wore heavy coats, and many carried black umbrellas, though the fierce wind rendered these almost useless. They came from all over the realm and the world to bid farewell to the man who had led Britain through its darkest hour. They stood in line for hours on end, winding their way slowly toward the dry confines of Westminster Hall.

Out in front of St. Paul's Cathedral, Harry Higgins was watching some of the preparations for the service. From his sheltered perch outside the building, he had a good view of the Royal Navy sailors as they practiced for their important role in the ceremonies. They marched up and down the street, solemn and efficient, their white uniforms striking against the old stones of the church and the grey sky above.

Harry lit a cigarette and watched as the sailors pulled a large gun carriage, preparing to carry Churchill's coffin through the streets of London and back again. *What a spectacle*, he thought, though his mind was focused on a different kind of spectacle. He had been given a key role in planning what was about to happen there the next day. And because of that, he knew the gun carriage would be making only one trip. Smiling, he lit another cigarette.

Not going to go anywhere from the church, he thought.

MANY PROMINENT MOURNERS had arrived from around the globe. The elaborate arrangements for Churchill's final farewell and the eagerness of foreign dignitaries to participate in the proceedings sealed his transformation from a controversial figure to a national hero. It was almost as if his passing had united the nation once again, and his death was being treated with the same reverence as his greatest triumphs.

Far from St. Paul's, where Harry Higgins watched the sailors rehearsing their duties, others involved in the plot were also making their own preparations. Most of the conspirators were low-level operatives, some of them not even knowing who they were working for. They had been given specific tasks without being told how those tasks fit into the larger plan.

"NO, WAIT," PHILBY cried. "I can tell you more—so much more." In his agitation, the wig that he still wore had shifted back somewhat and exposed his dark hair. He strained forward against his bonds and his glib façade was gone.

Angleton turned back and regarded him thoughtfully. Philby had struck that particular note that resonated with him—information. He had time to listen. The bomb was gone and that information was unsuspected by the Russians. He sat back down. "Go on."

Philby took a deep breath and gave his head a small shake as though trying to adjust his wig. He settled back against the chair. "As I understand it, the original idea came from Stalin. He hated Ch-Churchill and thought he'd outlive him but didn't. After his death, some of his associates—those c-called 'hardliners' here in the West—kept the idea alive for when the old man finally k-k-kicked off. The plan has a c-code name: KOBA

"Ah yes," Angleton said thoughtfully, "Stalin's early monicker."

Harvey King stood up abruptly and walked over to the prisoner. "Okay, Kim, here's what we're going to do. We'll put you back in your room while we check out your story. But we have our eyes on you. In the meantime, to show more good faith, you write down everything you know about this plan. Names, places, anything that can help us. Have that done in an hour. Then you call this room as if you're calling room service and order some coffee. You put your info in an envelope and hand it to the man who brings the coffee. Got it?"

Philby kept staring at Angleton, who was now standing with King. He seemed to be seeking further assurance of his safety from the quieter and more diplomatic of the Americans. He finally responded, "Yes, Harvey. It's all very s-st-straightforward."

"Well, you'd better be straightforward yourself, Kim. Or we'll hand you over to the gangsters you've been working for all your pathetic life."

CHAPTER FIFTY-FOUR

THAT AFTERNOON, THE Americans—minus Tiernan Brogan, who remained with Kaitlyn and the sedated Wheelan couple—assembled at Walter Thompson's flat. Hunt and Thompson had taken charge of the day's agenda. Edmund Murray was there, as well. Spirits were high. Angleton and King had brought along a two-page document in Kim Philby's own hand, and they looked like cats with a bowl of cream. It contained a treasure trove of valuable and actionable intelligence.

"Yes, the man came through. I think we must operate on the assumption that Kim very much wants to come to America," Angleton said.

"I agree," King added. Everyone in the room seemed very pleased.

"Now, it's clear timing will be everything here," Angleton continued. "We need to have good people in place at the key moment. The Soviets are operating on the assumption that their dreadful deed will happen at the appointed time."

Here King interrupted. "And when it doesn't, the Reds will smell a rat. They'll want two things: to know who sold 'em out, and to cover their shitty asses."

"Thank you, Harvey, for your usual colorful analysis," Angleton said. Mary Thompson, who had just brought another tray of sandwiches, chuckled out loud.

Howard Hunt spoke up. "We need to get some help—some more hands."

"Already on it, Hunt," King said brusquely. "I have some 'friends' on the way."

"Who are these *friends*? Some of our boys?" Hunt asked.

"Oh, we've worked with them a few times—like back in Florida a few years ago," King said, grinning.

Comprehending grins spread throughout the room. Angleton then said, "Excellent, Harvey. But let's make sure to task them compartmentally."

"Way ahead of you, Sport," King replied.

Howard Hunt, speaking in low tones, asked about the importance of keeping their inside information from being discovered by the wrong parties. "How many people know about this?" he asked.

"Just us," Angleton reassured him. "Everything's off the books. That way if the Reds smell a rat, they'll never find it."

"Good," Hunt said. "That should give us at least two days before they start plugging holes."

KIM PHILBY'S DOCUMENT was extensive and seemed frank, almost as if the man thought himself a ghostwriter of his own obituary. They were aware of the assassination plot, the bomb, but the notes they had acquired so richly filled in the blanks that one might believe the defector was determined to write his own way to a new life. Many gaps in their intelligence, particularly pertaining to Soviet operations outside the United Kingdom, now emerged crisp and clear.

Much of the fresh information focused on various other European cities, suggesting a network of mischief with multiple points of action. Accordingly, two of Johnny Romano's men were diverted to Paris within hours of Philby's missive landing in American hands and told to intercept Henri Girard. Their specific instructions were to ensure that Girard simply disappeared when he was most needed by his comrades.

Other operatives were sent to Berlin and Brussels with similar mandates and absolute orders to steer clear of official police and intelligence channels. Philby's document had revealed the names of two additional conspirators, each one charged with assisting in the Soviet effort at coordinated disruption throughout the continent.

The entire scheme was breathtaking in its audacity. For an operation of this magnitude, the Reds were involving an astonishingly limited number of personnel. Several key players in just the right places, acting under the cover of confusion. This small circle was meant to ensure that Soviet fingerprints would remain undetectable on the sordid deed they hoped to orchestrate, an act they believed would set the machinery of revolution and conquest into unstoppable motion. Ironically, this precisely calculated shortage of people went a long way toward ensuring its ultimate failure. It made it far easier for the Americans to disrupt the plan.

AS FRIDAY AFTERNOON gave way to evening, Lady Churchill and her daughter Mary made another appearance at Westminster Hall, this time accompanied by Randolph Churchill. Winston's son was not alone. He brought with him a large and raucous party of friends for what turned out to be a lengthy visit. Randolph acted true to form. His flamboyant gestures and loud proclamations made this the most boisterous occasion during the mourning period for Lady Churchill's husband.

In the car on their way back to the home at Hyde Park Gate, Detective Sergeant Edmund Murray revealed a piece of news to Lady Churchill: he had turned in his retirement notice to Scotland Yard. He thanked her for the privilege and honor of serving her husband and family for so many years. Clementine, touched beyond measure, wept at his announcement and expressed gratitude as best as she could without being overcome by emotion.

Despite—or perhaps inspired by—the increasingly foul weather, people wishing to pay their respects still queued up in masses. The line stretched back all the way over Lambeth Bridge, extending along the battered South Bank of the Thames. From the early hours onward, the everyday people wishing to express their admiration of the great man—whom they considered a fellow "commoner"— rubbed shoulders with monarchs and dignitaries. They too found it necessary to come and pay homage. These included The Duke of Edinburgh, Prince Charles, Princess Anne, and the Kings of Denmark, Norway, Belgium, and Greece.

The great and famous arrived in small clusters, never more than a few at a time. It was all part of the plan, and the next day they would assemble in a single place, completely unaware of the danger they had already evaded.

FAR REMOVED FROM the prying eyes of the public and the journalists who were gathering for the event of a lifetime, a veritable army of security personnel from Scotland Yard, British intelligence, and other law enforcement agencies worked methodically to ensure the safety of the procession that would carry the beloved leader from Westminster Hall to St. Paul's Cathedral, and from the Tower Bridge to Waterloo Station.

They searched buildings and rooftops along the entire route, double-checking corners and suspicious nooks for signs of danger. These men had been preparing for months—and in some ways years.

Long before the great man's final illness, the name of every single person with views along the route had been supplied to the police. Each of these names was carefully examined against a current list of what the authorities described as "politically uncertain" individuals.

The "official" security plan called for nearly four thousand soldiers, sailors, and airmen to line the route. The planners believed that the best chance for any kind of attack or action would be outside, in public, and in plain view, where the target was exposed. They gave very little thought to the funeral venue itself; they were too confident in their own assumptions.

The Russians were aware of this oversight, thanks to their well-placed source, Harry Higgins. Every report from him was the same: "no unusual security measures inside." Higgins had spent months carefully preparing his role for the event. He knew the Soviets, with their meticulous planning, were depending on him as their point man. He was determined that his performance would be flawless.

As Higgins attempted to sleep that evening—a night he thought of as the prelude to a new chapter in world history—he grew restless. It wasn't the fact that he was the key player in a moment that would change the world: an event whose significance would eclipse the assassination of Archduke Ferdinand. The thought of being the trigger person was exhilarating. No, what disturbed him was the long silence. He hadn't heard from anyone else in the tight-knit circle of conspirators. Nothing from Michael and Molly Wheelan, and no word from Kaitlyn Dorsey.

This was unusual—and it gnawed at him.

After tossing and turning for several hours, Higgins finally convinced himself that radio silence prior to a major operation was the usual, indeed the expected, rule. But this particular long silence had come with no warning and was very unlike the conspirators he worked with. He drifted off to sleep, uncertain, but calmed by his own self-assurances.

A small box sat on the nightstand next to him, its presence a proof of his crucial role. It was something he thought he could not possibly forget, a thing of importance, but he wanted to be completely safe and sure. The box contained the device he would use to activate a timer on the bomb in the casket. This, he believed, would give him more than enough time to make a hasty escape into the chaos, celebrated by comrades, knowing that the terrible deed would forever carry his mark. At least, that was what he thought.

In fact, the device in his possession was designed to bring about an *immediate* explosion. The room would be reduced to shrapnel and carnage. The Soviets, shrewd in all things, wanted no loose ends. They did not tell Higgins this, nor did he suspect their murderous sleight of hand. Instead, he slept peacefully that night, dreaming of events he *thought* he was controlling.

CHAPTER FIFTY-FIVE

LONG BEFORE DAWN that chilly Saturday morning, Operation Hope Not was in full swing. Thousands of people from every walk of life had already mobilized for duty to pay their respects to the great man. The process of doing so had begun in earnest in the wee hours. The foul weather did not seem to bother anyone one bit. They all had a job to do.

Harvey King, James Angleton, and the other men on their team had worked long into the night and early morning on their own plan of action. They reviewed the funeral arrangements in great detail and surmised that the bomb would have been detonated after everyone was in place inside St. Paul's Cathedral, for maximum damage, meaning the window for the explosion would have been between eleven and eleven-thirty that morning. By eleven-thirty, then, it would be apparent to the Soviets and all the conspirators that their plan had been foiled.

Churchill himself had insisted on a relatively short service. Years earlier he had picked the hymns and plotted the order of things for his funeral. It seemed especially right and fitting that his man, Edmund Murray, would be the one inside St. Paul's with eyes on Harry Higgins. Security was so tight that he was also the only ally in the group who had a remote chance of getting inside the church at the appropriate time. Murray was determined that what would likely be his last day of service on behalf of Winston Churchill and his family would be one to remember. He might never be able to tell anyone about it, but he would know in his heart he had been part of something historic.

King and Angleton would oversee getting Kim Philby safely out of London and on his way to exile in America.

BIG BEN TOLLED loudly at nine o'clock that dreary morning. It would chime three more times that hour. But after nine forty-five, the great and iconic symbol would remain conspicuously silent until midnight, a solemn gesture to honor Mr. Churchill. For several hours, roads in the city had been closing. Eventually, vehicles would be banned from more than eighty streets in the surrounding sections of the city.

While the iconic clock was striking at precisely nine, several dark automobiles appeared at Hyde Park Gate. Family mourners, led by Lady Churchill, were transported to Westminster Hall. When she got out of the car, Clementine saw the Royal Navy gun carriage, complete with its cannon attached, waiting for the flag-draped coffin.

The funeral cortege assembled in stately fashion as soon as the family entered the building. They watched in solemn silence as a contingent of Grenadier Guards diligently draped the coffin with the Union Jack, handling it with the utmost precision. When that was done, one of the Guards laid the insignia of Churchill's Order of the Garter on top, the velvet gleaming.

Then the Guardsmen carefully lifted the flag-draped coffin and bore it with measured steps to the waiting gun carriage outside. With the cannon looming large at the rear of the carriage, Lady Churchill and her family led the way ahead of the coffin to its vehicle, then turned back to their own cars. When everyone was finally in place, the Duke of Norfolk, in charge of the arrangements, gave a quiet signal to the commanding officer.

The procession began its mournful journey to St. Paul's Cathedral, and more than two thousand military personnel walked slowly behind the gun carriage and vehicles, the pace of the march about sixty-five steps per minute. Along the route, military bands played somber funeral marches written by Chopin, Beethoven, and Mendelssohn, their notes echoing in the dreary morning air.

Huge throngs lined the entire route, at least six rows deep at most places. As the processional neared St. James Park and Tower Hill, artillery began to fire—the first of ninety such outbursts to be spread out over the course of the day. Each shot marked a year of Winston Churchill's monumental life. The gathered crowds barely stirred at the sounds, remaining resolutely in place despite the rain.

Those unable to find a spot along the roadside watched from rooftops, fire escapes, and even trees to get a glimpse of the proceedings. British subjects in full mourning dress stood next to tourists in parkas. Military officers stood next to dock workers. It was an occasion that cut across all strata of professions and society, and everyone seemed to understand that they were momentarily part of something larger than themselves.

EVEN AS THE earliest notes of the funeral march began to sound, all eyes were upon London. The world was paying close attention. Hours before dawn, in cities like Washington, D.C. and New York, offices and homes were already lit up by the ghostly glow of television screens.

Across the globe in Moscow, where it was now approaching midday, Soviet leaders huddled around their own monitors. It was a mark of just how much the world had transformed in the span of Churchill's long life that more than three hundred and fifty million people from every corner of the earth could tune into even a small portion of the coverage.

This broadcast was the largest television audience recorded in history to that moment, surpassing even the massive viewership that had been seen just a little more than a year earlier for the funeral of President John F. Kennedy. It was a reminder of the era that was passing and the new one unfolding before them.

It struck many as almost unfathomable that the funeral of a man born in the time of Queen Victoria, in an age when neither the automobile nor airplane had yet come into existence, was being relayed around the world by satellite technology—Telstar—the likes of which he could never have imagined as a child. Many felt a deep instinct that they were witnessing more than the ceremony of farewell for a political giant. Observers everywhere seemed to awaken to the notion that, with the passing of Churchill, the lights of a bygone age were on the brink of being extinguished forever, and that the world would never return to what it once had been.

PRESIDENT JOHNSON WAS also up early and watched from the Oval Office. He was painfully conscious of the widespread criticism he was facing for not being at Churchill's funeral. He knew that few would ever know the true reason he had chosen not to go. And should that truth ever be revealed, it would most likely be seen as an act of weakness. The press and public might seize upon it as a confirmation that he lacked the courage to confront danger head-on.

Yet Johnson was convinced it was for the greater good. He knew that peril was never more than a breath away, the Presidency had lost before to acts of violence. He believed the world needed a steady figure in these hours, someone capable of reacting to any turmoil that might unfold, a leader to guide the free nations through the chaos that would follow such an attack—if the worst should happen.

So he remained in Washington, trying to convince himself that he was being wise, and not merely cautious. But his thoughts did little to ease the bitter sense of isolation he felt as he watched the event unfold on the three networks playing simultaneously on the specially installed television console in his office.

The images on all three screens were identical—the somber procession moving at an agonizingly slow pace through the rain-slicked streets of London. When Johnson turned up the volume, he heard the solemn words of Eisenhower, who had made the journey and was attending the funeral of the man he once fought alongside in the war.

LBJ felt terribly alone.

IN THE KREMLIN'S shadows, a continent away, a group of men sat in a grand conference room, eyes glued to the television screen. These men, the architects of Operation KOBA, watched the solemn procession a world away, confident in their machinations as events unfolded in London. They had activated their plan with precision, and now, believing success was certain, they gathered to witness the final, triumphant moment.

Firewood crackled and popped in the large fireplace, casting a warm glow over the room. Across a long table, a buffet was spread to mark their anticipated victory, laid out with delicacies of elitist opulence. Vodka bottles gleamed, ready for the ensuing toasts, and tins of caviar lay waiting to be relished. These men awaited the culmination of their orchestration: the timed explosion, the chaos it would spark, and the new era of change they expected to sweep across Europe in its wake.

One of the conspirators, out of impatient excitement, suggested an early toast to the impending success of KOBA. All those present heartily agreed, exhilarated and dismissive of tradition, raising their glasses to drink even though the clocks had barely struck noon in Moscow. They anticipated their plan would become a fait accompli in just over an hour. A slow, self-congratulatory cheer arose as the vodka burned its way down.

WHILE THE RUSSIANS were celebrating their presumed triumph, Edmund Murray was already in place at St. Paul's. He had arrived there at seven-thirty that morning and managed to slip through the heavy security using his credentials and with the advantage of his well-known association with Churchill.

Once inside, Murray was able to move about with remarkable ease, examining all corners of the church unimpeded by the guards or any other personnel who might otherwise have obstructed him. It wasn't long before he located Harry Higgins, who was positioned discreetly in a loft area overlooking the main hall. Murray's instincts told him Harry was exactly where he wanted to be when the moment came to strike. It was a cat-and-mouse scenario that Murray had played out a hundred times in his head.

The shrewd security man found a spot close enough to keep Harry within sight but far enough to remain unseen himself, biding his time confidently. He watched intently as, at one point, Higgins pulled a small box from his coat pocket, examining it surreptitiously before tucking it back out of sight. Murray immediately surmised it was some sort of triggering mechanism for the bomb.

Briefly, he considered moving in on Higgins and undoing the plan's last remaining threads before the funeral began, but he ultimately resolved to let the drama play itself through. He knew the conspirators' mission had already been thwarted, so he was content to wait and do his part to ensure that things would stay that way.

THE HOPE NOT PLOT 350

the conspirators' mission had already been thwarted, so he was content to wait and do his part to ensure that things would stay that way.

CHAPTER FIFTY-SIX

AS THE GUN carriage solemnly carried Winston Churchill's coffin through London's streets, leaders from every corner of the globe had already taken their seats at St. Paul's. In the cold January light, the American delegation was notably prominent, led by Ambassador David Bruce and Supreme Court Chief Justice Earl Warren.

However, there were glaring omissions among the American attendees. Although Secretary of Defense Robert McNamara and Secretary of State Dean Rusk had been expected to join the delegation, they were both conspicuously absent. Their official reason for not attending was sickness, but in the midst of Cold War politics, their absence led to much speculation and whispering among those gathered.

Yet, it was the Soviet presence that provoked the greatest intrigue and murmuring. As the procession of official vehicles smoothly deposited dignitaries at St. Paul's, the notable exclusion of high-ranking Kremlin officials caused quite a stir. Despite the historical alliance between the United Kingdom and the Soviet Union during the Second World War—and the fact that much of it was orchestrated through Churchill's direct dealings with Josef

Stalin—none of the familiar Soviet power brokers were in attendance.

Instead, Moscow sent a delegation whose leaders were less well-known in the West. It was helmed by Konstantin Rudnev, a deputy Prime Minister, and Ivan Konev, a military figure infamous for his role in crushing the 1956 uprising in Hungary. The choice of these men seemed to carry a message, though its precise meaning was unclear, and it left experts and commentators debating the implications.

Around ten-thirty, the royal party departed Buckingham Palace. The Queen, accompanied by Prince Philip and a young Prince Charles, traveled in their customary maroon Bentley, making the short journey through London's rain-slicked streets. Their early arrival at the Cathedral was a calculated gesture, meant to signify the depth of the Queen's respect and affection for Churchill and his family.

Sir Lionel Denny, the Lord Mayor of London, stood waiting at the church steps, clutching London's ceremonial mourning sword with a velvet handle. The Lord Mayor received the royal family with quiet deference, and they slowly ascended the stone steps, where they were met by Michael Ramsey, the Archbishop of Canterbury, standing solemnly at the entrance.

Meanwhile, General Eisenhower was also notably absent from the crowd at St. Paul's but was instead stationed in a remote television studio, joined by the respected BBC veteran Richard Dimbleby. Together, the two men offered live commentary on the unfolding historic event.

At one juncture, Eisenhower could not help but comment on something he observed during the televised procession: among the throngs of onlookers lining the route, he noticed one individual who stood out. As the gun carriage passed by, this man audaciously continued to puff on a pipe and failed to doff his hat, an action

Eisenhower interpreted as a glaring mark of disrespect. He shook his head, unable to hide his disdain for the man's apparent insolence.

ROGER HOLLIS, UNDER the intensely scrutinizing eyes of the Americans, ventured to Philby's hotel room that somber morning before the Churchill funeral. He was anxious about the operation that was so carefully planned and wanted to personally brief Philby that everything was ready. Hollis understood that Philby was the point man of the Kremlin's intricate activities in London that day, and he felt it was imperative to meet face to face.

But when Hollis arrived, he found that Philby was gone, bag and baggage, and that unsettling discovery sent a chill through him. His eyes scanned the room quickly. It looked as if a violent commotion had taken place, as if someone had left in a hurry or had been removed by force. The furniture was askew, and several items were strewn haphazardly across the floor. Amid the chaos, Hollis's attention was drawn to the waste can near a desk. He noticed some scraps of paper and instinctively grabbed them.

He left the room, and as soon as he got on the lift heading down to the hotel lobby, he nervously began to read what he'd found. The fragments on the crumpled bits of paper made him feel sick with dread. The words were scribbled in an almost indecipherable scrawl, and he struggled to make out the meaning. Even though many of the words were unclear, only two words mattered.

Those two words told him everything he feared: KOBA and Angleton.

It now dawned on Hollis that Kim Philby might be orchestrating a ruthless game, playing both sides against each other for his own advantage. But this revelation left Hollis in a state of desperate uncertainty. He was powerless and unsure about what to do with his suspicion. Without knowing whom to trust, he feared making any official move.

He was reassured by the fact that Alex, a trusted operative, was on duty in the men's room downstairs. Taking a significant risk and with no better option, Hollis broke with strict protocol and confided in Alex. He told him that Philby had vanished and was possibly in league with the Americans. Hollis instructed Alex to pass this critical information up the chain and to warn his superiors of the turn of events. The initial reaction was swift. Alarm bells—stealthy ones, of course—began to go off, signaling a profound urgency to those who needed to know.

AS THE CLOCK struck ten forty-five, the gun carriage bearing the formidable weight of Winston Churchill's lead-lined coffin reached the foot of St. Paul's Cathedral. The scene was magnificent in its grim splendor. Members of the Household Cavalry, clad in their ceremonial uniforms, stood rigidly along the steps.

Nearby, the Ceremonial Pallbearers awaited the coffin's arrival.

This distinguished group included Clement Attlee, the former leader of the Labour party and the former Prime Minister who had succeeded Churchill. His presence, like that of the Queen earlier, was a show of utmost respect. Eight Grenadier Guards, handpicked for this austere duty, were charged with the formidable task of hefting the more than four hundred pounds of the casket up the broad staircase and into the church.

For a moment, as the pallbearers ascended with meticulous precision, it seemed that the march might meet with disaster. The eighty-two-year-old Attlee found himself faltering as he climbed the steep steps. He halted his progress halfway, and the unexpected pause sent a ripple of tension through the proceedings. The majority of the casket's considerable weight shifted abruptly onto the guards at the rear.

Seasoned veterans all, they managed to maintain their balance and hold the line steady. After what could only have been a brief instant, but one that seemed longer to those bearing the burden, Attlee resumed his climb. Perhaps aware of the difficulty his interruption had caused, he pressed forward with new determination. The entire group reached the top and made their way into the cool shadows of the cathedral's vestibule.

Inside, the Britannia pall had been placed on a table in the entrance. The casket was placed on it and was then carefully draped with the pall. The casket was then carried toward a black and silver catafalque positioned directly under the iconic dome. It was gently placed on the catafalque.

Large candlesticks stood at each corner of the platform, their presence dignified and historic. These particular candlesticks, revered relics of England's past, had last been used at the First Duke of Wellington's funeral, held in this same sacred place over a century earlier, when Churchill's grandfather had been a young man.

For a moment, the only sound was the solemn tread of the funeral party leaving the casket behind. Then, as the guards retreated to their assigned places, the organ swelled, and the gathered dignitaries and members of the general public rose to their feet.

WHILE THE STRAINS of Beethoven's Funeral March Number Three began to emanate from the church, more immediate strains were being felt back in the hotel where Hollis had discovered the scraps of paper. Soviet operatives were soon sweeping room 312 with a fine-toothed comb, searching for any clue about Hollis's suspicions and the American presence.

The operatives had no idea that the former occupant of the room was still close by. Up one floor, in room 408, the man who had once been the Soviet Union's most valuable asset was enjoying his view of events. Harvey King had ravaged and hurriedly abandoned Philby's room with careful purpose, leaving behind a few telltale hints in the process. Nothing too obvious or incriminating.

Just enough to make the Russians smell the unmistakable scent of the Americans' orchestrating hand. He knew the Soviets would soon be onto the deception, but that wasn't his concern.

As for Philby, he was sitting quietly with Angleton and watching the funeral coverage on the television. The room was filled with silence as the two men focused on the unfolding events. Philby checked his watch frequently. The moments seemed heavy and portentous, each one laden with the possibility of exposure or escape, treachery or freedom.

Finally, Angleton broke the tense silence with a knowing observation. "I suppose in a few minutes that your friends in Moscow, who must be watching as we are, will know their plan has been stopped."

CHAPTER FIFTY-SEVEN

THREE THOUSAND MOURNERS packed themselves into seats beneath the towering arches of St. Paul's Cathedral, their solemn voices filling the vast space with reverent silence. A congregation of elite and commoners alike, all gathered to honor the extraordinary life of a man who had defined an era. As the casket and funeral procession moved down the long aisle toward its appointed place beneath the towering dome, a choir's somber notes unfurled a hymn called "The Sentences."

The first lines echoed with poignant clarity as the singers' voices intertwined, chanting the words of the Gospel promise from John, chapter eleven: *"I am the resurrection and the life, saith the Lord. He that believeth in me, though he were dead, yet shall he live: and whosoever liveth and believeth in me shall never die."* Winston Churchill had orchestrated this funeral service with exacting precision, a final testament to the meticulous planning that had marked his wartime leadership. Even from beyond the grave, he ensured that not a note was out of place, not a scripture out of order.

Churchill's vision went beyond personal commemoration; it was a powerful statement of Anglo-American unity that reached back through a century of shared histories and struggles. This was nowhere more evident than in the inclusion of "The Battle Hymn of the Republic," a uniquely American anthem born from the crucible of its Civil War. The song felt like a loud pronouncement of common purpose, binding together two nations that he had worked so fervently to align.

As the strains of the anthem soared through the cathedral, mourners could almost feel the spirit of Churchill himself, orchestrating this moment as a final gesture of diplomacy. The theme of unity became more than an idea; it was a lived moment, drawing listeners into its embrace.

When the choir and the crowd rose to sing the majestic hymn "O God, Our Help in Ages Past," the culmination of Churchill's final plan began its sacred choreography. The coffin was gently lifted, and the pallbearers, their footsteps measured and solemn, began the long, deliberate journey back toward the entrance with its weight upon their shoulders. All eyes followed this last march of Churchill's physical presence, which seemed to glide as if on air. It was a beautiful service, flawless in execution, a fitting tribute to a life that had touched so many and shaped so much.

Just as Churchill had envisioned, everything went according to plan.

HARRY HIGGINS SURVEYED the solemn scene from the safety of his hidden vantage point. High above in the shadows, he could see everything. The mourners, the music, the coffin—all exactly as planned by the great man who now lay within it. Yet, neither Winston nor those who loved him had anticipated Higgins's presence and his own plan for the day.

He had not been explicitly ordered *when* to push the button and start the timer that had been embedded inside Churchill's casket— left to his own devices, so to speak. His Soviet handlers had trusted his instincts to detect the most opportune moment. Patiently, he had waited for just the right instant, considering how best to disrupt not only the service but the very legacy of the man being honored.

When the trumpeters lifted their instruments to play their tributes, Higgins knew the moment had arrived. He reached into his pocket, unhurried, and pulled out a small electronic trigger. He firmly pressed the button on it, not once, but three times to be certain. The information given to him by Soviet intelligence was that the timer would detonate in two minutes, ample time for him to disappear into the streets of London. Confident in his actions, he placed the device back into his pocket, then turned to make his exit.

That was when he heard a voice from the shadows.

"Hello Harry, going somewhere?"

The voice belonged to Murray, who was pointing a gun at Higgins, its barrel unwavering.

"Who the devil are you?" Higgins demanded, visibly shaken by the unexpected encounter.

"Name's Murray. I'm with Scotland Yard and assigned to Mr. Churchill's home. I'd like to ask you a few questions."

"You can ask me anything you bloody well want, but let's move out of here," Higgins insisted, eyes darting nervously.

"What's wrong, Harry? You afraid of something?"

"We need to get out of here! Now!"

"Not until we've had the chance to chat a bit."

Higgins made a desperate attempt to escape, lunging toward the door. Murray, anticipating the move, tackled Higgins and pushed him through the heavy door. He was relieved the choir and congregation were singing at the time, drowning out the noise of the scuffle. Once in the echoing stairwell, he threw Higgins to the floor.

Harry anxiously looked at his watch, disbelief on his face.

"Checking the time, are we? Expecting something, Harry?"

Harry sat in silence, sweat forming on his brow.

"Well, let me ease your mind, old boy. You see, the other day, yours truly and a friend of mine, another man who loved Mr.

Churchill, paid a visit where the casket down below was waiting for the great man's body. And we managed to find the material and device that some friends of yours put there. So that gadget in your pocket is worthless. There is no bomb. Your treachery has failed, and you are about to answer for your crimes. We're going to wait here for the church to empty, so you just sit tight."

THE MEN GATHERED in the conference room at the Kremlin found it increasingly difficult to maintain their composure. They sat solemnly around the expansive, dark wooden table, eyes fixed on the televised funeral of Churchill as it streamed via satellite hookup. Tension thickened the atmosphere, palpable in the growing silence, as news from their operatives on the ground was late in arriving. A sense of dread permeated the room when the assembly began to sing "The Battle Hymn of the Republic." The hardliners felt the irony sting even more as the distinctly American battle anthem magnified the failure they were not yet ready to concede.

Finally, a young assistant—his face betraying the urgency of his message—entered the room with a cable from the embassy in London. It bore grim news: Kim Philby was in the custody of the Americans. The dispatch further suggested that the Americans had dangerously precise information about the entire KOBA operation, leaving no doubt that their grand scheme had collapsed disastrously.

The men reached for their vodka glasses, but the spirit with which they had started the meeting was now wholly absent. The resolute toasts and defiant talk that had echoed earlier were replaced with a somber resignation. An uneasy hush prevailed, punctuated only by the clinking of ice and the muted sounds of the funeral they were no longer certain would change anything.

Finally, after what felt like an interminable period of anxious silence, Leonid Brezhnev, drumming his fingers on the table as he reflected on the concessions they would have to make to others who had been privy to the plot, broke the tension. In a calm but decisive voice, he addressed his comrades, acknowledging the harsh reality with a command. "Comrades, it is clear our plan has fallen short. We must now make sure it never becomes public. Please pass the word down the line for everyone to stand down. And get Philby back."

The edict went out swiftly, cascading through the ranks of Soviet operations across the globe. Each call to stand down brought with it ripples of confusion and frustration, as well as an uneasy relief. It was more than an hour later when the message reached Henri Girard in New York. He received it with utter incredulity, especially considering the timing.

The transmission arrived a scant five minutes before he was scheduled to launch his violent scheme and execute his target. He had planned to murder his boss, whereupon he would vanish from sight. The stand down order reached the other Soviet-backed assassins with the same puzzling timing. One by one, they abandoned their plans of attack and scattered quietly, unsure of what had unraveled their tightly woven plot. This put them beyond the reach of Johnny Romano's goons who had been hired to stop the assassins, leaving the goons to stare at the empty spaces where their marks had been.

By the next day, the hired Italians were back in Rome. They sat in Romano's office, trying to explain the strangeness which had enveloped their operation. One man scratched his head, visibly perplexed by the sudden shift. He looked to be wrestling with thoughts of betrayal or incompetence, neither of which he was accustomed to countenancing. His suspicion gave way to confusion as he asked his men, "What the hell was that all about?"

It was a rhetorical question, one for which they had few answers and even fewer explanations. The men shrugged in embarrassment while Romano, whose notoriety for precision was legendary, contemplated the unprecedented disarray of his operation with a mix of irritation and disbelief.

TIERNAN BROGAN WAS finishing a call to Harvey King. Harvey told him things were chaotic for a while, but the storm was passing. The troubling news was he needed to bring Kaitlyn with him. They couldn't risk her talking. Brogan was told to be careful and apologetic, but very firm.

His instructions were to bring Kaitlyn and Michael and Molly Wheelan to Thompson's flat, which would be the staging area for the team's end game and escape from England. He had to figure out what to do with the girl—she was a potential complication.

He knew she was not going to be happy about the plan.

Kaitlyn was drinking a cup of tea as though nothing were going on. She thought the operation was over and that she'd be back in Belfast in a matter of hours. She serenely sat at her kitchen table and looked over at their prisoners still drooped in their chairs. Michael and Molly didn't seem to have moved at all; still unconscious.

Tiernan poured himself a cup and sat down across from her. "That call was from one of the men I've been working with, Kaitlyn," he said as he prepared for her wrath.

She smiled back at him, and he wondered if he had the nerve to do it. "Ah, very cloak and dagger, love. You're quite the handsome man of mystery," she said with a brilliant smile.

He winced, knowing how long that smile would last. "Well, it appears we need to prepare to move out."

"Out where?" she asked, not even considering the possibility that she wasn't going out on her own.

"There's a flat that's being used by the team," he said gently. "From there we'll be moving to Essex and Stapleford Aerodrome. There's a plane there waiting to get us out."

"And where, pray tell, is this mysterious airplane going to be headed?"

"America," he replied.

"You're going to America?" she asked, her voice rising in both pitch and volume.

"Yes," he said, "for now, I must. That's where this whole story resolves. Our orders are to make sure none of this sees the light of day here in Britain."

"Isn't MI-5 working with your friends?" she asked. "I thought you said the British were in on it?"

"Actually, no. Not at all. This is strictly a Yank operation," he said.

"And what of me? I know all about it."

"Yes, and that means you need to come with us to America for now," he said, bracing himself.

"The devil you say!" she yelled as she slammed her mug onto the table. "I'm not getting on any airplane to the United States—that's for fucking sure."

"I'm afraid I must insist."

"I was thinking maybe you cared about me," she shouted. "You've just been using me? You bastard!"

"Calm down, darling—"

"Don't darlin' me!" she said as she threw her tea in his direction. "I can't believe I allowed me-self to get taken in by you and this bloody plot."

Brogan realized that he had to come up with an alternative. He did care for her. So thinking quickly, he provided another way. "Kaitlyn, I do care for you. If you don't want to come to America, I don't want to force you. How about I set you free and you go back home to Belfast. I was thinking I could meet back up with you in a month or so, after this all settles down."

Kaitlyn's scowl turned swiftly to a smile. "Now, that's the man I've been loving. 'Tis more like it."

"Great. Then I think you should make your way from this place quite soon. Do you have money? I have some you can use."

"Aren't you the gentleman? I'm fine. Save yours for when you come to Belfast. We'll have a proper fling. Let's meet at Bittles Bar one month from today. I'll be there waiting."

"It's a date."

A few minutes later, Kaitlyn had packed a bag and was on her way. Her plan was to make her way by train to Manchester, catch a ferry there, and be in Belfast early the next day. Neither Kaitlyn nor Tiernan were aware that Michael Wheelan had been awake for some time and had heard their plans.

CHAPTER FIFTY-EIGHT

AS WINSTON CHURCHILL'S casket was borne down the stone steps of St. Paul's, members of the Cathedral Guild began the mournful tolling of the church's great bells. There were twelve bells in all, yet it took thirteen people to ring them, a testament to their great size and weight. The tenor bell alone, a mighty instrument, weighed more than three tons, its resonance echoing through the cold air.

The somber peal cast a profound and lingering silence over the gathered crowd, a silence amplified by the massive throng of dignitaries, political figures, and those who simply admired the man. After the casket began to move further away from the famous church and onto the waiting gun carriage, Queen Elizabeth made her discreet exit, returning swiftly to Buckingham Palace.

There, she prepared to host a formal luncheon for the many foreign heads of state who had come to pay their respects to one of the most towering figures of the era. They joined her shortly thereafter, even as a lengthened procession followed the path of their revered leader through the city.

The stately gun carriage made its way slowly and majestically to Tower Hill via Canon Street, flanked by long lines of soldiers in formal dress. As it approached its destination, it neared the

Havengore, the hydrographic survey launch waiting at Tower Pier. This teak and oak framed vessel built nearly a decade earlier would ferry Churchill on the next stage of his final journey.

Onboard the vessel, General Dwight D. Eisenhower stood ready to speak. The former U.S. President had been asked to deliver the tribute to his long-time ally. Waiting for the moment to begin, he stood solemn and poised against the clear winter sky. The crowd hushed as he started his remarks, declaring in a voice filled with admiration and sorrow, "Upon the mighty Thames, a great avenue of history, move at this moment to their final resting place the mortal remains of Sir Winston Churchill." The dense throng of assembled mourners, straining to hear, fell silent as the General captured the poignancy of the occasion with his stately words.

"He was a great maker of history," Eisenhower continued, "but his work is done, the record closed. We can almost hear him, with the poet, say—'Sunset and evening star. And one clear call for me! Twilight and evening bell and after that the dark! And may there be no sadness of farewell, when I embark." This powerful and evocative quotation from Alfred Lord Tennyson stirred those in attendance, its profound sadness mingling with notes of pride and gratitude for Churchill's vast legacy.

The General spoke with dignified eloquence for several more minutes, his delivery imbued with the deep respect and friendship he had for Churchill. With each emphatically spoken word, the enormity of the loss grew more palpable, touching each heart in the audience and binding them in collective mourning. He concluded his tribute at last, with a moving, "And now, to you Sir Winston— my old friend—farewell!" The impact of this final farewell resounded, and the great vessel finally began its progress down the River Thames.

EDMUND MURRAY WALKED alongside Harry Higgins, escorting him through a short period of bright sunshine—at odds with Harry's mood—to the home of Walter Thompson—a simple flat which had hosted King and his team during the week of planning and operations.

The team was waiting on the results of Tiernan Brogan's round-up. Jim McCord was on his way to assist and help with the transport of the prisoners to the airfield. There was a sense of urgency and anticipation in every step they took, knowing that failure was an ever-looming possibility. As Murray and his new charge arrived, Harvey King chose the waiting moments to express his gratitude to his hosts.

"Walter, Mary—you have been so gracious to us," King said. "I want you to know that I will personally commend you to the President of the United States. Now, because this whole mission has been top secret, there's not much that can be done publicly to thank you. But I assure you that all of us 'across the pond,' as you like to say, will make sure you are rewarded for your efforts."

Thompson replied in a voice both humble and proud. "Mr. King, nothing for us. Please, no. We have served our nation and history. You have given an old man one more moment of service to my nation and Mr. Churchill. For that I will be forever grateful."

Howard Hunt added, "You are a remarkable man, Mr. Thompson. A real hero. It has been an honor to serve with you."

"Hear! Hear!" the Americans all said, with respectful laughter.

"Where the hell are Brogan and McCord?" King interrupted, the anxiety creeping back into his voice.

BROGAN WATCHED AS Kaitlyn disappeared down the street, then stepped over to the Wheelans to prepare them for travel. Working in a kind of daydream about Kaitlyn, he was oblivious to the fact that Michael had been awake and working on his restraints for quite a while. As he bent down, Michael came up with an elbow to Brogan's chin, knocking him to the ground. Brogan's gun was on the kitchen table and Michael lunged for it, the chair still roped to his hips, He snatched it up and got a shot off before Brogan could grasp him.

Brogan banged his head on the table as he fell, clutching a wound on the left side of his chest below his shoulder, and his world went black. He came back to consciousness in a pool of blood in time to see Michael bundling his muzzy wife out the door. He then fell back with a groan.

Three minutes later, McCord rushed in through the open door and saw Brogan. The Irish operative was alive, but he had lost a lot of blood. He was conscious enough to report what had happened. McCord called Harvey King at the Thompson flat, who told him to immediately head for the airfield.

"How the hell do I know how to get to Essex?" McCord asked. "Especially with a man who needs a hospital?"

"Stop the bleeding the best that you can and get out of there. We're blown. Who knows what that couple knows? And find a map. Just be there—you got that? I'll try to figure a way to get a nurse or doctor to the airfield."

"Roger. We'll be there."

Harvey then placed a call to Dulles in Washington. "We're blown," he said. "Heading to the airfield now. Brogan's been shot. Not sure of his condition."

Dulles replied, "I'll let the President know. Is Philby with you?"

"Yes, we have him. The Russians probably know this and are on the trail."

"Is there any way they know where you're headed?"

"Well, two bad guys escaped—the ones who shot Brogan. It's possible that they may have picked up on our plans before they ran. We'll operate on the assumption that the Russians are not far behind us."

"All right. Get a message to us when you are airborne. And be careful."

"Count on it."

McCord attended to Brogan's wounds and readied him for travel. He grimaced. "Come on, Brogan, you're going to have to stay with me. We're heading to the plane. It's going to be a bumpy ride. And I hope to hell that one of us knows the way to Essex."

"I know the way," Brogan gasped.

King kept his word. It turned out that Blair Lithgow's brother was a doctor. It took one discreet telephone call and medical help was soon waiting for Brogan at the Stapleford Aerodrome.

AS THE HAVENGORE continued its journey along the River Thames, it approached a location known as Hay's Wharf on the South Bank. There, thirty-six crane drivers, determined to pay homage to Winston Churchill, prepared to deliver their own unique tribute. These men had assembled at their posts on a Saturday, not drawn by the promise of overtime wages, but instead by a profound sense of respect for the monumental passing of history they were witnessing.

As the casket bearing the mortal remains of the former Prime Minister came into clear view, the laborers, in a carefully coordinated expression of honor, began to dip the jibs of their cranes. This was a bold and public salute, and it was performed with precision. The sight was so unexpected and moving that their foreman, overwhelmed with emotion, decided to award his crew with overtime pay, acknowledging the powerful and sincere gesture they had made.

The Havengore pressed on, passing beneath the London Bridge and then Waterloo Bridge. As the vessel drew near to Festival Pier, a massive crowd had converged at the riverbank to watch the casket taken ashore for the next leg of the journey—a scene of mourning both solemn and grand, with flags lowered in honor up and down the embankment.

The casket made its way to Waterloo Station, where a gleaming Pacific steam locomotive of the Battle of Britain class awaited, its engine hissing with anticipation. Named, appropriately, "Winston Churchill," the funeral train stood poised to carry the statesman on the final stretch of his last journey.

It was stationed at Platform 11, surrounded by British Rail officials in immaculate uniforms. An enormous black and white photo of Churchill was placed at the front of the locomotive. The train pulled out of the station, rolling steadily towards Hanborough, a small village not far from Blenheim Palace, Churchill's birthplace and where he would be laid to rest among his ancestors.

The front of the locomotive carried three large white discs arranged in a striking V formation. Although the discs were traditionally used to mark that a train had broken down and was delayed, on this particular day of days the intention was entirely different. It signified, for all the world to see, Churchill's most famous battle cry.

"V for victory."

CHAPTER FIFTY-NINE

SHOWING UP AT the Soviet Embassy in London might have appeared reckless to outside observers, but the Wheelans were convinced it was their only option. For Michael and Molly, it was the sole place that felt remotely secure. Despite the uncertainties, they realized the Soviets would be interested in what they knew.

On arrival, after some tense moments and urgent phone calls from the uniformed guards at the small station, they found themselves being escorted into the elegant building. Important-looking men in suits swarmed around them. Their presence and the information they revealed set off a swift flurry of activity and concern as men disappeared into corridors and rooms, making rapid calculations and plans while speaking in hushed and then frantic tones.

Soon, a helicopter team had been assembled and dispatched to the Stapleford Aerodrome. The Russians were determined to get there first and to secure the coveted target before the Americans even realized what was happening.

No one spoke as the London skyline receded; all were aware of the urgency. A veteran of the war, the pilot had proven himself in much more precarious circumstances than this, but even he couldn't help but feel the tension. He flew low, just above the trees and rooftops, ensuring nothing would stop them from reaching their destination.

From the other side of London, McCord drove toward Essex at a furious pace, trying to keep Tiernan Brogan conscious and engaged in conversation. Bleeding but alive, he struggled to stay awake as McCord pressed the accelerator, desperate to make it to the airfield before time ran out. He shouted toward Brogan in the back seat to keep him focused.

THE RUSSIAN OPERATIVES mobilized rapidly and were already deployed on the ground long before Lithgow and the Americans arrived. Their helicopter had touched down in a secluded clearing just beyond the airfield's perimeter, using the surrounding trees as cover, and ensuring their approach was unseen. With precision, the agents advanced toward the main building, noting that a DC-3 was positioned conveniently near a hangar, parked close to an attached administration building.

The crew's absence confirmed the belief that the pilot and others, perhaps forewarned, were already inside the plane, potentially waiting for the Americans to arrive. Keeping the main building between them and the waiting plane, they entered the main building through the rear door.

Inside, they observed two men going about their duties. One worker sat at a desk in an office adjacent to a small lobby area, while the other stood behind a service counter. The Russians moved with practiced swiftness, their actions synchronized. Within moments, they had subdued the two employees.

Dragging them into a nearby storage room, the agents stripped them of their uniforms, which they pulled on. The two disguised operatives took their positions, while another went to a window to scan the perimeter with a pair of binoculars. He soon spotted the convoy of American vehicles speeding toward the Aerodrome. The undisguised Russians quickly split into two groups and ducked out of sight in the back.

THE GRAY PANEL van, driven by Lithgow, was first to arrive at the airfield. He guided it skillfully toward the main building and parked, expecting no more than the typical light activity of a Saturday, particularly since much of the public was preoccupied with the national spectacle of Churchill's funeral. But something seemed off as soon as he stepped inside.

"Afternoon, gents," he greeted, making his way toward the counter where one of the disguised Russians stood, pretending to read a manual. The man met Lithgow's gaze silently, raising suspicion. "Where's Alfred? I expected to see him today. Is he sick, or just watching the telly somewhere?" Lithgow asked, now uneasy. He glanced towards the office and saw the other stranger, neither of the workers' clothes fitting convincingly.

Realization struck when he closed the distance to the counter and saw the name tag—Alfred—on the shirt of the silent man. He turned on his heel, attempting to flee, and managed to shout a warning, "Russians!" But that was all he could summon before a bullet tore into him from behind.

The Americans getting out of the van and car had not heard Lithgow's scream, but the crack of the gunshot reached them instantly. Instinctively, they went for their weapons, taking defensive positions. The Russians inside had already bolted through the back, and as the rest of the Americans moved to intercept, three operatives appeared from around the building's corner, firing with precision and putting Harvey King and his men on the defensive.

The Americans scrambled for cover, ducking behind vehicles and any available structure as bullets flew around them. Meanwhile, the two Russians from inside executed their plan with cold efficiency, circling around the building in pursuit of the vehicle carrying Kim Philby.

As Harvey's team engaged in a hasty firefight, the two Russians spotted the second car and saw their target. Kim Philby was in the passenger seat, accompanied by Ferguson Matthews behind the wheel. The shots fired by the other Russians created confusion and had drawn much of the return fire away from Matthews and Philby, leaving them initially oblivious to the immediate threat.

For all his tactical knowledge and experience, Matthews had made a critical miscalculation, leaving a clear line of approach for the Russians to exploit. The bad guys wasted no time on subtlety. One of the agents shot Matthews in the head through the window.

The other Russian moved with precision, reaching Philby and pulling him out of the vehicle and dragging him toward their escape route. With Philby in tow, they quickly retreated, taking a direct line back toward the helicopter, which awaited their return. The two Russians did not linger or turn back for their comrades but instead crossed the open field with determined speed, focused solely on securing their objective and making a swift departure.

AS MCCORD DREW closer to the airfield, the situation remained a mystery he was desperate to solve. Anxiety knitted his brow as he noticed another car trailing him, about three hundred yards behind. He had no way of knowing who was tailing him, but he was alarmed. "May have picked up a follower," he said, casting a glance at Brogan, who lay in the back seat, bandaged and weakened but stoic.

"Bloody hell," Brogan muttered. "Russians?"

"No way to tell," McCord replied, his voice tense with urgency. "The car has turned with me three times now."

"How far to go?" Brogan asked, his breath shallow but determined.

"Should be to the plane in less than five minutes, barring any problems." McCord gripped the steering wheel with renewed intensity.

"Yeah, well, let's try to do this problem free, old man," Brogan said, attempting a smile that turned into a grimace.

"I'll do my best, Brogan. You hold on." McCord pushed the car to its limits, every second feeling like an eternity. As they neared the airfield, their plane came into sight, a solitary promise amidst the chaos. But then they heard the staccato bursts of gunfire piercing the cold air.

"Tell me that you're seeing fireworks," Brogan gasped, struggling to speak as pain clawed at him.

"I wish. It's definitely gunfire coming from the airfield. Holy shit!" McCord's heart raced with the realization.

"What are you going to do?"

"Get as close as I can to see what's going on." McCord maneuvered with precision, closing in on the scene. He saw the van and the other members of his team pinned down by gunfire. The din of shots masked the sound of his car's approach. He pulled close to the far side of the building, using it as cover. Quickly, he glanced in the mirror. The car tailing him was nowhere in sight.

"You stay put, Brogan. I'm going to take a look and see how I can help our boys," McCord ordered, his resolve steely.

"Look at me, McCord, you asshole. Do I look like I'm going anywhere?" Brogan shot back, a mixture of defiance and discomfort in his voice.

"Roger that," McCord replied, flashing a quick smile as he slipped out of the car. He snuck along the length of the building, then paused to survey the chaos. The Americans were outgunned but holding their ground. McCord peered around the corner, identifying three shooters.

From his experience, he guessed they were Russian operatives. They would shoot him on sight if he made a move. But a plan was already forming in his mind. He spotted a ladder leading to the roof and scaled it with quiet agility. From this vantage point, he could see the shooters clearly. He knew he could get one good shot off if he was quick enough. He aimed and took down one of the Russians with a single shot.

The sudden strike threw the attackers into chaos. As the other Russian operatives spun around, McCord adjusted his aim and took another down in the confusion. The last remaining Russian ran for cover behind the building, heading straight for the vehicle where Tiernan Brogan lay wounded. McCord swept his view for the shooter. The Russian moved cautiously toward the vehicle, drawing closer every second.

Meanwhile, Harvey King, Howard Hunt, Frank Sturgis, and Howard Perlstein hesitantly emerged from their cover. They sensed a shift in the battle, realizing that their attackers had somehow been eliminated, at least for now.

"Go check on Philby and Ferguson," Harvey barked, urgently pointing to Howard Perlstein.

With his gun drawn, Perlstein crept around the side of the building. He spotted the Russian closing in on the car, and next to the vehicle he saw a body sprawled lifeless. Before he could react, the Russian turned and fired a single shot, hitting Perlstein in the leg. Perlstein fell, clutching his wound. McCord, now on the other side of the roof, tried to get an angle on the shooter, but the car was too close to the building.

The Russian looked into the car and saw Brogan in the back seat. He needed the car for escape, but not a hostage. He leveled his gun, ready to finish Tiernan Brogan once and for all. In that crucial moment, McCord managed to graze the Russian's head with a shot, knocking him to the ground. But the resilient operative scrambled up, got into the driver's seat, and began to back the car away.

By this time, the rest of the American team could see him attempting his escape. They raised their guns and McCord yelled,

"Don't shoot! Brogan's in the backseat!" They dropped their arms in dismay as the vehicle was speeding across the field in the direction of the Soviet helicopter.

"Don't shoot! Brogan's in the backseat!" They dropped their arms in dismay as the vehicle was speeding across the field in the direction of the Soviet helicopter.

CHAPTER SIXTY

"GET IN THAT van and chase that car," King yelled, urgency lacing his voice. Howard Hunt was closest to the van, and he sprinted to jump behind the wheel and sped off in hot pursuit. As the Russian drove furiously across the terrain, attempting to reach the helicopter, another vehicle suddenly appeared, seemingly out of nowhere.

It barreled directly toward the Russian's car.

"Who the hell is that?" Howard Hunt muttered, startled.

The mysterious vehicle closed in with fearless determination. When it came within range, a single shot rang out. The Russian slumped over the steering wheel and his vehicle plowed uncontrollably into a grove of bushes. The Americans approached the scene with caution, eyes wide in disbelief. They watched a figure emerge from the mystery vehicle. It was a woman with flaming red hair. She opened the back door of McCord's car and disappeared briefly from view.

"Identify yourself," Howard Hunt demanded as he neared the wreck with his pistol raised, his voice echoing across the field.

"Brogan, Tiernan Brogan," a voice answered, resolute despite the chaos.

"Brogan? You alright? Who's that with you?" Hunt shouted back, bewilderment giving way to curiosity as he closed the distance.

"My Irish angel—that's who."

A cautious smile crept across McCord's face. He knew now that his follower had been Kaitlyn Dorcey.

KAITLYN HAD NOT been far into her escape when she had second, then third thoughts. She craved freedom from it all—the fear, the chaos, the threats, the death. That craving had propelled her out the door. But as she walked away, doubts like hornets had followed, stinging and making her rethink.

Soon, she turned around and returned to her flat to talk further with Brogan.

Instead, she found a bloodied scene, the room in violent disarray. She prayed he was not dead, yet the absence of a body did nothing to reassure her. In a panic, she remembered Sean's talk of the airfield in Essex, and her thoughts raced to the near certainty that he was in serious trouble. She had enough experience to know danger, enough heart to know she couldn't abandon him.

Borrowing a car from a neighbor—she left a note but took it all the same—she sped toward the Stapleford Aerodrome. She had not the slightest idea what awaited her but was determined to be part of whatever it was. When she fell in behind McCord on the road to the airfield, she gleefully recognized the red head propped up in the back seat and followed it until the airfield came into sight and she heard the unmistakable sound of gunfire. She slowed to a stop to survey the scene; it took only moments to understand. Then the sudden silence as the guns stopped, a voice shouted, "Brogan's in the back seat!" and the car she'd followed roared away from the building. She was after it like a wolf after a weasel. That was *her* man in there.

Simple as that.

As she reached Brogan, she feared it was too late. She saw the blood and his wound, his eyes barely open. But she had been part of enough operations to push aside the worry. She had been frantic enough times to know when to calm down and act decisively. And she had held on to hope through harrowing circumstances before now. She prayed this would be no different.

As she gently tended to his wound, Kaitlyn spoke softly, "If I'd known you were going to be in this bad shape, love, I might have thought twice about leaving. It's clear that you need me."

Brogan smiled weakly, more at her presence than at her words.

"You know I used to be a nurse, right Sean? Back in Belfast?"

"I had no clue," Brogan replied. He struggled to keep his head from lolling against the seat.

Kaitlyn knew he was in agony but still in good enough condition to joke with. "Well, me father used to ask, 'You know where you find clues, don't you?'"

She paused, waiting, and sure enough Brogan filled her silence. "Like I said, no clue."

"You find clues in the clues closet."

He laughed though the pain stabbed through his left shoulder and forced him to sit up a bit straighter. But he saw Kaitlyn's eyes and felt a warm relief wash over him.

Then she said, "Brogan?"

AS THE REMAINING members of the American team gathered at the scene, they cast a collective eye to the sky and saw the unmistakable outline of a helicopter disappearing in the distance. "Son of a bitch," Harvey King exclaimed, barely able to contain his outrage and frustration. "I'll give you ten to one that Kim Philby is aboard and already spinning a tale about us trying to kidnap him. The bastard!" His words hung in the air like a bitter curse, the reality of their predicament beginning to settle like a heavy fog.

The Americans—plus one—carefully retraced their steps toward the main building, each man deep in his own thoughts about the failed operation. The anticipation they had felt was now replaced by the dull ache of inevitability, but they were nothing if not resilient. As the pieces of the puzzle started to come together, Howard Hunt took the lead in debriefing. "As I see it," he said, rallying the team, "the Russians got wind about our whereabouts from that Wheelan couple. The bad guys scrambled over in that chopper, beating us here. Their target was Philby, and they got him."

He paused, letting the impact of his assessment sink in.

"Well, this is a royal pile of shit," King replied, his tone a mixture of resignation and defiance. He looked around at the team and their surroundings, assessing the damage done. "But I don't think there's much left for us to do. Our work here is done." His matter-of-fact acceptance of the situation was a rallying cry for the others to start thinking about their next steps. Hunt nodded in agreement, already considering the logistics of cleaning up and moving on.

They had suffered a significant blow, but he wasn't about to let them wallow in defeat. "I can get some people to clean up here," he said. "I doubt the Russians will be back. They have what they wanted. I guess it's a consolation prize, considering they didn't get their big-ass revolution." He was already mentally calculating how long it would take to scrub the scene of its incriminating evidence as his mind raced ahead to the next phase.

"We need to be airborne in fifteen minutes," King said with urgency, ready to put the entire mess behind them. "Did that doctor get here?" He was determined to make a clean getaway and regroup, far from the scene of their latest failure.

"Yeah. He's taking care of Brogan and his brother," McCord responded. "Lithgow is bloody but not badly hurt. He was shot quickly from behind and had the sense to play dead. It just caught him high in the side and bounced off his ribs. Brogan is in rough shape, but he'll make it. The girl is in there with him now."

He paused as if grappling to understand how anyone had survived the onslaught. "Last I heard, he was trying to explain why he never told her his real name. Probably better that he has a bad wound when breaking news like that, especially to that broad." There was almost admiration in his voice, as he imagined Brogan's predicament.

"What about Ferguson?" King asked, his voice carrying the weight of the day's casualties. "He bought it," McCord said with the same grim acceptance. "Never had a chance. We'll put his body on the plane." He paused as the thought struck him. "By the way, Brogan's new girl is a trained nurse, so she can watch Brogan on the flight back. Don't want to lose another good man." It was a small piece of luck on a day that had had precious little of it.

Hunt was already on his radio, calling in some cleaners, and they had the area sanitized by the time the DC-3 was at cruising altitude over Ireland. The cleaners were also tasked with gathering and disposing of the two bodies on ice back in Walter Thompson's freezer.

No loose ends.

CHAPTER SIXTY-ONE

THE TRAIN, KNOWN as the "Winston Churchill," pulled up to the modest platform at Hanborough Station shortly before three-thirty in that afternoon. It had completed the final leg of its journey from London, marking the end of an era and carrying with it the hopes and memories of a nation.

From there, a hearse accompanied by several vehicles formed a dignified procession, winding its way through the quiet English countryside to St. Martin's Church at Bladon. This tiny hamlet, peaceful and serene, offered a modest final resting place befitting the statesman's wishes.

The rector of St. Martin's led the solemn gathering, receiving the coffin and accompanying funeral party with due deference. Accompanied by his son, he guided them directly to the graveside. There, surrounded by a small circle of family and close friends, the rector recited a brief word of committal, allowing just a few moments of reflection before the simple and private burial.

As tradition and privacy dictated, the casket was swiftly and respectfully lowered into the ground. All the while, Lady Churchill, showing a moment of private resilience, remained by the graveside, gazing pensively into the grave for several minutes as she absorbed the magnitude of the moment.

Once the grave had been backfilled with the rich, dark earth, a gesture of finality and renewal, it was adorned with several wreaths. Most notable among them was one from the Queen, a special tribute from the crown to the man who had served it so tenaciously. The wreath was composed of a variety of flowers: lilies, carnations, and freesias, all in shades of pure white, signifying remembrance and honor. It carried the heartfelt words: *"From the Nation and the Commonwealth in Grateful Remembrance, ELIZABETH R."*

AS THESE EVENTS were unfolding in England, the DC-3 carrying the American team—and the remains of Ferguson Matthews—made its way back across the Atlantic. Angleton had gotten to the aerodrome a few minutes before takeoff. Meanwhile, another aircraft—a DC-8—sped across the same ocean in the opposite direction. This plane, much faster and larger, had been chartered by *Life Magazine* with the singular purpose of covering the funeral. Transformed into a flying newsroom, it bustled with activity.

The cabin had been meticulously converted to include a photo lab for a staff of forty, a ten by fifteen-foot darkroom, tables crowded with typists and writers, and even a small reference library dedicated to books by and about Winston Churchill. This airborne studio was an ambitious attempt to produce a very special edition of the magazine at thirty-three thousand feet, a tribute that would remain a collector's gem for many years.

None of the writers, photographers, or editors on the Life Magazine charter were aware of the dramatic plot that had been foiled by members of American intelligence. Had the Soviet operation been successful, they would have been crafting a very different kind of story, one that chronicled shock and despair rather than tribute and memory.

IN THE GRIM aftermath of the catastrophic failure of KOBA, those within the Soviet power structure hastened to assess the wreckage and tally the blame. Kim Philby was spirited away to Moscow in a cloak of secrecy. Under intense scrutiny, Philby proved himself once more to be a master of deception. Wielding his formidable skills as a trained prevaricator, he argued convincingly that his supposed collaboration with the Americans was nothing more than a ruse meant to deceive.

The tale he wove was intricate and persuasive, managing to sway at least some of his skeptical superiors. According to him, he had been brazenly abducted by the Yanks, who had miraculously unearthed the details of KOBA on their own and rendered it powerless long before the grand funeral at St. Paul's Cathedral. His narrative was plausible enough to deflect the most damning of accusations.

But Philby could not entirely shake the shadow of doubt. Within the labyrinthine corridors of the Kremlin, whispers persisted. A faction of hardline voices continued to voice their suspicions. To them, the possibility remained that Philby was, in reality, a double agent and that suspicion would haunt Kim for the rest of his days.

The hardliners were never in the majority, but their influence was such that it could not be ignored, and they had the ear of enough key figures to shape Philby's future in critical ways. They ensured that he would remain a sidelined participant in the espionage intrigue which he loved to grandly refer to as "the great game." The consequence of their mistrust was a slow and painful punishment: Harold Adrian Russell Philby found himself in a reluctant exile within the cold confines of his Moscow flat.

He maintained a semblance of activity by writing and editing in the intelligence community's margins. But mostly, he was a man adrift, devoting himself more and more to drink and to the depression that, like the long Russian winter, seemed to settle in for an eternity. Even his few allies, men who were once ardent in their support, began to avoid him, fearful of being tainted by association. The greatest betrayal, it seemed, had not been his own, but that of the people he trusted.

MEANWHILE, ACROSS THE Atlantic, another narrative—this one triumphant—was being authored in the deepest shadows of American intelligence circles. The successful disruption of KOBA had not gone unnoticed or uncelebrated at the highest levels. Harvey King, the legendary spy and architect of the operation, received personal commendation for his exceptional service. In a secretive off-the-record meeting held under the cover of night, he was summoned to the Oval Office by Lyndon Johnson. It was a full two weeks after Harvey's return from sorting out the dangerous mission in Great Britain.

"Harvey, you are James Bond, after all," said the President with a broad grin, wrapping one of his long arms around the operative.

King replied with uncharacteristic humility. "Just serving at your pleasure, sir." He managed to extricate himself from the awkward embrace with some difficulty, much to his own relief.

The meeting was intimate, with just the two of them present, and the atmosphere was congenial if somewhat conspiratorial. They shared several glasses of Cutty Sark as King provided Johnson with a detailed briefing on the mission's success. The President was deeply impressed.

"Sad thing is this can never be known," Johnson said with a knowing shrug. "It would be too easy to trace it all back to this office. Can't have that. Maybe one day the story will be told, but you and I will be long gone by then, Harvey."

King took it all in stride. "I'm used to working in the shadows anyway," he said. "I do have one request, though—something you may be able to help with."

"Name it. If I can do it, I sure as hell will," Johnson replied, leaning in with genuine curiosity.

"Get me the hell out of Rome!" King's tone was half-serious, half-pleading, reflecting his readiness for a change of scenery after the high-stakes drama in Europe.

"Consider it done," said Johnson confidently and with a broad smile.

A few months later, Harvey King found himself appointed to lead a new division for the CIA at Langley, where he enjoyed a central role in shaping American intelligence strategy for years to come. It was a position of great influence and little public recognition, a perfect fit for a man who thrived out of the limelight.

AMIDST THESE CLANDESTINE maneuvers and reassignments, other transitions were quietly taking place. The British Ambassador, David Ormsby-Gore, stepped down a few weeks after the events in London. He paid another visit to President Johnson in the Oval Office—this one on the record and covered by the press. The two would never meet again. Ormsby-Gore took a seat in the House of Lords as Lord Harlech, succeeding his father, who had died a year earlier.

His wife died in a car accident a few years later, and David was often seen thereafter in the company of JFK's widow, Jackie, prompting rumors of a romantic relationship. But she eventually chose another.

Roger Hollis, the man in charge of MI-5, understood with alarming clarity that the end of his tenure was nearing. The dramatic failure of KOBA, the covert Soviet scheme, had rattled the intelligence community, and Hollis knew that his exposure as a double agent was no longer a distant improbability. Realizing the precariousness of his position, he made the calculated decision to quietly retire.

The suddenness of his departure left Prime Minister Harold Wilson and the Cabinet reeling with surprise. Before long, suspicions mounted, and whispers of his betrayal grew louder. These accusations gave way to a flurry of publications, with several books attempting to make the case for Hollis's treachery. Throughout the years that followed, Sir Roger remained resolute in his denials. He consistently maintained that he was a man whose loyalty was steadfast to Queen and country, a claim he defended vigorously until the end of his life.

Howard Hunt, meanwhile, returned to the United States and settled back into his dual existence, juggling his role in the espionage world with his vocation as a prolific writer of spy novels. This balancing act had always been his way of life. Following the Churchill funeral and the collapse of the Soviet plot, Hunt occasionally accepted CIA missions that appealed to his taste for intrigue. He was a man who thrived on the undercurrents of clandestine operations.

Several years after the events in London, Hunt found himself drawn into political orbit once more, this time by Lyndon Johnson's successor, Richard Nixon, who enlisted Hunt to join his administration, capitalizing on his expertise in covert affairs. Eager to serve, Hunt dove into this new challenge.

He brought with him a few trusted allies, including Frank Sturgis and James McCord. Together, they were tasked with stemming the tide of leaks to the press. That operation, fraught with its own risks, would unfold with far less success than the clandestine triumph in London in 1965.

CHAPTER SIXTY-TWO

A FEW DAYS had passed since the solemnity of Churchill's funeral. At the White House, journalists gathered in anticipation of President Lyndon Johnson's first public appearance since his "recovery" from the cold that had kept him from London.

They found him uncharacteristically sullen.

He seemed to know what the first question would be and, though he was prepared with an answer, the members of the White House Press Corps could tell he was more than slightly vexed. Unlike his predecessor, who was famously adept at charming the group, Johnson's interactions with the reporters often revealed his irritation and, more dangerously, his vulnerability. A few of the senior members exchanged knowing glances. The new President was as thin skinned as ever.

"Mr. President," one reporter ventured, his voice melding authority with insinuation, "there has been some criticism both abroad and here because Vice President Humphrey was not sent to London to the Churchill funeral. Would you care to go into your reasons and what motivated you in selecting the American delegation?"

His choice of words was pointed, framing the question as an inquiry into Johnson's very competence. The President seemed to fidget at the accusation, then responded in a manner that was both rambling and defensive, almost as if he were sorting out the narrative for himself as much as for his audience.

"Well, at first," he started, "I hoped that I would be able to go if my physical condition permitted. I asked that we defer final decisions until the doctors could act. But I had my staff contact President Truman and President Eisenhower and express the hope they could accompany me. President Truman was unable to go, and President Eisenhower informed us that he had accepted the invitation of the family, and he would be going and that he would be in attendance and would be doing other things there. I urged that he go with us in our delegation and sent a plane to California to pick him up.

At the same time, I personally called the Chief Justice and asked if he would agree to go with me in case we made the trip. I also was informed we had Senator Fulbright, the chairman of the Foreign Relations Committee, and Senator Hickenlooper, the ranking Republican of that committee, and eight other Senators in London at the time, some of whom would be paying their respects as representatives of this country. I felt that with the former President, with the Chief Justice of the United States Supreme Court, with the distinguished Ambassador of this country to the United Kingdom, that we had a good delegation and a high-ranking delegation."

Johnson took a breath, allowing his audience a glimpse into the psyche of a leader submerged in a swamp of insecurity. He continued, "I had no particular reason for not asking the Vice President to go, although the Vice President, as you may or may not have observed, was addressing the delegates from 50 States at noon the day the plane left at seven-thirty in the morning, on his new responsibilities in the field of civil rights.

I am glad to have the press reactions and the reactions abroad on the protocol involved in connection with funerals. I had served as Vice President for three years and it had never occurred to me and I had never had it brought to my attention so vividly that it was the duty and the function of the Vice President to be present at all official funerals.

On occasions during the three years I was Vice President I attended one or two funerals representing this country, but there were many representatives from many walks of life. I did review the list of delegates representing their countries at the Churchill funeral and I did not observe that other nations sent in most instances either their top man or the next man necessarily. I thought we had a rather well-rounded delegation in the former President, the Secretary of State, the Senators who were present, the Chief Justice of our Supreme Court."

Sensing a perception of weakness in their subject, the reporters remained silent, letting their quarry furiously rationalize his position in the belief that he was his own best advocate. "In the light of your interest and other interests," he conceded, "I may have made a mistake by asking the Chief Justice to go and not asking the Vice President. I will bear in mind in connection with any future funerals your very strong feelings in the matter and try to act in accordance with our national interest."

Even in backing down, Johnson seemed intent on telegraphing that he, and not the press, would ultimately dictate the nature of his presidency.

A FEW MONTHS later, a new term made its way into the American vocabulary—and it was first used by the media to describe how Lyndon Johnson tended to handle the truth. The term seemed to describe the new spirit of an age that had seen the death of a President under mysterious circumstances, as well as a growing military involvement on the other side of the world. An involvement that Lyndon Johnson was determined to guard by what Winston Churchill once described as "a bodyguard of lies."

Credibility gap.

EPILOGUE

THE DC-3 LANDED heavily on the rain-slicked tarmac, and before the propellers had even ceased their final spinning gasp, an ambulatory team rushed forward from a nearby hangar. Tiernan Brogan, pale and swaddled in the woolen lap-belted blanket that had been his comfort since Lithgow's brother had tended to him at Stapleton Aerodrome, was shepherded down the metallic steps under the glow of floodlights.

The entire welcoming committee—a baffled airport manager in a windbreaker, a paramedic, and a woman in a green skirt-suit whose presence was a guarantee that none of this would reach the morning papers—moved with the choreography of practiced secrecy. It was 3:17 a.m., the hour of the wolf, when secrets and wounds tend to fester.

As they pushed Tiernan through the corridor to a waiting ambulance, Kaitlyn pressed close at his side, her face fierce and unyielding against the onset of fatigue. The journey from the UK had been a patchwork of fever dreams and adrenaline spikes—Reykjavík, where a grim Icelandic doctor had poured Bushmills Black Bush whiskey on Brogan's shoulder and half-heartedly stitched the wound; Gander, where they'd idled for a customs agent who never asked a question; and now Virginia, cold and wet, with its undertow of secrets.

When they reached Fairfax Hospital in Falls Church, the intake staff already stood at attention, having been summoned by higher authority. The attending physician, a Dr. Abelard, greeted Brogan with the solemnity of a priest. "We'll have you sorted out in just a few hours, Mr. Brogan," he said, not bothering to mention that the room they'd prepared had no windows and two locks. In the intake forms, the line labeled "Cause of Injury" was left blank, and the nurse—hand trembling only slightly—scribbled "accident" in the margin before whisking the paper away as though it were a loaded weapon.

Brogan drifted in and out of consciousness during the first few hours, the sedatives warring with whatever stimulant had been administered to keep him alert on the flight. It was during one of those lucid moments that he realized Kaitlyn hadn't left his side. She dozed in an orange-tinted vinyl chair, hands folded primly in her lap, but when he shifted in the bed, she was instantly awake, eyes searching his with the intensity of a field agent and the fear of someone who had seen the barrel of fate pointed her way before.

"What's the prognosis?" Brogan croaked, voice thick as congealed blood.

"Four weeks off your feet, but they think you'll keep the arm," Kaitlyn replied, her accent softening as the tension drained from her. "They say you were lucky."

He tried to laugh, but it came out a cough. "Lucky is not the word I'd use."

She reached out, brushed a lock of hair from his sweaty forehead. "You're alive, Tiernan. That's luck enough."

In the days that followed, the rhythm of hospital life rubbed the rough edges from the trauma. Kaitlyn became a fixture on the ward, bringing in books and crossword puzzles, dazzling the nurses with her wit, and evading the questions of the plainclothes men who came daily to peer through the glass and jot notes in their little memo pads. Tiernan, for his part, grew stronger. The bullet had missed bone but hit enough muscle to require a scaffold of stitches and a schedule of physical therapy. He relished the pain—it meant he was still in the game, still a piece on the chessboard.

During the hush of visiting hours, with only the hum of machinery and the static of late-night news reports as background, Kaitlyn confessed the full extent of her deceptions. She described the coded communications, the web of alliances and betrayals that had ensnared both of them. She leaned in, her lips brushing his ear. "No more secrets, Tiernan. Not with you." They sealed it with a kiss, mouths tasting of antiseptic and hope.

Less than a week later, a hospital orderly wheeled Brogan out to a waiting Ford sedan that Allen Dulles had provided. Kaitlyn drove, her hands steady on the wheel, and as they wound through the suburbs of Northern Virginia, he realized that he'd never felt safer than in the company of this woman whose capacity for loyalty matched her appetite for danger.

KAITLYN, USED TO running toward chaos, chafed at first at the monotony of homebound convalescence. Tiernan, for once, found comfort in domesticity. He cooked elaborate breakfasts, lost himself in books, and spent long afternoons tracing the scar on his shoulder as a kind of ritual. The two of them, always circling conflict, finally learned the contours of peace.

Autumn burned through the maples, and they decided that they would marry before the year's end. Brogan asked Harvey King to be his best man, while Kaitlyn's side was represented by an old nurse from the hospital who'd taken a shine to her. Allen Dulles escorted her down the aisle.

The ceremony was held two days after Thanksgiving at a Lutheran Church near the home they had purchased in Vienna,

Virginia and officiated by a retired Air Force colonel. Outside, a freezing rain turned to sleet. They honeymooned at the Greenbrier Resort in White Sulfur Springs, West Virginia, in a cottage on the property owned by a friend of Allen Dulles. The only sounds were the pop of the fireplace and the occasional cry of a distant fox. For a while, it seemed possible to be ordinary.

But the world had other plans.

By the following Easter, their son was born—a pale, writhing knot of raw energy who Kaitlyn instantly named T.J., for Tiernan Jr. They took to parenthood with the same recklessness they'd applied to espionage, never sleeping, always improvising, always watching over their tiny, vulnerable charge as though every passing cloud might conceal an assassin. This time, the stakes were real, and the cause—defending the future—was the only one that ever truly mattered.

Brogan tried to leave the world of shadows behind. He took a series of consultancies, then started his own firm specializing in what he called "proactive risk mitigation," a phrase that sounded dull enough to keep the CIA from meddling. But it was never so simple. The phone rang, sometimes at 2:00 a.m., and the caller would address him by one of his old code names. He never refused a mission, not out of duty, but because he knew the game would go on with or without him.

Kaitlyn, amazingly, never looked back. Motherhood suited her; she layered all her drive and cunning into the arcane logistics of playdates, preschool, and pediatric visits. When T.J. turned five and began kindergarten, she returned to nursing, half-expecting to chafe at the routine, but instead discovering that the hospital, with its crisis and camaraderie, was as close to the old life as she would ever want to get. She was good at it—better, perhaps, because she could see the angles, the lies, the buried motives in every interaction. She became the nurse everyone trusted in an emergency, the quiet center when things fell apart.

They kept the old scars hidden. Brogan's bullet wound faded to a white crescent, easily concealed beneath a shirt. Kaitlyn's traumas were less visible. They seldom spoke of London, or Belfast, or the electric nights on the run. But sometimes, when T.J. slept and the darkness settled, they would sit together on the porch, her hand in his, and the world would shrink to that small circle of safety they'd carved out together. Tiernan would eventually be called upon again by the President of the United States.

But that's a story for another day.

AUTHOR'S NOTE

DETECTIVE: "Is there any other point to which you would wish to draw my attention?"

SHERLOCK HOLMES: "To the curious incident of the dog in the night-time."

DETECTIVE: "The dog did nothing in the night time."

SHERLOCK HOLMES: "That was the curious incident."

THE ABOVE DIALOGUE is from a book published in 1892 by Sir Arthur Conan Doyle and it appears in a story titled, *Silver Blaze,* a mystery about the disappearance of a famous racehorse the night before a race and the murder of the horse's trainer.

Holmes solved the mystery by noticing that no one heard a watchdog barking during the night. The legendary detective used a "negative fact" to help solve the crime. Something absent from the record.

I have long been intrigued by those moments from the past when something that should have happened didn't. The "what if's" or "why didn't's" of history.

And that's how this book came about.

I wondered why Lyndon B. Johnson *didn't* go to Winston Churchill's funeral.

The cast of characters in THE HOPE NOT PLOT includes some familiar names from history including Lyndon Johnson, Bill Moyers, Allen Dulles, Clementine Churchill, James Jesus Angleton, Leonid Brezhnev, E. Howard Hunt, Walter Thompson, Robert Kennedy, Frank Sturgis, Queen Elizabeth II, Harold Wilson, Yuri Andropov, Edmund Murray, Roger Hollis, Kim Philby, and Dwight D. Eisenhower.

But at the center of this story is Winston Churchill himself. His accomplishments. His mistakes. His admirers. His enemies—even at the hour of his death.

Then there are other fascinating (I hope) invented characters. Some are based, at least in part, on real people. For example, readers familiar with Cold War espionage might notice how Harvey King resembles a real-life spy by the name of William King Harvey who led the construction of the Berlin Tunnel in the 1950s and was involved in "Operation Mongoose."

President Kennedy was drawn to him because of the rumor that the spy was one of Ian Fleming's models for his creation—James Bond.

I hope you enjoyed reading this story as much as I did writing it.

David R. Stokes
Haymarket, Virginia
June 2025

ABOUT THE AUTHOR

DAVID R. STOKES is a ghostwriter, bestselling author, broadcaster, columnist, and retired minister. He is married to Karen Holland Stokes. They live in Virginia near picturesque mountains, idyllic horse farms, and bucolic vineyards. Please find out more about David's books and ghostwriting work at www.davidrstokes.com.